Daughters

Paule Marshall

DAUGHTERS

ATHENEUM   *New York*   *1991*

MAXWELL MACMILLAN CANADA   *Toronto*

MAXWELL MACMILLAN INTERNATIONAL
New York   Oxford   Singapore   Sydney

Copyright © 1991 by Paule Marshall

Atheneum
Macmillan Publishing Company
866 Third Avenue
New York, NY 10022

Maxwell Macmillan Canada, Inc.
1200 Eglinton Avenue East
Suite 200
Don Mills, Ontario M3C 3N1

Macmillan Publishing Company is part
of the Maxwell Communication Group of Companies.

Library of Congress Cataloging-in-Publication Data
Marshall, Paule——
Daughters / Paule Marshall.
p. cm.
ISBN 0-689-12139-3
I. Title.
PS3563.A7223D38 1991
813'.54—dc20
91-8219
CIP

10 9 8 7 6 5 4 3
Printed in the United States of America

For my father, Samuel Burke
and
For my brother, Frank Burke

BOOK I

Little Girl of All the Daughters

Little girl of all the daughters,
You ain' no more slave,
You's a woman now.

EPIGRAPH TO
AN ALVIN AILEY DANCE

1

Ursa Beatrice Mackenzie

Not even a good two hours and it's all over. The receptionist, a woman in her late twenties with sculptured nails and expertly made up Latina good looks, places the bottles containing the capsules into a mini shopping bag—like the kind used for cosmetics in a department store—and hands it to Ursa over the counter, along with a thin, bound sheaf of postoperative instructions that resembles a chapbook of poems.

"Any questions, any problems, just give us a call." The woman waits, smiling, her back to a clock on the wall that reads 4:20 and her hands with the red flawless nails resting patiently on top of the counter that takes the place of the usual desk or glassed-in booth in the reception area.

Across from her, Ursa slips the instruction booklet into the

little shopping bag and the bag over her arm and resumes buttoning her coat, taking her time, waiting, still waiting for something to make itself felt, and thinking "beauty parlor" as she takes
a final look around her. The place could pass for a beauty parlor,
one of those fancy hair design salons, as they're now called. Why
out of all the places listed in the yellow pages did I have to pick
this one? With this resurrected Art Deco decor. And this harem
wallpaper. All these calla lilies staring at you from the walls with
their petals spread open like some poor woman's exposed sex in
the centerfold of *Hustler*. Calla lilies. They're not my favorite
flowers.

The wallpaper, a soft-focused design of the pale, long-stemmed
lilies against a background of mauve and dusky pink, has set the
color scheme for everything that meets her eye. Everything's been
done in one or more of the colors. The counter in front of her,
which almost overreaches her because she's so short, is in the
dark pink; the carpeting under her feet is mauve, and the modular
furniture inside the waiting room next door, where nearly every
seat is taken—women, their heads bent, leafing through magazines—the furniture there alternates among mauve, pink and
the creamy white of the lilies. Even the window blinds screening
out the office buildings across the way and the traffic ten stories
below on West Fifty-eighth Street match the flowers. And she'll
be carting them home with her, because calla lilies are all over
the decorator shopping bag and the cover of the booklet.

A beauty parlor. She had taken one look around when she
entered and might have turned and left if not for the receptionist.
The woman's smile reaching out to her at the door had been
more than just one that went with the job. And it's still there.
Although she's taking up time now by stalling with the coat
buttons, the smile's still there—patient, solicitous, saying, Hey,
mira, it's all right. Take your time. I'm not about to hurry you.
I know how it is. Which one of us hasn't stood on that side of
the counter? So take all the time you need. It's that kind of smile.

Thank you. Ursa, her eyes averted, thanks her for it.

The buttons done, she starts on her gloves, slowly drawing

them on and then repeatedly pressing the leather down between her fingers. Taking a year and a day with them also.

"You can still speak with the counselor if you like." Said after another long minute and in a voice that matches the smile.

"No, I'm fine."

"Then we'll see you in a couple of weeks."

Without calling attention to themselves, the woman's hands slip down from the top of the counter to the paperwork on the ledge below, and come to rest there. Under the lab coat she has on, she's wearing a print blouse of strong yellows, reds and a bright Caribbean blue. Where the colors erupt at the open front of the lab coat, they clash with the tame ones on the walls.

Spanish Bay. She could be from Spanish Bay back home with that face and those fighting colors she's got on.

The thought makes Ursa like her all the more.

"And there's no need to make an appointment for your checkup. Just come in any Tuesday or Thursday morning between nine and eleven."

"I see. Thanks."

The gloves are on skintight. Her long woolen scarf has been arranged, taken down, and then rearranged for the third time around the turned-up collar of her coat. The strap to her shoulder bag had been adjusted and readjusted on her shoulder. She's sorry now she never wears a hat; a hat would have bought her more time. Because suddenly there's nothing left to put on, button up, adjust or arrange, nothing left for her to do but to turn from the pink counter and the lilies and the unfailing smile and to force her legs to bear her away, across the reception area. And finally to leave the place under the eye of the security camera trained on the door.

Downstairs, on cold, crowded West Fifty-eighth Street, Ursa feels well enough to walk home. I don't understand it, Viney. The March wind has already cut through the fleece lining of her shearling coat and closed in a vise around her head, yet she feels well enough, game enough to walk the forty-odd blocks to her apartment on West 101st Street. Walking will be easier than trying to get a taxi out here at rush hour on a Friday—thinking this as she stands at the curb in front of the office building she's just left, an arm raised, her body set to lunge toward the first empty cab that appears. And praying. Praying she won't have to do battle with some cabbie who'll swear she's headed for Harlem and will try locking his door on her. Please. I'm not up to a fight today . . .

And once she reaches her apartment after walking there, she'll turn around and go right back out if she still feels this good and do the shopping, which hasn't been done in over a week. Nothing in the refrigerator but a couple of eggs and the supply of coffee beans the PM sends her faithfully every three months. That man! And once there's some food in the house, she'll fall to and clean the place, which hasn't been touched in over a week either, not since the popsiclelike stick in the home test kit turned blue. Dust turds up under the bed. The blackened fallout from the City sheeting the windowsills on the inside, and every dish to her name piled in the sink . . .

Or maybe she'll just leave the mess till tomorrow—one more day won't matter—and call Viney, tell her to find a sitter and the two of them hang out, have dinner someplace first and then hang out, this being the weekend. Go hear Carmen McRae at the Blue Note, if she's in town. Or Betty Carter at the Village Vanguard. Maybe Abbey Lincoln is singing, screaming some-where. *I need to hear Abbey do some screaming tonight!* And they'll stay through the last show, till the echo of the final scream has dissolved and the silver trim on the drums is the only thing visible in the darkened club. The management will have to ask them to leave. The same thing'll happen later at the after-hours spot they'll ferret out uptown. They'll be the last to leave there too. And hungry again by then, they'll hop a cab down to the Empire Diner like in the old days and eat a trencherman's breakfast seated at the counter with the musicians from the clubs, the interstate truck drivers with their giant rigs parked outside, and the night people from the Village.

Dawn will find them still in the streets.
She feels that good physically.

"Since you seem to have forgotten, may I remind you that the number here in Brooklyn is still one, seven one eight, two six nine, thirty-eight forty-seven. Please make a note of it: one, seven one eight, two six nine, thirty-eight forty-seven. This message will not be repeated. In other words, I'm not calling again. . . . Seriously, Ursa, what's up? Why have you got this machine on all the time? Why won't you call me back? Something's happened. I know something's happened and you've crawled into some manhole on the Upper West Side again and pulled the cover over it. Call me. You know how I worry."

Please don't worry, Viney. I'm fine. I'll call you this weekend or next week for sure. I promise. Forgive me.

Ursa stands beside the answering machine next to the phone on her desk, asking her friend's forgiveness and listening anxiously for one other message. Silence. Only the soft whirr of the empty tape on the spool. Not another voice besides Viney's. No word from the people at the Meade Rogers Foundation about the follow-up study in Midland City, New Jersey, they want her to work on. Whether the money's come through for it. And after promising they'd call and let me know something by the end of the week. What's wrong with them? Don't they know how much I need the job?

In her annoyance, she forgets and turns off the machine and without stopping to take off her gloves, scarf or coat or to put down all the things she's carrying—her keys, the change from the taxi that she took after all, the mini shopping bag, her own bag, as well as the large stack of mail she collected from her box downstairs, which hasn't been emptied in more than a week—carrying all this she goes and stands over at the one window in the apartment.

The window, a high, wide triple bay that takes up most of the wall, offers a sidelong view of Riverside Park at the foot of 101st Street, the icebound river next to the park and the West Side Highway, and beyond the river, New Jersey and the Palisades, with a rampart of high-rise condos on top of the cliffs, diminishing their height.

The sun has all but disappeared behind the condos, but for the moment, before night closes in completely, the sky over Jersey is a painted desert—bands of purple, magenta and flame yellow—and the few white clouds higher up have been drawn so thin by the cold and wind they could be vapor trails left from the planes taking off from Newark Airport.

Arms laden, Ursa stands gazing for a long time at the dying day and the darkness that follows it, and then for an even longer time at the lights from the condos reflected on the black and frozen river. Waiting. Still waiting for something, anything to make itself felt. But with her mind also on the job she should have heard about today.

A glance down at the mail piled in the crook of her arm. Maybe they decided to write instead of calling, and the letter's somewhere in all this junk. . . . Quickly she gropes her way over to the bed through the darkness that's more than an hour old by now. The bed hasn't been made in over a week either. Aside from the desk it's the only sizeable piece of furniture in the apartment. As she turns on the bedlamp, the apartment itself is revealed to be only one large room with a kitchen tucked into an alcove on one side, a cramped bathroom on the other and an oversize steam radiator noisily throwing off its heat over near the bay window.

Give!—The United Way of New York. *Time* magazine—a special introductory offer. The Christian Brothers Cleaning Company. The Council on Economic Priorities. The Literary Guild —four books for a dollar . . . One by one Ursa tosses the envelopes, unopened, to the floor, just wide of the anarchy of books, papers and printouts that surround the bed and cover the desk across the room. Research material, all of it, for a still-to-be-written master's thesis, her second one.

Before starting in on the mail, she put aside the shopping bag containing the booklet with the calla lilies on the cover and the bottles of ergotrate and tetracycline capsules. And she took off her gloves and scarf. She still has on the bulky fleece-lined coat, though. She has unbuttoned it and slipped her arms out of the sleeves, but keeps it pulled tightly around her shoulders.

She can't even feel the heat in the room.

Catholic Charities. Save Our Wildlife. Nuclear Scientists Against War. Committee for Democratic Renewal. The city controller's report. Get thee to the floor! And there, suddenly, beneath the controller's report is the familiar blue airmail envelope with the striped border and the official seal of the government of Triunion.

The PM.

Wouldn't you know it! Amazed, she almost laughs out loud. That man! He had known, somehow he had known, and had timed the letter to arrive today. He had consulted his crystal ball, or a little birdie had flown the eighteen hundred miles from New York down to Triunion to tell him about her appointment on West Fifty-eighth Street today, and he had seen to it that the blue envelope with the government seal would be waiting for her when she got back. As a reprimand for her carelessness . . . Ursa, you're not being rational—the monitoring voice inside her, that keeps itself apart from her, scolding her. / I know but I can't help it.

He used to stand at the edge of the swimming pool everyone said he had installed more for her than for the guests at the so-called hotel he owns, keeping an eye on her while she made like a little chocolate Esther Williams in the water. His shoulders in the shirt-jac suit he wore on Sundays—their day to go to the pool—would look to be a mile wide above her. His head with the high domed forehead she had inherited, and that had earned him the nickname PM when he was a boy, would appear larger than the sun. Sometimes, as she glanced up and found she couldn't see the sun or even a blue patch of sky because of his being in the way, she'd do a sudden flip, annoyed, pull the water like a blanket over her head and dive to the bottom of the pool and sit there. Just sit in the wavery blue, sunlit silence until the last bubble of air floated up from her lips and disappeared and her lungs ached to breathe in anything, even the blue water. She did it to impress, tease and frighten him a little. She always surfaced with a grin and a wink. Then to get back in his good graces, she'd do more minilaps than they had agreed on for the day.

For long minutes Ursa sits motionless on the bed, the blue envelope in her hand, remembering the PM's head eclipsing the sun and his shoulders that got in the way of everything. Suddenly she makes as if to toss the envelope to the floor with the junk mail—still teasing him after all these years—then sets it lovingly down on the bed. But without opening it. Let it wait. It can wait. It's probably just more about the government's big new resort scheme that he's all fired up about these days. The latest in what passes for development in that place. And then he wonders why I can't bear to come down there anymore!

Con Edison. American Express. *The Social Research Journal* . . . These three she places on the bed, next to the letter. Inside a compartment at the head of the bed sits a digital clock with a black face and a grid of raised glass studs that spells out the time. The appropriate studs fill up with a ruby-red light to note the hour and minutes. It's already past seven o'clock. . . . Citibank —her canceled checks and statement. Is there enough in her balance to cover the check today? Don't look now. She speeds up her search for an envelope with "Meade Rogers Foundation" in the upper left-hand corner. Val-Pak coupons. Publisher's Clearing House Sweepstakes. She consigns them to the floor. The Mt. H. Alumni Newsletter . . .

Ursa falls motionless again.

How many letters has she written, how many times has she called that alumni office to tell them to take her name off the mailing list? She's lost count in the twelve years since she graduated. And none of the calls or letters has done any good. The damn newsletter turns up regularly in her mailbox, and before she throws it out without reading so much as a word of it she always feels as if she's right back on the Mt. H. campus again, back in the office of her senior adviser on that fateful day. She's standing in front of the man's desk again, taking careful aim through her tears with the musket that's suddenly materialized in her hands. Her aim is so perfect that when she fires, the hole appears in the exact spot she wanted, right between the grayish blue eyes on the other side of the desk. And she doesn't run after firing, doesn't bolt out the door; she stays on to watch the last agonized twitch, the final death throe. Standing there, the still-smoking musket in one hand and in the other the proposal for her senior paper that the dead man rejected only minutes ago.

A neglected area in the study of the social life of New World slave communities has been the general nature of gender roles and relationships. This paper examines the relatively egalitarian, mutually supportive relations that existed between the bondmen and women and their significance for and contribution to the various forms of resistance to enslavement found in the United States and the Caribbean.

The man had the proposal waiting for her the moment she stepped in his office that Wednesday morning in late November, the first half of her senior year. Before she even reached his desk he had picked it up and was holding it out for her to take. His usual smile was missing.

It was unacceptable, he informed her. Her topic, the sources she intended using, her methodology, and most of all her thesis—which he found highly doubtful—all were unacceptable. There was no way he could agree to her continuing with the study. She would have to find another topic. His voice terse, distant, final.

Normally, the man would have asked her to sit down before anything else. And he would have offered her a cup of coffee from the two-cup Norelco he kept amid the clutter on his desk. An irreverent touch, that coffee maker. Ursa liked it. As she did the linty brown cardigan the man wore all the time, and his pepper-and-salt beard. Everything about him was an antidote to the Gothic gloom of the place, all those beamed, dark-paneled classrooms and halls and the gray, battlemented buildings over-run with ivy. And the man was known to be the most progressive-thinking member of the small history/sociology department and the friendliest, so that whenever she had a conference with him there was always the chair waiting and the offer of a cup of coffee before they began discussing her work.

And he liked her work! She had received A's in the three courses she had taken with him, and only that summer he had recommended her for an internship at NCRC, the big consumer research outfit in New York.

That Wednesday morning he didn't so much as ask her to sit down, and he had the rejected proposal ready to hand back to her before she crossed the room.

How long had she stood there? Later on, when she tried remembering, it seemed she had spent the entire day in one spot in front of his desk pleading with him to reconsider his decision. She could have sworn she saw the sun reach its zenith at noon and then slowly, hours later, go down behind the administration building she could see through the window behind him. Had stood there from morning till night, pleading with the man and trying to fathom the change in him: the eyes that were suddenly as remote as the sky outside and the same grayish New England blue, and the expressionless voice that kept repeating whenever she paused that the proposal was unacceptable and she would have to find another topic. *Why?* What was wrong with the one she had? She didn't understand his objections. She didn't buy the reasons he had given. I don't buy them, you hear! Her inner voice rising to a shout as her anger began to build. Her methodology? Why not? She wanted to try something different. Her sources? The slave narratives and oral histories, the old plantation records, Aptheker, the Angela Davis article. Why not? They were just as valid as the scholarly texts. "I remember you once said in class that all history no matter who writes it is only factual fiction at best," she reminded him, and saw the face fringed by the black-

and-white beard grow whiter and the eyes harden, taking on more gray than blue. What was it? Her mind struggling to understand, to get at the real reason for his no, even as she continued to plead.

". . . Please, Professor Crowder, I'd really like to go ahead with the paper. It's a subject that genuinely interests me. I'm curious to know what relations were like between the slave man and woman. How did they get along? What was the nature of their social, sexual and family life? How did they feel about each other, treat each other? My theory is that in spite of the circumstances their relations were mainly positive. I'm convinced of that. It's something that goes back to when I was small . . ."

She paused and the voice inside cried, Tell him! Go ahead and tell him! What've you got to lose? Can't you see the bastard's not going to change his mind? Tell him about those two warrior-lovers on the monument back in Triunion. How you once reached up and touched them . . .

"See if you can touch her toes, Ursa-Bea! Reach all the way up and try and touch her toes!" Estelle, her mother, whom she couldn't remember ever calling anything but Estelle, had gotten down on her knees at the base of the statue just minutes ago and put her to stand on her shoulders. Diminutive Estelle down on her knees in slacks— which she got away with wearing because she was the wife the PM went and "find" in America. And as Estelle rose to her feet again, both of them wobbling a little, Ursa had felt herself being slowly lifted toward the oversize stone woman in a lace shawl whose head appeared to be grazing the sky. A musket in one hand, a cutlass in the other, the stone woman was marching in place with three stone men on a pedestal that stood about eight feet above the ground. "Stretch all the way up and touch Congo Jane's toes, Ursa-Bea. Go ahead. Stretch! I'm not going to let you fall!" With her feet planted on Estelle's narrow shoulders and her ankles in Estelle's tight grip, with her arm straining out of its socket, she had reached all the way up until she could just touch the toes on the giant foot thrust forward from the edge of the base. "And make sure to touch Will Cudjoe's toes while you're at it.

You can't leave him out . . ." She did as she was told, leaning dangerously over to her left to get at the other colossal pair of feet. Warmed by the sun, their toes had felt as alive as her own.

Congo Jane and Will Cudjoe. Coleaders, coconspirators, consorts, lovers, friends. You couldn't call her name without calling his, and vice-versa, they had been that close. Ursa had planned to organize the entire paper around them, and had said as much in her proposal. They were to provide the methodology. No, she decided. Don't say another word about them to this man. It'll only make matters worse. He probably can't stand the thought that those two actually existed.

". . . Won't you at least let me try, Professor Crowder? I'm sure that once I really start digging I'll come up with the kind of material you'll find acceptable and that will support my thesis. I know I can write a good paper. Besides, I've put in so much work on it already, and it's so late now to have to look around for another topic . . ." Why, goddammit, would you wait until almost the end of the semester to turn it down? There're only three weeks of classes left, do you realize that? Only three weeks. That's all. How could you do a thing like this? Wait all this time before saying anything. I thought you were my friend. What am I supposed to do now, will you tell me? How am I going to come up with another topic, write another proposal—which you might also decide to turn down for whatever reason—do the research and all the reading and write a sixty-page paper between now and April 15? How in the hell am I to do that with all the other work I have . . .

By then the closed face with the beard and the vaulted windows framing it like a bishop's miter had begun to blur. And when Ursa quickly looked down to hide from the man what was happening, she had trouble making out the title of the paper and her name on the cover of the proposal in her hand. How am I supposed to do all that, will somebody tell me? There's no way. April 15? I'll never be through by then. I won't be done in time to graduate. Do you realize that, Professor Crowder? I-won't-get-to-graduate. And oh, God, what'll *he* say? *What's the PM gonna say, motherfucker?*

Ursa sends the alumni newsletter sailing to the floor and resumes her search for the letter about the job. Why after twelve long years does that thing still rankle so?

Eight-thirty by the clock at the head of the bed. She's been sitting idle for over an hour now, the bedlamp turned off, her lap emptied of all the mail, which hadn't included anything from the Meade Rogers people, and her body still feeling no different from when she got up this morning.

With the lamp off, there's only the ruby-red glow of the clock in the room, each lighted stud on the grid calling to mind those perfectly round, jewellike drops of blood that form when the tip of a finger is pricked. The only sounds to be heard are the noisy radiator and the wind rattling the bay window. An occasional car hurtles by. Sounds that are merely part of the silence of the night. Ursa doesn't hear them. Until voices begin to float up from outside, accompanied by bursts of laughter and a parade of footsteps climbing 101st Street, which slopes sharply up from the river.

This she hears. Her neighbors—the singles, couples, live-togethers, graduate students (including the aging, part-time ones like herself) who live in the old converted graystone houses like her own that line the hilly street—are on their way to "eat Chinese" on Broadway two blocks over, a Friday night ritual on the Upper West Side. They'll stand waiting for a table in the crowded entryway of their favorite restaurant or out on the cold sidewalk even, while those already inside, behind the steam-fogged windows, will linger over the winter melon soup, the Lake Tung Ting shrimp, and the quartered oranges that come with the fortune cookies at the end of the meal.

Should've called you, Viney. Should've called and said, Find a sitter, girl, let's hang out.

* * *

Because of the heavy shearling coat that she has yet to take off, she has to step sideways between the wall and the tub in the narrow bathroom to reach the toilet in the corner. Finished, she inspects herself. Hardly a stain. Her third trip since coming in and still hardly a stain. What's going on, Viney?—calling on her sister/friend again. You can't tell me this is normal. That other time I got caught it was like the Red Sea had relocated between my legs afterward. Remember me telling you that? But this time is completely different. This I don't understand at all.

Back over at the bathroom door she flips off the lightswitch and makes her way across to the bed in the darkness.

A marching, chanting, screaming legion with signs. Mounted police in full riot gear. The walleyed horses rearing, charging, frothing at the mouth, their breath long jets of steam in the freezing air. A fleet of ambulances and police vans waiting. And West Fifty-eighth Street between Ninth Avenue and Columbus Circle cordoned off. That's what she'd half expected to find when she arrived downtown: cops everywhere, the street cordoned off, and bodies chained to the door of the office building she was headed for. Or if the cold had kept the rank and file home, there would at least be a lone fanatic with a Bible, kneeling at the entrance. Some Hoosier type who'd never know what it was to count the days on a calendar and feel his heart drop. She would've had to climb over him to enter the building. Or worse, just as she stepped inside the beauty parlor upstairs, before she could even close the door, he would have slipped up behind her and pulled the pin out of the thing hidden under his coat, tossed it in, and fled. Her limbs and those of the Latina sister with the smile, who reminded her of people from Spanish Bay back home, as well as the limbs of the women inside the waiting room, scattered amid a wreckage of calla lilies . . .

Ke'ram. Ke'ram. Ke'ram. Seated on the side of the bed, eyes

closed and spine held straight to allow the energy to flow, Ursa silently repeats Ke'ram. Ke'ram that is nothing more than a sound designed to quiet the mind and suspend all thought. Peace; be still. Ke'ram, that when it's working, takes her in her head down to Triunion and a beach there that's her favorite in all the world. A two-mile stretch of sand, sea and sky that's so perfect and peaceful no thoughts can reach her there. That's if Ke'ram is working. Ke'ram. Ke'ram. Ke'ram . . . *Fly me to the moon, and let me play among the stars . . . /You go to my head and you linger like a haunting refrain . . . /The very thought of you and I forget to do the little ordinary things that everyone ought to do . . .* Songs to match the harem decor had drifted in from a hidden speaker as she sat in the disposable gown in the final waiting area. Lilies on the walls there too. Songs from one of those radio stations that plays the oldies-but-goodies virtually nonstop. She had blanked them out, was repeating Ke'ram, trying to get herself centered and calm before her turn came, when the music was suddenly interrupted by a woman announcer's voice, a husky, come-hither bedroom whisper of a voice. "Love songs," the whisper came. "Nothing but love songs." And the Mancini violins had welled up again.

The laugh that had gripped her felt as if some crazy had rushed up to her on the street and stabbed her in the chest. A laugh that had hurt. And she had failed to stifle it quickly enough, so that the two white women in the room with her, also sitting waiting in the gowns, had darted her a look. That look. She came to understand it only when she read Baldwin in college: At any moment the beast may spring, filling the air with flying things and an unenlightened wailing. That kind of look. And an attendant had hastened over, a middle-aged woman with teased platinum hair, blue eye shadow, and a whisper as she bent close to her ear that was as husky as the announcer's. "What's it, hon? Are you all right? Sure you don't wanna see the counselor?"

That laugh, knifing through her for a second, has been the closest she's come all day to feeling anything like pain.

Something's definitely wrong, Viney. You can't tell me otherwise. Do you think maybe the doctor was some incompetent who only half did the job so that whatever it is, is still there? That's possible. It could happen. Something like that could happen . . . Let it go, Ursa. Herself speaking to herself again. Just let it go for now. Ke'ram. Ke'ram. Ke'ram . . . 10:37 glows in the dark. And why didn't those people at the foundation call when they said they would? I don't think the study's going to come through, you know. Over two months and the board still won't say yes or no about the money. I've had it with these foundations and nonprofit outfits. This free-lancing! Should've stayed at NCRC. Let that go too, Ursa. Call the people the first thing Monday morning but let it go for now. Try to stay with Ke'ram.

Ke'ram. Ke'ram. Ke'ram . . . "*Mal élève!* You should have had it, *oui*, and know you're not getting any younger!"

The large, lined, biscuit-colored palm of the hand poised to strike her is as clear as day in the dark room. It's Celestine's hand and Celestine's voice. Celestine who helped raise her and who still considers herself more her mother than Estelle. She's standing over her at the bed, threatening her with that hand. Every day for more than a week she's made her appearance. If Ursa could have talked to anyone, sought out anyone as a counselor, it would have been Celestine. If she didn't always crawl into some hole whenever anything happened, she would've gotten on the phone to Triunion and tried explaining to Celestine about the trip downtown today. Why she had done it, and without hiding the tears in her voice. Celestine's the one she would have turned to, talked to. Not Estelle. She couldn't have told Estelle, not after all Estelle had gone through before finally managing to have her.

". . . You should have had it, *oui*, and sent it down for me to raise . . ."

Celestine's voice drowning out the sound of Ke'ram.

11:00. The two rows of lighted studs to the left of the grid form two perfectly straight blood-red tears down the black face of the clock. The zeroes to the right are two wide-opened red mouths about to emit a scream that will shatter the bay window and send glass raining down on 101st Street, on the heads of her neighbors returning from the meal on Broadway. The mayhem is about to happen any second, she's about to clap her hands over her ears and add her own scream—the one that's been building in her for days—to that of the clock, when suddenly the phone on the desk across the room freezes all sound.

One ring; another follows; and then abruptly the phone falls silent, only to resume ringing after a small eternity.

Go away, Lowell.

She knows it can only be Lowell.

The Friday night workout at the Sixty-third Street Y is over. A half hour on the machines and forty-five minutes around the track. He has come in, reaching his door at exactly ten o'clock or as close to ten as possible, and then gone right back out to walk Mitchell, whose pit-bull snarl of a face only a mother could love. Back in the apartment again, he has emptied his gym bag into the hamper—sweat-soaked shorts, T-shirt, towel and jockstrap—and taken a shower; and afterward, wearing pajamas and robe, ready for bed at ten-thirty on a Friday night! early to bed, early to rise to catch the milk train to Philly in the morning, Mitchell left to the care of the dog walker in the building, and he'll be on the 6:40 out of Penn Station to spend the weekend being a stand-in daddy . . . afterward, dressed for bed, he has eaten the small portion of food he saved from his dinner earlier to serve as a snack when he came in from the Y. The plain white dinner plate, the equally plain knife and fork have been thoroughly washed, carefully dried, and put away. (His ex-wife when she left had taken the best of the wedding-gift china and silver, crystal and linens.) The garbage has been taken out and deposited in the chute down the hall, the dead bolt and chain put on the door, and at eleven sharp he has picked up the phone, has dialed, hung up after the second ring, waited the small eternity and then redialed to let her know it's him.

Go away. Said almost gently. The voice inside her is almost gentle. She's long ceased being annoyed by Lowell's ritual with the phone. And by all his other irritating little rituals and habits.

Just go away. Please. *Vas-y, t'en prie*—pleading with him in the Creole she learned from Celestine. Just hang up and go on to bed. I'll see you next Friday.

He's forgotten she said she'd be spending the weekend in Hartford. He probably hadn't even heard her when she told him.

The fifth ring. Why won't he give up? And how could she have forgotten and turned off the machine? That would have cut off the ringing and answered for her: Hello, I'm not here just now, but if you leave your name, number and a brief message I'll get back to you.

Where does he think I could be in this one room that it would take me so long to get to the phone? Ursa, he's never been here, remember? He doesn't know how large or small the place is. The man's never spent so much as a night here. You banned him, remember? True, but he brought it on himself. He had no right asking me how I was going to pay the rent free-lancing . . .

Straining to see the ringing phone in the darkness: If I thought for a minute that you could have handled it, if you hadn't let that job of yours ruin everything, I would've called you as soon as the stick turned blue. Go away.

The job. That's it, I bet. Something happened at the office today. Another run-in with his nemesis and he needs to talk it out. He'll be on the phone all night if I answer. Oh, Lowell, why don't you quit that job? For the thousandth time just quit! Pleading with him.

Eight? Or is it the ninth ring? She's lost count. Besides, they all seem to have merged now into one long, shrill, unbroken ring that comes not only from the phone she can't see over on the desk but from inside her head as well. A massive telethon with the phones ringing off the hook is going on inside her head. The din is wreaking havoc on her eardrums, it's threatening to do in what little sanity she has left after the ordeal today, the scream she didn't get to vent minutes ago is building again, and suddenly, as if the bed under her has exploded, she's on her feet.

"Wha' the rass! Lef' muh in peace, nuh! Just lef' muh in peace!"

Ursa's on her feet, clutching the heavy coat around her so it won't slip off and shouting toward the desk in the darkness. And she keeps on shouting, the same words over and over again and in an accent thick enough to cut, until the phone across the room and the one inside her head—which keeps on ringing much longer—both fall silent.

Trembling, awash in perspiration, she slowly sinks back down on the bed.

His damn hand must have finally gotten tired holding the receiver. Or he finally remembered what she had told him, the lie about going up to Hartford. It must have dawned on him at last that this is where she is, spending the weekend at her uncle's, in the family house not far from her old high school, the same roomy, two-story brick-and-fieldstone house where some thirty-four years ago and after any number of "slides" on Estelle's part, she had somehow managed to be born.

Oh, Estelle.

A perspiring Ursa lies drawn up under the coat in the middle of the unmade bed, thinking about Estelle. About all those "slides."

2

Estelle Harrison Mackenzie

A little boy, an iron stake in one small hand, a mango which was probably all he was having for breakfast in the other, was leading to pasture a goat with legs as thin and knobby as his own. From her window of the car, Estelle watched him come speeding toward her along the dusty shoulder of the road, watched him hail her and the PM with the hand holding the stake, and then abruptly vanish as the Buick shot past him.

The same thing in the next village they came to: a little girl no bigger than the boy, who was being given a shower on her way from the standpipe by the brimming pail of water on her head, was there one second and gone the next. The child close enough for a second for Estelle to see the sun that was just rising reflected in the large eyes under the pail—and then she too was gone.

In Mangrove Town up ahead, some early bird already had her wash spread out to dry on the cactus hedge in front of her house. The ragtag clothes were a snatch of color as they sped by.

A gaunt cow in Heywood Village came and went in a flash. So too the old man milking it in his dust bowl of a yard.

All the early-morning scenes in the little villages and towns were being snatched away before her eye or mind could register them, before she could use them to distract her from the pair of hands kneading bread dough inside her.

Driving as if hoping against hope it wasn't too late and his speeding could still make a difference. Estelle almost turned to the stonefaced man beside her on the front seat, almost reached over and touched him, almost said, What's the point, Primus? It's already over. Slow down.

Earlier, when she had reached over in the bed to wake him, his eyes had flown open almost before she touched him. And the dread in them as he abruptly sat up had spared her having to say what had happened again and that they would have to leave for town right away. He had remained hunched over in the bed for the longest time, too stricken to move or speak. Neither of them saying anything. The light around them the dun gray of a mourning dove. Finally, in a hoarse voice, his head bowed: "I begged you, Estelle." Then he was heaving himself out of the bed.

He was up and dressed and in the Buick before she had recovered enough to put on her clothes. He hadn't stopped to shower or shave or to drink the cup of coffee Celestine hastily prepared for him. Had just sat waiting for her in the car, his gaze already fixed on the road that would take them the eighty miles to the capital, Fort Lord Nelson; and then, once they were underway, driving as if he had blinders on that didn't permit him to look anywhere but dead ahead.

"I begged you, Estelle." His sole words for the morning.

Estelle kept her face to the window on the passenger side of the car and her arms folded over her stomach. Like someone angrily kneading dough. That's what it always felt like afterward.

Priory Village. Roselle. Hightown. Concepcion. Each little

clutch of sunbleached houses that insisted on calling itself a village or a town disappearing almost as soon as the Buick came charging toward it, along with the canefields and banana groves that separated it from its neighbors.

Pointe Baptiste. She glimpsed the dirt road off to their left that led to the sea two miles away and to the long finger of land called Pointe Baptiste that stretched out into the sea. She sat up, remembering, her mind latching onto the memory to dull the cramping. The victory celebration after the last election had been held at Pointe Baptiste, in the large thatched-roof dance shed that stood halfway along the spit of land that faced the sea on both sides.

The rum, she remembered, had started flowing long before the final count was in, so that by nightfall both the crowd inside the shed and the overflow gathered outdoors alongside the sea and under the stars was more than a little sweet, more than a little salt. "Which is it, salt or sweet?" she had asked him in the beginning. "I don't understand the difference between the two."/ "It's a matter of degree," he had said. "Salt, when you've fired one too many and you start making an ass of yourself. Sweet is when you've had just enough to be feeling good, to be feeling sweet."

Early in the evening any number of people in the packed shed had made the customary toast, their shot glasses of rum raised into the glare of the Tilly lamps hanging from the rafters that held up the thatch. "To the PM, yes! Primus Mackenzie might only be a member of the House in that so-called government they got in town, but lemma tell yuh, bo, he's the PM, the one and only PM as far as the North District is concern. He was from a boy and will always be!"

After each toast the drumroll of bare feet on the dirt floor and the thunderous "hear-hears" had threatened to bring not only the roof but the sky with its oversize stars down on their heads.

Later, during the dancing, one of her many partners had gotten carried away, and before she managed to pull back from him and fix a space the size of a small moat between them, the man—an elderly coffee grower from the mountains—had swept her in close, held her against him with a rock-hard arm, rolled the muscles of his stomach like a belly dancer's against her, and breathed white rum in her face.

She had marched over afterward to where Primus Mackenzie stood "firing one" with his right-hand men, those who got out the vote for him at each election and looked after the district when he was in town. She sent a smile around to them all. "It seems," she said, "that everyone at this party wants to dance with me except the man I came with. If you'll excuse us. I'll have him back in a minute."

Out on the crowded floor she pressed up against him and did a mean jelly roll.

"What one of your constituents just did to me," she said as he pulled back sharply. "I thought you might like to know how it felt."

"Was he salt? He must have been good and salt and didn't realize who he was dancing with."

"He was salt and sweet and everything else, and he had a nest of snakes in his stomach. There're some things, Primus, that go beyond the call of duty." Said angrily, although her anger had evaporated now that she had made her point. Besides, the belly dancer had been an old old man.

"Are you still vexed?" he said with a laugh, perhaps sensing the change in her. "Should I go and cut out his liver? Where is he? Show me who he is. The damn scamp." Laughing with the light from the gas lamps reflected on the high rounded forehead that sat like a dome above the rest of his face. Then abruptly his laugh died. "He forgot himself, Estelle. The poor fella thinks we actually won something today and got besides himself. I beg for an excuse for him. Now let's finish the dance without all the winding and grinding."

It wasn't the drive up yesterday. He's sitting over there with the blinders on waiting to blame it on that. Or on all the excitement at the dedication of the new market. But it had nothing to do with either one. The minute he finds an excuse he's going to say that the market would've opened and been dedicated without my being there and I should've stayed in town. Keeping his eyes glued to the road and his foot on the gas, holding it all in. Oh, Primus—again she almost looked over at him—why not just say it and get it over with?

Vincennes. Hastings Village. Wellington Town. *Gone!* The sun at a slant now that it was beginning to sting the side of her face turned to the window. And a thick molasses smell from a nearby sugar mill was pouring into the car. Then they were hurtling in a wake of dust and ground stones toward Government Lands, the large unused tract of public land that had the most beautiful beach in all the world at its far end. How she'd love to be there right now—all by herself! Government Lands came and went. *Gone!* in minutes. Everything fleeting. Only the sun was keeping pace with them, along with the mountain that dominated the North District. Estelle saw it off in the distance, its great spurs and the foothills where the coffee was grown taking up half the sky and lording it over the lesser mountains and hills scattered around it. Gran' Morne. She spoke its name to herself. Like an anxious mother, it hadn't once let her out of its sight since she stepped in the car an hour ago.

"Morne said like mourn." He had taught her how to pronounce it in the beginning. "It means mountain."

Gran' Morne was one of the first things he had taken her to see her first visit to Triunion . . . Another memory to distract her from the kneading . . . Eight years ago she had gone to a luncheon at an estate outside Hartford, had met there this silent man beside her, who couldn't even bring himself to so much as glance at her now. Had talked with him for the better part of an hour standing beside a marble swimming pool, and in parting later that afternoon he had held her hand and kept on holding it as if he couldn't bear to let it go, and had urged her to visit Triunion.

Estelle closed her eyes, tightened her arms over her raging stomach, and reached back for that day.

She had just become the newest member of the Deltas' Hospitality Committee in Hartford when they were invited to meet a group of young lawyers from the islands who were touring the States as guests of the Carnegie Endowment on International Relations. The tour was part of the endowment's policy of offering young professionals from countries that might soon be independent a chance to see America, those who might one day be high-level civil servants, development planners, government officials, even presidents and prime ministers. The two-week tour always began with a luncheon at the estate of the man who chaired the endowment's board, and whenever the visitors were from Africa or the West Indies, the Deltas in Hartford were invited to come and meet them.

It was Estelle's first time attending one of the affairs.

"Robber-baron money, probably," she said to her friend Gladys as they drove onto the grounds and she saw the huge Italianate house surrounded by formal gardens of sculptured boxwood and statuary. "One never knows, do one, what's hidden away in the backwoods of Connecticut?" She rolled her eyes like Mantan Moreland in the movies. And then was suddenly serious: "I want to talk to whoever is from the place called Triunion," she said. "I've got to find out whether some of the things I read about it are true. . . ."

". . . Over twenty wars in two centuries! I couldn't get over it when I read it," she exclaimed, standing with him beside the marble swimming pool that looked to be Olympic size. In keeping with the spring day, she was wearing her Easter suit for that year, which had a peplum to the jacket and the new longer skirt.

"Twenty-three, to be exact," he said.

"That's an average of a war nearly every eight and a half years, isn't it?"

"That's right."

"Good Lord. And you hold the record, I guess you know. That's the most wars of any of the islands, according to the book I read. And the fighting wasn't just between the English and the French. The Spanish were in it also."

"Right again. Spain was also after us. We were considered quite a prize back then."

"Habla español?" Smiling up at him suddenly. Because of her scant five feet one, she was having to hold her head all the way back to see his face.

"No, not a word." He returned her smile and stood waiting for her next question, a tall, solidly built man with a broad composed face and the striking forehead, wearing a suit of heavy English wool left over from his student days at the Inns of Court in London. The suit was much too warm for the spring day.

"But I read that some of you speak Spanish."

"Only a handful of people in a remote part of the island."

"What about French? I bet you *parlez* a little *français.*"

"Only when the spirit moves me," he said. "And it's Creole, not French. Some people in the district I'm from speak it along with English, which is the official language."

"Yes," she said. "England won in the end. Eighteen fourteen. That was the last of the twenty-three wars and they won it. September second, eighteen fourteen, is when the treaty was signed."

"You even know the date!" He laughed, amazed, and gave her his full attention.

All during their conversation his gaze had been subtly divided between the intense buff yellow face raised to his, and his surroundings: the huge palazzo of a house close by, the gardens, the stables, the tennis courts, the great lawn sloping down to the Connecticut River, and the marble pool beside them, where a pair of nymphs stood at each corner waiting for spring to end and summer to begin, when water would flow from the urns they held tilted down in their arms.

The pool had repeatedly drawn part of his gaze.

Now, though, he turned his full attention to her; was suddenly, totally absorbed in her face.

"Tell me," he said. "I'm curious. Did you do the same for my colleagues? Read up on their little islands as thoroughly as you did mine?"

"Oh, yes. I was determined not to show my ignorance, which

would have been the case if I hadn't. I'm ashamed to say I knew almost nothing about the West Indies, except what I saw on travel posters. Palm trees and romantic beaches. So I went to the library and looked up all six of you. Don't tell your friends, but I found Triunion the most interesting. I couldn't put down the book when I started reading about it. To have been bandied back and forth like that! All those wars nobody's ever heard of. And all the slave revolts! I should have mentioned them first. I love the woman who was one of the leaders. Her story . . . It was a real education for me . . ."

"I teach grade school," she told him later when he asked her what she did. This was after the luncheon. They had been seated apart, Estelle next to a lawyer from Jamaica, and Primus Mac-kenzie at another table with their host, a white-haired man with a long-jawed, Abe Lincoln–like face who looked as if he had stepped down for the occasion from one of the portraits of his family members on the walls.

". . . I teach grade school," she told him. "As did my mother and my grandmother—she lived in Tennessee. There're nothing but schoolteachers and social workers in my family. The best part of teaching for me is that I get to put on the school play every year. And I also have a drama club at the community center my father runs. He's the social worker. I love the theater, especially directing. I love bringing it all together and making it work."

At the end of the afternoon they stood side by side for the group photograph taken out by the pool. Estelle was to come out looking lighter than she was next to the plum tones of his blackness, and she would appear shorter than her five feet one because of his height and the long, forties hemline of her skirt. To compensate there would be her smile, which always seemed to be projected toward the last row of seats in a theater.

"I appreciate the review lesson," he said in parting. "Perhaps one of these day you'll visit Triunion and see for yourself the place that was once considered such a prize. I'd be honored to show you around. Please. You must come."

Holding her hand longer than was called for, his manner al-

ready that of the foreign minister or head of state he was sure
to be someday.

"Dear Homefolks," she had written the following year,
"Gladys and I are being treated like visiting royalty. Our picture
in the Visitors to the Island column in the paper. An interview
over the radio where I talked about my drama club. A cocktail
party in our honor at one of the big hotels. A grand tour of the
island, which is more beautiful than any travel poster. Poor but
beautiful, especially the mountains in the north where Primus is
from. We've gone swimming under the sun *and* the stars. And
on and on. All of it Primus's doing. He's our host with the most-
est. And he's seeing to it that we meet everybody who's somebody, including his friendly enemy, the premier, whose job he'd
like to have now that they have home rule and are pretty much
governing themselves. Our folks are in charge of nearly everything down here. Love it! Love it! Love it!"

Mwen renmen ou, he confessed in a letter shortly after her visit,
making up a phonetic spelling for the Creole words and trans-
lating them for her: He had loved her from that spring day beside
the swimming pool when she had looked up and said, "Over
twenty wars in two centuries! I couldn't get over it . . ."

"Just say it and get it over with."

"You should have stayed in town, Estelle."

"And how could I have done that?" She turned sharply to
where he sat almost hunched over the steering wheel. The silence
that had gone on for close to two hours had finally ended. "You
know as well as I do, I couldn't have done that. It wouldn't have
looked right for me not to be there. After all, I was beating the
drum for that market shed as much as you for the past four years.
Promising everybody in the district that we'd get it. And then
when it's finally built I don't show up for the dedication? It
wouldn't have looked right. People would've felt slighted, you
know that." She had kept her face turned to her window for so
long, her neck was stiff now that she was looking at him. "Besides,

who would've arranged for the fete afterward if I hadn't been there?"

She had seen to it that there were sweet drinks for the women and children, rum for the men, and that everyone got at least a small wedge of the CARE-package cheese and two or three crackers at the reception following the dedication.

The large shed with its shiny new corrugated roof had replaced the open-air market in the district seat. The Ursa Mackenzie Market. It had been named after his mother.

"The market would have opened, it would have been dedicated, there would have been the little fete afterward without your being there. You should have stayed in town as I asked you to. As I begged you to."

His head was thrust all the way forward, a habit of his when he was upset. And the voice he was holding in check was hoarse. The phlegm in his throat could have been a cold coming on or tears he was choking back.

He had cried the last two times she had had a slide, Estelle suddenly recalled. Had held her, stroked her, and cried.

"You should never have come on this long drive. And on this road. You know what this damn road gives."

As if to hide its shameful state, the stretch of road just ahead of them—with its fissures, potholes and the broken *pavé* surface of matched stones the French had laid when they built the road long ago—slid swiftly out of sight under the hood. Only to be replaced the next instant by another stretch in the same condition.

"It wasn't the road. The one thing to be said for this car is that it gives you a smooth ride." Which was true. The big patrician-looking Buick sedan, a gleaming black in the sunlight, treated even this old road as if it were newly laid macadam.

("Dear Homefolks," she had written, "I don't know what possessed him to buy it. Nobody here drives an American car. They're too big for these narrow roads. Besides, we can't afford it.")

"It wasn't the road," she repeated.

"You should have stayed in town in any case. That way you would've been close to Roy and the clinic."

"I practically lived at the clinic all the other times and did it help? And don't you think I asked Roy if he thought it was all right for me to take the trip?" Like him she was struggling to hold her voice in check. "You know I did. He didn't feel it would be too much. And I was fine all of yesterday and last night . . ."

Until just before dawn this morning, when someone began kneading bread dough inside her and woke her up. Some angry housewife, it seemed, had gathered up all the organs below Estelle's navel and was kneading them as if they were dough on which she was venting all her frustration and rage. That's what it felt like. And there had been a slickness between her thighs. Please, she had prayed, let the kneading stop. Let this woman with these angry hands go away. And the slickness, let it be nothing more than perspiration—this room can get so hot at night—or love come tumbling down, as they say in the song. Yes, that must be it! She had rolled over against him in her sleep, against the warm, partly swollen knot below his belly, or he had reached out in his sleep and drawn her to him; had moved, dreaming, against her and her love had come down.

If I count to two hundred before smelling the coffee, it'll be nothing more than love or perspiration.

And she had actually counted, lying beside him in the bed in the old Mackenzie house up-country in which he had been born. When the long slow count ended with no smell of the coffee Celestine prepared especially for him each morning, she had reached slowly under the sheet covering them—Please, God— believing in the sign she had been given but praying nonetheless. Seconds later when she withdrew her hand and held it up, the stain on her fingers had looked black in the mourning-dove gray light in the room.

". . . It's not as if I didn't plead with you not to come," he was going on, the hoarseness like a cold or tears in his voice. The invisible blinders he had on still keeping him from looking at her. "I begged you, Estelle!" Said with such despair she quickly turned back to her window and to the string of little woebegone villages and towns fleeting by. The silence returned.

Marigot at last. A half hour later they reached Marigot, the last town in his district, and then, a few miles farther, they came to the intersection where the old north/south colonial road they were traveling met up with the main road that led to Fort Lord Nelson, the capital, ten miles away.

He swung the big car onto the main road, and suddenly there it was again, worse than ever. The kneading had abated when she returned in her thoughts to meeting him that first time in Connecticut. But now for some perverse reason, just as they reached the one decent road on the island and the long drive was almost over, the unhappy creature inside her began bearing down again on the bread dough. And she was working it harder and faster this time, harder and faster, with a pent-up fury in each stroke that finally brought Estelle sitting up sharply in her seat and then doubling over with a cry, her head almost striking the dashboard as the pain sent her pitching forward.

"Stel . . . ?" His own head spun around. There suddenly were the anguished eyes he had kept hidden. "Oh, Stel . . ." He started to pull over.

"No! Just get me to Roy."

———

"You know, Roy, I've come to appreciate the way people here put certain things. When I first came and would hear women in the district saying 'So-and-so just had a slide, you know' or 'What's wrong with that woman—every time you look she has another slide,' I couldn't understand how they could speak of it like that. Slide seemed like such a callous way of putting it. But I've come to think otherwise. They couldn't have found a better word. Slide fits the bill, especially in my case. Don't you think so, Roy? Don't you think it's exactly the right word for someone with my problem?"

The man at her bedside stood with his head bent and his hand resting on hers in such a way that he might have been taking her pulse or simply holding her upturned palm. Or both. He kept his gaze on their hands and remained silent.

"I asked you a question, Roy. Wouldn't you say that slide's the perfect word for someone like me? Even you have to admit that I seem to have a sliding pond instead of the usual organs.

"I'm talking to you, Roy. Wouldn't you say . . ."

He looked up finally, a pair of hazel eyes coming to rest on her face. He was a stocky man with wiry sandy-red hair, freckles spattered across his broad nose and cheekbones. And skin that matched his hair.

Colored folks come in every shade but green, her father always said. She had thought of it the first time she met Roy.

"What I say, Estelle, is that you're to go home the next time." He spoke quietly. "The minute you don't see your period you're to get on a plane and park yourself in Hartford. Maybe, just maybe that'll do the trick. Because we've tried everything else . . ."

It was true. She had stopped working any number of times, stayed in town, stayed in the house, even stayed in bed for weeks, even months. Just lying there like an invalid, taking vitamins and the array of pills Roy prescribed. Her thighs sore from all the injections. And none of it had helped.

". . . Not even those big ob/gyn fellas in New York your husband spent all that money to take you to see could figure out what it is. So you're to go home. That's what I have to say."

"All right. But you still haven't answered my question. Don't you think that slide is—"

"I'm not making sport, Estelle. The next time—if there is a next time, because you can't go on losing them like this without damaging yourself, that's what has me worried—you're to form yourself back home."

Baby. Nobody said the word baby around her anymore. She didn't even say it to herself.

"All right, Roy, all right."

Through the lingering fog of the anesthesia and her tears, she saw that he had already changed from the surgical gown to one of the casual Guayabera shirts he wore instead of a medical jacket. His Spanish Bay shirts, he called them, because he had them custom-made in Spanish Bay to the south of the island. There were white ones in cotton for work and silk pastels for social occasions, including receptions at Government House. The sight of the shirt with its open collar and stitched pleating down the front was somehow reassuring. Reassuring also was the garden of the clinic which she could glimpse through the French doors of her ground-floor room. Great beds of amaryllis, tall red cannas and the prized pagoda flowers Roy lovingly cultivated in his spare time. She shifted her gaze to the downcast face above her. Roy, not only her doctor but her good friend. And Primus's friend as well. They had gone to the same school as boys.

"You're going home the next time if I have to put you on the plane myself."

"All right, Roy, I hear you."

"I've already told Primus . . ."

A panicked look toward the door. "I don't want to see him just yet." The dread in his eyes as they flew open this morning . . . She hadn't had to utter a word. He had known what she was waking him up to say.

"He's not here," Roy said. "I told him to go home and shave and come back. But I've already let him know that if he won't see to it that you go up to the States the next time, I will, because I don't think I can bear looking in your face or in his or my own for that matter with the same bad news again. You're to go home."

"All right, Roy, all right."

———

Late the following year Estelle would give in and allow the baby to be named Ursa, after his mother. She would insist, though, on calling her by her middle name also: Bea, short for Beatrice, which was her mother's name. Ursa-Bea. Estelle alone would call her Ursa-Bea, thus claiming her for the homefolks as well.

3

Lowell Carruthers

"... Can you believe it! The bastard waited good until I was away from the office last Thursday to call the meeting. Had his secretary get on the phone and set it up as soon as he knew I'd be at the Yonkers plant for the day. Supposedly it was to discuss the new budget for the division, but I hear he spent most of the time talking about what he sees as the problems in my unit. Can you imagine, holding a meeting that concerns my unit and I'm not there . . . !"

Another week, another Friday, another one of their bimonthly dinners out on Columbus Avenue, and Lowell Carruthers has been going on about his nemesis and the job ever since they entered the restaurant. Across the table Ursa sits half listening, hungry, waiting for the soup she's ordered, her thoughts moving back and forth between the present moment and this same day a week ago.

She's a little high from the sake they're both drinking. The alcohol on her empty stomach.

". . . He's suddenly got it into his head that the compensation unit needs an assistant manager. Somebody, he says, to take some of the pressure off me and to help the unit run more efficiently. Somebody who'd be more of an administrator. What's the fool talking about? I run the tightest ship of anyone around there . . . Thinking of bringing in someone to be second to me, discussing it with the entire division and not a word to me first? I mean, have you ever heard of anything like it . . . ?"

As always, Lowell Carruthers is being careful to keep his outraged voice reined in to a conversational low so as not to call attention to them.

"Sounds to me like your friend Davison is having another one of his seizures," Ursa says. "He'll get over it and forget about this latest brainchild in a couple of weeks. He always does."

Has he heard her? Does Lowell Carruthers even see her? She doubts it, although he's looking directly at her across the table. Davison. Davison's face is in the way. She sighs to herself and continues to half listen and have her own thoughts. It's going to be one of those Davison nights.

Her soup arrives, thank God. It's a clear miso with a few scallion tips and a thin cross section of mushroom floating tranquilly on top. She alone is having soup. Lowell Carruthers never has anything other than the sake, a large serving of sushi, and tea whenever they eat in this particular Japanese restaurant.

It's a restaurant they both like, a place as simple, stark and tranquil as her soup. Glancing around her, Ursa takes in the black-painted ceiling and walls, the white-covered tables, and the roses. A single fresh white rose sits in a vase on each table under the recessed lighting overhead that has the softness of candleglow. Over at the windows a double thickness of shoji screens shuts out the carnival atmosphere of Columbus Avenue on a Friday night, and the tape of a koto playing quietly in the background lessens the rumble of the trailer trucks that use the avenue as a highway through the city.

And the waiters match the decor. They're all slender, smooth-faced, gay young men in white karate jackets and black tights, their long midnight hair swept up and skewered like a sumo wrestler's on top of their heads. Ursa thinks of them as the Asian dancers in Alvin Ailey's troupe. They're part of the appeal of the place. Lowell Carruthers refuses to eat in those Japanese restaurants where the waitresses wear the traditional dress. The mincing steps they're forced to take in the hobble-skirt kimonos always make him think, he once said, of bound feet.

That one comment, made back when they started going together six years ago, remains high on the dwindling list of things she still likes about him.

". . . Sure, I'm under a lot of pressure with all the cases I've got. Sure, I could use a couple more people in the unit. But not someone he hires without first consulting me, or some member of his little cabal he might decide to promote. Someone to report back to him about how often I even go to the john. He thinks I don't know what he's up to. But I've got this latest ploy all figured out. It's about bringing in some white boy for me to train. I'll train him, and then as soon as there's a cutback my friend'll see to it that the white boy stays and I go. I will've been training my replacement. It happens all the time. That's what the bastard has in mind. I know how he thinks . . ."

Would it have come into the world with the frown across the table already affixed between its eyebrows?—her thoughts move back to last Friday as she drinks her soup. A frown like a knot from a fresh blow that had caught Lowell Carruthers just above his nose, between his eyebrows. A frown like the keloid of an old wound that keeps compulsively piling on scar tissue long after it's healed.

Blacks are predisposed to developing keloids. She had come across that piece of information while working on a study for the Minority Health Council a couple of years ago. Keloids, sickle cell, sarcoidosis and a host of other predispositions and tendencies. She'd been glad when her part of the study was over.

". . . Three hours! They tell me the goddamn meeting went on for three hours! And they say he sounded like he was all ready to go out and hire someone on the spot!"

He snatches up his small cup of sake and drinks.

Would it, when grown, have found itself working in the Personnel and Employee Relations Division of Halcon Electronics Incorporated of Hempstead and Yonkers, manufacturers of electrical parts and components for major home appliances? As manager of the compensation unit? Would there have been a Davison in its life and a Davison crisis every three to four months?

The main course finally. Their smooth-faced waiter serves it with a dancer's flourish. There's shrimp-and-vegetable tempura for her and for Lowell Carruthers a minibanquet of sushi arranged on a black ceramic platter.

He falls silent for the first time since they sat down. Head bowed as if saying grace, hands clasped on the edge of the table, long, shapely fingers meshed. Hands with a look of both delicacy and strength. They could easily, it seems, snap a phone receiver in two—like the one he held onto last Friday night, ringing and ringing, trying to destroy the little sanity she had left—and then turn around, those same hands, and delicately peel a grape. They always make her want to hide her two broad, dark, short-fingered stubs. "Gimme those hands!" she used to demand during the love years—those first couple of years at the beginning—and laughingly try to pull them off his wrists.

Silent, he is studying the array of raw fish and short, seaweed-wrapped tubes of rice the way he would a still life in a museum, marveling at its composition and color, while closely examining it for the slightest flaw.

He always does this when he eats sushi. Another one of his habits.

With his head bent, the pattern of his receding hairline is revealed. Two deep bays at his temples. The bays meet across the crown of his head, leaving a small island of hair to the front. Triunion, Ursa secretly calls it. Triunion stares back at her from above Lowell Carruthers's forehead. She's been thinking of the place all week . . .

A long, quiet moment. Then another. She waits, her tempura untouched. There're about thirty diners at the other tables and another half-dozen or so at the sushi bar across the room, and they too seem to have stopped eating and talking and to be waiting also. The sound of the koto has faded. Even noisy Columbus Avenue outside has fallen silent.

Almost a full minute. By now all trace of the frown is gone. His entire face has smoothed out. And his agitated heart has slowed down, Ursa imagines. Behind the flesh, muscle and bone of his chest, his heart has slowed to a meditative beat. Ke'ram. It's beating, she would like to think, with the sound and rhythm of Ke'ram.

He looks up finally. Gazes across at her, actually seeing her now. No other face in the way. He smiles. *Perfect.* He mouths the word perfect, meaning the sushi, and underscores it by holding up a forefinger and thumb joined in a circle. The Yogic sign of wholeness and unity. He doesn't know it, but that's what it is.

Next, he picks up his chopsticks with the same hand that shaped the circle, lifts a California roll of crabmeat and avocado from his platter, and deposits it on her plate. "Your appetizer," he says, his smile holding, and the meal is under way.

That's it. That's all there's likely to be for tonight, what with the latest crisis. Just a long, quiet minute that had the feel of grace being said, and afterward the smile and his eyes clearly focused on her face. I know, Viney, I know. You don't have to say it. It's not enough. Her sister/friend is always telling her it's not enough.

"Always up to some shit!" From across the table. The knot, the wen, the keloid reappears. Lowell Carruthers has returned to Davison and the job.

At least he has a job, Ursa thinks and is almost envious. She has spent the entire week trying to line up something. On Monday she called the people at the Meade Rogers Foundation about the follow-up study in Midland City, only to be told they were still waiting for the money to come through. She then called and went to see her contacts in other organizations for whom she had done work, including even the Minority Health Council again. To let them know she was available. The five days spent running around town. In the evenings she tried working on the thesis for her second master's, but had made little progress. Each evening spent sitting at her desk fighting panic and paralysis. Why? What is it? All the research is done. She has enough notes and material for a five-hundred-page dissertation, never mind a modest thesis. And as much as I want to write about Congo Jane and Will Cudjoe! Because that's what she's doing; the thesis will be an expanded version of the senior paper she was forced to abandon twelve years ago.

And it's been a week spent waiting, still, for something to make itself felt. She knows she's being irrational, but there were moments over the past five days when she seriously considered going down to West Fifty-eighth Street and accusing them of not having done anything. Not so much as a cramp! I don't understand it, Viney.

Then there's been the PM's letter to deal with all week. That's been weighing on her heaviest of all.

". . . Hit with the news of some meeting the minute I step in the office. Next thing I see this long memo about it on my desk. And before I can even finish reading the damn thing here he comes sticking his head in my door. Smiling. All set to mess with me again, and smiling. 'How did it go in Yonkers? See you're reading my little note. We had quite a powwow around here yesterday. You and I have to talk.' What's there to talk about? He's already announced his move. I felt like slamming the door in his goddamn face. Why doesn't he stay in his office? Always up and down the halls, barging in your door, bugging you. I swear the cat doesn't spend a good five minutes at his desk except to fire off some long-winded, convoluted memo about one thing or another . . ."

Do you realize that for a hot minute there you were what the Welfare Department calls the putative father?

Lowell Carruthers puts down his chopsticks. He has hardly touched the sushi he's been so busy talking in the reined-in voice. "What're you smiling about?" His face is tight, the frown between his eyebrows all the more pronounced. "Here I'm telling you how the cat is trying to shaft me again and you're sitting over there smiling."

This thing on my face a smile? It sure doesn't feel like one.

She also puts down her chopsticks and slowly finishes chewing the piece of zucchini in her mouth, giving herself time, searching. Then: "When you said memo I suddenly thought of the time he sent around one that was fifteen pages long and single spaced to boot. Remember that one? It was to everyone in the division. You said you had a mind to Xerox the thing, switch around the 'to' and 'from' on the copy, and route it to him. He'd be running from office to office trying to find out who did it, but everyone would have the original. I thought that was pretty funny. Anyway, as I said, the man's just having one of his periodic seizures. It'll pass. He'll soon drop the whole idea and leave you alone for a while. I wouldn't worry about it if I were you." Then, without pausing: "I heard from the PM last week."

A noticeable flicker across the shoulders opposite. The sportscoat Lowell Carruthers has on might have suddenly become uncomfortably tight across the shoulders.

"What did he have to say for himself?" He resumes eating.

"Just the usual," she says. "The letter was just more about the big resort and conference center the government's planning to build with this group of developers from Canada and the States. I told you about it. Another one of their wrongheaded ideas. I don't even like to think about it. And I certainly don't want to see the thing once it goes up. But that's all he writes about these days. And the latest is that he's planning on putting money in it too. They've got this new law that permits members of the House to invest in a so-called development project once it's a public-private joint venture. Not that the thieves running the government haven't been doing it all along. Only now it'll be legal. Where the PM's going to find the money I don't know, but that's what he intends doing, he says."

"He can always borrow against his hotel."

Ursa laughs. "Mile Trees? Are you kidding?" She thinks of the dozen little nondescript cottages that call themselves the Mile Trees Colony Hotel, which the PM has owned for as long as she can remember. A hotel that is scarcely more than a guesthouse. Its clientele mainly old retired schoolteachers and civil servants from Canada. He used to take her there every Sunday to swim in the pool he had installed when he bought the place. Every time she'd look up from the water, his head would be in the way of the sun . . . And there had been the woman who still manages the place for him—the "keep-miss manager," as everyone calls her. She would also come and stand beside the pool every Sunday, holding a bath towel to dry her with and a glass of her favorite soursop juice on a tray. Miss Astral Forde. She too has been at Mile Trees for as long as Ursa can remember. Indeed, were it not for Miss Forde running the place with an iron hand, it probably would have closed down long ago.

"The PM couldn't get a dime on poor old Mile Trees. It's already mortgaged to the hilt. He'll have to scare up the money somewhere else." Then, again without pausing: "The other news is that elections have been called. They're to be held at the end of May, he tells me."

She's been waiting all evening to tell Lowell Carruthers this. Waiting all week, in fact, ever since she woke up last Saturday morning to find the blue envelope with the Triunion seal lying unopened next to her on the bed. Seized by guilt she opened and read it before taking off the heavy coat she had slept in or going to the bathroom. Read the part about the elections over and over again, becoming more dismayed each time. She finally put the letter in the compartment of her headboard that she reserved for his mail alone. The sound of his voice on paper within easy reach. She had trouble sliding shut the panel, the compartment was so full.

Ever since then she's been waiting to tell Lowell Carruthers that one piece of news.

"And naturally you're going to end your boycott and go down for the big event."

By boycott he means the four years she hasn't been to Triunion on a visit.

"Why must you go down there so often?" he used to complain during those first couple of love years. For the past four years, though, there's been no need.

"I said naturally you'll be going down for the big event. Didn't you hear me?" He has yet to look up from the sushi.

"Do I have a choice? I promised him, remember? You know that as well as I do."

Two years ago there had been a virtual barrage of the blue envelopes and any number of overseas calls. What was wrong? What had gotten into her? Why had she taken to staying away for so long? Was she vexed over something? Her uncle Roy, Celestine, her aunts, her cousins—everybody kept asking for her. Did she know what she was doing to him and to her mother behaving like this? Did he have to fly up to New York and bring her home by force of arms? He needed to lay his eyes on his girlchild! Letters and calls that went on for months until she finally capitulated and wrote promising him that she would come down for the next general election, whenever that would be.

And two years later here it is. To be held in two months.

"The only way I might get out of going is if the study I'm waiting on comes through," Ursa says. "Then I'd have a legitimate excuse. But I've about given up on that. The people at Meade Rogers are still waiting around on the money. I'm so fed up with that foundation! And it's the one study I'd really like to do. Midland City, after all, was my first real job when I started free-lancing. But I started looking around for something else this week. Just in case. It's been a while now since I finished working on that study for the Minority Education League and I'm getting low on funds. Sometimes this free-lancing makes me wish I had stayed at NCRC."

Another flicker of discomfort and irritation across Lowell Carruthers's shoulders. But he remains silent. He has already, years ago, had his say about her leaving the job at NCRC to free-lance.

". . . Do you know how many niggers there are running around out here claiming they're free-lancing, consulting and shit? Do you? And what do they have to show by way of proof? Not a goddamn thing, most of them, but the job section of the *Times* and a bologna sandwich for lunch in those fancy attaché cases they carry around. The Second Reconstruction is over, baby, haven't you heard? Hasn't anybody told you? It's over! Don't you see where the country's getting ready to put some cowboy in the White House come November? We might find ourselves back in the cotton patch. And this is the time you pick to quit a perfectly good job to free-lance? You gotta be out of your mind. . . ."

He didn't stopped talking for hours. He had come over to spend the night in the apartment in Park West Village she had at the time, a large two-bedroom on the fourteenth floor with a terrace that faced downtown—all of Manhattan displayed before her—and when she told him that she had resigned her job just hours ago, he went on nonstop.

". . . Walking out on a good-paying job where nobody bugs you, and just when you were up for another promotion, which would've meant more money . . . I mean, how could you have done something like this? What's gotten into you? I don't understand what's gotten into you all of a sudden. And worse, leaving without giving the people so much as a day's notice . . . !"

True. She had simply walked.

Earlier that day, alone in her office at the huge NCRC complex in Mount Vernon, she had suddenly taken a deep breath and, reaching over, switched off the terminal in front of her. Gone in a green flash was a wealth of data pertaining to one of several surveys NCRC was carrying out for American Leaf and Tobacco, this one to measure the effectiveness of a massive advertising campaign the company had recently conducted in the special markets. She had been studying the data in preparation for writing her portion of the report.

A flip of the switch and the monitor went blank.

She had then wheeled herself in her desk chair over to the typewriter, afraid to stand up, convinced that if she did, her legs would give way under her and she'd never make it out the door. Over at the typewriter she had taken off the dustcover, turned on the power, slipped in a sheet of her letterhead with "Associate Director of Research, Special Markets" in the upper left-hand corner. Had somehow managed in spite of her shaking hands to type the necessary sentence or two, and afterward, with what felt like the flutter kick she used to do in the pool at Mile Trees years ago going on in her chest, around her heart, she had signed it.

The resignation came two weeks after her last visit to Triunion.

". . . Don't you know that these foundations and half-assed advocacy outfits you'll find yourself working for don't pay any money. You can't get anywhere fooling around with them. You should know that. How're you going to pay your bills, the god-damn rent? Send an SOS down to Daddy the first of every month . . . ?" The voice flailing away as much at himself as at her, she knew. Because his troubles with Davison had already begun by then. He had already started talking about letting Halcon Electronics have their job, but only saying it.

"Quitting a job you've had for years to work on your own. Taking that kind of a chance. I don't understand how you can take that kind of a chance . . ."

"Are you done?" she said when he finally fell silent. She spoke almost gently, knowing who he was really shouting at. She then told him that she had also decided to go back to school for a second master's. To take care of the unfinished business he knew about. She had unearthed the rejected proposal for her senior paper when she came in that afternoon, NCRC behind her forever, and had made up her mind.

*　*　*

When she could no longer put off writing home to let them know what she had done, the flutter kick started up around her heart again.

"She's with the National Consumer Research Corporation, y'know," the PM loved to say, his voice underscoring each word. "It's one of the biggest companies of its kind in the States, bo. One of the Fortune 500. Their profits for a month alone are probably more than our national budget. They could buy and sell Triunion in a minute. She's second only to one of the big directors there."

"Stop it," she once said to him. "You make it sound like I'm about to take over the place."

"And why not?" he laughed. "I don't know about you, but I'm expecting to see president or vice president or some other big title on the door to your office one of these days. After all, that's a country where the impossible is possible. Why do you think I sent you to live up there? CEO big on the door, my lady!"

"I wouldn't hold my breath if I were you."

But he did just that. Drawing up the solid mass of his body, he took a deep breath and held it, and kept on holding it until she cried laughing, hugging him, "All right, all right, I'll go for it. Now start breathing, for God's sake."

The PM. He could charm the devil himself.

Three months went by without a word from him once she wrote. No call, no blue envelope for three months. She heard only from Estelle, which surprised her, since Estelle rarely called and seldom wrote—aside from a hurried postscript at the end of the PM's letters. "Leave her alone. Let her live her life. Don't ask her to beard the lion for you," Estelle was always telling him. She had promptly replied, though, to the news of Ursa's leaving NCRC. A telegram consisting of a single word arrived. HOORAY! The telegram simply read HOORAY!

She gave up the apartment in Park West Village she could no longer afford, sold her furniture, her car—a new Toyota Corolla she had bought only the year before—even sold the better part of her clothes, all those NCRC suits, as she called them. She didn't bother to renew her membership at the health club on West End Avenue, where she had gone to swim at least twice a week. And as if reverting to the sixties even as the eighties were getting under way, she got up one morning, washed and washed her hair—all the TCB relaxer down the drain!—then, once it was dry and standing in a bush all over her head, she parted it down the middle, divided the hair on either side of the part into two thicknesses and carefully plaited it to form a single wreath of a braid that started at her forehead, trailed down behind her ears, and was joined at the back. Her hair was just thick and long enough to manage it. It looked, she decided, inspecting herself in the mirror afterward, like the braided loaves of hallah bread in the bakeries along Broadway.

It was the way Celestine who had helped raise her always wore her hair.

Afros, dreads and braids had not been allowed at NCRC.

And the braid brought her luck. Because shortly after she began wearing it she was hired for the project in Jersey. The Meade Rogers Foundation was conducting a study of the mayoral race in small, mostly black Midland City, just across the Hudson, and she became part of the team working with the black organizations in the city that had joined in a coalition to elect their candidate. It was to be a hands-on study with the foundation directly assisting the black candidate in his campaign. "Can't get away from the special markets," she had said to Viney with a laugh. "But this time I love it. We're actually going to be involved, putting some money where our mouth is, instead of just getting in people's business and collecting data. It's the kind of study I've always wanted to do."/"It's the most challenging and satisfying work I've ever done," she wrote to Triunion. Still no word. Until, some weeks into the study, she came in from Jersey one evening to find the familiar blue envelope in her mailbox.

Estelle, she later learned, had stopped eating until he changed his mind.

"One thing. If I find I can't get out of going down there for the election, I won't stay any time. I'll arrive two or three days before all the hoopla and leave the day after it's over."

She has finished most of the tempura on her plate and can't eat any more.

"You should go early and help with his campaign. You'll be able to give him some pointers from what you learned over in Jersey that time."

Steady eating. By now his head with the deep bays at the temples looks permanently bent over the almost empty platter.

"That old pro." Ursa decides to ignore his sarcasm and laughs. "He doesn't need any pointers from me. It's just that he likes for everyone in the family to be on hand for his big windup speech the last night of the campaign. He insists that the entire family be there—my two aunts, their husbands, my cousins, their children, everybody . . . Maybe I can get Viney to go with me!" The sudden thought brings hope. Viney had accompanied her that last visit to Triunion. Perhaps she could be persuaded to come along again.

"And how's the assistant vice president these days?" Lowell Carruthers looks up finally. Now that they're no longer talking about the PM, he raises his head.

"She's fine." The tone again! Down on everybody tonight because of the run-in with Davison. "I talked briefly with her this week, and I'm going over to Brooklyn tomorrow to spend the day with her and Robeson."

"Ah, the little wunderkind."

There it is again. Oh, Lowell, why don't you quit that kiss-muh-ass job? "Yes, the wunderkind," she says.

"Your godson."

"My godson."

"And he's fine too, of course."

Ursa gives him a look across the table, and shamefaced, apologetic, Lowell Carruthers quickly pours her a cup of tea, and then one for himself—he's finished the sushi. He'll have exactly three of the small ceramic cups of tea, Ursa knows, and he will pace himself drinking them so that he'll be through by ten forty-five. By no later than eleven, the bimonthly dinner will be over, the check paid, with her contributing her share, and they will be on their way out of the restaurant. "How're you going to pay your bills, the goddamn rent?" he had shouted at her four years ago, and ever since then she has insisted on paying her share of the check. And her one-room apartment on 101st Street has been off limits to him as well since then. "It's this hole-in-the-wall scarcely big enough for me, with papers from one end to the other," she had told him. "You couldn't stand the mess. I'll just come over to your place from now on."

She watches now as he raises the cup of tea to his lips and slowly drinks, already pacing himself, and last Friday comes flooding back. It would have been a girl. She's suddenly certain of it. A compulsive little girl born with a permanent frown above her flat little nose and all of Lowell Carruthers's irritating habits. When she took her on visits to Triunion, people there would look at her—take one look at her—and say she was one of those children who was living its last days first. An old child, in other words. A worrier. And organized to a fault. The kind of girlchild who would keep her room neat as a pin even when she was a teenager. What would she have said about her mother's sloppiness, her disorder? The books and notes for the still-to-be-written thesis littering her desk and the floor beside her bed? And the bed itself that still hasn't been made although another week has passed?

Ursa pushes away the cup of tea Lowell Carruthers poured for her in his effort to make amends and reaches for her pocketbook.

4

Outside on Columbus Avenue the night is surprisingly mild, windless, springlike. Earlier in the week, March—true to form —abruptly abandoned the numbing cold and wind that had gripped the city since the month began, and for the past four days the weather has suddenly been like spring verging on summer.

Old two-faced, not-to-be-trusted March, Ursa thinks, it could turn cold again tomorrow; nevertheless she welcomes the feel of the mildness against her face as she and Lowell Carruthers, who has reverted to the subject of Davison and the job, turn from the door of the restaurant and head uptown.

The change in the weather has swelled the weekend crowd on the avenue. The entire Upper West Side, it looks like, is either strolling along with them in the direction of Eighty-sixth Street, their cutoff point a dozen blocks ahead, or moving in an opposing tide downtown, toward the Chagall murals and the fountain at Lincoln Center. Couples, small groups, lovers, friends—all of them in as many different combinations as there are races and sexes—are window-shopping in front of the boutiques, book-stores and antique shops that line the street. They throng the bars, the gourmet food stores, the twenty-four-hour Korean fruit stands, and are still crowding into the restaurants although it's less than an hour from midnight. And where the owners of the sidewalk cafés have taken advantage of the false spring and brought the tables and chairs outdoors, every seat is filled. The faces flow by, black, white, Latina, Asian but mostly white, the Young and the Restless Upwardly Mobiles—she has her own name for them—the YRUMs who have taken over the lower half of Columbus Avenue, remade it into their image, and are continuing the march uptown.

Isn't she one of them? A YRUM in blackface? It's a question she avoids if she can help it, and she sidesteps it now by thinking of the avenue in its "before" days, before the cafés and the bou-tiques and the high-rise condos that flank it on either side. The first time she lived in the city for any time, which was thirteen years ago during the summer of her internship at NCRC, Co-lumbus Avenue had been a run-down stretch of old-law tene-ments and SRO hotels, little dingy mom-and-pop stores, bodegas that reeked of *bacalao*, and a roadway that put her in mind of the old north/south colonial road back in Triunion. Potholes for days! Some of them so deep you could see the steel tracks of the former trolley line lying embedded like the ribs of a dinosaur beneath the worn-away macadam.

"Don't you so-and-sos realize that one of these days this city is going to go tumbling into all of these potholes you leave all over the place. The entire city. It'll just disappear like Atlantis." She used to rail at City Hall as she drove down Columbus Av-enue, with the VW beetle she had at the time being shaken apart around her.

A couple—two of the YRUMs—are strolling just ahead on the crowded sidewalk. She sees the winter pallor to their whiteness in the sleeveless tops they both have on. Rushing the season. They could end up with pneumonia . . . She sees, too, the arms they have wrapped around each other. The woman's hand is thrust deep into the back pocket of the designer jeans the man has on.

. . . *Sexual activity can be resumed once the red discharge has ceased completely and there is no likelihood of infection or irritation.* So had read the instruction booklet that resembles a chapbook of poems with all the calla lilies on the cover.

She hasn't seen a speck of anything since the second day, and the closest she's come to feeling anything like pain is the laugh that knifed through her for a second last Friday when the bedroom voice over the speaker at the clinic whispered, "Love songs. Nothing but love songs."

". . . He just won't get off my case! Not a good three months goes by without him sharpening his ax again. The bastard spends more time thinking up ways to do me in than running the division . . ." The runaway voice next to her; she doesn't have to look up to know the size of the frown. ". . . And the fool doesn't even see the irony of it. Here our job is to try to resolve any differences the guys in the plant might have with each other or with management. We're *Employee Relations*, for God's sake, there to help everyone get along. That's what we're trained to do. What we were hired to do. And just look at what goes on with the twelve of us in that office! We get along worse than the three hundred guys in the plant. And all because of him. Ever since they brought him in to head up the division it's been hell around there . . ."

Think of him inspecting the sushi with his head bowed and hands clasped as if saying grace. Think of him looking up, the keloid of a frown gone, his eyes free of that man's face, his lips smiling and saying the word perfect without a sound. Think of his forefinger and thumb joined in a perfect circle.

". . . Cats hacking away at each other and thinking nothing of

53

it. That's what it's all about. Even if I were to leave and go somewhere else I'd probably run into the same shit. There'd be some other clown to contend with . . ."

I know, Viney. I should turn and take a cool walk in the opposite direction and let Mr. Carruthers go on up Columbus Avenue raving to himself like one of the crazies out here. It would be blocks before he even noticed the hole at his side. Don't ask me why I don't do it. I know: you would've been long gone . . .

Seventy-fifth Street. Two short blocks ahead, the night has hung a fuzzy half-moon above the roof of the American Museum of Natural History that sits on the corner there. And along with the moon a few dim little stars have broken through the soiled ozone. In Triunion now, the stars are numberless and outsized, Roman candles that refuse to dissolve once they rocket to the sky and explode . . . One of the first things Estelle had taught her was how to find Orion, the hunter, and the North Star, already pointing her in the direction of this, her other home, when she was no more than three or four . . . Come the end of May and the final meeting of the campaign, which the PM always holds at night out at the Monument of Heroes in Morlands, she'll look up at the sky and see the stars arrayed above the heads of Congo Jane and Will Cudjoe. The real stars above the giant stone heads, while on the platform at the base of the statue, she, Estelle, Celestine and the rest of the clan will form another constellation around the PM as he stands before the entire North District giving the government hell.

I'm not ready yet to be a star in the galaxy again! Oh, God, let that study come through!

". . . Who knows, maybe it's not even my black face that's the problem so much, but just the way the cat is. The way Type A personalities like him operate. That's what the Buppie hotshot out of Wharton they hired in marketing last year keeps telling me. You try talking to him about color and he looks at you like you're from before the Flood. Color's got nothing to do with it anymore as far as he's concerned. It's about personality types and egos and power plays. That's what he—"

Lowell Carruthers breaks off. His eye's been caught by the display window of a bicycle store they're passing. The store was not there the last time they walked along Columbus Avenue, which was back in October, before it turned cold. The window is very wide and two stories tall, and the bicycles on display— ten-, twelve- and fifteen-speed Schwinns, Raleighs and Peugeots —have been mounted on wires to give the impression that they're racing each other up a steep hill toward a neon finish line and a checkerboard flag in the upper left-hand corner of the window. The only light in the display comes from the flag and finish line, which are a flashing electric blue and hot pink. Occasionally the neon flashes off completely, the huge window goes black, and the bicycles disappear, only to reappear in a second or two.

"Beauties," Lowell Carruthers says, and taking her by the elbow, touching her for the first time all evening, goes over to stand almost reverently before the glass.

The riderless bikes speed motionless up the invisible hill, toward the finish line and flag high up in the corner to the left. Ursa finds herself in the lower right corner of the window, her reflection superimposed on the back wheel of a Raleigh that is at the end of the pack. As usual, she's the shortest thing there, half the height practically of the suddenly silent, absorbed figure next to her, who disappears along with her each time the window goes black, and shorter than a white couple standing nearby, admiring the display also, whose faces linger ghostlike in the plate glass whenever the hot pink and blue lights go off.

And I look even shorter in this cape! When the weather turned mild she had switched to an old spring cape left over from her NCRC days, which had begun to look slightly worn even back then. Viney will get after her about it tomorrow. The cape makes her look shorter yet. But like the coat she slept in last Friday and the loose-fitting dresses and boxy suits she wears, it does the job. It hides the body she still sometimes blames on Estelle when she stands naked in front of a mirror. Small, slight, sawed-off Estelle . . .

"You's everything like him, *oui!*" Celestine used to whisper in her ear the first thing in the morning as she sat her on the potty and the last thing after lowering the mosquito netting over her crib at night. "You's everything like him!" Meaning the PM's plum black skin and the version of his forehead that sits atop her face. But Estelle's genes had also had their way. They'd seen to it that she barely reached five feet, and they never got around to supplying her with a pair of decent hips, a discernible waistline and breasts that were more than just two nubs.

A body that belongs on some prepubescent ten-year-old!

It has taken her years to reconcile herself to it.

"Which one are you riding?" Lowell Carruthers asks.

"I'm on the Peugeot up at the finish line."

"You beat me. I'm on the slowpoke Schwinn in the middle," he says, laughing. For the first time all evening he's laughing, and his hand is still cupping her elbow. The warmth and shapeliness of his fingers on her skin. Then, as they resume the walk uptown: "I didn't see any Rosses in that window. They should have had a Ross going up that hill too. Now, there's a bike for you. I had one of those babies when I was at Lafayette. A fourteen-speed. You don't see those very often. A beauty. It was a beauty. I had this friend on campus who every time he saw me go whizzing by on it would yell, 'It's a bird! It's a plane! It's *Carruthers!*' " Laughing again, and a long arm shoots out, taking off for the half-moon above them. "I'm going to get one for my oldest nephew as soon as he turns twelve."

Had he ever thought it would come to this? Ursa asks herself as his laugh dies and his hand leaves her elbow, and Halcon Inc. takes over his voice again. Had he ever suspected that the four years riding around Lafayette on the Ross, and the six additional years he spent there after graduating, working as a recruiter and counselor in their minority outreach program (he himself had been recruited from Overbrook High in West Philly, just in time to escape Vietnam); and then the seven long years he had put in afterward on his master's and doctorate while continuing to recruit for Lafayette on a free-lance basis, recruiting being what he liked most—and married by then, he was married by then to the woman who would later walk out on him, taking with her all the wedding-gift china and silver, crystal and linens—had he ever once thought, ever imagined that all of that, the long haul, the grind, the years staying steady on the case would come down to this: Davison and a job that has raised a frown like a permanent welt between his eyebrows, eaten away at his hairline so that at thirty-eight he looks almost the age of the PM, and is sending him raving up Columbus Avenue now like some poor crazy the state hospital had demobilized, ruining a Friday evening that tastes and feels like spring?

". . . I betcha I won't be in the office a good five minutes on Monday before another one of his memos . . . Shit!"

She is seriously considering heeding Viney's voice and doing an about-face and heading back down Columbus Avenue, when Lowell Carruthers suddenly cries "Shit!" and stops. He stops and for a long minute stands silent in the middle of the sidewalk, his head bowed and every muscle in his body reined in as his voice was in the restaurant. Steeling himself to be silent. A huge Mayflower moving van thunders past them amid the cars and buses. Someone moving in or getting out of New York under cover of night. And then Ursa feels it: his hand groping for her arm again, the part that lies outside the slit in her cape. He seldom says anything when he does this, just reaches down, searches blindly for her arm and once he finds it holds on. Holds on as if that one small limb alone has the power to save him from both his outrage and his runaway tongue.

With her arm pressed to his side, they make the turn at Eighty-sixth Street and head toward Central Park West one long block away. There they'll either continue walking or take the bus up to his apartment near the northern end of the park and the official beginning of Harlem.

———

Would it have had, whether a boy or girl, the two slight depressions she calls dimples at the small of its back? Dimples like grace notes. They're something else that rates high on the list of things she still likes about Lowell Carruthers. She brings her fingers to rest on them where they lie on either side of his spine, just above the two rounded hills of his behind—a part of him she would love to steal and graft onto herself.

Would it have been blessed with the dimples and the same shapely ass . . . ?

Tears, with the sudden violence of rain in Triunion. They add to his excitement: "Ursa, baby!" He has mistaken them for the welling up of pleasure.

5

Vincereta (Viney) Daniels

"Aunt Ursa!"

Robeson is so happy to see her he breaks into the boogaloo as he unlocks the basement gate of the brownstone. Dancing, he swings open the heavy wrought-iron gate, Ursa steps down into the entryway that lies beneath the high stoop of the house, and he almost topples her with a bear hug.

"Aunt Ursa!"

He's all long, solid limbs, sweaty heat and excitement in a Little League uniform. Cat's whiskers from the milk he must have gulped down before racing to answer the bell are at the corners of his mouth. And his mouth, she discovers, is almost on a level with her own. "Stop growing!" She playfully shakes him. "Seems like every time I come over here you've shot up another inch. You're not supposed to be taller than your aunt and you're not even nine yet. How's my favorite godson?" She hugs him back.

"Great! Look what I got on." Stepping back, he opens his arms to show off the uniform. "We started spring practice this morning and guess what, Aunt Ursa, I got two hits, drove in a run, stole second, and only struck out once. How's that for the first day?"

"Your mother should have named you Robinson instead of Robeson." Laughing, she hugs him again.

Behind him on the stone wall of the entryway a sign reads V. Daniels and Son, and under the name there's the silhouette of a woman's hand with the index finger pointing toward the interior of the house. Standing under the sign, waiting to be greeted, is a wiry little girl Robeson's age with large, watchful eyes under a beaded curtain of hair. She's also in uniform, complete with a cap over the beads, which come down to her eyebrows. Red and green beads against the black twigs of her hair. A pitcher's glove almost twice the size of her face hangs from her belt. One small, very dark hand holds a softball; the other she's exercising with a handgrip. She stands as if about to go into her windup and pitch.

"And how's Miss Dee Dee?" Ursa asks.

"Fine," the child says and allows herself to be embraced. "I'm gettin' my arm ready."

Dee Dee from down the block. From the unsightly group of walk-ups and old-law tenements that sits like a wart at one end of the gentrified brownstones that occupy the rest of the street. She and Robeson were inseparable as toddlers. And even now that they're older and go to different schools, they still spend their weekends together. Viney sees to that.

The children—with Robeson already launched into an account of the ball game—shepherd Ursa down the hall that runs the length of the ground floor. A large family room with a fireplace and an exposed brick wall opens off to the right. Separated from the family room by a pair of beautifully carved sliding doors is a formal dining room. At the end of the hallway, through a doorway flooded with sunlight, lies the kitchen; and there, waiting on the boundary between the sunlight in the room behind her and the partial dimness of the hall stands Viney, a hand on her hip and her tall frame angled to one side. Standing as if poised to take that first dramatic step onto a dance stage or the runway at a fashion show. She could be a dancer—a Judith Jamison in "Cry"—Ursa thinks, or a high-fashion model—some Imam being shot in silhouette—or a market woman in Triunion, getting ready with that hand on her hip to haggle you to the death over the price of her mangoes. Dancer, model, market woman. Viney could be all three.

"My mother's not speaking to you." A whisper in Ursa's ear. They are almost to the kitchen.

"I hope you know I'm not speaking to you."

"So I've just heard."

They hold each other for a long, silent minute. Her head scarcely reaches Viney's breastbone. "Here come the long and short of it," their friends on campus used to say when they saw the two of them walking across the quadrangle together or in the corridors of the old battlemented buildings on their way to class or coming toward the soul table in the dining hall. Viney's long-legged five feet nine next to her four eleven and three-quarter inches. "Here come the long and short of it."

"I mean it. I'm not saying a word to you, not directly anyway." Viney has stepped away from her. "Robeson, tell your aunt what the procedure is for today. But first, take that thing she calls a cape, which I had hoped not to see again this year, and hang it up and have her sit down."

He does as he's told, and when they are all inside the kitchen and Ursa's seated at the table that holds his and Dee Dee's unfinished lunch, Robeson strikes his mother's pose of moments ago, a hand akimbo and his body at a slant. "Okay, Aunt Ursa, this is how it goes. My mother's not speaking to you, right? Not directly anyway. So whatever she says to you has to come through me. I'm to be the inter—, the inter—" He glances over at Viney.

"Intermediary. What am I paying my money for at that fancy school?"

"You didn't have to tell me. I was gonna say it. I'm to be the intermediary, Aunt Ursa. Whatever my mother says to you has to come through me."

"And whatever you say to her has to come through me."

"Oh, am I to have an intermediary too?" She turns with a laugh to Dee Dee.

"I just decided you needed one. I wanna play too."

"All right, I'm putting you right to work then."

"Shoot." Dee Dee—all fifty pounds of her—readies herself, and Ursa's gaze shifts back to her friend. "Viney, I'm sorry. I know you don't want to hear that old, tired word, but I am. I've been apologizing to you all week. I know I should've called, but something came up, another crisis, and I just couldn't pick up the phone. You know how I am. I've been steady talking to you, though, in my head. Not an hour's gone by in over two weeks that I haven't called your name. Your ears just had to be ringing nonstop. But I know, you don't want to hear all that. I should've called no matter what, so you're hot—which you have every right to be—and I'm in the doghouse, where I belong. Anyway, when I tell you the reason for the silence, you'll forgive me. I know you'll forgive me." She keeps her eyes on the set face.

Her small hand working the grip, Dee Dee repeats as much as she remembers.

"You left out most of it!" Robeson cries.

Viney reprimands him with a look, and in the next breath says, "It had better be a good reason, that's all I have to say. I'm going to be all ears. Over two weeks and not a peep out of you. Haven't seen you in more than a month and then for weeks I can't even reach you on the phone. Each time I call all I get is the machine—and you know how I hate that thing. But I leave a message. Each time I leave a message. What's up? Why haven't I heard from you? Is anything wrong? I just knew something had to be wrong. Call me. Please call me. You think you called? Not a word—"

"I'm sorry, Viney."

"—I'm not speaking to you. And then when you do finally call it's only to say you'll be over today. Hung up before I could even get in a word. Is that any way to treat folks? Had me worried half to death. Was she in an accident and lying in a coma in a hospital somewhere? Or had a certain person whose name I won't mention finally driven her to end it all off the George Washington Bridge? . . ."

He had taken her tears last night as a sign of pleasure.

". . . Or did she wake up one morning and decide she was ready to go back to that island of hers and just took off without so much as a fare-thee-well. All kinds of horror stories kept running through my head. You know me and my overactive imagination. Anyway, I'm glad to see that whatever happened you're still here. And you seem to be all right. You look the same, down to that miserable cape you should have thrown out long ago . . . All right"—she pauses briefly—"now that I've got that off my chest, I'm going to remember my manners and make you a cup of coffee, which I know you need after that long subway ride over here, and then fix us some lunch. We're having a crab-meat and pasta salad, tell her, Robeson—and you're not to leave out a single word I've said—and a little vino to go with it."

Robeson waits a second or two to make sure she's done and then, bringing his right arm up halfway, fans her down. "Who's supposed to remember all that? Not me."

"Ya see! Ya see!" Dee Dee cries. They all laugh and the game is over.

Viney goes to prepare the coffee at a large island in the middle of the room that holds the stove, sink and work space, while over at the table, which is an extension of the island in the form of a counter with stools on either side, the children resume eating. Eating and talking, especially Robeson.

"So lemme tell you, Aunt Ursa, how I stole second this morning, okay? . . ."

He has hitched his stool so close to hers his face is only inches from her own. He has Viney's mouth, that full lower lip that always makes Ursa think of a hibiscus. There's the same curled-over, striated look as the petals of the hibiscus that are to be found growing everywhere on Triunion. It's the national flower. When Robeson's being stubborn, that lower lip curls down almost to his chin. And he has Viney's cigar-store-Indian nose. Some Chickahominy in Virginia long ago left his or her signature on the Daniels family tree before being force-marched on the Trail of Tears. The rest of his face—the square little jaw, the skin as dark as her own and Dee Dee's and the coffee being made, his smile—none of these can be placed.

"... I could tell the kid guarding me wasn't paying attention, so I just started easing off first, easing off first . . ."

"My arm's still a little rusty, but I did okay for the first day. Only gave up three hits . . ." Dee Dee, across the table, has placed the ball and the handgrip beside her plate, which holds a partly eaten chicken sandwich.

". . . and then I just took off and went flying into second . . ."

". . . They wouldn't let me pitch the whole game because the others had to have a chance, but I only gave up three hits when I was up and I struck out musta been five."

". . . and listen to this, Aunt Ursa . . ."

"I got this new pitch I'm working on."

Ursa listens, and inspects the two pairs of eyes crowded in on her. The whites in Robeson's match the milk in his glass and at the corners of his mouth. Eyes so clear, so unmarred that when they're brought up close like this they always cause a little flutter kick of anxiety around her heart. Why? She can't say. Not so with the eyes across the table. They appear to be on twenty-four-hour guard duty under the beaded curtain of hair. She listens, and sips the coffee when Viney places the large mug in front of her. Coffee grown on the foothills of Gran' Morne. The PM always includes a supply of the beans for Viney in the package he sends faithfully every three months. She listens, and from time to time looks over with a penitent smile to where the salad's being made.

Viney—tall, lean, angular, with the hibiscus mouth, majestic nose and skin the color of caramel. She has on her usual at-home outfit—long denim wraparound skirt, a Lady Hathaway shirt with the tails gathered and tied at the waist, and Swedish clogs. An Aunt Jemima bandanna hides the flyaway hair, and not a trace of makeup is to be seen on her bent face. There's the Viney of the plain denim skirt, head tie and no makeup, and the fashion plate who leaves the house five mornings a week dressed in the flawless suits, coats and dresses she calls her going-to-meet-the-Met clothes, the Met being the Metropolitan Life Insurance Company where she is an assistant vice president in annuities and other retirement products. Right after graduation, she entered the management training program at Metropolitan and has been there ever since. She was already living and working in New York the summer Ursa did her internship at NCRC. She stayed with Viney in her apartment on West Ninety-third Street.

"I hear New England, but what's that other accent you've got?"

Ursa told her. She was the freshman, newly arrived on campus, and Viney the junior and one of the RAs in charge of the freshman dorm.

"I ask," Viney said, "because I'm kind of a foreigner myself. And I know the hard time they sometimes give us in this place. My first semester I was all ready to give these folks back their scholarship and go on back to Petersburg. Petersburg, Virginia, that's where I'm from. You see, I'd forget sometimes and come out with a 'y'all' in class, and everybody would look at me like I just crawled out of a bale of cotton and still had lint all in my nappy head. And it wasn't only the little white girls looking at me funny but some of the siddity sisters we've got around here went to these white private schools all their lives. They'd be looking at me funny too. I used to feel like more of a foreigner than the real ones on campus. But I learned how to deal. Had to! And you know something: it wasn't all that hard. Anyone can do it. I just trained myself to save the 'y'alls' and such for Folks with a capital F—and to use 'you' singular *and* plural with everybody else, including the siddities. If you ever need it, I'll teach you how to deal too. Just hang with me."

"Here come the long and short of it," their friends used to say. "If you see one, you know you *gots* to see the other."

". . . Pick any name, Aunt Ursa, and ask me his batting average last season and I bet I can tell you." Robeson has brought out his collection of Yankee baseball cards and thrust them in her hands.

". . . Lookit how I'm gonna have to hold the ball for my new pitch." The small dark hand with the oversize white ball is also being thrust at her across the table.

". . . Just ask me, Aunt Ursa. Any name. I've got my eyes closed . . ."

"Lookit how . . ."

"Help," she cries, laughing, and over at the island Viney stops cutting up a green pepper, puts down the knife, the hand goes to her hip again; dancer, model, market woman; and the table falls silent. "You two have got exactly fifteen more minutes to try and talk her to death. Just fifteen more minutes, and then I'm going to send you packing so I can get in a word./You see what happens when you stay away so long? They can't get enough of you./Both of you seem to have forgotten you have a rehearsal this afternoon./They're in a play over at the center . . ." Viney's eyes and voice move back and forth between Ursa and the children. "Why don't you tell her about that instead of bending her ear about baseball? You're rushing the season anyway./I keep telling them it might be the last week in March and it might feel like spring but it's still March and we could have ten inches of snow tomorrow."

"It's this play about Harriet Tubman, Aunt Ursa. Ever heard of her?"

Dee Dee is on her feet. "I'm the star. I play her so I'm the star. There's a price of forty thousand dollars on my head."

"And I'm her father, Aunt Ursa, that she sneaks back down

south to rescue. I'm gonna have to wear this long white beard and put talcum powder in my hair. And I'm gonna have to walk all bent over." He too is on his feet, demonstrating.

"I'm wanted dead or alive," says Dee Dee.

"Only fifteen more minutes, remember, and you're to lower the decibel level and speak one at a time."

"They call me the General."

The General. One night it would be the story of the General, another night that of Sojourner Truth, with Estelle on her feet beside the bed where she lay, demanding, "An' ain' I a wo-man . . . ?" And repeatedly there would be Congo Jane and Will Cudjoe, their story as well. Celestine, whom Estelle had taught to read when she was teaching Ursa her ABCs, used to sit to one side listening. But she would also be waiting for Estelle to finish, lean over the bed and kiss her goodnight and leave. Then just before the lamp was turned off there would come the whisper through the mosquito netting: "You's everything like him, *oui*. Everything!"

"There's this real scary part, Aunt Ursa, when the paterollers with their big dogs are after us . . ."

"Me, I'm the only one who's never scared . . ."

Their voices home in on her again.

The smell of crabmeat, onions and green pepper drifts over to the table, while sunlight from the backyard pours into the room through a bay window that is as wide if not as tall as the one in her apartment. The first thing Viney had done after buying the house was to remodel the kitchen, Ursa remembers. The large island with the counter and stools at one end became the centerpiece, with a rack of gleaming copper pots above it. The cabinets and the brick-colored tiled floor are those of a French country kitchen, and a garden of culinary herbs—dill, thyme, basil and oregano in a row of green planters—takes up the wide ledge of the window. During the renovation Viney had the room stripped of everything except the old-fashioned coal stove that had been there since the house was built. This she kept and even uses occasionally. Last winter she taught Robeson how to bake bread in it.

This kitchen. Ursa takes another sip of her coffee. This house. It was number four on the list of indispensables Viney drew up on the day Robeson was born. Ursa arrived at the hospital just hours after Robeson's birth to find a radiant Viney propped up in bed, a pad on her lap, a pencil in hand, busy drawing up the list while waiting for her milk to come in.

1. *Sleep-in help for at least the first three years.*
2. *A private school if a decent public one is nowhere near.*
3. *Some kind of a black cultural center so he won't grow up to be a siddity.*
4. *A house with some stairs and a backyard so he'll be able to say he had an honest-to-God childhood . . .*

A house. A few months later Viney was to say to her, "You should see the look on your face. I keep telling you it's nothing a few repairs and some paint won't cure."

They were standing outside the partly boarded up brownstone that was missing one end of its cornice and several balusters to the stoop. They had just come from inspecting inside the house, which as far as Ursa was concerned was as hopeless as what faced them. Yet even inside, moving from one wreck of a room to another, Viney had been enthusiastic.

And it wasn't only the house. It was the treeless, run-down block on which it stood amid scores of others like it, and the blighted streets around it. Harlem, the South Bronx, the worst of the North End in Hartford she kept seeing as they drove through the neighborhood earlier.

"Your problem is that you can't imagine what it's going to look like once it's fixed up. Ursa, those are parquet floors in the living room—parquet floors!—and oak paneling under all that cheap paint. A few cans of stripper and it'll be oak again. And you saw the sun parlor upstairs. Who ever hears of a sun parlor anymore? And the size of the backyard. I've been looking for a house with a big backyard. I'm going to turn it into a playground for Robeson and friends. Swings, a sliding pond, a jungle gym, a sandbox, the works. What do you think of that, Mr. Daniels, suh?" She consulted the four-month-old Robeson who was fast asleep in a canvas Snuggli strapped to her chest. The October day was chilly and she had dressed him in a yellow sweater set and socks. "He approves," she said, looking up with a grin. "He further states that he does not want to grow up in an apartment on the Upper West Side with all the crazies and beggars on Broadway making him feel so bad every time he steps out the door. Nor does he want to live in the suburbs where he'll hardly ever get to see another little chocolate-colored minority like himself. Brooklyn, he says, will do just fine."

"I just don't see the point, Viney. Why sell an apartment that's worth its weight in gold to buy a dilapidated old house all the way over here?" She thought of Viney's large two-bedroom apartment on Ninety-third Street near Columbus Avenue. She had been lucky to find it only months after she moved to New York, and four years later, when the building went co-op, she had bought her place at the insider's price with a loan guaranteed by Metropolitan. "I fail to see the point—" repeating herself, although she saw the point only too well. It had to be someplace as far away as Brooklyn. Willis. Willis Jenkins. Someplace far from him. Oh, Viney. But why this old house? "Anybody can see this thing is going to be nothing but a headache and money," she said.

"To repeat: a few repairs and some paint. You're letting appearances fool you. This house is a diamond in the rough. And, yes, the neighborhood is strictly inner city right now. But don't let that fool you either. All this is going to be prime real estate in a few years, seeing as how close it is to high-priced Brooklyn Heights. The YRUMs, as you call them, are coming. Gentrification with a capital G is on its way. You won't recognize around here by the time Mr. Daniels here is ready to go to school."

She was right. By the time Robeson was in first grade at the Belfield School in nearby Brooklyn Heights, more than half the old brownstones on the block had been bought, renovated, and restored, and almost as many white as black and Latina faces were to be seen. The transformation brought trees evenly spaced along the curb, new sidewalks and streetlamps, and grass or inlaid slate in the front yards. A few like Viney even added an old-fashioned gas lamp out front. There was a block association. The children's softball team was organized. And a committee with Viney as chair was formed to pressure the owners of the walk-ups at the corner where Dee Dee's family lived to completely overhaul the buildings.

"The big G," Viney said. "What did I tell you?"

In restoring her house she insisted on stripping all of the woodwork herself. She brought in a contractor to carry out the other work, but no one save herself was allowed to touch the oak paneling on the parlor floor. Evenings and weekends found her with her head tied up and wearing a surgical mask and heavy industrial rubber gloves scrubbing away at the wainscoting, the baseboards and the tall, beautifully carved sliding double doors that separated the rooms on the second floor. She went through gallon cans of stripper, countless rolls of sandpaper and Triple 0 steel wool and any number of pairs of gloves. Working away until perspiration stained the old shirts she wore and her headtie where it stretched across her forehead.

Willis, Ursa would say to herself, watching her. It's still about Willis Jenkins.

The evening she met him in Viney's apartment on Ninety-third Street, he had his large black-leather portfolio spread open on the coffee table in the living room and he was showing her and Viney sketches for a book jacket he hoped to do for Macmillan. Everything had been cleared off the table and it had been moved a little away from the couch to make room for the portfolio. In fact, she had the impression that everything in the room—all the furniture, books, the prints and paintings on the walls—had been shifted around, rearranged to accommodate not only the oversize leather case but Willis Jenkins as well—his long legs, his long narrow feet, his shoes that came she could tell from one of those men's stores where there are no prices in the window, his close-cropped beard, his voice like Ron Carter's singing double bass, and the elephant-hair bracelet in gold around his wrist. Gold against his blackness. A man all black and gold.

She was happy for Viney, but envious. Envy for a moment soured on her tongue the wine she was drinking with them. Because those were the years—years that felt like an entire lifetime—when there wasn't even a Lowell. An inventory of her life then would have turned up only NCRC—the job morning, noon and the better part of her evenings—the pool at the Park-view Health Club on West End Avenue twice a week, a night out with Viney on the weekends—a club, a concert or a party. Viney and her parties! And the occasional date that was seldom repeated. And there were the faithful visits to Triunion. She spent the holidays and every one of her vacations there, up-country, in the old Mackenzie house up-country. Sometimes, on the spur of the moment, she even took the plane and flew down for a long weekend. And she never missed an election.

"How do you expect to meet anybody running down to that island every minute? You tell me there're no men there to speak of. You need to stay on the scene more." Viney, acting the part of her RA in the dorm again, would lecture her. "All right, so it's rough out here. But you need to do like me. I refuse to think about all the things ag'in' us. The black men–black women ratio thing to begin with, more of us than them. That's a downer right there. And these fancy-sounding job titles a few of us have—assistant vice president this, associate director that—that scare the brothers away, and the little white girls out here eyeing what we eyeing, and the brothers who only have eyes for them. And not to mention, not to mention *pu'leeze* those among the brothers who have eyes only for each other, or for themselves—you know, the me-me-mes; or the ones who believe, really and truly believe, that things go better with coke, and love that more than they can ever love you. And you know I know of what I speak. I've been there and oh, that can be some heavy competition. But I refuse to let my mind dwell on any of it. And that's what you need to do. Don't think about all that mess. Don't let it get to you. Just hang in there. You got to hang in there! You get discouraged too easily."

For years Viney zealously followed her own advice. There wasn't an opening at the Studio Museum uptown or the Cinque Gallery downtown she didn't attend. She was at every exhibit, screening, symposium and panel discussion, every book signing and poetry reading held at the Schomburg Center for Research in Black Culture on Lenox Avenue. At every concert of the Up-town Chamber Society and nearly every jazz concert, dance recital (Alvin Ailey, the Dance Theatre of Harlem) and cultural festival. Viney on the scene at every major Black History Month event in February and at the round of African receptions at the U.N. in the fall. "Looking for an ambassador. Won't settle for anything less than an ambassador." And there were the parties, those she gave, those she was always being invited to, and the ones she ferreted out and appeared at uninvited.

"Party!"—said like a battle cry over the phone when she called to get Ursa to come along. "I feel tonight's our lucky night. Put on something outrageous and come."

"I don't have anything outrageous."

"Well, put on one of those mumu dresses of yours and come anyway. You need to get out."

"I was out until six in the morning with you last Saturday, remember? Nina, crazy Nina, at the Village Gate, remember? The woman kept us waiting two hours before she even showed up and then another hour before she decided to sing. Then you just *had* to go to that after-hours club after that, and when that closed you just *had* to have breakfast at the Empire. It was dawn's early light before I saw my bed. No, thanks. Not tonight. I can't keep up with you and the marathon, Viney."

"Please, Ursa. I really feel lucky tonight. Please."

A long silence during which she saw her friend's face over the phone, the strain and pleading there . . .

"All right."

For a time she put her faith in something called Black Professional Selective Introductions—"It's all done by computer, Ursa. You should try it."/"No, thanks."/—and the Black Singles Vacation Club. Later on, in the desperate years just before Willis Jenkins, there had been the Friday and Saturday night take-home men from the bar for the Beautiful People on Columbus Avenue not far from her apartment. "It clears the tubes, Ursa. You think and feel better the next day. You need to get out here and get you some." A Viney who didn't even sound like herself anymore. And for a long frightening year, when she was involved with an account executive at Merrill Lynch, she became a fixture along with him at the other, more notorious bar for the BPs that was even closer to where she lived on West Ninety-third, the one nicknamed "The Pharmacy." Every and any remedy could be purchased there.

Ursa rarely saw her then.

Viney. She partied hearty, always looking with her long, lean angular frame and the flawless clothes she wore as if she were about to step onto the runway at the annual Ebony Fair Fashion Show, a hand at her hip, her body at a model's slant, and the red hibiscus mouth in bloom under the icon of a nose.

"You got to hang in there!" She had taken her own counsel, had hung in there, had refused to think of all the things ag'in' her, and had finally met Willis Jenkins, who not only drew beautiful illustrations and talked of book jackets, art editors and the publishing business, but whose daddy longlegs outstripped her own.

In no time the second bedroom in her apartment was converted into a studio, the bed and other furniture there moved out to make room for Willis Jenkins's huge drawing table and stool, his clothes and the special cabinets he used for his art supplies.

"You're shining like new money," Ursa said to her friend.
"Can't help but."
"I'm jealous." Hugging her.

Five years later Viney was to move the bed and other furniture
back into the room. Five years. It took her that long before she
could bring herself to tell Willis Jenkins to take his drawing table
and stool, his cabinets, his clothes and shoes—especially the
shoes: "You can have them! Every last pair of them! Just take
them and go!"—and everything else belonging to him out of her
apartment, and hand over her keys.

"And come to find out, Ursa, he didn't even have that far to
go. Had his next sponsor already lined up down on the second
floor. And look who it is. The final kick in the teeth . . ." Then,
turning her anger and disgust against herself: "Fool! How blind
can you be."

She was in the pool on the top floor of the Parkview while Viney,
wearing a bathing suit with an overskirt because of the weight
she had put on, was sitting, meditating, on a bench against the
wall. The wall of white tiles reached three stories high to the
banked lights on the ceiling. Seven o'clock on a Friday evening
in late January, and almost a year since Viney had demanded
back her keys and Willis Jenkins had moved downstairs. On the
streets below the Parkview the blackened remains of a snowstorm
from earlier in the month lay piled along the curbs, and the
sidewalks were slick underfoot where the snow hadn't been removed and had turned to ice. They had had to hold on to each
other to keep from falling on the way over.

Since the breakup Viney had taken to accompanying her nearly
everywhere. Sometimes, no matter how late Ursa got in from
work she found her waiting. Viney would have let herself in the
apartment with her set of keys and would be sitting, waiting, in
the dining area off the kitchen, snacking on whatever was to be

found there. Or the phone would ring sometimes as soon as she stepped in the door: "Whatcha doing? I'm coming over." Or: "I don't feel like cooking. Let's go out to eat." On Saturdays she neglected her own chores to trail along with Ursa to the shoe repair, the dry cleaners, the bakery; and although she couldn't swim aside from a dog paddle and had never approved of swimming pools—"You can't meet anybody there. The brothers don't swim"—she had even taken to accompanying her to the Parkview.

Eyes closed, legs drawn up in a partial lotus, she sat on the bench set back from the water. Her long hands, the caramel of a Sugar Daddy lollipop, lay on her knees with the thumb and forefinger joined. Wholeness and unity. Inner peace and calm . . . "I'm not going back out there, Ursa," she announced one evening, speaking grimly out of one of the long numbed silences that would come over her from time to time. "I-am-not-going-out-there-again. You hear me?"/"I hear you."/To give her the strength to hold to her vow, she sought out a TM group uptown and began attending meetings and talking about being initiated. "I won't do it, though, unless you do too."/"Oh, come on, Viney, you know I don't go in for all that spirituality stuff."/ "Please. Just do it for me."

So that one Saturday afternoon Ursa found herself along with her friend in a stuffy, overfurnished little apartment in the Riverton on 135th Street, not far from the Schomburg. A middle-aged brown-skinned woman whose body, clothes and dyed wavy black hair, "good" hair, gave off the smell of sandalwood, ushered them in and took the gift-offerings they had been instructed to bring: a few pieces of fruit, a small bouquet of flowers and a brand-new white handkerchief. The main part of the initiation took place privately in the adjoining bedroom. Viney went first, and when she was done, Ursa followed the woman into the bedroom, where a large picture of the Maharishi—flowing white beard, a kindly face the same nut brown as the woman's—hung on the wall across from the bed. There, engulfing her in the smell of sandalwood, the woman repeatedly whispered "Ke'ram" in her ear. She was to say it silently with her eyes closed and her spine held straight for fifteen minutes at the beginning and end of each day, and whenever she felt the need . . .

The pool was virtually empty that Friday evening. There was Viney seated like a Buddha against the soaring white wall and herself in the water along with one other swimmer, a white woman about her age whom she saw nearly every time she came to the Parkview. A solitary swimmer like herself. For exactly a half hour each time, the woman did a series of smooth blind laps that scarcely brought her goggled face out of the water. Even when she climbed out at the end of the half hour and disappeared into the locker room she remained hidden behind the goggles and her expressionless face. She never spoke, smiled, or looked at anyone there. What would an inventory of her life turn up, Ursa often wondered, watching her retreating back.

The woman left. She had the huge pool all to herself. Or so she thought, until glancing over as she reached the wall at the deep end and started to make her turn, she saw that Viney had joined her.

Occasionally, when there were only a few people around, Viney would come in the water, paddle briefly back and forth across the shallow end, perhaps do a few scissor kicks holding onto the gutter, then climb out and return to her bench. Tonight, she had entered the pool up near the diving board, and instead of her usual dog paddle she was simply dangling in the water, her back against the gutter, her arms outstretched along the ledge, holding onto it, and her head thrown all the way back.

Ursa was at her side in seconds.

"Viney . . . ?"

The head remained flung back, almost touching the gutter; the eyes were wide open, and there was this river on her face.

"Oh, Viney."

She held her. She reached around, and with her undersize arms gathered in as much of her as she could, this stranger with the thickened waist and fleshy arms and shoulders, and breasts that were twice their normal size. Not even the familiar fragrance of her cologne and the Lustrasilk she used on her hair made her feel and look any less strange. Ursa spoke to her, saying in one breath: "Don't, Viney, please. Don't upset yourself. I thought you had put him behind you . . ." And in the next breath: "Go ahead. Get it out of you. It's about time. You'll feel better . . ." Not knowing what she was saying or what to say. Not that it mattered, because there was no sign that Viney was either listening or could hear her. Was she even aware of the arms around her? It didn't seem so. She simply hung there like a human plumb line that had been dropped over the side of the pool to measure the depth of the water, staring up at the lights in the high ceiling, while the silent river made its way along the ridge of her cheekbones down to her ears and then through the intricate channel of her ears before emptying into the gutter behind.

Ursa held her—as much of her as she could manage—and she felt her own river, which couldn't be blamed on a Willis Jenkins, or on any one person or thing yet, at times, was about everything, all the shit; a river that was simply there, ever present, always threatening to catch her unawares and overrun the levees she had built against it: NCRC, the pool here, the faithful visits to Triunion—she felt it rising in her as well. She tried gently rocking Viney, she kept repeating the words that went unheard, tried comforting her friend, and it was like trying to rock and comfort herself.

Around them the water in the pool was as warm and placid as the sea at her favorite beach in Triunion, the one at Government Lands up-country. "You have to come with me the next time I go home, all right?" She spoke softly. "As often as I've gone with you to Petersburg, you've yet to visit my little island in the sun. That's not fair. You have to come with me the next time I go down. I'll take you to the best beach in all the world. Don't worry, you won't have to go in the water. You can just sit under a palm tree and look glamorous. And have the sagaboys falling all over you . . ."

Silence. The water lapping against the side of the pool and flowing in the gutter was the only sound. The only other movements, aside from the water in the gutter, were the light pumping of her legs below the surface, the rocking motion she kept up, and the river winding through the watercourse of Viney's ear just inches from her.

Nine-forty by the clock on the wall behind the diving platform.

"It's time to get out of the water, Viney. The pool'll be closing soon. Come on."

Still no sign that she was even capable of hearing.

"Let's go eat. I only had a little something when I came in from work and I'm starving. Come on, dinner will be on me. I'll treat you to Chinese on Broadway since it's Friday . . ."

She heard it then: a deep, racking sound that could have come only from the source of the river. Viney's head remained thrown back, her arms rigid along the gutter, her flooded gaze on the banked lights overhead, but her body had begun to heave with a sound like the tearful raging of a mute. "Oh, Viney, don't—" holding her tighter, cradling her all the more, while the racking sound and the heaving went on and on, growing stronger, until soon she could feel it beginning to drain the body dangling like a plumb line over the edge of the pool. She found she had to pump harder to keep herself afloat, and suddenly there was the same rapid kick going on around her heart. "Please, Viney, let's get out. It's time we got out."

The water that had been no higher than the swollen waistline when she first spotted her and came racing over now stood above the bra of the matronly bathing suit. And there was this drag, this pull to her body as if the more than twenty pounds she had piled on in the past year had suddenly settled around her ankles. And the weighted ankles in turn were causing her hands to lose their grip on the ledge. Her outstretched arms were slowly sliding, slipping down.

"Viney!" She was struggling now to keep afloat not only herself but this large slack body that felt as if it had suddenly grown weights around the ankles. The strength in her shoulders and in her arms and legs from all the swimming she had done over the years was suddenly nothing against the growing dead weight in her arms.

"Viney!" Her cry drowned out by the choked raging of the mute.

One limp, fleshy arm slipped from the gutter, broke the skin of the water and disappeared.

"*Viney!*"—screaming into her ear now at the terrifying thought that the custodian might come to turn off the lights and find both of them up to the game she used to play long ago in the pool at Mile Trees—diving to the bottom of the pool and sitting there to impress, tease and frighten the PM.

"*Viney!*" This time her scream reached all the way up the acres of white tile to the high ceiling and the bank of lights, and as it came sheering down in what sounded like a hail of shattered glass and splintered light the weighted, near lifeless thing that was bearing her down with it suddenly started as if struck by the raining glass, and the head on the thing, which was arched all the way back, slowly, inch by painful inch, righted itself.

The moment Viney brought her head up, into place again, the river altered its course, and after a millennium it stopped.

"I'm all right now." Said with her face turned away.

Ursa held on. There was still the slackness and the dead weight, and the heaving could still be felt.

"I said I'm all right. You can let go now."

She continued to hold on until Viney finally turned to face her, and then she abruptly dropped her arms. One look at those eyes and she let go. The last of the river had dried to form what looked like a high-gloss, scuff-proof polyurethane finish on a hardwood floor. One glance at it and her arms dropped of their own accord. Seconds later, as Viney turned and started her little primordial crawl over to the nearest ladder, she simply followed behind.

* * *

They could have been merely two small sample vials of perfume Viney had placed for some reason in the freezer compartment of her refrigerator. Perfume the odd color of concentrated grapefruit juice or, Ursa thought, peering in the freezer, the soursop juice she used to love as a little girl. The same grayish white, clouded-over color.

"The closest you can get to an immaculate conception, I'll have you know," Viney said with a laugh, and closed the freezer door.

It was two months after the scare at the Parkview, and she was beginning to take off the weight and to sound like her old self.

"Naturally, Jewell Daniels is not going to approve. But I'll work on her. I'll have to get her to think of her grandchild as one of those little charges of hers that she loves so much. . . ." For years Viney's mother had run the day-care center at her church, the Triumphant Baptist Church, which stood a few doors down from her house and directly across the street from a large Civil War battlefield. Petersburg was famous for its battlefields. For a second, Ursa saw Viney's mother's house, the large steepled church just down the block from it, and the battlefield that was a tourist attraction across from both the house and the church.

"Oh, she'll have at least a couple of seizures, but she'll get over it," Viney was saying, "and be running around proud grandma with its picture when it comes."

Nine months later at the hospital: "Isn't he beautiful? I'm going to name him after Mr. Robeson. My granddaddy would have liked that." Her grandfather, who had helped raise her when her father died, had been a dining car waiter in the forties, and once on a run between New York and Chicago he had waited on the great man. "My granddaddy said he acted just like Folks. No siddity airs. It was the highlight of his life. He used to talk about

Mr. Robeson all the time, even to people who didn't know who he was . . . So that's to be his name."

Robeson. Hours after his birth, Viney had sat propped up in the bed drawing up a list of indispensables. And before he was a year old she had sold the apartment on West Ninety-third with Willis Jenkins down on the second floor and bought the house in Brooklyn. And once the renovations were done, including the stripping of the woodwork that she insisted on doing herself and the old turn-of-the-century brownstone restored like some aging grande dame who had been given both a face-lift and a new heart, she had placed a gas lamp like a beacon in the front yard, hung a sign that read V. Daniels and Son in the entryway under the stoop, and planted a small garden of herbs in the kitchen window.

This house. Ursa drains the last of the coffee in her mug. The children, their fifteen minutes almost up, are trying to get in a final word before they have to leave for the center to rehearse the play.

". . . I know all my lines already, Aunt Ursa . . ."

". . . I got this gun, see, that I carry with me all the time, and when this lady I'm rescuing gets scared and starts talking 'bout she wants to go back, I just take my gun and put it to her head and say you better come on now if you know what's good for you. . . ."

Dee Dee from down the block.

Viney, the salad done, is taking a bottle of wine out of the refrigerator. She holds it up for Ursa to see the label. Waggles it by the neck. "Party!" The old battle cry said with a self-mocking grin.

("Wait a minute, have you stopped meditating?"

"Oh, that," Viney said. "I don't need that anymore."

The two of them were cleaning up after the big housewarming she had held, complete with a case of Moët, once the renovations were done. It was at the housewarming that Ursa had met Lowell

Carruthers. One of Viney's old boyfriends had brought him along.

"What about you? Do you still bother?"

"Yes, once in a while," Ursa said. "It comes in handy sometimes."

"You see! And I had to drag you there kicking and screaming.")

This house. The moment Robeson swings open the basement gate and she steps down into the entryway, she always feels as if the small rowboat that she imagines her life to be, which Estelle had launched her in before she knew how to work the oars properly or could read the stars well enough to know which way was north, has finally made it to port. There're only two havens left in the world as far as she's concerned: this house, especially the kitchen, and the beach at Government Lands, which she hasn't seen in four years.

6

A hurt and baffled Viney sits on the wicker love seat in the sun
parlor upstairs, her long legs drawn up and folded under her and
her hands fallen open in her lap. She's swaying. The upper half
of her body is swaying lightly from side to side without her being
conscious of it, a clear sign that she's upset. Swaying like some
elderly mother of the church moanin' low in her pew up front.
She's old Mother Daniels of Triumphant Baptist in Petersburg
from the waist up and Buddha—legs folded lotus fashion—from
the hips down.

Ursa, seated across from her in an armchair that matches the
love seat, knows better than to say anything more for the moment. She's just told her about the trip down to West Fifty-

eighth Street last Friday, and it's best, she knows, to remain silent until the first wave of outrage passes, the swaying subsides, and Viney recovers enough to speak.

Waiting, avoiding the face opposite her, she looks out of the solid wall of windows that takes up three sides of the room, which is at the rear of the second floor of the house. The parlor floor. The longest stretch of windows faces west and looks out over the backyard below.

On a wicker coffee table in front of her lie the remains of the meal they finished a little while ago, the empty salad bowl and plates and their partly filled wineglasses. Both the glasses and the wine—a pale Chablis that has absorbed the sunlight around it —seem made from the air and light in the room. Someone might have taken a handful of the unseasonably mild air and heated and blown and spun it to fashion the glasses with their slender stems, and afterward taken a portion of the sunlight flooding in the tall unshaded windows and distilled it to make the wine.

This room. Ursa looks around at the white-painted wicker furniture with its colorful cushions, the raffia rug Viney bought in Triunion when they were there the last time, and the plants that claim the rest of the space. Huge hanging ferns, corn plants, potted palms, crotons of every color and design. A small rain forest fills the sun parlor. This house.

"Why are you like that? Why is it that whenever anything happens you go and crawl into the nearest manhole and pull the cover over it?" At last the voice from across the coffee table. "Why do you do that? Why won't you pick up the phone and call me when there's trouble? Aren't I on the phone to you the minute anything happens? Suppose something had gone wrong and they had to rush you to the hospital . . ."

Ursa doesn't feel like it, but she has to laugh. "Why do you always have me lying up in a hospital half dead or in a coma? What's that all about? And what could have gone wrong, for God's sake? I wasn't even three weeks, I told you, so there was nothing to it. I was in and out of there in less time than you spend at the hairdresser's. In fact, the place looked a lot like that fancy salon you go to. And I was perfectly all right afterward. Didn't feel a thing./*Why don't I feel anything, Viney?*/Not so much as a cramp. In fact, I felt so good when I left there I was all ready to call you and say find a sitter, let's hang out."

"Well, why didn't you?" Said angrily. Anger overtakes the hurt in her voice. "At least I would have found out before now."

"I just couldn't. You know me. Instead, I stayed up half the night talking to you in my head. All kinds of craziness."

"Such as?"

"I don't want to go into it."

"Such as?"

"Just craziness. Everything was over and done with so quickly I had to ask myself if they actually did anything besides draw a little blood. Maybe whatever it is, is still there."

Viney's puzzled, even alarmed face on the other side of the table. The swaying has ceased. "What're you talking about? How could that be? You're not making any sense."

"I know. I haven't been making any sense all this week."

"I don't understand you sometimes!" The anger again. "You pulled the exact same thing that other time. I haven't forgotten . . ." She means, Ursa knows, the only other time she ever got caught. A summer fling, the summer of her internship at NCRC. An exchange student from the University of Calabar who was finishing up his degree in engineering at Columbia. She had met him at one of Viney's parties. A man with two perfectly sculpted quarter-moons on his high cheekbones and a way of holding her in bed, of fitting himself to her, of moving with her that swelled the bud of her flower till it exploded. He had returned home at the end of the summer. And two weeks after his departure, she had missed her period.

". . . Had me thinking you had gone to spend the weekend with your folks in Hartford, and it wasn't until a month later that I found out what you had really been up to. And now the same thing again. I'm being told after the fact. All these years we've known each other and you haven't changed. It's still go it alone, keep your business to yourself, maintain a stiff upper lip no matter what, and all the other nonsense they taught you in that place you're from. Massa really did a job on you folks down there."

Ursa sighs, holds her tongue, picks up her unfinished wine. Here we go again. It won't do any good, she knows, to remind Viney that she had been born in Hartford, had gone to high school in Hartford—dear old inner-city Weaver High in the North End—and that by now she has lived more of her life within a two-hundred-mile radius of Hartford than anywhere else. "Hartford, Connecticut, for God's sake! Do I have to show you my birth certificate," she used to shout at her. It never did any good, and wouldn't now. Whatever Viney doesn't understand about her, whatever she sees as her defects, shortcomings, failings, she blames on the first fourteen years of her life spent in Triunion. They're the fault of the British and Triunion. She holds them responsible, lays the crime at their doorstep whenever she's baffled or annoyed by something she's done. That's the only side of her she chooses to see then. And she's not the only one. Others you would call Folks with a capital F would catch the island lilt in her voice she couldn't even hear anymore and without stopping to listen to the strains of New England, New York and the mean streets of Hartford's North End would immediately color her immigrant, alien, islander without a green card, not realizing they were lopping off more than half her life. People who were supposed to be Folks thinking pushy, arrogant, different, difficult; thinking small island go back where you come from, thinking monkey chaser, some of them, when they detected the faint lilt. So that instead of them or herself stepping forward to shake hands or to embrace with their faces and bodies touching, instead of one saying, "Hey girl, hey sis-tuh, how ya doin'?"/And the other: "Hey soully-gal, how yuh keepin'?"/One: "It's a bitch out here having to deal with these men *and* the white folks, ain' it?"/The other: "Is true. But we still here, bes' proof." Instead of the handshake and embrace, power flowing between their clasped palms, healing between the dark cheeks pressed against each other; instead of the intimate, loving palaver, they hold off, shy away, step back, setting distrust between them.

"Dammit, one of my grandmothers—I'm named after her—came from Tennessee!" she would have shouted at Viney years ago. Now she just sighs, forgives her, loves her, and takes a sip of the wine that is the color and texture of the light encircling them both.

". . . Keeping something like that to yourself. Do you know what a strain you sometimes put on this friendship?"

"For the hundredth time, Viney, I'm sorry. I'm sitting here in sackcloth and ashes. What more do you want?"

She watches then, steeling herself, as a question joins the aggrieved look on the face opposite. The question slowly forms, and the mouth that is like the national flower of Triunion—especially its lower half, that swollen furrowed underlip—begins to curl out and down, all the way down.

Her Lowell lip.

"And what did your gentleman friend have to say? I hope you made him foot the bill."

"No. He doesn't know a thing about it." *He had taken her tears last night as a sign of pleasure, and early this morning she had gotten up while he was still asleep, put back on her clothes without stopping to shower, had eased open the bedroom door, faced down the pit-bull rictus of that beast of his, that Mitchell, who always posts himself outside the bedroom whenever she sleeps over, and after the beast gave up and with a low-level growl moved out of her way she had snatched her cape out of the closet in the foyer, taken down the chain on the front door, opened the deadbolt, set the other lock to slam shut behind her, and gone about her business without leaving so much as a note. And later, when she reached 101st Street and the phone rang—two rings, the silence, then the ringing again to let her know it was him—she had let the machine answer for her as she stepped into the shower to prepare for the trip to Brooklyn.*

"What do you mean, he doesn't know a thing about it?"

"Just what I said."

"You didn't tell him either?"

"No. Nor do I intend to."

"You don't intend to? You don't intend to? What're you talking about? Why not?"

"Because it's got nothing to do with him."

"It's got nothing to do with him? . . ." Viney repeats dumbstruck. "What're you talking about? Who does it have to do with? Who else are you sleeping with? What is this? Why are you coming out with all this off-the-wall stuff that doesn't make any sense? . . ." The long legs unfold, the long feet hit the floor; Viney, the alarmed look on her face again, needs solid ground under her. "Ursa, I'm asking you what you mean by that?"

"I don't know. I told you my mind's been throwing up all kinds of craziness this week. Anyway, I didn't tell him. What good would it have done? Do you think he was going to say great, have it and come move in with me and Mitchell? That man's never going to risk having anyone walk out on him again, you know that. He would've just gotten into a state and talked nonstop. He'd still be going on. Besides, I was the one who decided to switch from my old reliable to some new foam thing out on the market that doesn't work. Stupid. Just plain stupid. And it's not about letting him off the hook, which is what you're sitting there thinking. I can see the wheels turning."

"That's exactly what I'm thinking."

"It's just that it didn't seem to have anything to do with him . . . And I don't know what I mean by that. But it's what been in my head all week."

Another long and baffled silence from Viney. This time without the swaying. Old Mother Daniels in her pew up front has vanished. So has the Buddha.

Voices of children playing in a backyard a few houses away reach them through the windows, a few of which they had opened when they came upstairs. Because of the sudden silence in the room, the voices outside sound so near the children could be in the yard just below, playing on the sliding pond, the jungle gym

and swings Robeson and his friends seldom bother with anymore.

"And I really don't understand you when it comes to that man.
Never have and never will."

"Viney." She holds a hand up to warn her.

"I know. I'm not to say anything about you and Mr. Carruthers. The subject is strictly taboo. I'm to mind my own business as you told me that time. My own you-know-what business.
I refuse to repeat what you really said . . ."/Rasshole, she had
said in her thickest Triunion accent. She had blown up and told
Viney to mind her own rasshole business./". . . Went all native
on me. Using cuss words nobody'd ever think could come out
of your mouth. And you know how I feel about that. If someone
can't hold a conversation or discuss something without using a
lot of four-letter words, I'd rather not hear what they have to
say. And that includes you. Jumped all over me that night just
because I—"

"Viney."

"I know. You'll storm out of here again like you did then.
Decided you weren't going to stay over after all and went home.
You preferred to risk your life taking the subway as late as it was
that night rather than spend another second in my company. And
all because I dared to tell you what I thought about that relationship."

"Stasis," she had said, "meaning stagnation, meaning at a standstill, meaning going absolutely nowhere as in constipation. Stasis.
That's the first word that comes to my mind whenever I think
of her and Mr. Carruthers. Stasis. And I ask myself why. Why
does my friend who is a sensible, self-respecting, no-nonsense
black woman, why does she continue in a relationship that's
clearly suffering from stasis? I keep trying to understand why
she's doing this to herself. Because normally she's one to put up
with 'stuff' for just so long. Didn't she walk out on a good-paying
job at NCRC? . . ."

"I sure did."

". . . She got fed up with all the whiskey, beer and cigarette surveys she found herself having to do when they promoted her to special markets and upped one day and walked. Felt she couldn't take it another minute, that it went against her principles, it was another way of doing in Folks, so she walked . . ."

"To repeat: I'd *ruther* drink muddy water and sleep in a hollow log than work another day for NCRC," Ursa said. It's what she had told her friend when she left NCRC four years ago. Driving over to Brooklyn with the news that time, she had searched her mind for how to put it to Viney. And something came to her by the time she reached the foot of Manhattan and started across the bridge. It was a line from a blues her uncle in Hartford— her uncle Grady—loved to play. During the sixties he had gone South to work in the Movement and had been arrested, jailed, and badly beaten, a hip broken, so that he still walked with a limp. And sometimes he played him some blues. Suddenly, driving over the Brooklyn Bridge, a line from one of his favorites had come to her. So that later, when Viney questioned the wisdom of her having left NCRC, she had her answer ready. "Viney," she had said, "I'd *ruther* drink muddy water and sleep in a hollow log than work another day for NCRC."

She repeated it now.

". . . So she walked . . ." Viney made as if she hadn't heard her. "Then got rid of car, apartment, furniture, everything to live like a peon in one room. But she did it. Just cut everything loose. A couple of weeks before that, she got very upset when we were in Triunion on vacation. Said she couldn't take anymore what was happening there, and she hasn't been back since. Won't go near the place. After running home practically every other month, she just stopped and has her poor father going out of his mind . . . My friend doesn't play, in other words. She might not look the type, with her petite little self, but she'll *move* on you in a minute. Why, then, I ask myself, can't she do the same with Mr. Carruthers? Why does she continue in a state of stasis with a man who doesn't even have the decency, for example, to offer to share that big apartment he has with her and get her out of that one room. Although—"

Ursa had laughed outright at that, almost spilling the Tia Maria in the cordial glass in her hand. "Woman, what are you talking about? Who in her right mind would want to live with Lowell? Please, Viney, come and sit back down. All this pacing up and down isn't good for your powers of reasoning. And who's this 'she' person you keep referring to when I'm sitting right here?"

Early September three years ago, a Saturday night, and the two of them in the family room on the ground floor of the brownstone, with Robeson asleep upstairs. As soon as Viney had started in on Lowell she had leaped up from her chair and begun pacing the floor. And for some reason, the moment she took to her feet she began using the third person. She was acting as if she were alone in the room, speaking aloud her thoughts to the unlit fireplace, the exposed brick wall around it and the furniture as she swept back and forth in a pair of red challis lounging pajamas with ballooning Turkish pants. A matching headwrap hid her hair. Red against the caramel-colored skin. A woman all red and caramel-candy brown.

Ursa, reclining in a lounge chair over near the fireplace, the small glass of coffee liqueur in her hand, might not have been there.

". . . Although she'd be out of her mind to think of living with someone like that. But he could at least make the offer after all the years they've been going together. I mean, the dude won't do right even in the smallest ways. Take tonight. What's she doing baby-sitting along with me on a Saturday night? Not that I'm not glad for her company—she knows I am—but wouldn't you think she'd be stepping out someplace with Mr. Carruthers? A lousy movie, if nothing else?"

"I saw the gentleman last weekend," she said. "And I'll probably see him in another couple of weeks or whenever. We'll do our stepping then. Go out to dinner somewhere. No lousy movies, thank you. And who knows, the evening might be rather pleasant if something hasn't come up on that job of his. A nice meal. I like eating out. A little male company through the night. You know what I mean. That's about it, though. It's got nothing to do with any high-powered romance, I keep telling you. Not anymore. It's just a little something in this desert out here. A break in the routine. Force of habit. Whatever . . ."

For a while, for those first couple of years, the love years, it had been more than just a little something. There had been the free zone from time to time back then. She had secretly called it the free zone.

"Doesn't she ever wonder what he's up to all the times she doesn't see him?"

"No. Mr. Carruthers goes his way, I go mine. You don't seem to understand that I don't need to see the man every day of the week. Frankly, I wouldn't even want to see a husband every day of the week."

"Where's he right this minute, for instance?" Viney has yet to hear her. "Right this very minute? You can't tell me he's spending Saturday night working out at the Y or walking the dog or cleaning that big spotless apartment of his."

"Right this minute the gentleman's in Philadelphia," she said patiently, "where he is every other weekend, helping out his sister with those three boys she was left to raise on her own when her husband was killed in the stupid war." (The husband had died in Vietnam, and every other Saturday, Lowell Carruthers took the 6:00 A.M. train to Philadelphia to spend the weekend with his nephews, a set of twins and an older boy.) "You know as well as I do where he is right now. And, yes, I sometimes resent the fact that he won't let anything get in the way of those visits, yet it's also one of the things I like about him. So do you. That's probably the *only* thing you like about him . . . Viney, I'm talking to you!"

The tall figure in the lounging pajamas swept past, blind to her presence, deaf to her voice, addressing the furniture and walls. ". . . For all she knows he might also be tipping out on her down to the second floor, in a manner of speaking. She might be in for the same kick in the teeth."

Willis! I should have known. It's still about Willis after all this time. Oh, Viney! (The large slack body in the swimming pool at the Parkview had felt as if it had weights attached to the ankles, twenty-pound weights that were threatening to pull them both under.) Don't say another word, Ursa. Let her talk. It's as much about Willis Jenkins as anyone else.

"She acts like she doesn't know how some of these dudes out here will mess over you . . ."

Just let her talk. Think of the couple of love years. Think of the free zone . . .

It had had both time and space, she remembered. Space was the circumference of the bed on which they lay, as well as the length, width and height of the bedroom, either hers in the apartment with the terrace she had at the time or his, twelve stories above the northern end of Central Park. Time was the half hour or longer that followed her final *"Don't stop!"* Crying out to her body not to come down from its high, not to let go of the pulsing in her flower and along tiny nerves she never knew existed. All of her a pulsing, soaring heart. *"Don't stop!"* Time in the free zone was the long, loving aftermath when their limbs remained entangled, their bodies inseparable. Everything was held in common then—arms, legs, eyes, ears, buttocks, breasts. Everything about her belonged as much to him as to her, and vice versa. He was stuck, as she had been for years, with a body she thought of as a case study in underdevelopment. And he didn't seem to mind, maybe because the trade-off was that he got her full head of hair to fill in the bays at his temples. That thought always made her laugh. And she suddenly possessed arms and legs that were nearly twice the length of her own, a pair of strong, shapely hands that looked as if they could snap a phone receiver in two and then turn around and delicately peel a grape; also dimples like grace notes at the small of her back, and the waistline and ass she had long coveted.

When she spoke she imagined she heard the timbre of his voice in her own.

And every and anything could be talked of in the free zone.

"... I just stood there and cried I was so angry," she said one night at her place, speaking, it seemed, in both their voices and feeling that the pair of long arms around her belonged to her. "How could he have done something like that—wait until almost the end of the semester to turn it down? I still can't get over that. I open the mailbox, see the alumni newsletter inside, and get mad all over again. That man has ruined the memory of the four years I spent in that place. 'It's unacceptable. There's no way I can approve of your proposal.' I can still hear him!"

"What was it? Why was he so opposed to your doing the paper?"

"Because of what I was setting out to prove," she said. "Which was that there had been a time when we actually had it together. That slavery, for all its horrors, was a time when black men and women had it together, were together, stood together. That there were Congo Janes and Will Cudjoes—I've told you about them—both here and in the islands . . . We have a saying about those two in Triunion: You can't call her name or his, we say, without calling or at least thinking of the other, they had been so close."

"I like that." He nodded. "What it says, what it means. We need to get back to thinking like that, being like that again, if we're ever going to make it."

"Well, that man hated the thought. For all his liberalism—and he was the biggest liberal on the campus—he couldn't stand the idea behind my paper. 'You'll have to find another topic.' Which is what I had to do, hustle around and find something else so I could graduate. All I could think of was what the PM would say if I didn't graduate. So I pulled together something on the internship I had done at NCRC that summer. But you wait. One of these days I'm going to dig out that proposal, go back to graduate school, and write that paper. I won't rest till I do."

"Do it, Ursa," he said, drawing her closer. "Do it."

* * *

". . . I think I'd like to go back to recruiting someday," Lowell said.

They had left the bed and were curled up on the sofa in his living room, the lights off, the windows open to a summer moon over Harlem and the north end of the park and vintage Marvin Gaye on the stereo singing about the state of the country, Marvin asking, "What's going on across this land . . . ?/Make me wanna holler/And throw up both my hands."

And they were sharing a joint of the high-quality Mexican weed Lowell kept in a hand-carved mahogany box she had given him—a present from one of her frequent trips to Triunion.

"Not that I don't like what I'm doing at Halcon," he said. "But I still prefer recruiting. It doesn't pay anything, but those years I worked at Lafayette were the best of my life. I came across some really bright kids, and in some of the roughest places. Not to say they didn't need a lot of help or that some of them didn't mess up or just couldn't take the pressures of that near lily-white campus. But more made it than not. I felt good knowing I had helped snatch a few of them off the streets before they got sucked under. So I'd like to go back to that. And set up my own program this time. There's this guy I've heard of in Chicago who runs his own outfit right there on the South Side. That's the way to do it. He and his staff really work with the kids they recruit— tutoring, counseling, getting them ready. And he's done well, I understand. He's gotten some of the kids into the Ivy Leagues even . . ." He paused, suddenly hesitant. He took a deep drag off the joint as Ursa held it to his lips, sucking the smoke all the way in and holding it for a long minute. Then, as it flared out: "Of course, I'd be taking a chance stepping out there on my own. I worry about that. And there's always the problem of getting funded. But someday, if I ever get up the nerve, I'd like to set up something like that . . .

"Take my island woman as codirector," he added after a pause, a smile suddenly visible in the moonlight. "Move back to Philly and open shop."

"I'd kiss NCRC goodbye in a minute," she cried, laughing.

That was the time before the keloid of a frown had become a permanent fixture between his eyebrows. The time before Davison.

Winter, and the banshee roar of fire engines twelve stories below his bedroom. What sounded like every battalion in the city racing uptown through the icy streets and the iron cold of February. It was the third time they had heard them since they'd been lying there in the free zone of the bed, the lamp on the night table on, and he said, turning away his face, "She hated this apartment. She was always complaining about the fire engines passing all the time. The noise. As if you can get away from the sound of fire engines and ambulances in any big city. Here we had one of the best views in New York, all the way over to the East River and downtown to the Empire State Building. We had four large rooms, rent we could afford, a doorman day and night; I even got the dog so she'd feel safer, and she still hated it."

"Look at me, Lowell."

He shook his head.

" 'Nigger,' she'd say when she really got angry, 'I didn't leave my daddy's good house to come and live in no Harlem.' I'd tell her this wasn't exactly Harlem. That we were four blocks away, albeit four short blocks. Don't look north when you look out the windows, I'd tell her. Joking with her. Just trying to get her to stop being so uptight about it. Needless to say, she didn't appreciate my jokes. Maybe there's no escaping Harlem, I'd tell her, not even for the white folks—which is something I believe. That would really make her angry. It got so she hated everything about this city.

"Then there was me. Something about me she just couldn't stand after a while. It had to be. Because nobody can tell me she was unhappy over some noisy fire trucks and an apartment. But all I tried I could never get her to talk about what she found so wrong with me, with the marriage . . . What was it?" he suddenly cried, bewildered, his face still turned away. "I wasn't making enough money? Was that it? I wasn't ambitious enough for her? I talked too much about myself, maybe? I got to be boring? I had bad breath? I wasn't any good in bed anymore? What? What was it? She wouldn't say and she wasn't interested in us going for some help. Instead, one day she just upped and split. Waited good until I had to spend a couple of days at the Yonkers plant and cleared out. I get home and her closet's empty and half the fucking wedding presents are gone . . ."

"Don't ever do that!" He turned sharply to her, baring the pain and angry bewilderment he couldn't put behind him. "Whatever happens, don't ever just pick up and walk out without a word! I couldn't live through that again . . ."

Slowly, Ursa disentangled herself from his limbs and sat up. Slowly, she drew the quilt on the bed up around her nakedness. "I'm Ursa," she said quietly. "Ursa Mackenzie. Please, *Please!* don't go confusing me with anybody else. And Ursa Mackenzie's not walking anywhere. She's here for the duration."

To seal her word, she bent down and kissed the worn place at his temple. Both places. And then the small island of hair to the front she called Triunion.

". . . He'd stand there in the hot sun with the perspiration pouring off him and would forget to use his handkerchief. He'd be holding it right in his hand, but he'd be so busy making sure I did my little laps he'd forget to use it. Only when I had finished and come out of the water would he think to wipe his face. So tense all the time. I don't know why it meant so much to that man to see me racing up and down that pool every Sunday."

"Maybe he had dreams of the Olympics. You were going to prove that not only can black folks run and shoot baskets and swing a bat but we can swim too."

"With these arms! With these legs!" Laughing, she held them

up for his inspection. It was summer again, their second summer, and they were lying together with the top sheet bunched at the foot of the bed, the windows open, the lamp on as usual and Mitchell asleep outside the bedroom door. "He should have known better. But there he'd stand—he and the keep-miss manager of the place I've told you about—the perspiration pouring down his face and not using that handkerchief till I was done . . ."

Another night: "The first thing we're going to do when you come down with me on a visit is to sit in the sea and dip and eat mangoes."

"Sit in the sea and dip and eat mangoes . . ." Lowell puzzled over it for a moment, then smiled. "Okay, I'm game. Only tell me how it's done and why."

"Why," she said, "because it makes any mango you eat taste ten times better. And the way you do it is to just sit in the surf, peel your mango bit by bit and before taking each bite you dip it in the water to get the salt taste on it, and then sink your teeth in. Mmh! *Li bon, oui*! Which freely translated means some 'good eatin'.' There's nothing sweeter than a mango with a little seawater on it. When I was small, the PM and I used to sit in the sea and dip mangoes whenever we went up to the country. Oh, we had fun! He used to love doing it as a boy, he told me. And you'll love it, too."

"I'm looking forward to it," Lowell said. "I'm also looking forward to meeting this other man in your life you talk so much about."

"Who, the PM? You'll love him too. There's no resisting him."

Yet another time she spoke of Estelle. "She was always in such a hurry for me to grow up. As soon as I turned twelve she went rushing off to town and bought me a training bra. All I had were

these two little things scarcely bigger than pimples, yet she rushed
out and bought this bra and strapped me in it. She got the smallest
size in the store, but it still was too big. No problem. She just
stuffed cotton down inside. A little cotton till you fill it out on
your own, she said . . ." Ursa paused. "Of course, that never
happened." She paused again, and this time turned away from
the face next to hers on the pillow. "When I came to live in
Hartford I used to worry that not a boy in Weaver High would
ever look at me twice. Who was going to ask me to the movies
or to a Weaver basketball game with this sawed-off body of mine?
And I had an accent to boot! I used to wish sometimes I could
turn myself in for another model, the way you do a car. I used
to—"

Lowell Carruthers gently placed a hand over her mouth, so
that there was sudden silence in the room. It was her bedroom
this time.

"I keep telling you that good things come in small packages,"
he said. "And that I dig this particular small package." With his
free hand he drew back the blanket and for long minutes gazed
quietly at her, from her copy of the PM's domed forehead to her
ten short blunt toes. Admiring it all. She might have been a
sculpture of herself he had just unveiled.

The hand still resting on her mouth, he then brought his own
mouth down to the two small nubs on her chest. Slowly, his
tongue traced and retraced the dark aureole around each. His
head rocking slightly as he savored them. From there after a long
time his mouth moved to her navel, and lingered there also. And
then slowly on down to her flower.

"Don't stop!"

The free zone she had secretly called it. Every and anything could
be talked of there. Every and anything could be done. During
that long aftermath when they lay with their bodies interchanged
and their voices melded, everything had seemed possible. If they

had wanted to, they could have picked up his fifteen-story apartment building or hers for that matter and moved them from the Upper West Side to another planet.

The free zone. She couldn't remember the last time it had happened.

———

". . . A relationship like some tired marriage to a man who does nothing but complain. Stasis. Why does she put up with it?" Viney asking it of the exposed brick wall, the fireplace, the furniture as she paced up and down the family room in the red billowing Turkish pants. "What does she see in someone like that? What's she getting out of it?"

"Hint," Ursa called from the recliner, unable to keep silent any longer. "Hint. It has one syllable and only three letters, beginning with s." Even louder: "Second hint. It clears the tubes so you think and feel better the next day. And that's not original with me. I stole it from a friend who used to say it all the time in her precelibate days."

The pacing on the other side of the room abruptly ceased. Slowly Viney came over and stood beside the lounge chair where she lay, one arm akimbo and her body at its familiar slant. She was looking down from what seemed to Ursa a great height.

That nose, she thought, that nose and the face that goes with it belong on Mount Rushmore. They've got as much right to be up on that mountain as Washington and Lincoln and those other two.

"Lowell?" The lip again, and curled so far over this time the pink lining was visible. "Lowell Carruthers? You could have fooled me. But all right, I'll take your word for it. He's a Feel-good, the good doctor himself, although you'd never guess it looking at him. But-what-about-the-rest-of-him?" Each scathing word stood on its own. "Is he useful? Is the dude really useful? Tell me that!"

Willis Jenkins. I forgot. It's still really about Willis Jenkins.

*　*　*

"It wasn't only the lies," she had said, sitting up, seven months pregnant with Robeson, in the living room of the apartment on West Ninety-third Street. "Oh, the dude could lie! Or the charges he ran up on my credit cards buying his four-hundred-dollar pairs of shoes and expensive art supplies. Bills into the thousands of dollars that I'm still paying off. It wasn't even the baby, although you know how much I wanted one . . ."

Ursa, seated across from her, had quietly nodded.

"Not ready for the weight. That's what he'd say whenever I brought up the subject. Marriage? Same thing. Not ready for the weight. Although we know the real reason now, don't we? And you remember how negative and critical he became about my work after a while. Always putting it down . . ."

Again all Ursa could do was nod.

"So what I do isn't glamorous or artistic!" she suddenly cried as if Willis Jenkins had slipped away from his latest sponsor downstairs to join them in the living room and she was telling him off to his face again. "It pays the bills, doesn't it, and all those annuity and retirement plans I help design and monitor are about people, including some Folks, having a little money when they grow old. It's respectable work. Everybody can't be an artist. Somebody's gotta make some money. Angry with me because I was in a position to help him! Treating me like an enemy instead of a friend, all because I saw what a rough time he was having free-lancing and was willing to help. I can't get over that . . . But it wasn't only his attitude, or even the final kick in the teeth—that white man down on the second floor—because I didn't know about that till the very end. Five years and I had no idea he went both ways. Any sponsor who can afford the four-hundred-dollar shoes will do. How blind, how stupid can you be! But as much as that still hurts, it was something else," she said and suddenly leaned toward Ursa over the swollen stomach. It was night and a nearby floor lamp caught the shiny, polyurethane glaze that had formed over her eyes that evening at the Parkview. The last of the river. "It was the fact," she said, "that when I finally started coming to my senses I understood the truth about Willis Jenkins. I took a long, hard look at him one day and could suddenly read into his life. And I saw, clear as words in a book, the truth about him . . ."

"Which is?"

"That he isn't useful. The dude and all those like him are not useful."

"I'm not sure I understand what you mean, Viney."

"I'm gonna tell you. 'The woods are on fire out here,' my granddaddy used to say, 'and we need everybody that can tote a bucket of water to come running.' He used to say that all the time, talking about the situation of Black Folks in this country, you know, and the need for all of us to stand up and be counted. To be useful. And one day I took a good look at Willis Jenkins and knew he was not one of those Folks. He might be bright, talented, good to look at, great in bed, someone who knew how to talk the talk in order to get over, but he wasn't really useful. Because Willis Jenkins wasn't about to tote so much as a thimbleful of water anywhere, for anybody, not even for himself if his own patch of woods was on fire. Do you understand me now?"

Ursa nodded, and satisfied, Viney sat back in her chair, the eyes with the scuff-proof finish moved out of the light and the oversize stomach settled itself again on her lap. "When I understood that, Ursa, really understood it, I could say to him, look just take your things, *all your things*, shoes, everything, and go. Just go! I could finally cut him loose . . .

"If thy right hand offend thee!" The flat of her hand came down like a scalpel, severing the air. It was followed a moment later by a little shamefaced apologetic smile: "I know. You don't have to tell me. As someone on the spiritual path, I'm supposed to simply bless and release him. Forgive, bless and release him, but I can't just yet."

* * *

"I'm asking you, is a Lowell Carruthers useful?" Standing over her in the recliner that Saturday night three years ago.

And because Ursa had asked herself the same question any number of times in her own way—Why are you sitting here, woman, listening to this man go on about himself and that job? Why are you taking this? There's nothing there anymore, no free zone, what's the use? *Is there any use?*—and had been unable to answer with a simple, unequivocal no . . . because of her own questions and her failure to give the answer that was called for: No, there's no use, she had blown up at Viney that night. Had jumped up from the lounge chair and shouted at her to mind her own rasshole business. And the next moment had abruptly changed her mind about spending the night as she had planned. Before Viney could stop her she was out of the room, had grabbed her cape from the hall closet, her overnight bag and pocketbook from the shelf there, and was out the basement gate.

Midnight and not even a gypsy cab to be found in the dark, empty streets.

Goddamn Brooklyn.

She had had to risk her life and take the subway home.

7

Ursa picks up her friend's neglected wineglass and hands it to her across the wicker coffee table. A peace offering. During the time they've been sitting there, the Chablis has deepened several shades to match the light in the sun parlor that has turned from pale yellow to gold. The afternoon rapidly veering toward evening.

"Come and go down with me for the elections if I find I can't get out of it," she says. "If the study doesn't come through."

During lunch she told Viney about the PM's letter with the news of the elections at the end of May, and about her fear that the follow-up study in Midland City would not be funded.

"It's called changing the subject," Viney says, taking the wineglass from her but not drinking from it. "We're discussing you and Mr. Carruthers, remember? Why you're letting him off the hook."

"I know, but I don't want us to get started on Lowell and end up having a fight. Besides, I'm through talking about last Friday. That's over and done with and I'll soon get over these post-whatever blues and the craziness that's been going through my head all week. So I don't want to talk about it anymore. Come go with me. Please. The break'll do you good. And Robeson won't be a problem because his school will be out by then and we can take him along, like we did the last time. Celestine will love seeing him again . . ."

"*Mal élève!* You should have had it, *oui*, and sent it down for me to raise!" For an instant Celestine's voice is loud again in her ear; her hard, biscuit-colored palm is about to come upside her head. Celestine has given her no peace this week either.

Viney shakes her head. "I can't go anywhere right around now. I'm sending your godson to computer camp this summer, re-member, which is costing me a small fortune. And I'm going to have to put him in day camp between the time school ends in early May and he goes away in June. More money. Then I've got to have the roof repaired. Another small fortune. You were right about this house. I love it, but it's nothing but a headache and money. All I do is spend. Sometimes I could swear Willis Jenkins has gotten hold of my checkbook and credit cards again and is buying himself four and five pairs of shoes a day . . ." She pauses, then suddenly laughs, "What was wrong with me back then, can you tell me? I should've known better than to be buying shoes for any man. Any black woman with an ounce of sense knows you're just giving him the wherewithal to walk out on you. But not Viney blinded by love. There I was buying Mr. Jenkins all those traveling shoes. Talk about a fool!" She laughs again. She can at last laugh about it. She's finally blessed and released it all. Then: "No, Ursa, I don't have any vacation money this year."

"Fly now and pay later."

"Can't do it. I can't face another bill. You'll be all right," she says. "Just don't go near downtown Fort Lord Nelson, that's all. You only went there so often that last trip because of me. Being as it was my first visit, you wanted me to see everything. But just stay away from that place since it upsets you so much. Do what you always did before. Spend a couple of days there seeing your relatives and then take off for the country. Just spare yourself the mess we ran into in that town, especially on the main drag— what's it called again?"

"King William Street," Ursa says quietly, her head down. She's flooded suddenly with the shame and despair she had felt before Viney on King William Street.

Seiko watches, gold chains of all lengths and thicknesses, earrings, bracelets, diamond-looking rings, contraband of every description kept appearing repeatedly from an unfolded handkerchief or newspaper or the pink palm of a black hand thrust in front of them as they strolled the crowded streets of downtown Fort Lord Nelson. "Price special for you, soul sister . . ."

"The mighty herb, darlin', the mighty powder, anything you head desire, darlin'." Whispers reaching them every day from the sagaboys in their dark shades limning out on King William Street, on the lookout for tourists. "Wait a minute. Where's the un-spoiled tropical paradise you promised me?" Viney, in a pair of designer sunglasses twice the size of those of the sagaboys, had tried making a joke of it. "I might as well be back in the Pharmacy on Ninety-fifth Street, my old hangout. Oh, don't look like that, Ursa. It's not your fault. The stuff is all over creation. If we were in Timbuktu, somebody would be sidling up to us trying to sell us some kind of smoke, dope, whatever . . ."

"Remember," she says now, putting back down the wineglass. She does so without having touched the wine. "Remember the smooth-talking Lothario who attached himself to me at the night-club? The one who was all ready to offer me his services for the night—for a fee, of course. It was understood there would be a fee. And when I told him I was into celibacy for the time being, how he came on even stronger. He thought I had said celebrity, that I was a celebrity." Viney laughs, although her eyes remain sad and somber. "Never came across so much black dick for sale in my life. Just steer clear of that town, Ursa. Head for the hills as soon as you can."

"That won't help. Not anymore. I can't hide from it anymore, even if I don't go near that town," she says, thinking of the woman with a baby in her arms who had accosted them one broiling-hot day on King William Street. How with the sleight-of-hand deftness of a magician the woman had quickly raised the filthy cloth from over the baby and then as quickly dropped it back. Now you see it, now you don't. The cloth raised only long enough for a peek at the sores covering the face, neck and little stick-figure arms. The woman held out her palm, closed it around the money they gave, and darted over to a group of sailors she spotted. They were from the battleship, the *Woodrow Wilson*, which regularly visited Triunion.

The woman was not the first they had encountered with her hand outstretched.

"You never saw that when I was small, Viney. That's what this government has come up with by way of progress. That woman, the U.S. Navy and tourists. And the PM's party can't do a damn thing about it. Some people here say they're even part of the problem. For years I've refused to let myself think that could be true, but I can't hide from it anymore either."

Viney gently took her arm. "Come on," she said, "let's find someplace that's air-conditioned and have a drink."

"Miss Ursa!" He came elbowing his way toward her through the crowd and drew her aside from Viney and Robeson, whom they had brought to town with them that day. A thin, ragtag man her age wearing a faded Hawaiian shirt whose missing buttons exposed his bony chest. Did she remember him, he wanted to know, smiling at her, the teeth to the side of his mouth already rotted away. "I was one the little children your mother uses to let come and play with you in the yard when you all came to spend time in the district," he said. "You must remember me . . ."/She didn't remember him./"I saw in the paper the other day that you was back in the island. I always know from the paper when you come down, but this is the first time I was ever lucky enough to butt up on you. How you keepin'? How you like America? That's a place I'm hoping to see one of these days. They saying here is getting just like over there, save for the money. We don't see the money over this side . . ." He drew closer, his voice dropped, and as if they were Siamese twins sharing the same heart, Ursa felt the heart in the man's bony chest speed up. He had heard, he whispered, his carious breath in her face, that they were hiring at a stone quarry outside town, but he needed bus fare to get there. Bus fare and a little extra if she could spare it so he could put something in his stomach. "Things hard in the Fort, Miss Ursa. If you's not a good thief or one of the sagaboys you see 'bout here selling some of everything, even themself, you can't make a living in this place. I have a mind to move back up to the country. At least there you can always find a mango to eat or somebody'll take pity on you and give you a piece of breadfruit or yam they're cooking, even if they don't know you. But not here. Not in the Fort."

She continued to stand on the hot, crowded sidewalk for some time after the man left, asking herself why. Why does it hit me so hard here? The same thing—worse even!—happens every time I go over to Broadway to buy a loaf of bread. I'm stepping over live corpses with their hands stuck out every time I go down into the goddamn subway. And I don't get so upset anymore. So why does it get to me so here? Why do I run and hide out up-country until it's time to take the plane back to Broadway to see the same thing there? The PM? She couldn't avoid the thought anymore that it might have to do with the PM and that party of his.

"What's wrong, Aunt Ursa? What's wrong? How come you look so sad? How much did that guy hit you for?" Robeson, who was four at the time, wanted to know.

She had forgotten he and Viney were there.

"I think I've seen all I want to of this town," Viney said from behind the sunglasses that took up most of her face. "I'm more than ready for the countryside."

The rest of the two-week visit was spent in Morlands, which was the official name of the North District, as well as the name of the principal town there. The old Mackenzie house where they stayed stood on the main square of the town, not far from the huge market shed Estelle had seen to it was built years ago. Nearly every day Ursa drove her guests over to the beach at Government Lands, using the jeep the PM kept up-country for the unpaved roads in the district.

On their final day at the beach Viney suddenly stood up on the mat they had spread on the sand, took off the oversize sunglasses, let the breeze swell the sheer, batwing-sleeved caftan she had on over her bikini, and opened her arms. And then tried with her long arms to embrace it all: the wide white-sand beach that went on for over a mile on either side of where she stood, the deep grove of palm, grape and almond trees that bordered it, and the sea that mirrored the flawless sky overhead. Water so clear you could see the micalike gold dust sprinkled in the sand at the bottom as you swam out to the reefs.

She next turned and faced in the direction of the Monument of Heroes, which stood out of sight two miles away on the other side of the road that ran alongside Government Lands. Ursa had taken her and Robeson to see the statue the day after they arrived in Morlands. She had told Viney to stand Robeson on her shoulders so that he might touch their feet—Congo Jane's feet as well as Will Cudjoe's. Just as Estelle had done with her when she was small. Her gaze reaching across the distance, Viney bowed deeply in their direction, then turned back to the sea. "I know there's no escaping anything," she said finally, "but we should have headed straight here the minute we got off the plane, put up a tent right where I'm standing, and not budged for the entire two weeks."

Her arms spread wide in the billowing sleeves.

* * *

"You did promise him, Ursa," she says quietly from the love seat. "Besides, you're going to have to go down there sooner or later, so it might as well be now."

"I'm not ready yet to sit through another end-of-the-campaign speech, can't you understand that? I can't take it!"

And there's the thesis. I can't go down there until I finish the damn thesis and get the degree. Something to show for the four years. Proof that I haven't been wasting my time since I left NCRC and he stopped writing for months . . .

She can't bring herself to tell even Viney that.

"I understand, but you can stay away just so long," her friend is saying.

"I've heard them all before. Those speeches. The same words. And what's the point of it all? He's just going to win again. Everybody knows that. His entire party could get wiped out at the polls and he'd still keep his seat. It's happened before. He did mention that there's some 'small boy'—his words, not mine—running against him this time, small boy meaning nobody for him to worry about. It never is. People in Morlands would never think of voting for anyone but him. So I don't see why the entire family, including Celestine, has to be at that last meeting. If he wasn't afraid of what might happen, he'd probably have the manager of his hotel there too."

Ursa sees her: Astral Forde, the iron-fisted keep-miss manager of the dozen little cottages that call themselves the Mile Trees Colony Hotel. She's standing with them on the platform out at the monument that last night, and she's holding a bath towel and a glass of soursop juice for her on a tray, just as she used to years ago beside the swimming pool at the hotel; and in the woman's veiled gaze, directed at her, is the look from years ago that had said if looks could kill, bo, you'd be dead.

She dreamed about Astral Forde this week. On top of all of the craziness she dreamed of that woman.

"I dreamed about her this week."

"Who?" Viney asks.

"Miss Forde. I was in the pool at the Parkview and she was standing on the side throwing towels and trays and glasses of juice at me and cussing me out but good."

"That one!" Viney fans down Astral Forde. "I'm surprised she even opened her mouth in a dream. The woman hardly had two words to say the day you took me over to the hotel, remember? She wouldn't even come and have a drink with us when you invited her. I don't think Miss Forde can talk or smile or look anybody in the eye. Miss Stone-face."

Viney's name for Astral Forde.

"Don't kid yourself. She can talk all right. You should hear her with the help. She's got what we call in Triunion a fowl-yard tongue. I used to sneak behind her when I was small and take in every word. Where do you think I get this purple language you can't stand?"

"I've often wondered."

"Astral Forde and Weaver High. That's where. They're the ones responsible." She laughs only to quickly fall sober. "When I think of the looks that woman used to give me! And yet the funny thing is, Viney, I liked her. Dirty looks and all, I liked her. . . . I've been thinking about her this week. About all of them down there."

"Your father especially, I bet."

"That man! You know I never think about that man!" Her laugh this time hurts her chest.

There's no way to say it to Viney, but the thought of the PM and the news of the elections has made her feel all week as if she still has on the heavy coat she slept in last Friday. As if she's still dragging around all that shearling wool and suede although the weather has turned mild. She's felt weighted down by it all week. Worse, thoughts of him have somehow gotten confused in her head with the trip down to West Fifty-eighth Street. Her suspicion that the people there didn't half do the job, that whatever it is, is still there.

Craziness.

Viney over on the love seat has grown very quiet, and she has begun the slight swaying again. She's once again old Mother Daniels in her pew up front at Triumphant Baptist. Swaying with her eyes averted and the hibiscus lip pulled in.

Ursa's tin cans and graveyard bones, she's thinking. She won't say it because she knows I don't want to hear it, but that's what she's thinking. "You remind me of a cat with a string of tin cans and some bones from a graveyard tied to its tail when it comes to your folks. And I don't only mean your parents but Celestine and especially Miss Stone-face. All that stuff about them and that island that stays on your mind . . . The cans and bones keep up such a racket you can't hear your own self, your own voice trying to tell you which way to go, what to do with your life. You can't hear Ursa. You know what you're gonna have to do with all that stuff, don't you?" Her hand, held ramrod straight, came up and then swiftly down, slicing the air.

Each time Viney delivers this particular lecture, her hand turns into a scalpel.

This time she holds her tongue and busies her hands clearing the coffee table.

The light in the sun parlor has lost nearly all of its summer brightness by now, and the sun itself is about to disappear behind the leafless trees in the backyard. And a sharp chill can be felt in the air. March about to show the other side of its Janus face again.

"Come and help me figure out what to fix for dinner." Viney, all lanky grace, stands across from her, holding a tray with the dishes and wineglasses. "Robeson and friend will be back here ravenous any minute. Motherhood!" She rolls her eyes to the ceiling and beyond, smiling.

BOOK II

Constellation

1

Astral Dolores Forde

2:10 **P.M.**

The friggin' watch scarce keeping the time good.

Astral Forde shook her wrist to start the second hand on the cheap little watch moving again as she bypassed the front door of the pharmacy and went around to a flight of steps at the side of the building. At least this time, unlike last week, she knew better than to go butting in the front door of the place like she was just somebody come to buy Cafenol for a headache or a packet of salts to move their bowels. She was to go round to the yard at the side, she knew now, where the man that ran the pharmacy kept his big motorcar, and climb the steps there to the hotbox of a waiting room on the second floor. Last week she din know any better and had gone marching in downstairs and the man with his funny-funny eyeglasses had taken one look at her standing there like a foolie-the-fifth—she couldn't see a thing for a minute, the damn place was so dark!—and had chased her right out. How was she to know where to go? All Malvern had told her was to look for the pharmacy that had the big glass jars in the window filled with all kind of different-colored medicines. She din say nothing about going around to the yard and climbing no stairs, and the man had ordered her out the door soon as he set eyes on her. Shooing her out the place like she was a yard fowl! "Go round to the side!" Talking to her like she had come to beg him for a few cents to buy a penny bread!

And when she turned and went back outside last week, she had had to contend with the other heathen sitting staring at her from across the road. Instead of him 'tending to the shoes people left for him to fix, there he was outside his little dungeon of a shop watching everybody going around to the side of the pharmacy. His eyes like somebody smear them with the white of an egg. The raw white of an egg. And smiling, all the time smiling, to let you know he knows more about your business than you. A busy-lickum! Even before she reached the pharmacy that first time, while she was still a good ways up Drayton's Road, she had felt his eyes running hot and sweaty to meet her. Never mind all the motorcars and lorries, donkey carts and people on the road, his two eyes had latched onto her the minute she got off the bus and started looking for the place.

And when she stumbled back out the pharmacy to go round to the yard, the smile and the eyes like egg white had followed her up every last one of the steps. Taking every last stitch she had on off her. Down to her small clothes. And later, after the man with the funny glasses sent her away with nothing but a few tablets because her money wasn't sufficient, the eyes of the hangman across the road that knew her business better than she did herself had followed her all the way back up Drayton's Road to the bus stop.

Making her feel so shame!

Today though was different. She knew where to go—no but-

ting in the wrong door—and her money was sufficient. She
had borrowed against her salary for the next month, the five dollars old Mr. Massad paid her by the week, and this time had
the money it would take. So that as she climbed the stairs to the
waiting room and felt the brute across the road stripping the
clothes clean off her again, she 'bused him good. Wha' the rass
you looking at, you nasty black rabbit. Who it 'tis you smiling
at with your teeth yellow-yellow like you bite the Virgin Mary.
Why you don't mind what you doing and stop licking in people
business. Is a wonder you don't bring the hammer down on you
blasted hand instead of the nail, or run the needle through it
you's so busy looking. If I had the will of you, that's just what
would happen. Mr. Hammer come down *wha'dax* on you hand
or the big needle you sews with run clean through it, and the
hand cripple for life. But you watch, one these days you eyes
gon fall out you friggin' head from all the looking and that next-
skin-to-nothing you got between you legs, that anybody can tell
just from the look of you does give out before it even start up
good, gon fall off too. Mark my words!

2:15 P.M.

Country! Bare country from her head down to the pair of old
shoes on her foot. The dress looking like she just run it up on
somebody's Singer this morning before she took the bus to town.
Hot needle and burn thread. And the hat on her head like it say
"heap-me-on." Bare bare country.

"First thing, get the rid of that hat," her friend Malvern had
told her. "People gon take one look at it and see bare country
written all over you."

In the girl seated opposite her in the waiting room Astral Forde
saw herself as she must have looked when she first came to live
in Fort Lord Nelson.

And what's that old woman in the corner doing here? A ol'
ol' woman. She's got to be close to fifty if she's a day. You would
think she would be all dry up by now. What man would want

to have anything to do with somebody that old? Her face all drag down. Over there in the corner looking like she gon bust out in a flood of tears any minute and holding onto the piece-a pocketbook in her lap like it got in her last penny in the world. I know one thing: if her money ain't sufficient he's not gon touch her. He'll just sell her a few tablets wrap in a brown paper like he did me last week and show her the door. He don't make sport when it comes to the money, 'cause you know it takes plenty greenbacks to pay for that big motorcar he has down in the yard . . . Thinking, Astral Forde thinking: his wife and whoever keep-miss he got must feel like the queen herself riding around in it.

As for the sailor hag over by the window putting on a lot of ol' style and getting in the way of the breeze, you know she don't have a worry about money. Not when Uncle Sam sends the *Woody Wilson* by here regular every three months. Is a pretty dress she got on, though, with that flounce at the waist they call a peplum that's all the fashion now. You know she had to pay good money for a dress like that. And the nice shoes and pock-etbook. The fancy wristwatch. But she got on too much lipstick and scent. The scent licking you down. A sailor hag. How else could somebody looking like her have such nice things? She and the rest like her does be down on the wharf thick as fleas the minute the *Woody Wilson* pulls in . . .

A jagged seam of light, a brighter gold than the sunshine raining down on Drayton's Road outside and filling the cramped waiting room, swept the walls as the woman over by the window brought her left arm up in a wide overhead arc to consult the watch on her wrist. A loud, impatient suck-teeth from between her heavily painted lips. She turned back to the breeze.

Showing off! The minute she catch me looking she had to show off Mr. Watch, so I could see it's bigger and better than the piece-a thing I got that's already giving trouble never mind I ain't finish paying for it. One thing: there's not a soul can say they see me down on the wharf picking fares to buy it. Is fifty cents a week out of my pocket that's paying for it. Just look at her! The mouth like somebody up hand and bust her in it and it ain't stop bleeding yet. Her nosehole like you could rent out rooms. Somebody s'black till she's blue. What's she doing here anyway? You would think she and the rest like her would know some of everything to do so as not to be sitting up here with the ignoramuses like myself.

Only the three of them before me, though, thank God, so I won't have to spend all day and half the night waiting this time. Last week in here was like federation. You could scarce find a seat. And it was the longest time before the man with the funny glasses finished in the pharmacy and came upstairs . . .

3:45 P.M.
"When's the last time you seen anything?"

Astral Forde told him, making sure not to look at the glasses.

The trouble was they wasn't clear like ordinary eyeglasses and they wasn't what you would call sunglasses neither. It look like somebody had taken and stained them the colors of the different medicines in the big glass jars the man had in the window downstairs. Had taken the garnet and the deep pretty blue and the dark yellow like sulfur and the other colors in the jars and mix them together with the dust and dimness inside the pharmacy —she hadn't been able to see a thing for a minute when she went butting in there last week—and stained the eyeglasses a kind of dark funny color that was like everything downstairs mix together.

I never seen anybody with eyeglasses like them. He musta had them made up special in England or America.

They gave her a bad feel.

"You sure that's the last time?"

"Yes."

To avoid the glasses she kept her face turned to a chipped and spattered enamel stand that stood next to the cot where she lay. Besides the stand, which had some hospital things on it, and the folding chair the man was sitting on next to her on the cot, she couldn't make out not a thing else in the room. Not a window there to let in little light or air. Only a Tilly lamp among the hospital things on the stand and a smell like somebody hadn't washed under herself in I-don't-know-when, mixed in with the scent from the sailor hag that still clung to the rubber sheet beneath her.

Brown. The sheet brown so you can't see he don't bother to wipe it off each time.

"The tablets you sold me last week wasn't no use."

Not only had they been useless, they had given her a feeling worse than death itself each time she took one, she wanted to tell him. Her heart racing to beat the band, her head spinning till she thought she would topple over any minute. And there had been a ringing in her ears like somebody, someplace, was calling her name and talking her business from morning till night. Then, all of a sudden, her heart would slow all the way down till she felt she was gon faint away. Was gon dead away even. That's all the damn tablets had done.

"They was no use atall," Astral Forde said and wanted to ask for her money back. He ought to give back the money she paid for them.

"That's 'cause you's further along than you letting on. You and all the rest of you that come in here."

He was busy fitting on a rubber thimble like the ones old Mr. Massad and his wife used when they counted the pile of receipts at the end of the day. Only this one was much longer, covering the man's entire forefinger. Never seen one like that before. He musta ordered it special from England or America.

"Cock your legs and hold still."

All of a sudden her bent legs trembling worse than old Mr. Massad's hands when he came muching her up behind his wife's back.

"Hold yourself still!"

The long rubber thimble all up in her insides.

The man raised up. "If you don't hold still," he said, "I'm gon give you back your money and let you g'long about your business the same way you came in here."

He waited, his eyes hidden behind the glasses, until the trembling stopped.

Then, the feeling-her-up-inside over, he was stripping off the rubber thimble and tossing it in a small basin on the stand with the hospital things. A moment later he was taking off his glasses and putting them on the stand too . . . But wait! Astral Forde almost sat up on the cot. Jesus, Mary and Joseph! His eyes, she saw, were the same dark, funny, mix-up color as the eyeglasses and the light in the pharmacy downstairs. The said-same color. Even the whites. Like a blind man eyes. It don't look like he can see a lick. *You can't tell me this man can see what he's doing!* And he's reaching down now for something on the shelf to the bottom of the stand . . . Oh, God, what's that? Where's he going with that long long thing? *Malvern!*

"You know sometimes you get on like you don't have the sense you was born with," Malvern had said last week, exasperated, pacing up and down the small rented room they shared. "Here you been living in town upwards to two years now and you still acting like you just down from the country. All I do, all I preach, I can't make you to understand that somebody looking like you, with that color you got and that Spanish Bay hair long down your back, could easy find somebody that's in a position to help you. Somebody to give you nice-nice things and to help you. I keep telling you you's not some little dark spot like m'self that's gon have to take the first thing in a pair of pants to come along and ask her a question. No, you could find somebody high up, some big shot that would send you to learn secretarial or book-keeping so you could work in a office or in one the banks, or even help you to open a little shop of your own. Cause you could run a business. You got a good head on you, never mind you had something wrong with you when you was small and din talk for the longest time. Look how quick you catch on down at the Syrian shop. Two years and you know more about yard goods than old Mr. Massad and his wife put together. But you won't listen. It's like you don't mind spending the rest of your life making five dollars a week and living up with me in this hellhole they call Armory Hill.

"Not to say I ain't glad to have you."—She had paused briefly from striking fire with her bare feet to the shaky floorboards of the room. Malvern. She's one those people can't sit one place for a minute. Always got to be on her feet moving about. A Miss Murray in a hurry even when she ain't got noplace to go. "Your mother, after all, was my mother good friend, God rest them in their grave. But you should be looking to improve yourself. These is modern times, I keep telling you. Things changing. Look it's people black as me running the government these days, what with this home rule we got. There's some that's even talking about getting rid of England altogether and making Triunion independent. Everything's changing up. So you best get some sense in you head and find yourself one of these barristers or doctors that's springing up about the place. Eighteen is none too soon to be looking.

"And who knows"—she paused again, but all set to take off at the next word—"you might be lucky to butt up on some big shot that might even want to married with you. Never mind you's not of a class with him, he might still be willing to married because of the children—you'd make him some pretty-pretty children. But even if he couldn't see his way to marrying with you, at least he'd be somebody that could help you. That's the sort of person you need to put your mind to and leave off these spree boys and footballers you keep licking about with. They can't give you a thing but the trouble you in now . . ."

"Wait, nuh!"

But the foolish boy was refusing to wait. Instead of letting her undo the buttons on the bodice of the dress, he was pulling her hands away and fumbling with them himself.

"I said wait!"—and she was no longer laughing with him, no longer play-teasing like when they first started muching up.

"What's wrong with you all of a sudden? Where you rushing going? Is a new dress I got on!"

His fingers scrabbling at the buttons. He's gon pop off every last one of them. And breathing the lot of beers he had at the dance all in your face.

Suddenly she didn't like him anymore.

And he had seem like such a decent fella up till now! Every time the band start up there he was the first one asking her for a dance. And he knew how to ask proper, not like some of these other footballer fellas that don't have manners the first! She wouldn't go two foot near a dance floor with most of them. And she hadn't wanted for a thing. Every time she looked he was running bringing her a sweet drink or buying her something to eat: fishcakes, a small dish of pudding and souse, toffees and mints from the hawkers outside the dance shed. And all the time he talking nice, telling her how he's hoping his team gets a chance to play a match in England, that he'd like to emigrate there one day. Thing so. Even when it was intermission and everybody went outside to catch little air, he was still behaving himself, still talking nice as they walked out with the other couples along Cannon Beach. The sea breeze felt good after the heat inside the shed. The stars when she looked up had put her in mind of a necklace, all in diamonds, she had seen in a magazine Malvern had brought home from some white people from America she had worked for one time. The little waves down the beach that you could hear but couldn't see in the darkness was like somebody talking to their sweetheart. And when she glanced back over her shoulder she had seen Fort Lord Nelson on the far far side of the bay: the lights along the wharf and a ship sitting out in the harbor that looked almost as pretty as the *Woody Wilson* when it was all lit up at night.

Is only when they passed the old fortifications wall, where when she glanced back she couldn't see the dance shed anymore and the other couples had disappeared, that he turned beast. Almost as soon as they sat down behind the wall and started muching up 'n' thing, he all of a sudden catch a fit and started pulling on the bodice of the dress she was wearing for the first time and talking a lot of nastiness up in her face, what and what he wanted to do with her, his breath stink from the lot of beers.

"Didn't you hear me say wait!" She slapped at the clumsy hands, tried snatching them off her, tried prying them loose. Doing all she could to save the buttons. She'd never find them if he popped them off and they fell in the sand.

All excited like it's the first time he ever been with a woman.

She gave him a good cuff, brought her knees up to try and shove him away never mind the size of him—he was the biggest one on the Triunion All-Stars—and he started in laughing: "Yes, go 'head, go 'head!"

It's like he wants me to fight him! A idiot!

"Look," she cried, "if you don't behave yourself and stop trying to tear the dress off me I'm going on back to the dance and leave you sitting here."

Still tussling with him, she made as if to stand up, she almost got to her knees, only to have the madman—still laughing and talking nastiness and begging her to fight him—take her, just take her although she was nearly as tall and big-boned as him but without all the footballer muscles and weight, and throw her back down like he would a sack of meal, flat on her back, *brug-gadung-dung* on her back; and leaving off the buttons, he was grabbing hold of her head now, grabbing and holding it between his hands like he thought it was the blasted ball he was butting and kicking about at the match that afternoon. And oh, God, bringing it down, bringing her head down hard on the ground *wha'dax*, then raising it up and bringing it down again on what felt like one of the cannonballs left over from all the wars long years ago that were half-buried in the sand. Every star above Cannon Beach tumbling down inside her head. The pretty new dress half off her now, and he's tearing at her small clothes, then back to her head, his hands bringing it down again *wha'dax*! The stars spinning and shooting off inside her as she scrambles over onto her knees when he orders her. Pleading now with the brute for her life. Sand all in her face, her eyes, her mouth, her nosehole.

All day, all night, Mary Ann / Down by the seaside siftin' sand . . .
They had played "Mary Ann" and he had come over and asked
her proper to dance. Wait . . . ? On her knees, her head spinning,
her face shove down in the sand: Wait, where's he putting himself? Where's he forcing himself going . . . ?

"*Malvern! Malvern!*"

"You like it? You like it? They say the girls in England like it
so."

"*Malvern!*"

Screaming Malvern's name even when the wicked boy stopped
his nastiness and came into her proper at the end.

4:35 P.M.

"You's to take a big spoon of this three times a day till it's
finished, and you's to keep yourself to yourself for a time."

The bottle had in it a dark green something that looked like
the bush tea her mother used to boil and give her when she was
sick. Seated on the edge of the cot, her small clothes in place,
her dress pulled back down and the pain lancing her, Astral Forde
watched as the man wrapped the bottle in a brown paper that
he then twisted tight at either end. The same way he had wrapped
the tablets last week that wasn't no use. He ought to give her
back the money she had paid for them—still angry over that. If
she had the will of him she'd make him give her back every red
cent!

The man handed her the bottle wrapped in brown paper and
waved her toward the door.

He had put back on the funny-funny glasses the same color
as his eyes.

4:52 P.M.

When she reached the bus stop, she made sure to bend and
scoop up a handful of dirt from the dry hot shoulder of the road.
For a long minute, though, she found she couldn't raise back

up. *Is like the idiot went and left the wire thing inside me. Forgot and left it right up inside me.* Pain holding her bent over double, pain blinding her. When she left the place, she hadn't been able to see the man's big motorcar in the yard as she crept down the stairs, or even, thank God, the busy-lickum watching her from outside his shop across the road. Couldn't see him or anything else for the pain. Hobbling like some half-blind old woman back up Drayton's Road to the bus stop.

Inch by inch Astral Forde slowly raised up, and when she was fully upright, she took the handful of dirt she had scooped up and threw it with as much force as she could muster back down to the ground. I don't care who see me.

"Throw down little dirt when you leave the place so the child won't come back to hag your spirit," Malvern had instructed her.

2

Primus Mackenzie

Dear Homefolks,

    . . . You ask how the honeymoon's going. Are you sure you really want to know? Well, then, here goes. *There has never been and there will never be another one like it*. Period. This honeymoon is not only one for the books, it *is* the book! Now, I know that sounds like I'm complaining, but that couldn't be further from the truth. I am absolutely loving every minute of it. I wouldn't trade it for all the Niagara Falls mooning and spooning in the world. But can you really call it a honeymoon when you spend nearly every night tearing around from one little village to another and one small town to the next and up and down mountains and hills in the pitch darkness trying to get the brand-new husband elected to public office? Well, that's exactly what we've been up to practically from the day we arrived, which is why I haven't been able to sit down and write you folks a decent letter. No sooner had we stepped off the plane than the government called elections, as they say here, and Primus, who's been waiting for them to do just that ever since he returned from studying in England, started campaigning right away. It's certain he'll win, because he's a favorite son in his district. People there think there's no one like him. The PM (as everyone here calls him) is already the PM as far as they're concerned. Anyway, he's still not taking any chances. He's out stumping day and night. And guess who's out stumping with him and having the time of her life? Right the first time! And I know I'm being biased, but the new husband is something to behold in front of a crowd. No fireworks. No theatrics. No Baptist preacher oratory. He doesn't go in for any of that. He hardly even raises his voice when he's giving the DNP, the party running the government, some much-deserved hell. (They're the Democratic National Party—or the Do-Nothings as Primus calls them—and we're NPP, the National Progressives.) He keeps his voice at the same quiet level all the time, and he speaks slowly. The man will not be hurried! And he sometimes takes these long pauses that you would think would kill the speech. Yet they work. Everything he does works. Everywhere we go people turn out in droves to hear him, and also to have a look at me while they're at it, "the wife the PM went and find *(sic)* in America." That's the way everyone refers to me. "The wife the PM went and find in America." I love it!

". . . I know you been asking yourself why every time you looked I was rushing up to the States. 'What's gotten into the PM, nuh? What's wrong with the man? Why, every minute you look he's jumping on a airplane—spending money he don't have—flying up to America? What calling he got up there? And even when he keeps his tail home for a few months he's down to the cable and wireless office in town every chance he gets talking overseas on the phone. And he's all the time putting pen to paper, keeping the post office busy. What's ailing him, nuh? What's wrong with him atall?' . . ."

Primus Mackenzie paused, and everyone and everything within the sound of his voice also paused. The acetylene-torch roar of the Tilly gas lamp rigged above his head on the platform abruptly ceased. The insects in their giddy orbit around the lamp came to a stop, with the fireflies' greenish glow holding steady in the darkness beyond the reach of the light. The breeze moving over the surrounding canefields and banana groves and over the empty tract of Government Lands nearby instantly died. And the crowd gathered in the darkness in front of the Monument of Heroes, where the meeting was being held, stopped breathing. Everyone became as stonelike as the four giant figures on the pedestal behind the speaker. The men in the crowd no longer exhaled the smell of the rum they had been treated to before the meeting began. ("It's the custom," Primus Mackenzie told Estelle when she questioned it. "You've got to treat the men to a little rum or a few beers and share a little rice out to the women; if not they won't vote for you no matter how much they love you. That's the way it is in Triunion.") The women, guarding the packets of rice they had been given, stood without breathing also, their babies in their arms and their other small children asleep with their eyes open in the folds of their mothers' skirts. And all of them, men, women and children of Morlands, the North District, reveling in the sight of Primus Mackenzie standing before them framed by Congo Jane, Will Cudjoe and the other two on the monument. Looking almost as tall as them . . . And he's dressed proper, y'know, in one the nice suits he brought back from England, and with that forehead that was made for figuring out the problems in this life raise up high to the light. Mis-Mack boychild come home a big barrister. She would be proud enough of him, God rest her in her grave. And if you was to see him in court in his wig and his long robe! He don't even have to do or say all that much and he's winning the case for you. And he's in politics now. He's gon put fire to the tail of those thieves running the government. The rector knew what he was doing when he gave him that pet name years back. (One Sunday, the rector of the parish church that stood across the square from the house in which Primus Mackenzie was born and where his mother, whom everyone called Mis-Mack, had kept a large shop on the ground floor—the rector had taken a look at the little oversize forehead and the Lloyd George round collar his mother had dressed him in for church that Sunday and had declared him to be true to his initials. He was every inch a prime minister never mind he was only three years old, the rector had said, and from then on took to calling him by his initials, and everyone else in the district followed suit.) And here he was, a big hardback man now, looking and sounding like a PM in truth and treating them to a long, delicious silence that they were sure had brought even the watch on his wrist to a stop.

"Well, I gon tell you," he said at last, and they began breathing again; and time, the breeze, the insects and the noisy lamp over his head picked up where they had left off. "When you saw me flying back and forth up to the States I was on another campaign. That's right. I was up there asking for a vote, just as I'm here tonight asking for your vote come the fifteenth of September. Not that I was running for a seat in the government up there, y'know. I was only after one vote. Just one. But lemme tell you, bo, I had to campaign day and night, yes! I had to sweat blood for upwards to two years for that one vote. But I won out. Just as I'm gon win with your help in September. She said yes, I gon give the brute my vote if only so he'll stop running up here every minute persecuting my life . . ."/I'm like someone split in two, he once wrote her. One half of me is on this little two-by-four island, while the other half, the part that has my head, heart and other vital organs, is you-know-where. There's only one person who can heal the schism. You know her, Estelle. Talk to her for me, will you? Reason with her. She'll listen to you. Get her to say yes./". . . And the lady from America who said yes, who got fed up with all the letters and the overseas calls and my face turning up at her door every time she opened it and finally said yes, finally gave me her vote, is here with me tonight. . . ."

A few steps over from where she waited to the side of the platform and she was standing next to him in the noise and glare of the gas lamp. And the smile that made up for her lack of height was projected all the way to the back of the crowd, to the very last face there, although she couldn't see it.

After a meeting one night in a place called Heywood Village, she watched as the cane cutter whose rock-hard, callused hand she had just shaken stubbed out his cigarette with his bare foot. She almost gasped out loud and for a moment could have sworn she felt the stub with its glowing tip burning the bottom of her foot.

Dear Homefolks,

We're getting to be quite a team. After Primus finishes giving the government "licks," as they say here, for doing so little for Morlands, I usually say a few words. It's not a speech as such, although I also let them know how I feel about conditions here. Can you imagine, not a single clinic or dispensary in the district, no electricity, not a decent road to speak of or a decent drain along the road. And that's not the half of it. We're the poorest of the districts. And of course I beat the drum for Primus's platform. But mainly I tell them I must have lived here in another life because I feel so at home already. Everyone seems to like what I have to say. Only last week an old woman came up after I'd said my piece to tell me she plans on voting twice, once for Primus and the NPP and a second time for me. How about that? I love it!

"*Merci, oui,*" he said, inching the car down a hilly road that in the light of their high beams both looked and felt like the cratered surface of the moon. Estelle was clinging to the window frame of her door to keep from being thrown against the dashboard. Far up ahead, on the next slope, she could see the taillights of the small truck belonging to his principal right-hand man, the one in charge of transporting and then distributing the rum and rice before each meeting. The taillights dancing in the darkness because of the potholed road.

"*Merci?*" she said. "What for? What're you thanking me for?"

"For running about with me at all hours of the night. For throwing in your lot with the small islander. For being Estelle."

Eleven-forty, almost midnight, and they were driving back from a meeting in the foothills of Gran' Morne where the people, all of them coffee growers with their own small plots, spoke mainly Creole, using English only when it couldn't be avoided. They had loved it when he showed off the few Creole words and phrases that he knew. The old people among them remembered his father and his father's father, who had bought their coffee to resell to the big company in town. And everyone over twenty remembered Mis-Mack, his mother.

His eye on the cratered road he said, "I was just thinking of how lucky I was to have been invited to the States where I met the Harrisons' girlchild. I have the Carnegie people to thank. Had not for that little tour I might have ended up marrying someone from this place, one of those ladies in town you've yet to meet. If I had, I'd be driving along this road by myself tonight."

His bulk seemed to fill the car in the darkness.

"Why? Wouldn't she have appreciated a honeymoon spent on the campaign trail?"

He laughed. "Not in the least. The lady—whoever she would've been—would have scorned going around with me to these little poor-behind villages in Morlands. I wouldn't even dare ask her. And as for standing up with me at a meeting and saying a few words to the people or shaking some fella's rusty hand, not in this life! She'd be too busy running behind the great people–them!—as we call them—in town, wanting to live like them. That's what being in politics means in Triunion, you know:

living like the great people–them! So I thank my lucky stars for the Harrisons' girlchild, who's not the sort to run behind anybody and who'll see to it that this country boy in his donkey cart keeps to the straight and narrow."

"Look!" She held up a pair of small, clenched, buff yellow fists that she had turned upwards. To show him the grip she intended keeping on the reins.

Reaching over, he took the fist nearest to him, drew it to his lips, kissed it, and kept on holding it while driving with one hand. *"Merci, oui."*

———

10:40 P.M.

She stood in the windy darkness on top of Bush Mountain, buttoning herself into the cardigan she always brought along when driving in the mountains at night, buttoning the sweater while watching Primus Mackenzie walk unhurriedly up the road in the path of their headlights, on his way to find help.

Late August, only a little over two weeks before the elections, and on the drive back from a meeting in the town of Marigot at the foot of Bush Mountain their sturdy, hardworking English Morris had finally broken down.

"Let's hope it's something we can fix," she had said as the engine sputtered and died and they got out. "Where's the flashlight?"

"Me!" he had laughed. "I don't even know how to open the bonnet on this thing. And you can bet that not another car will be coming along to give us a push if that's what we need. Not at this hour. Nobody drives up in these mountains this late."

"And the truck left early."

"Yes." He sucked his teeth in annoyance. "Tonight of all nights."

The truck that brought the rice and rum had returned to the town of Morlands before the meeting ended.

Just before the Morris stalled completely, he had managed to swing it away from the sheer drop on the side of the road they were traveling over to the safer side, close to the wall of trees that crowned the final slope of the mountain. For a time after getting out of the car he had simply stood with his arm resting on top of the open door, gazing silently into the dark wood of mahogany and cedar—one of those long crowd-pleasing pauses of his that brought everything to a standstill. He might have been waiting for a mechanic to step from among the trees to fix the Morris on the spot. Standing there as if he fully expected it to happen, until finally, without hurrying, he had started up the road in the direction of their headlights.

He had spotted it before she did: a small one-room house about thirty yards away, a trash house, as he had told her they were called, made of woven twigs plastered over with mud and capped by a roof of thatch. During the day the trash houses were to be seen clinging like burrs to the mountains and hills of the district. This one had been built on a ledge just below the side of the road that sheered off into the darkness, so that only its thatched roof and the upper portion of the mud wall were visible from where she stood beside the car.

She watched, hugging herself in the sweater, as he disappeared down the embankment above the house; she heard him call out, heard muffled voices answer, a man's, a woman's, followed by a baby's startled cry escaping into the night as the door was opened. The sounds reached her easily in the dark, windy silence. Not even a cricket or a tree frog to be heard up this high. Then his unhurried voice again. His up-country voice that spoke as they did, in an accent so strong it made English sound like a foreign language to her at times. A burst of laughter, shy and deferential, followed his voice. He must have made a joke about the Morris breaking down or playfully scolded them for not having attended the meeting tonight in Marigot. What were they so busy doing that they hadn't come, she imagined him asking. Then, the question followed by a suggestive look from him that caused more laughter. Or maybe he said it outright: "Too busy making more feet for stocking to come hear me speak?" ("Baby," he had told

134

her. ("It's our way of saying having a baby.") He would only forgive them if they promised to give him their vote next month. Joking with them, teasing them, knowing that like nearly everyone in the district they already considered him to be not only the member of the House from Morlands but premier, prime minister, president.

When he climbed back up the embankment he was accompanied by a long-legged boy of about thirteen who was sleepily pulling on a man's khaki work jacket that was as threadbare as the shirt and short pants he had on. Peering through the headlights she could see that most of the seat to the pants was missing. Oh, God. Another small ashy behind bared to the world. It was getting to be a familiar sight.

The boy stumbled off into the darkness toward Marigot several thousand feet below and Estelle watched Primus Mackenzie walked unhurriedly back to her and the car.

"How long do you think it'll take him to get down this mountain?"

"God only knows. Two hours maybe if he ever wakes up," he said. "But we might be here until tomorrow this time waiting on the damn mechanic to come."

"Why? Why wouldn't he come right away?"

"Because he's the DNP's man in Marigot, that's why. They keep him in rum and cigarettes to get out the vote for them. So when he hears who it is stranded on Bush Mountain, he's going to take his sweet time getting here. And if I were to ask him when he does come how he could have the heart to keep us waiting so long, he might get vex and leave without so much as touching the car. And if he does fix it he's going to charge me double. That's the kind of hangman we're dealing with."

"And there's nobody else you could have sent for? No other mechanic?" Asking, although she already knew the answer. It was only three months and a couple of weeks since she had stepped off the plane, wedding rice still in her shoes, yet she already knew the answer.

"Not a one," he said. "He's the only so-called mechanic up

this way and the only one who has a truck with a winch—bought with help from his friends in government—in case we have to be towed. There's not a thing we can do but wait."

He took off his jacket and with great ceremony draped it around her shoulders. "I don't want the Harrisons saying that I came and took their daughter out of their house only to bring her to catch her death of cold on Bush Mountain," he said.

11:30 P.M.

"Now, if this was any country to speak of there would at least be a little hotel or a guesthouse up here or one of those inns you see in England, someplace where we could go and relax until the hangman decides to come."

They were in the backseat of the Morris with all the lights off to conserve the battery. Darkness like a stage curtain or a pair of black velvet drapes they had drawn around the car to give them privacy.

"The only thing," he said, "we'd have to think up something to do to pass the time in the little hotel or guesthouse or inn."

She laughed. "Any ideas?"

"Not a one," he said. "I'd have to leave it to your American ingenuity to come up with something. Me, I'm just a little colonial, a small islander, a barefoot native, somebody not long out of all that bush out there"—a wave toward the heavily wooded slope they couldn't see—"so you know I wouldn't be able to think up anything for us to do. Except, of course, the usual."

"You mean *that* again? I know you don't mean *that* again!"

"I'm afraid so."

She sighed. "Oh, well, I guess we'll have to stick with that until my American ingenuity can come up with something better."

12:01 A.M.

"Mwen renmen ou," she said, as he had taught her. It sounds better in Creole, he had said. *"Mwen renmen ou!"* He brought his face back up to hers briefly. She tasted herself on his lips. "Creole with an American accent. I love it," he said, using her favorite expression.

12:20 A.M.

This time he didn't just drape his jacket around her shoulders after buttoning up the cardigan. Instead, with even more loving ceremony, he fitted her short arms into the long sleeves, then turned up the sleeves, but only to her fingertips so that her hands remained covered; he also turned up the collar and the lapels around her face. ("I don't understand it. I thought this was supposed to be the tropics," she had said the first time she found herself shivering as they drove along a dark mountain road. "Not this high up," he had said. "At night, this high up, we feel North America breathing down our backs.") They had gotten out of the car so that he could more easily bundle her back into the jacket, and as she stood looking up at him from her scant five feet one, the top of his head appeared to be grazing the black dome of the sky, while the white of his eyes was the largest of the stars to be seen there.

1:10 A.M.

"Quashie. That's what the English used to call us back then. Quashie instead of slave. They must have thought even slave was too good a name for us . . ." They were back inside the Morris and she had asked him to tell her again the story behind the monument that stood across from Government Lands. "Well, I know one day Quashie surprised the rass out of them. He started banding together from all over the island, just grabbing up the first thing he could lay his hands on—hoe, cutlass, a big stick, a stone—and started marching. The conch shell spreading the word from one estate to the next. The flambeau setting fire to everything in sight. This was the time, as I told you, when all three of the Big Three were here. One little island under three flags. The French up this way, the Spanish to the south, and the English everywhere else. *Gallia est omnis divisa in partes tres,*" he recited. "They used to drum that into our heads at school, but nobody ever mentioned that we had also been divided in three once, like the famous Gaul. Not a word in the history books they gave us to read about what went on here."

"The twenty-three wars in two centuries."

"Yes," he said. "Anyway, the three of them were so busy fighting each other they didn't realize what Quashie was up to until they saw him come marching with cutlass and hoe, ready to chase them into the sea. We had an army almost as big as theirs, they say, and for a while all their generals were no match for those four you see out at the monument."

Estelle closed her eyes to see them more clearly. To the left of the pedestal stood the old man from Gran' Morne they called Pere Bossou, the conch shell he had used as a bugle raised to his lips. To the right, brandishing the sword he had taken off a conquistador he had slain on the long march up from Spanish Bay was eighteen-year-old Alejandro, the youngest of the four. And in between the oldest and the youngest, striding just a little ahead of them, came the two coleaders, coconspirators, lovers, consorts, friends: he, Will Cudjoe, a cutlass in one hand, a stolen musket in the other and a bandage made of the finest Alençon lace around his head; she, Congo Jane, also doubly armed and wearing draped around her shoulders, the ends crisscrossing her chest like bandoliers, the shawl—Jane's famous shawl—that had supplied the bandage for the gunshot wound on Will Cudjoe's forehead.

"Tell me about the shawl again," she said quietly. She was really asking about what the shawl had hidden.

He told her: of how, just before the final blow was struck and the flambeau put to the great house, Jane had snatched the shawl off the woman who owned her, to save it from being bloodied, and draped it around herself. Laying claim to it as long-overdue compensation for the loss she had suffered when she was no more than eleven.

"And she never took it off, you know. Jane died—she was hung—wearing it. They say that the women who came from the Congo loved pretty things."

Jane, the child, had seen the hair ribbon where it had been thrown on the floor and stamped on in this strange place they had brought her to, and unable to resist it she had picked up the spurned thing when no one was looking and spirited it away, just to gaze at it and to touch it in secret and to even put it on her own hair sometimes, although she had nothing to show her how it looked. A pretty red hair ribbon for the yellow head of the girl no bigger than herself who they said owned her, the same little girl who had thrown the ribbon to the floor and stamped on it, trying to kill it under her feet. . . . Soon, though, having just a hair ribbon wasn't enough to satisfy her, and she began collecting other little things that she saw spurned, discarded, forgotten or thought to be lost. A bit of lace trimming for a flounce left on the sewing-room floor. The silk lacings from a pair of lady's shoes that had become frayed and been thrown away. A handkerchief that had the look and feel of the mist on the ground each morning lying unused in a drawer because of a small tear in one corner. A curl from the yellow head that she saved after the haircut was over and she was left to sweep the floor. A single small mother-of-pearl button that had rolled under a clothespress and been forgotten. These and a treasure trove of other pretty things that the mother of the little girl who owned her would list item by item in her journal when the cache was discovered. Because one day they found the hair ribbon and other things, and the same cowhide that was used in the fields had come down on Jane, on every part of her, sending her scrambling rolling crawling screaming begging in the yard in front of the great house. Until one small nub of a breast was gone. Torn to shreds by the nine knotted tails on the whip. The blood. Her screams. They had had to send for an old woman from Guinea who was the only one who might know what to do to save her. She had hurriedly made a poultice of cayenne and other herbs, and Jane had screamed and screamed again.

"We had some beasts around here in those days," he had said the first time he told her about Jane. Holding her as she sat with her face buried in her hands.

"When you think of it," he said now in the darkness of the car, "that monument to Jane and the others is the only worthwhile thing the DNP has done since it's been in office. I told you how they rushed out and had it made when we got home rule and they won the election. That was before I went up to England. They wanted to show what strong nationalists they were. But look where they put it. Instead of its being in town where everyone could see it, they stuck it all the way up here in Morlands, so as not to offend the white people in town."

"We'll put it where it belongs come September fifteenth," she said, still thinking of the shawl and the mutilation it had hidden.

2:50 A.M.

The night dew on the windshield was visible in the starlight that had grown stronger over the hours. Dew like a fine cold drizzle. She was certain it would be cold to the touch. And the air seeping in under the dashboard was beginning to feel like the breath of an early frost that had found its way down from Canada. Soon not even the sweater and jacket or the arm he kept around her would be enough.

"We might have to ask the neighbors to move over and make room for us," she said.

"What neighbors?"

"The ones up the road. What others do we have?"

He sat around to peer at her, clearly shocked. How could a thought like that even cross her mind? It took him a long moment to recover. "The neighbors," he said, "scarcely have room for themselves, never mind anyone else. It was people like peas in there. I've never seen so many little children crowded up in one room. If there was one, there had to be a dozen."

"That's the point. We'd at least keep warm with all the bodies."

"And what about the smell of baby piss and people that don't have enough water to wash every day? The smell would run you out in a minute. No," he said sharply, "it wouldn't do." He quickly caught himself and his tone changed: "No, Estelle, we can't go in there. . . . You don't know how people here have to live. Not a single housing scheme—what you'd call a project— in the entire district, and Government Lands sitting there idle. I'd like to see that place turned into a model village for all these people you see scattered about on these hills or into a cooperative farm, or both. There's enough land for both. But it'll never happen while the Do-Nothings are in charge. That's why we have to throw them the rass out come next month. The whole pack." He drew her closer to warm her with his body. "Their henchman should soon be here."

3:30 A.M.

She slowly came awake and sat watching them as if they were the dramatis personae of her dream: a long line of market women (hawkers, she had learned they were called hawkers) walking single file along the side of the road that could send them plunging down the slope if they missed a step.

Whenever they were out late in the Morris they came across them, ghosts bundled against the night dew in old sweaters and flour sacks for shawls, their bare feet carrying them soundlessly between the small settlements that called themselves villages and towns and along the mountain roads. The high beams on the car would single them out, give them and the oversize baskets on their heads and the occasional baby swaddled in the sacking shawl—oh, God—a kind of ghostly substance for a few seconds, and then drop them back into the darkness again.

Because today was Wednesday, she knew that the women across the road were headed for the huge open-air market that was held twice a week on the main square in Morlands, just outside the old Mackenzie house. 'Foreday morning on Wednesdays and Saturdays found hawkers from all over the district, even from up Gran' Morne, encamped between the house where Primus's mother had had her shop on the ground floor and the church on the other side of the square.

By sunrise everything would be in readiness for the daylong buying and selling. The breadfruit and yam, the mangoes that ranged from green to yellow to blush red, the green oranges/ ". . . they don't look it, homefolks, because of the green skins, but they're the sweetest oranges I've ever tasted . . . /"—everything, every vegetable and piece of fruit they had borne over the miles would be stacked in neat pyramids of their kind on crocus bags spread on the ground. And the hawkers would be ready as well—straw hats the width of umbrellas on their heads, broad Congo Jane feet planted on either side of their small stools, a hand on their hip although the first customer had yet to arrive, all set to spend the day haggling to the death over a penny difference in price.

"Wha' the rass! Take your blasted hands off my mangoes. I wouldn't sell them to you for that little money if you was Jesus Christ himself."

"*Mes amis!* Not a cent less, *oui!*" (The hawkers from Gran' Morne were forced to speak English on market day.) "I kiss my right hand to God I'm not taking one cent less for these cucumbers!" Kissing both sides of the hand, they would then raise it to the sky above the nearly treeless, dusty square.

Pure theater, Estelle had said to herself the first time she had witnessed the market from the veranda of the house. Every one of them should be on Broadway. They'd all win best actress of the year. But oh, God, something needs to be done about them having to sit out in the hot sun all day!

"Where two or three are gathered together you have a market. That's what we say of the ladies. The market is in their blood."

He lay with his head on the seatback next to hers. They were in the front of the Morris now.

"I thought you were still sleeping."

"No. The ladies woke me."

"Me too. They're not making a sound, yet still in all they woke me. Do you think they see us? They're passing by like they don't even see the car."

"I doubt that they do," he said. Sitting up, he peered along with her at what they could see of the silent procession across the road. "The ladies don't have time for us. They're busy concentrating on getting to Morlands before dawn. That's all that matters to them right now . . ." Then musing aloud: "Nobody realizes it, but those are some of the best business minds in the world you see walking about these dark roads at night. Never been near a schoolhouse, most of them, yet the ladies can buy and sell you in a minute if you're not careful. They belong on Wall Street."

"Or on Broadway."

"True," he laughed. "They love to put on a show, but we need them more on Wall Street. Or here running the Ministry of Finance instead of the jackasses we now have. But what to do? They were born the wrong color, the wrong sex, the wrong class and everything else on a little two-by-four island that doesn't offer anybody any real scope . . ."

"Dear Estelle . . . You could even call it an act of cruelty to invite those like myself to visit the land of opportunity only to send us packing in two weeks time back to places that offer so little scope," he had said in a letter written shortly after her first trip to Triunion. He could speak of the tour more openly now that they knew each other better, he had added. Hearing the word "scope" again, she remembered the letter, whole portions of which she had committed to memory.

The Carnegie people have no idea of how difficult it is for us to adjust again to life on a small scale, a life with so few possibilities, after being

Paule Marshall

in a country where everything's the size of the Grand Canyon and the possibilities are limitless. One of the farms they took us to visit was larger than the island of Nevis, where one of us was from. Corn everywhere we looked. Imagine, a farm belonging to one man that's larger than an entire country! And the General Motors plant we toured would make two of the town we call our capital. It was the same everywhere we went. Everything on a grand scale. Of course, the point of the show wasn't lost on us. We were to take heed and think "free enterprise" rather than any socialist nonsense we might have picked up while we were away studying, and perhaps something close to what we saw might be ours when we take over our little atolls. But is it too presumptuous to ask how we're to achieve this miracle with only a few bananas, a little coffee and rice and some sugarcane that we can't even get a decent price for anymore? Never mind, when the time comes we're still to model ourselves on Big Brother to the north and not give trouble. . . . This isn't to say that I don't admire your famous ingenuity and drive. What I call your "get up and do" spirit. God knows we could use some of it here. In fact, I'd like to treat everyone on Triunion to a two-week tour of the States, so that some of the "get up and do" could rub off on them. The only problem is they'd never come back. Not one of them. The island would be deserted. They'd all prefer to stay and become taxi drivers in New York rather than return and help develop the place. And you saw for yourself how desperately it needs developing. I don't have to tell you what our situation is like, what with the people in Spanish Bay running off to Cuba and Puerto Rico in some leaky boat the first chance they get, so there's scarcely anyone left at that end of the island. And the people up Gran' Morne behaving like they're still maroons fighting the French, refusing to even speak the official language; and the rest of us still with this colonial thinking, acting more British than the British. If only we could throw off all that, come together and start thinking "get up and do," you wouldn't recognize Triunion. The place would actually begin to live up to its name. And what that would mean for the rest of these little islands! We might all finally come together— French, Dutch, English, Spanish—all o' we one! so that even Big

144

Brother would have to respect us. It's the dream that keeps me going, Estelle. At any rate, one thing is certain, come independence we're going to see to it that no one man owns a cornfield bigger than another man's country, we don't care what the Carnegie people–them! say. . . .

She had memorized every word of that letter.

3:56 A.M.

"All right, never mind us," she heard herself almost shouting. The silent parade on the other side of the road had ended, the night chill had penetrated to the marrow of her bones, and she was close to shouting. "Forget about us sitting here shivering. But how could he do this to the boy? Keep him up half the night like this?"

She had been thinking about the boy off and on ever since he stumbled off into the dark, rubbing sleep from his eyes. She imagined he had come fully awake about a quarter of the way down to Marigot and had started running, flying, his stripling arms acting like wings and his bare feet causing a minor avalanche of loose stones and dirt each time they struck the ground. Running, with the wind pouring through the holes in his ragtag jacket and pants.

"It's a crime to keep him up so late."

"Do you think that vagabond cares? If I know him, he went back to bed as soon as he got the message and put the boy to wait out in the tow truck. And the boy probably doesn't mind. It's a spree as far as he's concerned. He'll be able to tell everybody when he gets back about the big time he had staying up all night in Marigot and riding in the truck. And he'll have some change in his pocket because I'll have to give both him and his father something. Better yet, he won't have to do a lick of work today. While the others are out sweating in the ground he'll be lying up in the house sleeping."

"I still think it's a crime."

4:10 A.M.

She squatted in the narrow space between the car and the solid wall of trees, feeling—with her behind bared to the elements—like their long-legged courier and all the little boys they encountered each day along the roads with the seat of their pants missing. And it was also the yearly trip down home to Tennessee when she was small. Déjà vu, Estelle said to herself, holding her dress and slip up off the ground. I've been here before . . .

Years ago, on the long drive from Hartford to Norway, Tennessee, each summer to visit her mother's family, she would occasionally have to use the side of the road as a bathroom once they left Washington. Sometimes, even Bea Harrison was forced to join her outside the car. Her father, on the other hand, had so trained himself he could wait for a toilet with a Colored sign to appear no matter how long that took. When her brother, Grady, was small they brought along a milk bottle for his use. It was her job to hold it for him in the backseat when he needed to go and to screw the cap on tight afterward. So that it was only herself and sometimes Bea Harrison squatting behind a bush, a rock, a tree or between their old Hudson and the shoulder of some road below the Mason-Dixon Line.

"You all right, Bea?"

Booker Harrison always waited at least a minute after they were back in the car before asking. And he kept his gaze out the windshield. He never once, that Estelle could remember, turned to look at her mother when she came and sat back down beside him. Not for that first minute.

"Yes, Booker, I'm all right."

"Estelle?"

He never looked in the rearview mirror either.

"I'm all right too, Daddy."

Only then would he start the car again.

The cold breath of Bush Mountain under her, the shock of it, almost made her lose the urge. Then, briefly warming her, steam rose from the noisy puddle.

As she was getting out of the car just now, Primus had given her his handkerchief without saying a word. And without looking at her. Booker Harrison all over again. She made use of it. Her own was still damp from when she had gone three hours ago.

4:31 A.M.

"Is there anything to be done with a people like this? With a damn country like this?"

The upper half of his body was thrust in the back door of the Morris. His face was just inches from her own. He had been pacing up and down the black and empty road for close to an hour when he suddenly came over, tore open the door, and leaned in to where she sat huddled in a corner of the backseat.

"Is there?" His angry breath visible between them. "Why am I bothering to run for anything in this kiss-muh-ass place? It's never going to change!"

She had never heard this voice before, nor seen him move as swiftly; and his head, she saw, was pulled so far forward it looked almost detached from the rest of his body. She had never seen that before either.

Reaching up, she took his face between her hands, trying to stop him from saying what he didn't mean.

5:05 A.M.

She shifted slightly to prevent his head from slipping off her shoulder, and it shot up.

"Don't write and tell them I don't even have a proper car to drive you about in."

The head with the forehead that had earned him his nickname when he was only a boy dropped back to the curve of her shoulder.

Talking in his sleep.

5:32 A.M.

"A swimming pool the size of a damn lake! And with a set of naked women to pour the water for it!" A loud suck-teeth sought to dismiss the marble swimming pool in Connecticut two years ago. "People with so much money they don't know what to do with it."

He was awake this time, sitting up beside her with his eyes on the slowly yielding night outside. Yet his voice sounded like the one that had spoken out in his sleep.

6:05 A.M.

'Foreday morning. The oversize stars had dimmed and retreated, and while they had both nodded off again, the sky had turned the gray of a mourning dove. There was even enough light all of a sudden for the road beyond the windshield to be dimly visible. As Estelle crept out of the Morris, stiff and aching and chilled to the bone, she could actually see the morning fog and mist slowly filtering down through the void across from where they were parked. Stage smoke. The whitish cloud would come to rest like stage smoke on the lowlands, causing every house, tree and mountain to levitate a few feet off the ground, till it finally dissipated by noon.

Primus had left the car just as she was waking up and had disappeared down the embankment above the trash house up the road. Smoke could be seen rising from the shed-roof kitchen out back. Estelle waited, smelling her unwashed body, her mouth stale, her joints stiff, her eyes encrusted, everything she had on damp, cold and rumpled, and thinking suddenly, wildly, helplessly: *I want to go home!*—thinking this while watching him make his way back to the car, followed by a woman who was bundled in layers of sacking like the hawkers earlier.

While they were still some distance away she smelled the coffee in the two steaming cups the woman was carrying on a plate she was using as a tray. But even as they reached her and she greeted the woman and gratefully took a cup of the coffee between her hands and felt the heat spread from her numbed hands to her arms and then down through her body; even as the wild thought of home evaporated in the warmth and aroma rising from the cup, she heard herself asking herself, in a voice that sounded close to hysteria: *What is this?* Why couldn't he have brought the coffee over himself instead of having the woman do it? All those children she has to look after, including the baby I heard crying last night, and he's taken her away to wait on us. Or why didn't he just call me over and we could have had the coffee there? Why does he just stand and wait for things to be done for him? Wouldn't even open the hood of the car to see if it wasn't something we could fix. Just stood there waiting for a mechanic or God to come out of the woods and take care of it. The same thing at the house. That woman who he says raised him. Celestine. "She knew me, understood me, before I knew or understood myself, Estelle," he had told her. "Celestine's more than just one of the servants about the place." The woman seems to appear before he even finishes calling her name whenever he wants anything. It's uncanny. Or she sends some little boy she calls a *'ti-garçon* running to see what he wants. And every morning she has his coffee ready the minute he wakes up, as if she knows just when he'll open his eyes . . . *Primus, you should have brought the coffee over yourself!* she was about to cry in the near hysterical voice when suddenly it didn't matter all that much; in a swift change of mind, it was nothing to make a scene about, at least not at the moment—she'd tell him about it later, when she was calmer and could put it in a light vein, when she had reminded herself that it was another country, another way of doing things . . . She wouldn't say anything for the moment, because the woman from the trash house had disappeared back up the road after serving them the coffee; and with a look that said he had heard every syllable of her thoughts and stood corrected and chastened, Primus Mackenzie was touching his cracked and steaming cup to hers and intoning with a playful yet solemn smile, "I, Primus Everett, take thee Estelle Beatrice—just as you have taken me—for better or for worse, for richer for poorer, in sickness and in health, and all the rest."

7:00 A.M.

From the way the tow truck came roaring toward them through the early morning sunlight, the man at the wheel might have been driving at breakneck speed ever since he received the message that they were stranded. Next to him in the cab sat the long-legged boy, clinging to the window frame because of the jolting and grinning from ear to ear, a prodigal son come home unrepentant after a night of riotous living in Marigot.

"Is there anything to be done with a people like this? With a damn country like this?" he had cried before, his head thrust all the way forward. And it had come jutting out again, Estelle saw, as the truck pulled up and he walked over to greet the mechanic, who was smiling.

———

SEPTEMBER 16

PRIMUS BY A LANDSLIDE. STOP. WE'RE STILL CELEBRATING. STOP. HIS PARTY DIDN'T DO AS WELL, THOUGH, SORRY TO SAY. STOP. IT GOT ONLY FOUR SEATS OUT OF TWELVE, SO THE OLD GANG IS STILL IN CHARGE. STOP. BUT WE'LL TAKE CARE OF THEM THE NEXT TIME AROUND. STOP. LONG LETTER FOLLOWS. LOVE.

ESTELLE

3

Celestine Marie-Claire Bellegarde

Mes amis, he don' want to go! Here Mis-Mack is spending good money to send him to the big school in town and he don' want to go. He'd rather to stay in the little two-by-four school here in Morlands, up with a lot of fowl-yard children that don't have no background, as Mis-Mack says. All today, *oui*, he's been giving trouble 'cause he has to leave for town tomorrow. Look what he did this morning when Mis-Mack sent me to pack his clothes. As fast as I'm putting them in the valise he's dragging them out and putting them back in the press or throwing them on the floor. Clean clothes, *oui*, he's throwing on the floor! The pajamas was too small. He din want to take them. The underwears was too old. I wasn't to pack the shoes he wears to church on Sunday. They was too tight and hurt his foot. He wanted new ones. New shoes, new pajamas, new underwears. He wanted everything new. The pants to his uniform was too short and the boys at the school in town was gon laugh at him. Persecuting me so I could scarce 'tend to what I was doing.

And he got on worse yet later this morning when the man from Pointe Baptiste came with a mare to sell to Mr. Mackenzie and ol' Borak broke out his stall and caused the big commotion in the yard. He was a hundred percent worse after that. The minute the man came in the yard with the mare, before he could even say what he had come for, ol' Borak all of a sudden give one kick, *blam!* and knocked down the railing to his stall that needed fixing, and when you looked he was up on the mare. All up on the young mare. Every servant in the place came running to try and pull him off her. But all the yelling and all the lashes they gave him din do no good. They ran and called Mis-Mack, but she was too busy dispatching to leave the shop. They ran then for Mr. Mackenzie who was in the office where he buys the coffee visiting with friends. And when he came out along with the friends he had visiting, he just stood there in the white suit and white shoes he wears all the time looking at ol' Borak up on the mare. He din have a word to say for a long long time. And then he just bus' out laughing. He don' never let nothing worry him. And everybody there bus' out laughing too, even the man from Pointe Baptiste that brought the mare to try and sell her. 'Cause everybody knows ol' Borak ain't no use no more. Mr. Mackenzie don' even bother riding him since he bought the box Ford. Too old. A horse that's been down here since they said come let us make horses. Who's only living 'cause he ain' dead. But I know he came alive today and was all up on the young young mare like he was still the Borak from years back.

And the amount of bawling from her! *Mes amis!* You wanted to stop up your ears. And the trampling! And the dust enough to choke you flying up under their hooves! The lot of blood on the ground! Is a thing you see all the time, *oui*, but this is one time I wanted to hide my eyes. The feeling it gave you. I was laughing, all of us was laughing, but I wanted to hide my eyes and stop up my ears all the same. . . .

And the poor little PM couldn't take it atall. He ran upstairs to the veranda and hide himself behind one of the posts. All you could see was two eyes peeping around the post. He wasn't laughing like the rest of us, only peeping down in the yard and looking like he was frightened. Then, as soon as it was over and ol' Borak was back in his stall and the man from Pointe Baptiste took the mare out the yard and Mr. Mackenzie and the friends he had visiting went back inside the office, he turned into a worse hellion than before. He ran and got his stick, the one that's just like Mis-Mack's cane with a handle to one end, and he start chasing after every dog and cat in the yard, every fowl, trying to hook them with the handle. And every time one of the little doormouth children that work in the shop and about the house came out in the yard, he tried catching them round the neck with the stick too. The cook had to run him out of the kitchen I don' know how many times. In there every minute persecuting her. And he had his own sister in tears. Just tormenting everything and everybody about the place. *Mal élève*! He's too used to having his way. Spoil up, he's been spoil up ever since the rector gave him that name. That's why he don't want to go to the school in town, 'cause he knows he won't have his way there. And he hasn't stopped yet, y'know. Here it 'tis almost night and he's still going on with that stick. I was sitting feeding the baby just now and he come pulling the spoon out my hand and trying to drag the child off my lap. Well, I know I grabbed the stick from him and gave him one with it, *oui*! And you would think I tried to kill him the way he got on. A flood of tears. A big eight-years-old boy in a flood of tears. And over nothing, 'cause I din hit him hard. Just one his legs with the stick to get him to behave. But he start in one big bawling and he's gone running now to the shop to tell Mis-Mack.

Let him tell, *oui*! Mis-Mack's not gon do a thing to me. If it was somebody else that had hit him, yes. But she's not gon have a hard word for me. He thinks he's gon get her to do me like she does the little doormouth children in the shop, but he don' know that I'm the only out of everybody that ever worked in that shop who has never felt that cane around my neck. Mis-Mack has never so much as raised it at me. From the day I came she always treated me special. . . .

"Form yourself here."

The red rubber crutch tip on the cane the woman was holding pointed to a spot directly across from where she was sitting at the counter.

"Form yourself here, I said."

The child standing in one of the tall arched doorways to the shop, the dense night and the empty square behind her, didn't move; and she kept her head bowed.

"What's wrong with you, eh? You don't have ears to hear? I said form yourself over here . . . *"Vini m'pale ou!"*

At that the child shot forward, and the fleshy woman behind the counter who was pointing with the cane laughed, only to scowl again the next moment. "All right," she said, "raise your head and tell me what you're doing standing in the doormouth of my shop this time of night? What is it you want? The market is finished for the day, every last soul has gone home—you can't see that?—and this shop is closed. So if you've come looking to buy something—a penny bread or a sweet—you're out of luck. I'm through selling for the day. What it 'tis you want, I'm asking. Are you looking to buy something or did somebody walk off and leave you here for me to feed and clothe till they decide to come back for you? Which is it? Speak up! Raise your head! Look at me! Who is it left you standing like some duppy or *loup-garou* in the doormouth of my shop?"

The head remained bowed, the tongue mute.

"But look at my crosses! They're leaving them now for me to raise that can't hear and don't have tongues in their heads . . . "Your name, *oui*! *Ki nom ou?*"

"Celestine."

"Speak up! *Plus forte!*"

"Celestine."

"And what else? The second name? I know you people from up Gran' Morne does have a string of names. *Ki nom bateme ou?*"

"Marie-Claire."

"Celestine Marie-Claire what? *Ki nom fammi ou?*"

"Bellegarde."

"Bellegarde, eh? You speak English? Speak up!"

"*Oui.*"

"How you mean *oui?* You think that's English? I'm not keeping another one of you Gran' Morne children that don't understand enough of the King's English to fetch a tin of sardines or a box of matches off the shelf when I call for them. How you mean *oui?*"

"I mean yes, Mis-Mack."

"Oh, so you've found your English and your manners!"

The fat woman paused, placed the cane she had used as a pointer down on the counter, sat up on the high-cushioned stool with a backrest where she spent her day, and forgetting herself for a moment she smiled—unseen by the child whose head remained bowed. She smiled and it was as if someone had suddenly taken a knife and made a slit straight down her middle, had cleaved her open from her throat down past her navel, and out of the great slit had stepped another woman, a young, large-boned woman like herself but stripped of the fleshiness; someone who had her features—eyes, nose, pretty mouth—but not thickened and blurred by the fat, and skin that was the brown of the penny bread sold in the shop. A young, big-boned country girl/woman who did not look middle-aged before her time. And this young woman who still thought of herself as Ursa Louise Wilkerson, daughter of a seamstress in Hastings Village, as she had been before becoming Mis-Mack, the shopkeeper, refused to spend her day like the overweight woman she now inhabited, surrounded by barrels of pickled beef and pork and hundred-pound sacks of flour, cornmeal and rice, and cheap yard goods stacked on a shelf. Ursa Louise Wilkerson did not come away each night with the stink of saltfish and the kerosene she sold by the pint all in her clothes, hair and the pores of her skin. She hid from the smells and the rampant disorder of the shop in the body of her host, and could only be glimpsed when the fat woman forgot herself occasionally and smiled.

"Celestine Marie-Claire Bellegarde, eh? You got more names than you got flesh on your bones. How old you is?"

"Eight years, Mis-Mack."

"Six, you mean. You're no more than six if you're a day."

"Eight, *oui*." The child brought her head up sharply, and the woman found herself confronting a pair of ancient eyes and a little broad-nosed face the color of the night outside, a face surmounted by a bush of rust red hair that should also have been black.

Starved out till even the hair changed color.

"When's the last time you had little meat?" Her eyes on the unnaturally reddish bush.

No answer.

"Where's your family? You mother and father?"

"They dead, *oui*, and the big cousin I was with said she can't keep me no more. She has too many of her own to feed."

Leaning over the scarred counter the woman inspected the child in front of her: the undersized body, the legs that held it up, the small splayed toes. She had expected the legs below the scrap of a dress the child had on to be bandy, but found them straight. Thin, dusted gray from the mountain roads she had walked down earlier, and leopard-spotted from yaws and a thousand insect bites, but absolutely straight from ankle to knee. And they were planted on the worn floorboards on the other side of the counter like gateposts that had been driven into the wood.

She drew back. Closed her eyes. Placed a hand on the swollen melon of her stomach that went unnoticed amid the general fat. (Seven months gone. Primus Everett, if a boy. The gentleman in the white suit and shoes had already named it. Left to him I'd have it right here in the shop, sitting up on this stool dispatching.)

She nodded to herself. This one would stay. The other door-mouth children were always running off because of the cane handle. Or their people, the same ones that left them without a word sometimes outside the shop when the market was over, would come for them once they got a little flesh on their bones and could help out in the ground. And bold enough sometimes to leave another one for her to feed and clothe and train in their place! Gran' Morne people! This one was different, though. She would never run off, and if the cousin or whoever came back for her, she wasn't going two feet with them. She had come at the beginning and she would be here at the end. The two little legs like gateposts . . .

"Odette! *Vini m' pale ou!*"

A reed of a girl, perhaps twice the age of the child at the counter and with a shriveled left arm, appeared at the back door of the shop. The door led to the large inner courtyard, the size of a parade ground almost, around which the old house was built. The work areas were downstairs, while the family living quarters occupied the second floor, with the veranda running its length. A two-story-tall wooden gate—like the gate to a stockade—closed off both the yard and the house.

"Yes, please, Mis-Mack?" Odette in the doorway awaited her orders.

"Come take this one here and have the cook give her something to eat. And tell her I said to put little meat on the plate. Then tomorrow see to it that she makes herself useful about the place."

"Stop the bawling! And not another word out of you about what-and-what Celestine did. She had a right to hit you. I've got eyes in the back of my head, m'sieur, and I've seen through this wall behind me how you've been carrying on in the yard all day. Stop the bawling I said, and form yourself over here." The cane that was like a part of her hand, an extension of her arm, ordered him to the spot across from her at the counter.

She had never used that tone with him before, nor had she

ever held the cane by the end with the rubber tip, the curved handle extended out, when summoning him for a scolding. That was for the doormouth children. With him she always held it properly, by the handle. So that he hung back, puzzled, apprehensive.

"Form yourself here, I said!"

He refused to budge. The few feet of space between himself and the counter had suddenly become dangerous ground. Everything familiar and pleasurable was steadily being overtaken by something unfamiliar that offered no promise of pleasure. It had been happening for weeks now, ever since she had announced that he would be going to school in town. The four or five feet over to the counter would mark, he sensed, both the end of everything he loved and the beginning of something new and terrible, and feeling this he bawled louder, his head back and his face raised to the soot-blackened ceiling of the shop.

Until all of a sudden he heard himself fall silent, his cries abruptly cut off, and he felt his breath being snatched from him. Someone had pelted him with a rockstone, it felt like, striking him right on the bone at the nape of his neck, and the shock of it had taken his breath away. And the same wicked person had also, at the same time, thrown a big hook around his neck and was hauling him forward by this hook across the dangerous ground that lay between him and the counter, hauling him up to the spot reserved for the doormouth children when they were being taken to task.

If they—the doormouth children—misunderstood the order and brought the wrong item from the shelves, or if they were too slow getting back to the counter with the box of matches or the tin of sardines, or if their measure of the cornmeal or rice was off, if they erred in any way, the cane would spring forward, handle first, and as they came within range, it would hook them by the neck.

He always laughed when it happened—everyone did, even the other doormouth children. Then one day he had found a small branch off a lime tree that was curved at one end just like the cane, and he would play "Shop" with it, chasing after the dogs, cats and fowl in the yard, trying to hook them.

"Tell me, where is it you're going to be living from tomorrow on?" She had removed the cane and placed it on the counter. He could breathe again.

"I'm going to be living in town, *Maman*."

"And what will you be doing there?"

"I'll be going to school there, *Maman*."

"What's the name of the school?"

"Edgarton Boys School, *Maman*."

"And who do you think you're going to be meeting at Edgarton Boys School?"

"I don't know, *Maman*. The other boys . . . the teachers . . ."

"And where will these other boys come from?"

He looked around him for help, but found only shadows, large mute *loup-garou* and duppy shadows gathered in the corners beyond the reach of the oil lamp on the counter. And the doors to the shop were closed, so that he couldn't even look for help from the crickets or tree frogs outside. While he had stood there bawling, one of the yardboys had slipped in and closed and locked the front doors for the night. And his father, in his white suit and shoes, had already left for his evening outing in the box Ford, wearing his panama hat. He was not there to help either.

"Where will these other boys come from, I ask."

"I don't know, *Maman*. From about the place . . ."

"They're going to come"—she spoke slowly and deliberately —"from Garrison Row and Raleigh Hill in town where the great people–them! live. In big pretty houses you've never seen the likes of, m'sieur. And these other boys are going to have last names like Allenby and Shepard, Forsythe and DaSilva. And some of them you'll take for white people at first, till you look good at them, and even then you might not be sure. And because they come from Garrison Row and Raleigh Hill and have those names and that color they're going to feel themselves better than you . . . I wonder if you understand that?"

"Yes, *Maman*."

"So what are you going to do then about these little ringtail boys at Edgarton Boys School who're going to feel themselves better than you?"

He shook his head. The bone at the nape of his neck was still sore.

"You don't know, eh? Well, I gon tell you. You're going to see to it that Primus Mackenzie from Morlands, a place behind God's back, gets a First every year. Your name, m'sieur, at the top of the class each and every year. I wouldn't want to have to close up this shop and come all the way to town because it so happened that one year you only got a Second or Third. Do you understand what I'm saying?"

"Yes, *Maman.*"

"Another thing." She noisily pulled open the cash drawer over which she sat, jamming it into her fleshiness. She was larger now than she had been when almost full term with him eight years ago: the great bowls of peas and rice she often ate while sitting there dispatching, the sweets she stole from the jars on the counter over the course of the day had settled on her in layers. "You see this?" Shaking the drawer, which was filled with a disarray of coins and crumpled bills that smelled of coffee, sugarcane and sweat, the yeasty tang of human sweat. "This looks like a big set of money, don't it?"

"Yes, *Maman.*"

"Enough money that if you had it you would run out this very minute and buy a motorcar like your father's. Am I right?"

A faint surprised half-smile. How did she know?

A derisive laugh: "Pennies, m'sieur! Bare bare pennies! You ain't seen real money yet. Wait till you go into a store like Conlin and Finch. Wait till you see the big banks and businesses in town. Those little boys at Edgarton Boys School will look like they're rich to you, but take my word, the white people who own Conlin and Finch and the banks and so—and I'm talking pure white now, from England and America and Canada—can buy and sell all the great people–them! Everybody, including the government, taking orders from them."

As noisily as she had opened the drawer she quietly closed it, and as quietly regarded him for a time. Her face the floury brown of a penny bread, her pretty mouth and every pound of her close to three hundred pounds looking suddenly, unimaginably weary.

"Tell me, why am I sending a little boy still in short pants to live all the way in big Fort Lord Nelson? Why am I putting the only boychild I have in this world—my heartstring, *oui*!—in some big school where he won't know a soul? Why am I doing this to him? Can you tell me?"

Another plea for help from the duppy and *loup-garou* shadows. "I don't know, *Maman*."

"Is it just so he can learn a few Latin words? Or so he'll be able to say when he's grown that he went to school with boys from Garrison Row and Raleigh Hill? No, m'sieur, it don't have a thing to do with any nonsense like that. It's so he'll understand from the early how things go in this world. It's so he'll know how to carry himself in this life and what-and-what he must do to find the means to live as he would like—the motorcars and whatever else he sets his mind to . . ."

"The means, the money"—and there it was again: the handle of the cane around his neck, pulling him so close this time he was practically lying on top of the counter, his feet almost off the floor and his face just inches from hers—"so that when you're of an age to have a wife you'll be able to provide for her decent. I don't ever want to hear, m'sieur, that you married somebody only to stick her up in a shop selling saltfish and rice from the time God's sun rise in the morning till it set at night while you sit in your office in a white suit and shoes entertaining your friends all day. Got to have on the suit and shoes even when he's around the coffee he buys. Calls himself a speculator, yet he spends the whole day visiting with friends and come evening he's off in his motorcar to see his keep-miss . . ." Raging, her angry gaze on the tall doors of the shop and the town beyond the doors, then returning to the small stricken face just inches from her own. "If I was to ever hear of you doing anything like that to a woman you married, or treating her in any way disrespectful, if you was to ever so much as raise a hand to her, I'm going to come after you with this cane"—she gave it a sharp little tug—"never mind you'll be a hardback man by then. I could be in my grave, m'sieur, I'd still come looking for you.

"Another thing"—and another sharp tug—"don't go looking for anyone blacker than yourself when the time comes to marry. And watch the company you keep. If you run with fowl-yard people that's how the world's gon see you."

Then, without warning, the weariness again. He felt the cane slip from his neck as the hand holding it went slack, along with the rest of her. The soles of his feet touched the floor again. For a time he stood waiting for her to recover enough to go on. They both waited, the scarred counter between them. The kerosene lamp nearby throwing up its monstrous *loup-garou* shadows. Until finally all she could manage to do was dismiss him. "G'long," she said in the spent voice. "G'long and tell Celestine to give you your supper."

She already had it waiting for him. She had intended saying as soon as he came out of the shop, You see, you see, it serve you right, you went running to tell on me and look what happen, it serve you right, *oui*. You's too mannish! I keep telling you you's too mannish! And she had meant to say it with all the authority of her sixteen years and the pride she took in being the only one of the doormouth children never to have felt the cane handle around her neck. But as he stumbled out into the yard, where she had stood listening behind the back door of the shop, and she saw his face, she said nothing. His face looked worse than it had that morning when he was up on the veranda peeking down at ol' Borak and the mare. And so Celestine said nothing. She simply led him upstairs to the dining room where his supper lay on the table under a domed, wire-mesh *couvre-plat* to protect it from the night-flying insects.

There was Ovaltine, a large cup of it, along with bread and a comfiture of guava—his favorite—to go on the bread.

———

The door to the room opened just wide enough for the light from a quarter-moon and the numerous stars to reach across to her pallet on the floor. Light the color of mother-of-pearl.

The door was one of several in the line of bedrooms on one side of the veranda upstairs. The darkened courtyard lay below.

"Where it 'tis you going with your mannish self?"

Whispering it—she always whispered it—so as not to wake the baby in her crib or his other sister, who slept in the small bed that had once been his.

———

'Foreday morning. The dun-colored hour before dawn found him slipping downstairs in his bare feet, the tin of candies that he had just unpacked from his valise hidden under his pajama top. A tin of peppermint creams and toffees from Conlin and Finch that he had won on Prize Day, his last Prize Day at the school in Morlands.

Only Odette, who supervised the doormouth children, was in the shop. She was also responsible for seeing to it that the place was in order by the time his mother came downstairs just as the sun was rising, the floor swept and the tall doors that fronted the square opened. She assigned the tasks. Odette, with her finny arm: the left one perfectly formed—all five fingers, the hand, the wrist and forearm, all perfect—but only half the size of her right arm. Her people from up Gran' Morne had left her outside the shop door when she was only five. She was over twenty-five now. Some wicked person, they said, had paid a *bocor* good money to put her arm that way when she was still in her mother's stomach.

He knew he could trust Odette to see to it that the thieves among the doormouth children didn't snatch the tin of candies off the counter and run off with it. He had planned to wait and open the candies at the school in town, so that the boys there could see the snowy scene pictured on the cover, all the little white children dressed in old-fashioned clothes ice-skating on a pond that looked like glass.

He would never get to show it to them now. Or to share with them the peppermint creams and toffees inside.

But it would be the first thing to greet her as Odette and the other doormouth children hoisted her into her high chair, and she settled in for the day spent dispatching.

4

Dear Homefolks,

   . . . I sometimes wonder what she thinks of me. I've nothing to go on, but I suspect Mam'selle Celestine doesn't altogether approve of "the wife the PM went and find in America." She probably feels he would have been better off marrying one of the ladies in town, someone who would conduct herself more like the wife of a member of the House, and not some foreigner with what I'm sure she thinks are some very peculiar ways. At least that's my impression. I'll never know, though, because the woman is the Sphinx itself. There's never the slightest hint as to what she might be thinking or feeling. Mam'selle keeps all such information strictly to herself.

   In any case, the two of us have finally come to a truce without the first shot being fired. She's to look after the house in town, and when we go up to Morlands she's to come along and take charge there too. Whither we goest, she goes, in other words, and with her latest little helper in tow, the *'ti-garçons* I told you about. She's to run things in both places, which is fine with me, because as you all know keeping house is not one of my talents. And I certainly wouldn't want to do it in a place where it means playing general to a small army of servants. Spending the day ordering the help around is not exactly what I see as my life's work. So I've gladly handed the job over to Miss Celestine. It's all yours, I've more or less said. Don't even ask me what to fix for dinner. You decide. Surprise me. And if you want to get up at the crack of dawn to make coffee for the PM because you've always done it, fine. If you want to appear like a Johnny-on-the-spot before he even finishes calling your name—which she does all the time— that's fine with me too. It's positively eerie, homefolks. Her name is hardly out of his mouth before she isn't standing there in one of her black and white mourning dresses (she's still in mourning for Primus's mother, whom she adored) and her one braid. She's got this beautiful thick black hair that she wears in a single braid around her head. Not only does she appear almost before he calls her, she seems to know what he wants without him having to say. Which is all the more eerie. So I've called a truce. Why try to take on the Sphinx? The woman's been here running things long before I came, and you can tell just from the way she stands—she's got these absolutely straight legs—that she'll be here long after ordinary mortals like myself have gone our way.

Besides, putting her in charge leaves me free to do what I like. And I herewith announce that I now have a job. Since the last time I wrote—and I have to beg for an excuse, as they say here, that it's been so long between letters; I'll try make up for it with this one. Anyway, since the last time I wrote I've taken over running Primus's office. It's really two or three offices in one, his government affairs office, his law office as well as headquarters for Morlands in town. People from the district always stop by when they come to town, so we keep abreast of what's going on up there. It can get pretty hectic at times what with all the clients and visitors around, but I love it. And I've also taken a second job since the last time you heard from me. I've joined the board of the Arts Council, which sponsors various cultural events and in general promotes the local arts and artists. Or is supposed to. I finally had to give up on the drama club I joined when I first came. That turned out to be an exercise in futility. The old guard running it didn't approve of any play written after 1900, and they certainly didn't approve of me and my ideas. But why put on one dull English drawing room comedy after another? Shaw, then Oscar Wilde, then Shaw again. Every time you look, *Candida* in black face! It's ridiculous. As Primus says, they're more British than the British in this place. Where are the plays about life here and now in Triunion, I asked those folks. Or why hasn't someone written about Congo Jane, whom I've told you about. What a play the story of her life would make! They looked at me as if I were out of my mind when I brought it up. Frankly, I get to see more genuine theater at the markets here or in court when Primus is arguing a case than at the drama club. So I kissed it goodbye. I'll work with the Arts Council, although it's not much better in its thinking. But at least there're one or two like-minded souls on the board, so maybe we'll <u>gradually</u> be able to change things. You will notice that I underlined gradually. That's the way everything has to be done here.

So I keep so busy. And that's a blessing because it saves me from some of the socializing that goes on day and night in this town, especially the luncheons and teas. Yes, teas, homefolks, high tea with little cucumber sandwiches and cakes, which I'm always being invited to as the wife of a member of the House and where the conversation ranges from children to servants with not much else in between except gossip. Gossip with a capital G. I can't take it. And then there're the soirees and dinner parties, card parties and drinking parties. Parties of all types and descriptions. Primus complains about them almost as much as I do, yet he seems to enjoy himself once we're there. The man can be so contradictory! And let me not forget the receptions at Government House. And cocktails on board the Gray Eminence, which is what I call the good battleship the U.S.S. *Woodrow Wilson*, which pays us a visit every three months. It's supposed to be on break from maneuvers, but everyone says it really comes to keep an eye on us for His Majesty's government. In any event, when it turns up, all the members of the House, plus spouses, are invited to the captain's cocktail party. There's no getting out of going to that, or to the big do's at Government House. Those are command appearances, especially Government House. I circulate, making the usual small talk and smiling, and it's all I can do sometimes not to go over and give the premier and his ministers a good shaking for doing so little for Morlands and the other country districts. They act like the rest of the country doesn't exist. And another good shake for the stuffy Englishman who's the governor general. I'd love to sneak up behind him and the premier one of these evenings and slip the ice cubes from my drink down their backs. I only restrain myself because of Primus.

But at least I'm spared the luncheons and teas. Too busy, I tell the ladies. Would love to come but can't get away, too much work. And I don't even have to lie because as I said I stay busy. The other good thing about my taking over the office is that Primus no longer needs a secretary and I—thank goodness—no longer have to listen to the gossip about him and the one he had. And that's all it was, homefolks, just gossip, the lifeblood of the luncheon-and-tea crowd. I didn't bother mentioning it before, but it went on for months, complete with anonymous phone calls and letters. Anyway, it's over, and I run the office with just a law clerk and a typist. We've had to find ways to cut down on expenses, because although Primus works practically nonstop—when the House isn't meeting he's either in court or seeing clients or driving up to Morlands to check on things there—we still can't keep ahead of the bills. There's the Buick, and you know how I feel about that car. The payments alone take nearly half of his government salary each month. And I also have a car now, a nice sensible little Ford Anglia. A present from loving spouse. But another bill unfortunately. Then there's this white elephant of a house we bought. I know I get on my soapbox about it in every letter, but I can't help it. I swear the place has at least a hundred and one bedrooms. What do we need this big a house for? And who's going to have the children to put in all these rooms? Not me. I've already told Primus I'm drawing the line at three. I would've been happy with a much smaller house, and I really don't have to live on Garrison Row, which is the highbrow part of town. But Primus fell in love with the thing and insisted it was a good buy, so here we are.

And how are we going to furnish it? That's our big headache at the moment, because he wants it all done by the time you folks come down for Christmas so you can see he's set your daughter up in style. But I can't tell you the furniture it'll take to fill the place. Where're we going to find the money for it? We can scarcely meet the mortgage each month. The only good thing to be said for this barn is that we won't lack for space when you come. You can each have a suite of rooms all to yourself, including Grady, and there'll still be rooms to spare. Oh, I can't wait for December. I'm longing to see my homefolks . . .

. . . Followed Roy's orders to the letter this time, homefolks, and it still didn't help. Stopped work, stayed at home, stayed in bed for close to two months and I still couldn't hold onto it. Another slide, as the women here call it. Nothing seems to do any good. And there're my two sisters-in-law producing one fat healthy baby after another every time you look. It's not fair . . .

Dear Homefolks,

Another grand slam for Primus! Except for a few misguided souls he got nearly every vote in the district again. And of course there was the usual victory celebration afterward with lots of rum, lots of toasts and dancing until dawn. It was an easy win for Primus, but another loss I'm afraid for the NPP. We managed to pick up one more seat this time but that won't make any difference. The Do-Nothings went around saying that England would never grant independence if we were running the government because there're too many radicals and hotheads in the party. That was their campaign line, and people fell for it. Primus was thoroughly disgusted. So the old gang is still entrenched and still making it impossible for him to do anything much for Morlands. They haven't even finished putting in the drains I wrote you about last year. Just a few humble drains so people's houses and fields won't get flooded all the time, and the Ministry of Public Works has yet to finish the job. Over a year now! And it took Primus another whole year just to get them to vote the money. The same with the clinic in Marigot. The Ministry of Health has been stalling on completing it for the past eight months. One small building, that's all it is. Everything Primus proposes is either voted down or put at the bottom of the pile. I'm after him to get them to build a market shed in Morlands so that the women won't have to sit out in the hot sun all day. We'll see how far we get with that one. . . .

. . . To murder a child for *supposedly* talking back to some white shopkeeper! And then to throw his body in a swamp! I can't tell you how upset I've been, homefolks. I lie in bed at night seeing him floating face down in the water and muck and I can't sleep. How could they do a thing like that? What kind of barbarians do they have there in Georgia? What kind of country is it? When is it ever going to change? It was all in the papers here and people have been asking me about it and what can I say? I'm so ashamed and angry. The way I feel right now I'd never come near the place again if you homefolks weren't there. When I read about it last week I was all ready to cancel the trip up to New York next month I was so sickened by the whole thing. But Primus has talked me into going ahead with it. As I told you the last time I wrote, he keeps insisting that I see these specialists there in the hope that they'll be able to help me. It's still the same old story. I don't have any trouble conceiving, but I end up miscarrying in no time, and Roy and the other doctors I've been to here and in Jamaica can't figure out what it is. By the way, Primus has decided to come up also, just to be with me. So you'll be seeing both of us next month. Let's hope those specialists can find the problem and fix it, although to tell you the truth, ever since last week I've been asking myself whether I really want to bring another child this color into the world . . .

. . . Hooray! Finally got the market shed. It's finally up. And I feel, homefolks, as if we've won the Hundred Years' War. The foot-dragging that went on. The delays. The excuses. The money misspent and pocketed. This was worse than the drains and the clinic put together. Primus got so fed up at times he talked about resigning his seat. He would just practice law, he said, and perhaps start some kind of business, which I've discovered is something he'd really like to do. Not that he'd actually resign. It's just that he finds it so frustrating having to deal with the gang running things.

The market shed is the good news. The not-so-good news, the bad news, in fact, is me. Yes, another slide. This one last month when we went up to Morlands to dedicate the shed. I didn't have the heart to write and tell you as soon as it happened. What's wrong with me, homefolks? Why can't any of these doctors and specialists I keep going to find out what's wrong and do something about it! It has me so depressed. And Primus takes it harder each time. It's put such a strain on both of us. We can't even bear to talk about it anymore. Anyway, Roy is sending me home the next time. He feels we might as well give that a try since nothing else has worked. Maybe he's right. Maybe I need to just come and sit in Hartford and let you take care of me, Mama. I'll have you bake a peach cobbler just for me each week. Oh, how I miss your peach cobbler! I sometimes dream about it. I can smell and taste it clear as day in my dreams. Maybe some cobbler along with some 100-proof Harrison love close up will do the trick. If they don't, nothing will . . .

5

"You mean that big muck-a-muck member of the House!? The one they does call the PM in his district!? That does drive the big American car!? That got the American wife!? *Voilà voilà voilà voilà voilà voilà . . .*"

Her head thrown all the way back, Malvern unleashed a string of *voilà*s that had the sound of a Muslim woman's shrill keen of praise giving.

She did a dance. First, struggling up from her chair and then hefting her swollen stomach in both her hands, she broke into a carnival road march that propelled her across her cramped sitting room and back, across and back again. She went weaving and swaying through the furniture that was her pride: the heavy, cushionless mahogany settee and two armchairs she had crowded into the room, the small center table that held a framed wedding picture and a vase of wax anthurium lilies, blood red in the lamplight, and an open-shelved larder over in a corner with a few flowered glasses turned down on top. Holding her outsize stomach Malvern danced in the narrow spaces amid the chairs. Still keening the *voilàs*. Her distorted shadow dancing with her on the raw pineboard walls. The loose floorboards under her feet and the tin-ning roof over her head danced also. Everything in the little two-room house on Armory Hill shaking for all it was worth. *"Voilà voilà voilà voilà . . . !"*

Astral Forde had to reach out and hold the photograph and the vase on the center table to keep them from falling each time she came tramping by.

Malvern can get on too foolish. Disapproving but pleased, always pleased: Malvern with her foolishness made real everything that happened to her, especially this latest stroke of good luck.

The road march, the *voilàs* continued until a child cried out in its sleep in the other room and, winded, perspiring, Malvern collapsed back into her chair. "Oh, God, you gon make me drop this load before the night's out"—her hands on her stomach. She was seven months gone. The floor and flimsy walls still trembled. And the flame in the oil lamp that sat amid the turned-down glasses on the larder had yet to steady itself.

"So tell me."

"Tell you what?"

"Everything."

"Everything like what?"

"How you meet him, nuh? What kind of person he is? When you start up with him? How long? How he does treat you? What he's given you so far? I know he must have give you those nice earrings I see you got on. Everything!"

"How you expect me to answer all that one time?"

"How you meet him, then?"

"In the ministry, where else? You know Mr. Forsythe put my name to the top of the list and got me the little job in Public Works. I told you that the last time I was here. Well, this Mr.

Mackenzie comes by the office to see after the things they're supposed to be doing in his district. And he started having a word for me. But I din think nothing of it 'cause I wasn't the only one there he was chatting up. And then one evening after work I was in the bus stand waiting for a bus to go home and he come along in his big car and gave me a drop."

"Yes . . ."

"Yes, what?" Impatience. There was always a note of feigned impatience with Malvern in her voice. "The man gave me a drop. That's something too? I din think somebody like that would have me to study, some big shot in the House . . ."

Malvern laughed. She knew better. They both did.

"But then I noticed he was stopping by the office more regular, and when he come he had more and more to say, always asking me about the courses I took, the bookkeeping and so. And two, three times a week he was right there at the bus stand with the car."

"Yes, yes?"

Astral Forde had stopped as though she was finished. Then: "It went along so till one evening late. I was in the little room I'm renting on Waterloo Road, getting ready to look for my bed, when I hear Mr. Car pull up outside. I knew it was his from the sound of it. I had to ask myself what the man wanted with me at that hour . . ."/*My heart racing to beat the band, Malvern, racing!/*. . . "I tell you, is a good thing Mr. Forsythe din come by that night."

"Yes, yes?"

Astral Forde had stopped with the same finality again.

It was a habit with her. When she spoke her voice was flat, grudging, indifferent-sounding, a don'-care voice that said she remained unaffected by every and anything. Sometimes she just stopped altogether in the middle of a sentence, as if she didn't intend saying another word.

"Yes, what?" she asked finally.

"What happen? What he said?"

"What you think he said?" The feigned impatience and irritation again. "He asked me a question, nuh."

The *voilàs* rose to the tin-ning roof again and Malvern was about to struggle to her feet, when the child who had only protested before began crying in earnest.

"That hellion. He's gon wake the other two."

Malvern disappeared behind a curtain strung across a doorway and moments later came back and sat down again holding a little moon-faced boy, a toddler, who was naked except for a skimpy undershirt that didn't quite reach to his navel. His cries had become a loud wail, and in what was all part of a single uninterrupted ballet, Malvern threatened him with a raised hand, then brought the same hand down to snuggle him close, her mouth at the same time treating him to several noisy kisses, on the flat little nose, on his chin, on his chest, on the navel that was slightly bung and with an even louder smack on the nub of a penis, and putting him to lie face down on what was left of her lap, patting him vigorously, she turned a pair of still hungry eyes back to her guest.

"So tell me how long you been seeing him?"

"Is a good three months."

"Three months! And you only now come to tell me! How you could do a thing like that? How you could keep news like that to yourself all this time?"

"You think I can be running up to Armory Hill every time you look?"

"Funny ways," Malvern cried. "You got some funny funny ways. Here, I don't see hide nor hair of you for months at a time, and then you'll turn up with a piece of big news that's enough to give me palpitations. Only last week I said to myself, but I wonder what happen to Astral Forde? I ain't seen that girl in a good while. She like she don' have time for poor people now that she's got a big government job."

Malvern was aggrieved but smiling. She understood. Falling silent she inspected her visitor: the prized hair and creamy skin, the straight white people features. She took in the ready-made dress from Conlin and Finch/*She's wearing strictly ready-made these days, no more hot needle and burn thread*/and the earrings that just had to be a present from the big muck-a-muck member of the House. And she's wearing stockings! Only the queen or the governor general's wife would put on stockings as hot as it is. And the nice-nice shoes on her feet!

She snatched her own bare and swollen feet out of sight under her chair.

In spite of the three children she had had in five years and the one under way, Malvern was as lean and sharp-boned as ever. There was not that much to her aside from the stomach and her intense little face that looked as if someone had poured a cup of melted bittersweet chocolate over it. And there were her eyes, of course, always eager, always hungry for news. Malvern. She was as restless and high-strung as ever, every part of her on the move even when she was sitting still.

"You looking good," she said. "These are some nice-nice things you wearing here of late. And you're beginning to put some flesh on those long bones. You even sounding good. Each time you come you speaking more proper, almost like one of the great people–them! And to think"—this with a laugh—"that you went for years when you was small without saying so much as a word. Those wicked people in Westfield District said you would never talk. That the wife of the mechanic fella from Spanish Bay paid good money to put you so when she found out he was licking about with your mother when he came to work in the sugar mill during the crop season. They was just jealous of your mother 'cause she had little color. The red woman, they used to call her. Then it was the red woman and her little Spanish Bay wild-dog puppy when you was born. And I know not a word crossed your lips till you was a big girl going to school. That thing used to shame your mother so."

"Why you wun open your mouth, nuh, and let people know you got a tongue. Wha' the rass ailing you? Why you wun talk? Shaming

me before the world." Wha'dax! *The hand like fire on her face. "And take the friggin' thumb out you mouth!"* Wha'dax! *Fire on her hand.*

And she used to think, her face and hand on fire: If the big, swell-gut man with the pretty hair had only stayed instead of going away at the end of every crop season, not one of those malicious, officious, fowl-yard people in Westfield District would dare to come and stand in the road outside the house to talk their name. The size of him would have filled the house, the yard outside and the road, so that not one of the brutes would have been able to get near them with their busy-lickum tongues. If only he had stayed. . . .

"So what you did with Mr. Forsythe?"

"What you mean, what I did with Mr. Forsythe? Finish with him!" A hand the color of churned milk laced with butterfat fanned the air.

Malvern's dark hand started up in turn, ready to fan down Mr. Forsythe and say finish with him also, but she hesitated, feeling perhaps that it wasn't right. Because hadn't she, no more than a year ago, jumped up from her chair to dance and cry *voilà, voilà* when Mr. Forsythe's name—big Mr. Forsythe who was the permanent secretary in Public Works—was mentioned for the first time? As she had done for Mr. Weekes before, the one who paid for her friend to take the course in typing and secretarial and so, and Mr. Sandiford who got her the little job bookkeeping that time, and there was the nice young fella name Conrad when she working at Conlin and Finch—that was right after she left old Mr. Massad shop selling the yard goods, almost eight years now—Conrad that had wanted to married with her s'bad. And don't lemme forget Mr. Sealy that paid for her to learn the bookkeeping. That man would have done I don't know what for her, had not for the disgusting wife he had who was always following him about and getting on like a blackguard whenever she caught him with her.

With each of the men friends, Malvern had staged a minicar-nival in the sitting room, and afterward, winded, perspiring, she had sat regarding Astral Forde across the anthurium lilies and the framed photograph on the table with the look of a mother whose child has done her proud.

The same look now.

Then: "You ever see she?"

"Which she you talking about?" As if she didn't know!

"The beautiful-ugly wife."

A suck-teeth. "How you mean? I used to see her all the time when I was working at Conlin and Finch. She was always in the store with him buying furnitures for the big house on Garrison Row."

"What she look like?"

A longer, louder suck-teeth that in order to sustain itself drew in nearly all of the air in the little hotbox of a room.

"Short," Astral Forde said. "A little dough-off something not much higher than this table here. No height to her atall. It's like God took the dough he was making her with and used the better part of it to make somebody else. True, she got little color. But the hair short. She short and the hair short. And she's one these women can't make a child all they try. The kind that every time you hear the shout they've had another slide. She's like that I hear—you know how these people in Triunion can talk your business. She can't hold onto them to save her life, I understand."

All of a sudden Malvern scooped up the child on her lap who had fallen back to sleep and, laughing, said, "Here, take this one and give her. She's welcomed to this little hellion that does wake up and cry at the least noise."

She held him—a live offering, a gift—out over the wax flowers and the photograph, which showed her in a short wedding dress without a veil standing next to a man in an ill-fitting suit. His was the same moon-shaped face as the child in her hands.

A startled outcry, a tuning up, and Malvern snatched the baby close again, quickly repeated the hugs and kisses she had lavished on him before, and redeposited him face down on her lap.

"No, bo, she can't have this one, or the other two inside. The bus driver fella I got would commit murder, and I ain't ready to die just yet. 'Cause that's a man loves his children to the point that it's turned him foolish. He don' like them out of his sight not for a minute, y'know. If he could he would ride them about with him in the government bus all night . . ." Then: "So you say this Mr. Mackenzie went and married with some spoil-up something that can't make a child."

"That's the way it looks. She's in the States now trying again to have one. Is a good two months now since she's been gone. He's not the one that told me—he don't have nothing to say to me concerning her—but that's what I heard." The voice flat, monotone, seemingly don'-care. "It's August so she should be having it sometime next year if she can hold onto it."

"Well, she best try and get through this go-round, 'cause if the man's anything like the bus driver fella he wants some children about the place. Another slide and he might tell her to stay where she is. She don't know these Triunion men. And then who's to say, you might see your chance. Things might turn out so you'll find yourself moving from that piece-a room you're renting to the big house on Garrison Row with the furnitures in it from Conlin and Finch."

Once again it sounded as if all the air in the room was being sucked up between Astral Forde's clenched teeth.

"It could happen!" Malvern cried. "You's almost of a class with people like him now. The way you dressing and sounding these days. Mark my words, you might find yourself stepping right into the American woman shoes. And you'd make him some big pretty children too."

Astral Forde had brought her arm up in a wide arc to consult the watch on her wrist while Malvern was speaking; now, abruptly, she was on her feet. She stood in silence for a few seconds, too annoyed, too disgusted with Malvern to speak. Around her the little overcrowded room could scarcely contain her—her height, her large bones, her wealth of black wavy hair—as well as her gargantuan shadow on the wall.

"Nine o'clock gone," she said. "Lemme g'long before I miss the last bus sitting up here listening to your foolishness and the man you got comes and finds me in his house."

*   *   *

As she always did, Malvern accompanied her part of the way down to the bus stop at the bottom of Armory Hill. She had brought along the sleeping child and was carrying him high in her arms with a towel draped over him against the night dew.

The house they had just left, which Malvern had moved to when she married, stood on a low ridge of land above the worst of Armory Hill. The sprawling shantytown itself, where she and Astral Forde had once shared a room, lay at the foot of the hill, on the site of the huge armory that had stood there long ago. The English had built the armory, although it had also been used by the French and Spanish during the many times Triunion had changed hands. The cannonballs once stored there could still be found half buried in the sand of Cannon Beach, which lay directly opposite the hill, on the other side of the main road. The armory had long been a ruin, and the scrap heap of houses that had sprung up in its place in recent years, as people abandoned the country districts for town, was rapidly spreading along the road toward Fort Lord Nelson less than five miles away.

A footpath cut by the floodwaters during the rainy season snaked its way down from Malvern's house through a rookery of little one- and two-room pineboard houses similar to her own that crowded the ridge. The wooden shutters that served as windows stood open to the night. Voices. Voices talking, shouting, laughing, cursing in the darkness around them. Voices quarreling, a man a woman, the 'buse-ing, the cursing threatening to raise the rusted tin-ning roof on the house and send it flying; and Malvern said, "Watch, they gon come to blows any minute now. Thank God for the bus driver fella. He has his faults, but one thing: he has never so much as raise a hand to me." Dogs barking as they picked their way down the footpath. The fitful glow of the oil lamps inside the dim hot rooms like the first fire in the cave millenniums ago. Sparrow sang "Write to me care of the Royal jail . . ." on a radio, and farther down the ridge a child cried and coughed, cried and coughed, each breath sounding like its last.

"It's got the croup," Malvern said. "They need to boil some bush tea and give it." A flashlight in hand, she was carefully watching her footing, the light beam and her eyes trained on the rutted path, until suddenly she looked up, stopped, caught her breath, exclaimed, "The *Woody Wilson!*"

There, anchored outside of Fort Lord Nelson, which could easily be seen from the hill, stood the huge battleship with all its lights ablaze. A starfield of lights on the sea. A band of wandering stars might have converged on the waters around Triunion—having mistaken them for the sky in the darkness—and created a new constellation, another galaxy.

Malvern: "The *Woody Wilson* looks pretty enough tonight. You would think it was one of the big tourist boats. It's like they've put lights on the very guns-them!"

"You can't remember a thing, can you? I don' know how many times I've told you about the fancy cocktail party they have on board every time it comes on a visit." Astral Forde's annoyance had grown stronger. Her eyes had been on the ship ever since they started down from the house. "That's what's going on there now. That's why you see all the lights. A big fete. The premier and all the ministers and all the members of the House are over there. Them and their wives. Even the governor general and his wife."

"The great people–them!" Malvern exclaimed and sucked her teeth. "They's like the poor. We'll always have them with us. The bus driver fella don' like to hear me say that, but is true." Then, with a laugh: "Y'know, the *Woody Wilson* looks so pretty tonight that if I get another boy this time I'm gon name him after it. Even if the father don' agree. He had his way with the others. They had to have a lot of old-time names after the people on the monument in Morlands I ain't never seen. But if this next one is a boy too I'm gon have my way and call him The Woody Wilson. *The* Woody Wilson. The whole name. Mark my words."

She stopped. She had come as far down the hill as she intended. The rest of the way was too precarious even with the flashlight. Besides, this was where the worst of Armory Hill began.

"Watch you pocketbook as you go past that hellhole down there," she said, and after the ritual "Get home safe," she turned and started the climb back up.

———

"... *You might see your chance . . . You might find yourself stepping right into the American woman shoes . . .*" Oh, she's an idiot! Who tell her he's gon chuck the woman out even if she loses this one too? He ain't done so yet, has he? How I could put my hopes on that? Idiot! And I'm just as big an idiot to be climbing up Armory Hill every time you look to sit listening to her foolishness. I don't know why I bother going around her. She's one these people like to put themself in your business too much. Who tell her I'm looking to married with anybody? Or to have any blasted children? Or that I can even have any when I still feel sometime like that man on Drayton's Road left the damn wire thing up inside me. She must want me to be like her. Her insides don't have a chance to heal good before she's tumbling big again. And each one she drops takes after the beautiful-ugly husband his picture sitting up big in the middle of the house his face like a cow step in it she mighta take the friggin' picture and hide it someplace. Always sending me to look for trouble! "*And what about the nice young fella Conrad that wanted to married with you s'bad?*" Every time I looked she was asking the same question. What I would want with a Conrad? What could Conrad do for anybody on the next-skin-to-nothing he was making at Conlin and Finch? Besides, he was a man liked to beg too much. You gon give it to him, he knows you gon give it to him, and he's still begging. One these men that get their pleasure out of begging. Oh, that thing used to vex me! He couldn't wait. Just like the brute on Cannon Beach that time. Tearing the pretty new dress half off me. "*You like it? You like it? They say the girls in*

England like it so." Bare nastiness! Not one of them—Conrad,
Mr. Weekes, Cecil Sandiford, Mr. Forsythe, Mr. Sealy with that
fowl-yard wife he had—not one of them ever so much as asked
me to trot. Riding you all night sometime and you still ain't
feeling shite. My spirit just couldn't meet theirs. Only this one
this time is different. The man don' have to say a word and you
feel he's telling you all kind of nice things. He don' have to so
much as put a hand near you and you feel he's touching you,
muching you up all over. There can be I don' know how many
people about the place you ain't seeing, you ain't hearing nobody
but him. You does hear women talk about men like him, men
that have a way about them, but I never thought I'd butt up on
one . . . Only thing: he keeps his business to himself too much.
Two months the wife's been in America and he's yet to take me
to the house on Garrison Row. Not to lay up there with him or
anything so. Just to see the place, yes, what it's like inside, the
furnitures they have and so. But not once. He must be frightened
the servants will tell her when she gets back. Or he feels I'm not
somebody to bring in his big house. Well, let him keep it, you
hear! I don' have to set foot near the friggin' place. He's talking
about some big plans he has. He keeps saying he has something
big in mind for me. All right, bo, that's all I'm interested in,
everything else you can keep to you damn self, 'cause I'm looking
to leave government work. The money's too slight and there's
too many people feel they have the right to order you about . . .
Never a word concerning her. He has yet to call her name to my
face. She's too great to speak of with someone like me. A little
dough-off something! You don' know where he went and find
her. Not that she's all that bad of a person from what I remember.
She always had a smile for you when she came in the store. And
she talked nice when you waited on her. She wasn't like those
others from Garrison Row and Raleigh Hill. Those bitches would
look at you like they smell something bad just because you was
only a clerk. She wasn't like that atall. I have to say that much
for her. She looked like she'd be an easy person to talk to, somebody you could ask about all kind of things—what it's like in

America, if it's as nice as people say it is, and what she thinks of this place; you could ask to borrow the fashion magazines she must get from the States—just talking about one thing and another, like the two of you been knowing each other for years. . . . Idiot! A bare idiot! Malvern is the Three Wise Men compared to you! You think, you idiot, that that woman would have you to study? She might be just like all those other bitches, never mind the big smile. She would have to be. Even if she started out decent, after associating with them since she's been here she couldn't help but turn like them. They're her friends, after all. She's always with them at the big cocktail parties and the receptions at Government House. She would have to be like them, putting herself above other people the way they do. Always skinning her damn teeth! Making out like she's so friendly. I know one thing: she'd piss blood if she knew she wasn't the only one riding about in that big car he's got. And not the only one laying up with him in a bed.

6

While he talked on and on about the swimming pool he was planning to install, Astral Forde slowly, with her acute eye, inspected the dozen small, boarded-up stone cottages that had once been the Casuarina Beach Hotel. She was thinking—her mind making rapid calculations—of all the repairs it would take and all the money that would have to be spent before the place could call itself a hotel again. Plenty work, plenty money. But he's gon do it. You can tell from the way he's talking, Malvern, he's gon do it.

The cottages, six on either side of an open space where the pool would go and where they were standing, were joined at one end, the end facing the driveway and the road, by a pavilion-like building that housed the reception area, a lounge and a modest restaurant. Together the buildings formed a U. A large stand of the tropical pines that gave the place its name screened out the road at the end of the driveway and filled the air with a cool, grayish green light and the sound of the intimate conversation the trees kept up with each other even when there wasn't a breeze.

The Buick stood parked in their shade halfway up the driveway.

The open end of the U faced a white-sand beach and a wide tranquil bay that was a clearer, more sunlit blue than the afternoon sky it mirrored.

The line of surf was no more than a few yards away from the two cottages to the front.

What you need with a pool and the sea is right at the doormouth? Why expense yourself putting in something like that? A place this small don't call for no pool, she had started to say when he first mentioned it. She had thought better of it, though, as she glanced at his face. There was a look in his eyes . . . "Yes," she had said instead, "that might be a good idea, because with a pool you can always charge more."

Astral Forde had also made note of the flat roofs on the cottages and the fact that the six buildings on either side were attached to each other, thinking: another whole set of rooms could go right on top. He should build that before any pool. That way he'd be pulling in double the money right off.

Then there was the house where whoever he hired to manage the place would live. After showing her the cottages, he had taken her to see it. The manager's house. It stood off to itself on the other side of the grove of tall pines that surrounded the hotel. There it had stood as they emerged from the path through the casuarinas, an old-style bayhouse bungalow with twelve-inch-thick stone walls built to withstand a hurricane, solid wood shutters instead of glass at the windows, and an extra pair of heavy metal doors at each entrance to be latched and bolted into place at night. She had liked the house right off: the metal and wood, the thick stone, the trees that kept it separate and private.

"Another thing," Primus Mackenzie was saying. He had finally left off discussing the pool for the moment. "The Canadian who owned the place before used to cater mainly to old retired people. But I'm thinking of making it more a family hotel since the cottages have their own kitchens. People with children could do their own cooking if they wanted, and they'll have the pool right outside the door."

"I don't know," she said. "You might do better to stick with the retired people. They'll come more regular and stay longer. Besides, those bad-behave children I hear they got in America and Canada will only mash up the place. No, you'd be better off with the old people."

She saw them, remembered them from when she had worked at Conlin and Finch and they would come in to shop. Some of them ol' ol' people look like they had been down here since God said come let us make man, come let us make woman, their skin bare white from the cold up there in North America, their legs like two blue sticks—blue from all the veins showing—in the Bermuda shorts they ain't shame to wear at their age, and their hair like the snow you see pictures of in the magazines. She placed them now in the dozen little cottages that was gon take plenty work and money to fix up—and suddenly the ragged bougain-villea vines she saw trailing half-dead over the moldy walls and around the doors sprang to life again, the flowers bright red and white, peach and purple and a color she couldn't name that was red and purple mix together. She put them—the guests—to eat in the small restaurant, those who din feel like cooking for them-selves, and afterward to help them digest the food she stretched their old bones out on the lounge chairs beside the pool he's set on having, never mind there's no call for it. Later on, ignoring Mr. Pool, she urged them, the retired people from Canada, the States and England, to go and take a sea-bath. "Triunion water will make you feel so young, you'll be jumping up in the band come carnival," making a little joke with them as she took a few minutes out from whatever she was doing to lead them on the blue sticks for legs down to the beach.

"Yes, you might be right about the children. Maybe I'd better stick with the old people, at least in the beginning," he said. "The other thing is finding the right person as manager. That can be the biggest headache of all, they tell me, in a business like this. I'm going to need someone I can rely on not only to run the place but to see to the accounts and make sure that the people when they come are satisfied . . ."

He paused. His usual pause. One word today, the next tomorrow, Astral Forde thought. That's the way he speaks. And it's like everything has to stop and wait on him when he stops. Sometimes he takes so long between the words you think he's done finish altogether. She didn't mind, she understood. She also believed in taking her time. Sometimes when she was with Malvern she'd just stop in the middle of a sentence as if she didn't intend saying another word.

To besides, there wasn't no need for a lot of talk between them. No need to be always explaining their explanatories. They were both from the same little two-by-four place, after all, and knew how things were done here, were said here: the unspoken that lay not only behind the words spoken but in a look, the wave of a hand, a cut-eye, a suck-teeth. You talking to the other person but without having to say a word. So much in common between them.

"And it'll have to be someone who can handle the maids and yardboys and so."

"That's number one," she said, her heart racing. "You have to have someone who knows what these people give and won't tolerate any nonsense from them. 'Cause first thing, they won't do a lick of work if you don' keep after them, and next they'll steal you blind if you don' watch them like a hawk. Triunion people! It takes a Hitler to handle them, bo."

He laughed. Then: "Have you heard about the hotel training school the Ministry of Tourism is planning on opening soon?"

"I think I heard something about it."

"I understand they're going to be giving a course on how to manage small hotels and guesthouses. Do you think you might like to take up something like that?"

Oh, God, Malvern will dance the house down to the ground when she hears!

"I might," she said. "Because one thing: I'm looking to leave government work."

"You too?" he said and laughed again.

For the time being that was all that needed to be said.

On the way back to the car he suddenly stopped and looked up at the pines overhanging the driveway. "Casuarina Beach Hotel. I'm wondering whether I should keep the same name? What do you think?"

"I don' much care for it," she said. "Nobody born here calls these trees casuarinas, never mind you tell me that's the proper name for them. Only somebody who's a stranger to the place would call them that. Mile trees. They're mile trees. That's all I've ever heard them called. And you too, I know. You should name it Mile Trees something. That would sound better to me."

"Mile Trees Beach Hotel? Mile Trees Cottages? Mile Trees Bungalows? Mile Trees what . . . ?"

"Remember the Colony Hotel we had here some years back that was only for the big muck-a-muck tourists from England? You could name it that."

"Mile Trees Colony Hotel?"

"Why not? The white people will love it."

This time when his laugh died, he stood looking at her, shaking his head slightly, impressed, amazed, seduced. But also a little wary. There was that voice of hers with its flatness and apparent indifference, as well as her eyes that kept her thoughts and feeling carefully veiled.

"You seem to know all about the hotel business before even setting foot in the school," he said.

"What's there to know? The people come down from all the snow and cold in North America looking for a little sun and a chance to spend their money and enjoy themselves, and it's up to us on these little poor-behind islands that need the money to see that they do just that."

Once inside the Buick he sat silent for a long time. His eyes had grown both somber and distant, and his head had moved out from the socket of his neck.

His head long out like a sea turtle all of a sudden. Oh, God, he must be changing his mind about me running the place . . .

Above them the mile trees kept up their hushed tête-à-tête full of sighs and promises, and occasionally the breeze sent a few of the pine needles—that were like long green hatpins, but without the head—showering down on the roof and hood of the car.

Finally: "I don't know when I'll be able to start all the work that's needed. I'm going to have to try and get another loan from the bank or find somebody to come in with me. Another thing"—and his head came thrusting forward even more—"I might have to go up to the States any day now. And I might have to stay there for a while . . . "/*He's gon call her name!*/ " . . . Which is to say you're not to leave the government work just yet. All of this is going to take some time.

"Are you in a hurry?" Asked with a dim smile that brought him back to her, to the Buick and the present moment. He had turned around to face her with the question, so that his head, his shoulders and the top half of his body blocked out everything beyond the window in back of him. He seemed to fill the entire car. Stay just so, she almost told him. If possible, she would've had him stay just like that till Thy Kingdom Come, facing her with the smile and his body shutting out everything beyond the car.

"Are you Miss Murray in a hurry?"

She had to laugh with him. They both knew the expression from when they were children, he in Morlands, she in Westfield District. But looka she or looka he, people would say of someone walking fast, going down the road like Miss Murray in a hurry. She often said it of Malvern.

So much in common between them.

"Will you wait, in other words, till I can see my way with this hotel thing? It might take a few years . . ."

"Why not? Rome wasn't built in a day and I don' have nothing better to do for the moment."

His laugh again. "Astral Forde! What to do with you? You always say yes with a no. I love it," he said and sat around to the steering wheel to start the car.

The man don' have to so much as put a hand near you and you feel he's touching you, muching you up all over. You don' want him to ever go away. I din think anybody could turn me so.

"Who's to say? Things might turn out so you'll find yourself moving into the big house on Garrison Row . . ." That almost seemed possible later that afternoon when he truly touched her and moved inside her as no one had ever done before. Holding her in such a way that every stroke caressed the wick of her lamp. And moaning as if he never wanted to leave inside her. Malvern might not have been just running her mouth. She might turn out to be right after all . . .

———

She must be losing this one too! That's the only reason he would leave for the States in such a rush, without even saying that he was going. Astral Forde thinking this as she sat at her desk in the Ministry of Public Works months later. She had just read in the *Triunion Daily* that he had departed for the States the day before. They musta called from there to say she's losing this one too never mind she held onto it for a good while this time . . .

Another slide, Malvern had said, and he might just tell her to stay where she is.

He might do that in truth, y'know.

———

Waving her hand from the door of the plane like she's a movie star or the queen come on a visit! Skinning her damn teeth! And he's just as bad, standing next to her skinning his teeth too. Two idiots!

American-born Ursa Beatrice . . . named after both her grand-mothers . . . making her island debut . . . arms of her proud . . .

Her eye leaping back and forth between the words in the caption and the photograph on the front page of the newspaper. A furious steeplechase that knocked over words and raced past details in the picture. Until finally both her eye and her mind slowed down enough for her to take in the details she had missed. She was able then to see that the dough-off, skin-teeth woman wasn't the one holding it, as you would have expected; no, it was him, the father, the big member of the House, he was the one cradling the little dark spot of a baby in his arms.

7

"You's everything like him, *oui*." A whisper over the raised bars of the crib and underneath the mosquito netting that hung like a bridal veil from its hoop near the ceiling down to the floor, encircling the crib. "Everything."

She inspected the small foot she was holding—the blunt, plum dark toes, the pink sole and heel, the broad little instep. "His foot, *oui*! And his legs, when he was no bigger than you!" She playfully pinched a leg that at four months was still encased in rolls of baby fat. "And you'll never be able to hide from him with that head"—reaching up to tap lightly and with awe the little high domed forehead. "And fat! *Mes amis!*" Another thrilled whisper. "Fat just like you grandmother, *oui!*"—bending even farther over the crib to nuzzle the almost nonexistent neck whose folds and creases were white with Johnson's Baby Powder.

For a second the baby's mouth stretched wide in a reflex smile, then it tried pulling away.

A tiny heart-shaped locket hung around the roly-poly neck. There were miniature hoops at the ears, a beautifully etched bangle at each puffy little wrist, and an elfin ring on the third finger left hand. All of them in gold.

As though taking inventory, Celestine touched each piece of the jewelry, the same awed light tap she had given the forehead. Then she again reached for the small foot. She began caressing it now, stroking it, gently massaging it between her hands, which, like the foot, were the same combination of black one side and pale pink the other.

Every night, as soon as Estelle left the room, Celestine would stand openly marveling at those feet, legs, arms, that forehead as if they had all been formed in the secrecy of her own flesh.

8

O ciel eternel! How-could-the-woman-do-a-thing-like-this? Get up in the middle of the night, *oui*, take the man's child out of her bed, take his keys, take his car, and when we find out where she went to she's out to the airport, the car parked near the runway—the runway, now!—and she's sitting up behind the steering wheel in her nightie and robe with 'ti-Ursa in her nightie too—the madwoman din even stop to put on the child's robe—curl up beside her on the seat. Near the runway! The only one the little two-by-four airport has. *Seigneur!* What if it had been daytime and a airplane was coming in? All right, so she was at the end part where the airplane stops to let the people off, but still in all it could have hit the car. The two of them could have been hurt bad or dead for all you know. A madwoman, *oui*! She's nothing but a madwoman. Only somebody clean out their head would take a three-years-old child out to a airport in the middle of the night to sit on a runway like she's waiting for a airplane to come and crash into them . . . 'Foreday morning, *oui*, and I went in to put 'ti-Ursa to pass water so she wouldn't wet the bed, only to find she's not there. The child gone! The nice new bed the father just bought for her at Conlin and Finch empty. Oh, God, my heart dropped. *Tête chargé, oui!* A feeling came over me worse than when Mis-Mack died. You couldn't tell me that some wicked person din break in the house and kidnap her. But when I ran to tell them she was gone is only his one I found sleeping in the bed. And when I woke him and he jump up and ran outside he saw that the car was gone too. Her car was in the shop having something on it fixed so she took his. We din know what to think. Where to turn. What to do. Who to call. The man frantic over his child. *Tête chargé!* It wasn't till the watchman out to the airport called that we knew. He said he saw the PM car—he recognized it right off—drive up and stop out near the runway, and when he went over to it there she was at the wheel with 'ti-Ursa asleep next to her, and all he begged her to move the car, that that was no place for it to be, she wouldn't budge. She even rolled up the windows on him, he said, saying he was gon wake the child. *Mes amis!* The PM had to run then and call Dr. Roy to come and drive us out to the airport. And when we reached, there she was in truth sitting up in the car in her nightie and robe, the windows rolled up, all the doors locked and 'ti-Ursa still sleeping next to her on the seat. And you couldn't get a word out of her, *oui*. She acted like she din hear a thing you said. She refused even to look at you. Just staring off like a madwoman and holding the steering wheel like she thought the car was a airplane and could fly. Is only when 'ti-Ursa woke up because of all the commotion and start to cry that she open the door. If you had see the PM when that woman stepped from the car! He turned on her like he was gon kill her on the spot. Dr. Roy and the watchman had to run and hold him. Then he dragged his child from her. And he wouldn't let 'ti-Ursa go. Just holding her, holding her, holding her. Even when he drove the car home he had her on his lap. He wouldn't even let me take her. And he's in the room with her now, still holding her and trying to get her to go back to sleep . . . Don't that woman realize that the child could be marked for life by a thing like this? As for the scandal! *Mes amis!* Dr. Roy had to take the watchman to one side and give him quite a few dollars. But who's to say the man won't run his mouth all the same. Then he had to turn around and take the madwoman home with him, so as to give the PM time to calm down. She might have to stay over there for months, the state that man is in . . . The *blanche neg*'! There's no understanding her. Look what she did last week when we went up to Morlands for the cropover fete: letting a gang of fowl-yard children into the yard just to aggravate him. First off, the minute he left the house in the car, she went and took off the nice dress 'ti-Ursa had on and all her gold things and put some pants that the grandmother sent from the States on the child—a pants now! some overall-looking something with a duck in a sailor suit on the bib. *Mes amis!* Is that any way for her to dress the PM's child? Every chance she gets she drags off the pretty dresses he buys for her and every piece of gold and puts her in a overall like she's going to weed in a canefield. She's not raising the child proper. Letting her call both her and the PM by their names. "Let her call me Estelle if she wants to, Celestine. She knows I'm her mother and the PM's her father. She doesn't have to go around saying Mommy and Daddy." And she got the PM to agree to it. The creole is *Quel bêtise!* Whoever heard of such a thing? And she don' want me to do for the child, *oui*. All I hear is "Let her try and dress herself, Celestine. She's big enough./ Let her feed herself, Celestine, even if she makes a mess./Let her bathe herself, Celestine. There's not going to be a soul to wait on her hand and foot when she goes to live in the States." Already rushing the child off to America and she only just came into the world yesterday/. . . She put her in this overall with a duck on it as soon as the father left out and then opened the gate herself to let a gang of fowl-yard children in the place. Is that any company for the PM child? The yard was overrun with them. And if you had seen them grabbing at the tricycle the PM got her last Christmas! Each one had to have a turn on it. 'Ti-Ursa could scarcely get to ride on it. The little brutes interfering in all her playthings, making her cry. And the mother talking to her, talking to her, telling her she must learn to share. *Seigneur!* What three-years-old child can understand that? "She didn't have anybody to play with." That's what she told the PM when he got back and found the gang of them there. "Who let all these little children in the yard?" He was good and vex. "She didn't have anybody to play with." All he's fussing she's only saying that. And when the little whelps got frightened and ran from the yard, one of them had the brass face to turn and pelt a rockstone at the gate as the yardboy was closing it . . . *Toujours une histoire!* And all because of the woman he has running the old-people hotel he bought. But what must the man do? He has to have somebody to look after the place for him. The *blanche neg'* could never do it. She wouldn't know how to handle the maids and so. They'd get away with murder with her. And what if the woman is his keep-miss? Show me the man in this place that don't have one and sometimes more than one. This ain't America where they must do things different . . . "If I had a *loup-garou* running the place for me they would say it was my girlfriend. You've been here long enough now to know what these people give. Their middle name is malicious. The next time you get one of those phone calls just ask the idiot who won't give her name where I eat my meals each day and where I sleep each night." He was right to tell her! 'Cause it's true. All his meals right here in this house and he's in the bed next to her each and every night. And she don' want for a thing. The man spends money he don' have trying to keep her satisfied. Look how she made him take down all the shutters in the house at Morlands—saying the place was like a tomb at night—and put in glass jalousies and screens. He went and expense himself buying a generator so the old house would have in current and hot water. All for her. She wouldn't rest till she had him change over Mis-Mack shop to a office and meeting place like the one he has in town. He was keeping the shop just like it was when Mis-Mack was alive, but I know she made him tear down every shelf and get rid of everything, even Mis-Mack chair and cane—I can't tell you how that thing hurt my heart, *oui*—so people in Morlands would have a place to come and meet with him. She must have her way in everything. Even went interfering in the kitchen up there. The cook must have a gas stove 'cause she can't stand to see her working in an inferno. Burning *charbon* keeps the kitchen like an inferno, she said, and to besides the *charbon* is destroying the trees on the island. And I know he went and put in a stove, never mind the food don't taste right when you cook it on the gas. Everything she asks for he strains himself and gets for her. And she still ain't satisfied, *oui*. You don' know what it is she wants from his life. And she's all the time upsetting herself over the least little thing. Snatching the PM's child out of her bed and driving out to the airport in the middle of the night to sit like a madwoman near the runway all because of some woman the man hired to do a job the way he would hire anybody else. *Mes amis!* He has a cross to bear in the *blanche neg'*, *oui*. A cross.

9

"You have three choices, Estelle," Roy Shepard said quietly and waited for her to ask what they were.

He sat with his chair—an old-fashioned planter's lounge chair with a polished mahogany frame and wicker seat—pulled close to hers on the veranda. A few feet from their chairs a trellis of bougainvillea in red, white and magenta, along with large ferns and orchids in hanging wire baskets of sod, screened out the sun that had been up for almost two hours now. They had seen it rising above Armory Hill on their way back from the airport.

Roy had driven her straight to his house, a stately old Victorian great house on Garrison Row with a profusion of gingerbread trim, windows as tall as doors and louvered shutters everywhere to keep out the sunlight and heat while allowing the breeze to enter. The breeze along with the fragrance of the garden that lay between the house and his clinic next door. The garden that would have been his life's work if it had been left to him, he always said.

Except for the servants, Roy lived alone. He had never married, although there was the unofficial marriage he had had for years with the supervisor of the nursing staff at the clinic, a woman from nearby Jamaica who was as close to black as he was to white—his sandy-red skin and hair. In the beginning the affair had caused an even greater furor than the Guayabera shirts he wore everywhere. Roy, the maverick, the dissenter. Yet, as with the shirts and the sight of him working like a yardboy out in his garden, his unofficial marriage had come to be accepted over the years. Because no matter what, he was still Royston DeQuincey Shepard, one of the great people–them! with the big house on Garrison Row that went back generations in his family and his private maternity clinic that only a few could afford.

"One of the choices," he said finally when there was no re-sponse from the mute figure in the chair next to his, "is that you can believe the talk going around and leave the man. You can say finish with Primus Mackenzie, finish with this place and these bad-minded people, and take your child and go back to the States. You can always do that. The harpies who started the whole thing will be only too glad to know that they've run you out. Or you can do like some of them when the talk is about their husbands. Start following the man about. It would be beneath you, but you could always go and hide in the bushes around Mile Trees to spy on him. That's what they would do. And if and when you got the goods on him, so to speak, then take your child and leave. That's another choice . . ." He again waited. "Are you listening, Estelle?"

No answer. No sign that she had even heard him. She was unaware, it seemed, not only of his voice but of his very presence: his thickset body leaning close, his concerned gaze, his broad face with its spattering of freckles; unaware of being on the veranda even. In her mind, she might have still been in the Buick out at the airport, the car parked on the apron with all the doors locked, the windows rolled up, and her eyes trailed on the scarcely visible runway—sitting there behind the steering wheel in her nightgown and robe and wearing a pair of blue satin mules with Louis XIV heels and a fuzzy pom-pom on the vamp; waiting for dawn and the first plane of the day to make its appearance in the sky north of the control tower.

Roy placed a hand lightly on hers, which lay on the armrest of her chair. He said, "Or, third, you can be sensible about this thing, Estelle, and first of all refuse to listen to the harpies. Just hang up the phone on them when they call and tear up the letters when they come. You can tell yourself—and it'll be the truth— that all you have to go on right now is hearsay from a few malicious women who don't have anything better to do than write letters and not sign their name and get on the phone to whisper nonsense in your ear. Talk. Gossip. That's all they have to do with their time. You should know better than to believe anything they say. Besides, so far the man has given you no grounds to take their word over his—"

"Word! What word?" She snatched her hand out from under his, and as she turned to him and Roy saw her face in full he quickly drew back across the narrow space between their chairs. "You can't get anything out of him. He won't say yes or no! Why won't he just say yes or no?"

"Just say yes or no, dammit!"

"Estelle, I'm going to tell you as I did when there was all the talk about the secretary I had that time: I'm going to leave it for you to say. This has been going on for weeks now. A big noise almost every night over this thing. And all I try to explain the reason for the woman being there, it doesn't do any good. So I'm leaving it for you to say." His voice unperturbed, unhurried, giving no more weight to one word than to the next; his gaze, which didn't waver, meeting hers. He was preparing for bed and stood undressed down to his underwear. There, in front of her, the dark solid mass of his body whose every contour, every feature, whose entire geography she knew better than her own, and the forehead that had made him look as if he was already a foreign

minister or a visiting head-of-state when they first met. "You know better than I do how and where I spend my time so you decide for yourself."

Last night and the same nonanswer again. For hours she lay seething next to him in the bed, until unable to bear it any longer she had sprung up, grabbed her robe, her slippers, his keys off the dresser, and had gone for her child and the car.

"A no from him," Roy said, "and there'd still be no peace because you'd swear he was lying. A yes and you'd be gone before he could get the yes out of his mouth good, back to the States, you and Ursa, and Primus Mackenzie would be no use to himself anymore. You can take my word for it. He'd be a man finished, as much as he loves you and that child. So I guess he figures it's best not to say anything one way or the other. And even if there is some truth to the talk—and I'm not saying there is, mark you!—he'll never *do* anything to run the risk of your leaving. Not if I know him. You'll never see him parading any woman about the place the way some of them do . . ."

Suddenly he leaned close again, into the furious circle of her eyes, face and uncombed hair. "The best thing, Estelle, is for you to put this whole business out of your mind until you know for sure what's what. Just rid your mind of it till then. After all, the man had to hire somebody to manage the place. You wouldn't have wanted to do it—"

"Me!" The enraged eyes turned his way, her voice, were enough to drive Roy back again. But he sat firm. "Me! I didn't want him to bother with that thing in the first place! All the money he had to borrow to buy it and then more money to fix it up! Why he would want to give himself another worry and more debt I don't know."

"Well, he bought it for whatever reasons," Roy said. "Maybe with the DNP having such a stranglehold on the government he feels he'd better look to something other than politics. That might be it, because Primus was always about making his mark. I re-member that from school. He always had to be a step ahead of the next fella. If one of the boys got a new satchel or a fountain pen he had to have a bigger and better one. He'd write home, and his mother would send him the money. He was always trying to make up, I guess, for the fact that he was from the country. And you know the hopes he has for this place. When he first came back from England he was all for overhauling Triunion along strictly socialist lines—and a part of him still is, I believe, although I doubt that the bandits in charge will ever give him and the NPP a chance to try anything like that. Then, when he got back from the Carnegie tour that time he was ready to send everybody on the island up to the States to learn how to do things the American way . . . I don't know," Roy said. "Something happened to him in that place. It's like he butt up on a federation of Sirens singing sweet in his ears . . ."

"The contradictions, Roy."

"Ah, you're finally beginning to understand the person you've been married to all this time . . ." Roy paused, spread his freckled hands, shrugged. "He has his demons, Estelle. Like you, me, everybody. He might even have more than his share. Maybe you'll have to decide whether you love him enough to live with them. Or whether, in spite of them and everything else, there's enough about the man to make you want to stay.

"One thing: Mile Trees is a fact. So you might as well get used to it. And since you disapprove of it so much, it's best that you not have anything to do with the place. Just put it from your mind. If Primus wants to take the child over there on a Sunday to swim, let him. Don't make a big noise. You don't have to go with them."

"Me! I never go near the place anymore!"

"And the same with the woman. You don't have to have anything to do with her either. Put her from your mind too. Just say she's there managing the place like anybody else he might have hired, until if and when you find out otherwise. And from what I hear she's doing a good job. He's taken some poor girl from the country and given her a chance to better herself. You could look at it that way, Estelle."

"I don't care where she's from or how poor she was!"

"All right. Just ignore her then, and ignore the talk. You can act like she doesn't even exist as far as you're concerned. That's the way you might have to handle this thing for the time being. It's going to be hard, as I said. There's your pride, after all, and the fact that you come from a place where people run and divorce the minute one of them so much as looks at somebody else. But that's what you might have to do until you know something for certain."

While talking, Roy had quietly replaced his hand on hers. This time she didn't pull away. His slightly bent fingers were resting on her wrist, reminiscent of how he used to hold her hand as she lay in the clinic after she had had a slide, as if taking her pulse, while at the same time comforting her. He heard a slow, deep intake of breath, saw her eyes begin to fill, and he quickly bowed his head, just as he used to back then to avoid the sight of her tears.

Earlier, he had sent word over to the clinic for his assistant to take charge, so that he continued to sit with her, holding her hand, talking to her, quietly reasoning with her while the decorative trim around the veranda and the bougainvillea and ferns kept out the mounting heat. The eight o'clock sun was almost as strong as it would be at noon.

Around nine o'clock, he called for breakfast, and when the maid came with the tray he went over and took it from her at the door and set out the food himself on a small table he placed in front of their chairs. The meal consisted of two large slices of papaya, each with a wedge of lime, the lime cool and green against the bright orange-yellow of the fruit. And there was toast in a sterling silver basket and coffee from the foothills of Gran' Morne. Everything protected under a wire-mesh *couvre-plat*.

He poured her a cup of coffee, squeezed lime over her slice of papaya, urged her to eat. She shook her head. Her tears had dried, and from the closed, bitter look that had returned to her face, she was back out at the airport again, sitting waiting in the Buick for the first plane of the day to come in.

Roy finally set aside the food without touching it himself.

Turning back to her, he brought his hand to rest on hers again and continued to talk in the quiet tone. But he spoke of other things now, telling her at one point about his last visit to the clinic in Marigot, where he went two mornings a week. (She had enlisted him as one of the doctors for the clinic when it opened.) "You need to get Primus to keep after the bandits to build a hospital up there," he said. "It could go right on Government Lands."

Talking as both of them waited.

Beyond where they sat stretched the driveway, which was lined in jacarandas. Two, sometimes three times a year the trees showered the drive and the impeccable lawn on either side with blossoms that were so deep and rich a blue they looked purple once they came to rest against the green. Thirty yards away, at the end of the driveway, stood the opened gateway in the high stone wall that surrounded the house and grounds.

He was telling her about a new strain of daylily he had ordered from the States when the Buick rounded the wall and moved slowly toward them under the jacarandas and a fretwork of sunlight, its black hood gleaming. It was the same patrician late-forties model Primus Mackenzie had bought after the first election, with great curving front fenders that called to mind a tidal wave and a radiator grille that resembled a breastplate. It was almost an antique now.

The car scarcely came to a stop before the door on the passenger side opened and Ursa wearing the overalls with Donald Duck on the bib came tearing toward the veranda steps. He had dressed her in the outfit both he and Celestine disapproved of. "Estelle! Estelle!" Running, her arms open, and anxiously calling Estelle.

Primus Mackenzie followed. He was walking even slower than he normally did, taking a step back, it seemed, for every one he took forward. He had on sunglasses—something he seldom ever used—and at his side he carried a small suitcase with a change of clothes for Estelle to put on in place of the nightgown and robe.

10

"You call this bathroom clean?

"You call this bed made proper?

"You call these sheets washed?

"Who the rass told you to put the spoons to the left of a plate when you's setting a table?

"What kind of yardboy you call yourself? Look at all the bush you left out back where you thought I wouldn't see it. You's no use atall. I have a mind to give you what little money's coming to you and show you the gate.

"What the bloody hell is happening with the cooking oil, Millicent? Every time I look another gallon's finished and you're asking for more. You must be drinking it one, or taking it home to sell.

"*You!* Blast you! You can't move any faster than that? One step today and the next tomorrow! You think Mr. Mackenzie is paying you good money to drag about his hotel doing next skin to nothing?

"Wha' the rass! You call this floor polished? All right, I finish talking. Come get your money and get from round the place!"

The voice lashing out from morning till night in the kitchen, the laundry shed and other outbuildings behind the U-shaped row of cottages and out of earshot of the elderly guests. The voice sometimes helpless to stop itself even after the cook, the maids and yardboys had left for the day and there was only the night watchman to listen. The voice railing on in her sleep even, on and on as if to make up for the time long ago when she had said nothing for years, couldn't talk, had refused to talk for years, and the malicious, officious people in Westfield District had gone about saying that the wife of the man from Spanish Bay—the swell-gut man with the pretty hair who had been her father— had paid somebody to put her so. *"Why yuh wun open yuh mouth and talk, nuh, and let people know you got a tongue. Shaming me before the world . . ." The red woman who was her mother. Her hard stinging palm coming down. Fire on her face.*

"I'm getting rid of that Bertha," Astral Forde said. She had just served the great Mistress Ursa, as she secretly called her, the glass of soursop juice and given her the bath towel to go and dry off and get dressed, so that for the moment there was only herself and Primus Mackenzie beside the swimming pool, and she was using the time to report to him on the help and other matters. "She won't do the work right. And when I speak to her she's cutting her eye at me when she thinks I'm not looking. If looks could kill, bo, I'd be dead."

" 'All right, Miss Bertha, I finish talking. Come get your money and get from round the place.' "

His imitation of her was so flawless she almost laughed along with him.

"I think I'll buy you a cane like the one my mother had," he said, "so you won't have to use your vocal cords so much. When Miss Bertha or any of them won't do the work, you can just catch them round the neck with the handle and lead them to the gate. Out, *oui*! You's no use atall." An invisible cane in his outstretched hand, he made as if hauling away some miscreant.

"Buy it!" She was laughing openly now. "I need something for these do-nothings."

"Yes," he said, "we don't only have them in government in this place." And he was suddenly sober.

Astral Forde continued her report, standing big-boned and nearly as tall as him in the outfit she had adopted as manager: a nice shirtwaist blouse in white from Conlin and Finch and a gored schoolteacher kinda skirt that came down to her calves. Her hair swept back in a large neat bun. Face powder, a touch of lipstick, but no lot of makeup they had taught her at the hotel training school. A lacy handkerchief was tucked in at her waistband, and the principal keys to Mile Trees hung on a ring attached to the band. An appearance to suit the guests, the old retired white people–them! from Canada and America.

The water in the pool had settled from the great Mistress Ursa's swim, and beyond the pool, down on the beach, a few of the guests were sitting in the surf, the blue sticks they had for legs stretched out in the low-breaking waves. They scarcely ever bother with Mr. Pool. A waste of money. He had that thing put in just for Mistress Ursa, if you ask me.

The waves broke and retreated in a runner of lace. The mile trees standing tall above the roofs of the cottages whispered their endless promises of fidelity and love in the breeze. The Sunday morning sunlight being filtered through their branches caught the high dome of the forehead in front of her, the clear white of his eyes, and she said, "Another thing. I don't mean to put myself in your affairs, but maybe you should think about adding on to the place. Another set of rooms could go right on top of what's here. And it wouldn't take no lot of doing, because each row of cottages is attached and the roofs are flat . . ."

This was the first time she had brought up the subject in the five years since Mile Trees had opened.

"I've thought about it," he said, his gaze on the roofs, "but I can't see my way to do that just now. I've got too many bills and loans to attend to first."

"Well, just so you have it in mind. 'Cause that way you could make double what you're making now. Besides, an upstairs would turn the place into something big."

His gaze shifted back to her face and he smiled, amazed as always and utterly seduced, not only by the large-boned, cream-colored body and the hair but by the head she had on her shoulders, that "get up and do" spirit of hers. Her business mind. Even after eight years—it was eight years since he had first seen her in the Ministry of Public Works—he was still astonished and humbled by his good fortune in having found her to manage the place for him. At the same time, he remained wary. There was that veiled look of hers and her habit of saying yes with a no. There was the seemingly indifferent, don'-care voice and manner she affected most of the time. Things that both exasperated and excited him.

Astral Forde coolly submitted to his scrutiny, thinking: He's got on one of those shirt-jac suits the men are starting to wear nowadays. She liked it. The short-sleeved jacket left most of his arm bare. The skin black but pretty. And the way the collar opens down almost to his breastbone. You could slip your hand right down inside.

"I see you wearing shirt-jac these days."

"Do you like it, Miss Forde?"

She looked off, mildly sucked her teeth. "It's all right, I guess. One thing, it makes more sense in this heat."

"You're saying yes, aren't you?"

His look, his smile making her feel like he was touching her, muching her up all over.

And then the great Mistress Ursa came running up, dressed and ready to go home.

———

"... I ask you, Malvern, how does it look for me to be standing at a swimming pool holding a towel and a glass of juice on a tray? Right out in the open for everybody to see, the guests, the maids, the cook, the yardboys, everybody. How does that look, I ask you? Why won't he let me send one of the maids to do that? But no, the minute the two of them step from the car on a Sunday morning, it's 'Astral, bring a towel and something cool for Ursa to drink when she's done. Some soursop juice, if you have it.' And I must drop whatever I'm doing to go and stand next to him with the towel and juice while the great Mistress Ursa has her swim. Every Sunday the same blasted thing. He seems to think I like standing there watching her as much as him. Like she's some child belonging to me. And the old people who come to stay there are just as bad. They're always asking me for her. 'When's the little water baby coming over again?' They're always making a fuss over her in front of him. 'She's going to be another Esther Williams, Mr. Mackenzie.' Some big movie star in America that used to swim in all her pictures. 'She's going to be in the Olympics one of these days, Mr. Mackenzie.' If you was to see him grinning all over himself! One child has him turned foolish. Always acting like the sun rise and set on her-one."

Malvern waited to make sure she was done before speaking. Then: "He best watch himself," she said, " 'cause these spoil-up children can be the very ones to hurt your heart." She shifted the baby she was nursing to her other breast. It was a little girl with her stringy limbs and the bus driver's moon-shaped face surmounted by a thicket of the blackest hair. It was her third girl since the boy she had had seven years ago and named The Woody Wilson.

Night, the dense heat, and Malvern's cramped sitting room in the house on Armory Hill. Since Astral Forde's last visit the room had been reduced to half its size. A length of flowered yard goods strung down the middle now divided it in two, creating a second bedroom in the part that had held the larder with the turned-down glasses on top. On the side where they were sitting the hard cushionless settee and chairs were jammed even closer than before around the little center table that held the wedding picture and the vase of wax anthurium lilies. Malvern would have almost no room to perform her mini carnival if and when Astral Forde brought her a choice piece of news.

"Here I don' see you for months at a time," she said. "And then when you do come, all you can talk about is that child. Always upsetting yourself over her. I can't understand it. Here, you got a big big job. You, one, running a hotel. In charge of everything to do with the place. Hiring and firing people like you's God himself. I tell you, if not for all these children I've got I'd come and beg you for a job. Here you got your own house, with furnitures bought and put there by your friend. And even though you has yet to invite me to see it, I know it must be nice . . ."

"How you mean? You can come and see it any time you like!"

Malvern ignored her. She wasn't complaining. Nor was she offended. She understood. "And here your friend might get to be the prime minister now that we have independence. 'Cause NPP is all the talk here of late. Even though to tell the truth, I don' like all I'm hearing. There's too much of this Black Power talk from the States flying about the place. Do you read about all the demonstration and rioting and burning and thing going on up there? The American black people—them! are saying they want their rights."

"Me! You think I have time to be reading any newspaper as busy as I stay. All I know is that my friend can't wait till the five years are up next year and the DNP has to call elections whether they want to or not."

"Well, everybody is reading about what's going on in the States and you're beginning to hear some of the same kind of talk around here nowadays. Even from the bus driver fella I got. He and all talking Black Power. I'm always telling him to shut his damn mouth before he lose the piece-a job he has driving the government bus and then who's to feed this head of children. You should hear me in here with him. Is a wonder you don't hear my mouth all the way over to the hotel."

The baby had fallen asleep at her breast, and with a touch of the anger from her outburst Malvern pulled her nipple away, covered herself, and almost roughly laid the child face down on her lap. "No, I don' like what I'm hearing, and I don' like what I'm seeing neither. There's too many people here on Armory Hill walking about flashing a lot of money these days. And they're the worst vagabonds we have up here. Where they getting all this money I ask myself and they ain't working no place. No, I don' like what's going on. Still in all, things are looking up for the NPP. People are saying it has a chance this time. So, who knows, your friend might be the big muckamuck running the country this time next year, the PM in truth and not just a pet name."

"And the great Mistress Ursa will be First Lady, even more so than the wife!"

Her outcry startled the sleeping baby so that its curled little fists flew open for a second, and then closed tight again.

Malvern sighed, shook her head, surveyed her guest, taking inventory of her as she did each visit. "I don't understand it," she said. "Each time you come you's wearing the best of clothes. Everything bought ready-made from the big stores in town. And even though it's none of my business and I'd never ask you to loan me one red cent I know you must have money save in a bank someplace. And look how fat and pretty you're getting in your skin! Just look at you!" Pride in what she viewed as her handiwork glowed in the sharp-boned face that was the color of bittersweet chocolate and in the eyes that remained greedy for news. "It must be the fancy candies you say your friend is always sending you that's putting so much flesh on your bones."

* * *

McBurney's Toffees. Cadbury Chocolate Dragees. Harrods Peppermint Creams. Pearce and Whitehead Truffles . . . All of them in pretty tins with pictures on them or boxes with sweetheart bows. Only today a tin of Windsor's Mints and Fruit Drops— her favorite—had arrived. And he himself had stopped by later. First, to go over the accounts with her, the two of them seated together at the desk in the manager's house that stood off to itself behind a grove of trees.

Afterward, with no more than an hour of daylight left, he had taken off his suit jacket and vest and hung them on the contoured hanger of the silent valet she had bought and put in the bedroom for him . . . Did he have one like it in the house on Garrison Row? Don't even bother asking, she had told herself when she first presented him with the valet. You know he has yet to say a word about that house or the beautiful-ugly wife . . . He had then placed his tie and belt on the rack provided for them. His shirt and pants on the hanger also, under the jacket and vest. His keys, wristwatch and wallet into the accessory tray on top of the valet, along with the small change in his pockets. The sound of the coins striking the wood. Listening to the sound where she had lain already undressed down to her small clothes, which she always left for him to take off. And the two handkerchiefs he carried with him at all times lying next to the tray. Then finally his underwears on the chair she had placed for them beside the valet.

His hand all in her hair. Always the hair. He can't get enough of it. And his body, the weight and heft of him, filling her up, and not only her but the wide bed, the room, the house; the bulk of him stacked high against all the windows and doors like they had taken all the furnitures he had bought her and was using them to barricade the place so no one could get in ever. All of him straining because of the sweetness, moaning because of it, getting on like he would give up everything for it, even the little water-head child, and night would find him here and tomorrow and the day after tomorrow and he wouldn't know or care. And the little skin-teeth woman from America would be there waiting, sitting up in the swell house on Garrison Row waiting. Refusing, never mind weeks and months went by, to get in the car he bought for her and come looking for him. Won't set foot near the place. Scorning people. I come like nothing to her . . . His hands on her backside. Oh, God! And he's begging her to turn over now, raising her to her knees. One hand, as he goes inside again, reaching around to cup and cradle and milk her bubbies; the other hand—the fingers only—reaching Oh, God! for the wick of her lamp that's all swell up. A touching, a stroking sweeter than I don' know what. And he's talking now. Telling her, his face pressed into her hair—always the hair—his mouth to her ear, whispering about the two horses in the yard that time when he was a boy—always those horses, the trampling, the screams, the blood on the ground, how he run and hide . . . She'd piss blood if she was to see them now. Waiting. Over on Garrison Row waiting . . . One thing to say for her: she looks like some-body you could talk to . . . Oh, God, wait! Primus? Wait, I can't wait!

"Primus!"

Sweeter than all the candies he sends here put together.

She had lain in the bed this evening listening to him in the shower and thinking: he won't touch the cake of nice lavender soap I put there. It'll be sitting dry as a bone in the soap dish after he's finished. Only the water. So he won't have the smell on him. And he's not lingering once he puts back on Mr. Clothes. Oh, no, he's not gon let night catch him here. It's home in time to have supper with the great Mistress Ursa and the wife from big America.

". . . He gets on like everybody has been put on this earth to wait on Her Highness . . ." The voice pursuing its obsessed, relentless course. Malvern had given up by now and simply sat hearing her out, the baby across her knees, and the knees themselves crowded against the small center table in the room that was now half its size. ". . . Take last Sunday. One of Mistress Ursa's braids came loose when she was dressing to go home and don't you know the man had the gall to want me to fix it. I was to put my hands in those hard nigger knots. Always getting on like she's some child I had for him. So here she come running. But she must have read my thoughts because all of a sudden she stopped, just stopped and stood there looking at me with that big head just like his and the little square-off shoulders that belong on a boy . . . She's not afraid of anything, y'know. If you was to see the way she jumps off the diving board into the deep deep water . . . Standing looking at me. Then she's shaking her head, no, she don't want me to fix the braid. All he tried coaxing her to come to me she's shaking her head no. And then Mr. Thumb in her mouth. She's still with that thumb, y'know, a big seven-years-old girl . . ."

"She's you all over," Malvern said. "You sucked yours till you was a half-a-woman going to school."

"And take the friggin' thumb out you mouth!" Wha'dax! *Fire on her hand.* The memory again, and then the voice plunging ahead: ". . . And I know the great Mistress Ursa went home with the braid loose rather than have me touch it. Every Sunday it's something with her. Look what happened the week before . . ."

In one of her tightly wound up movements, Malvern sprang to her feet, the baby in her arms. A startled Astral Forde fell silent. "But what it is with you, nuh? Here it 'tis, you living good, you living swell, there's scarce any difference anymore between you and the great people—them! and yet you letting some child scarcely old enough to wipe herself good hag your spirit. I can't fathom it atall atall. It's like you don' know what you feel about her. You get on sometimes like you love her as much as you can't stand the sight of her."

A long, loud suck-teeth from Astral Forde.

Malvern stood there, disappointed. There had been no real news this visit. And who could say when she would see Astral Forde again? Another three four months if not longer. No news tonight. Malvern silently sucked her own teeth and, negotiating her way through the crowded furniture, went to put the baby down behind the length of yard goods strung across the room.

An ignoramus. A half hour later, Astral Forde stood at the bus stop calling her friend an ignoramus. Behind her stretched the lower half of Armory Hill, that fowl yard and hellhole, as Malvern calls it. The noise worse than Babylon, the kerosene lamps flickering in the jumble of scrap houses, the stink of the open drains and the WCs that're nothing but holes cover over in the ground. Right on the main road now! The tourists have to drive past it on their way from the airport and then back again when they're leaving. It's a wonder the government ain't shame . . . Across the road, in the near distance, lay Cannon Beach and the sea. The salt drift on the air lost in the stink around her. Above her, a dense and starless sky. An idiot. All I try to explain to her how he gets on over the child, she still can't understand. And it's like she don't even want to listen anymore. But you wait, she won't catch me climbing Armory Hill anytime soon again!

———

The following Sunday, yet another thing to vex her spirit. She was in the open-sided pavilion that joined the two rows of cottages when the Buick pulled up and the great Mistress Ursa came bounding out the car and up the steps at the entrance, already in her swimsuit. But no swimcap this time. *Oh, God!* Astral Forde felt her heart give a lurch. Look what that foolish woman went and did to the child hair! A Black Power haircut! How could she do a thing like that to the child? That woman! She needs to be put away in a madhouse someplace! And the father's just as bad! He needs putting away too! How could he let her do such a thing?

Later that morning she was forced to look on in the same

silent outrage as Her Highness, showing off, combed out the Black Power hair after her swim. With some long-tooth comb that looked like a pickax. The damn thing sending a bright shower of water flying up around her head.

11

Dear Homefolks,

Well, it's all over but the shouting. And there's not even too much of that to be heard, not even from the DNP gangsters who out-and-out stole the election. Even they're too ashamed to be celebrating. In fact, it feels and sound more like a wake than anything else around here. And that's as it should be, since our little three-year-old independence is just about dead as far as I'm concerned, along with all of the changes we hoped it would bring.

But first, before anything else, let me "beg for an excuse," as we say here. I should have written you all long before this, or I should have tried getting through on the phone right after everything happened. I just couldn't, though. I was too upset, too depressed, too angry. I've been practically paralyzed for weeks. I hope that you at least got my telegram saying that we were safe. That's about all I could manage at the time. Anyway, now that the worst is over and I'm a little calmer I'm going to try to get it all down, since I'm sure there was hardly a mention of what happened here in the papers up your way. Only if the bombs had actually started falling or they had gone ahead and sent in the marines would we have rated a notice.

The train of unhappy events went something like this. When it became clear that we were really going to win this time—and win big, a clean sweep—the Do-Nothings turned vicious. The name-calling, the mudslinging, the scuttlebutt were worse than ever before. And the Red-baiting. Yes, they started that too. Suddenly the NPP was in the pay of Moscow and if we won we'd not only nationalize everything—the big estates and all the businesses in town—we'd even take away the small farmer's little half-acre of land or tell him what he could and couldn't grow on it and throw anybody who complained in jail. The country would be poorer than it is now. Nothing to eat, no money in your pocket and nothing to buy in the stores even if you had a little money. Did Triunion people want to live like that? Every speech was the same pack of lies. Worse, we found out that the so-and-sos had been secretly organizing an army of thugs before they even called the elections. When the campaign started going in our favor, suddenly there were all these hired thugs all over town harassing and even beating up anyone they saw wearing one of our buttons or T-shirts. The DNP even sent them to the countryside to burn down the houses and crops of people they knew to be our supporters. Morlands was the only place they didn't dare go near. You never saw anything like it, homefolks. The entire country just changed character overnight. It's as though it went back to the time when there were all the wars here. My friend Roy was the only one who wasn't surprised at what was happening. He had warned us that the DNP would stop at nothing to keep us from winning. It got to be so dangerous in town we had to take Ursa-Bea out of school and send her up to Morlands with Celestine. And as if the thugs and violence and lies weren't enough, we woke up one morning to find the Gray Eminence sitting out in the harbor with its sixteen-inch guns aimed straight at us. It had stopped by at the invitation of the government. And it had brought along a friend. Sitting next to it was this aircraft carrier the size of a football field. Enough shells and bombs, homefolks, to wipe little Triunion from the face of the planet in a matter of minutes.

Well, that did it. People got the message. They remembered what happened to our neighbor just a couple of islands away when the same two friends paid it a visit a few years ago to help out the same kind of do-nothing government there. That time the guns actually went off, the marines landed, and as we know they're still there. So before you knew it, every NPP button and T-shirt disappeared, and on Election Day most of our supporters stayed home. They heard that the thugs would be around the polling places (which they were, and the police did absolutely nothing!) and that they now had guns. Some people were so frightened they didn't leave their house for the day. And the few who were brave enough to go to polls swore they saw the DNPs stuffing the ballet boxes and allowing their people to vote more than once. So there was that going on too. The upshot, of course, was that the old gang won hands down. They got more seats this time than ever before. Only Primus and one other member of his party survived.

I can't tell you what the whole thing did to me, homefolks. I was in a terrible state. I could have taken a gun to every DNP in sight. As for our supporters, all those people I'd seen wearing our buttons, who had come out in droves to our meetings, it was all I could do not to go up to them when I saw them in town and call them cowards to their faces. At the same time I wanted to put my arms around them because I knew how badly they felt. And I did with some of those I knew personally. I just went up and hugged them, never mind I was furious with them. Because, truthfully, everybody was frightened, even those of us who went out and voted. And all of us, even the ones who voted

DNP, are walking around ashamed and in mourning. The whole island is in mourning.

I needn't tell you that Primus was devastated. If he could have walked away from Triunion the minute the final count was in, he would have. And he would've never looked back. He's completely given up on this place. And it's not only because he was robbed of his one real chance to head up the government. Or the fact that our people behaved so cowardly—although I don't think he can ever forgive them that, especially since he campaigned all over the island this time to help the other NPP candidates. He worked so hard, homefolks! But more than all that, what he can't get over was the sight of the U.S. Navy sitting armed to the teeth out in the harbor. *Sent for by the government!* With permission from said government to turn the guns and bombs on us, if necessary. Its own people! And there wasn't a thing he or the NPP could do about it. I don't think he'll ever recover from that. As Roy says, the country is about as independent as Primus is actually a PM. All of it, he says, is a "puppy-show" (meaning puppet) with no longer England, but guess-who now pulling the strings.

And wouldn't you know it! After calling in the navy and setting the thugs on us, after stealing the election, out-and-out stealing it, as I said, the Do-Nothings now want Primus to serve on some planning and development board they and the moguls in town have come up with. It's to be a joint public and private setup and to operate independent of the government. So they say. If you ask me, it's nothing more than the DNP trying to put a good face on things after what they did. In any case, practically every day now there's an article in the paper about this soon-to-be Planning and Development Board. How it's going to transform the economy, bring in new business, put people to work, put Triunion on the map, promises and more empty promises. They've already gotten people calling it the P and D Board and talking about it as though it already exists. And they're after Primus to be part of it because under the charter they've drawn up, the board has to have at least one permanent member from the opposition. (What little opposition we now have.) He can only say no. He tells me he's going to say no. Then the next minute he'll say something that almost sounds like he might consider it. At this point I can't say what he'll decide. I'm afraid to think about it even. I've seen so many strange things go on in this place over the past six months, things I never dreamed could happen, I'm not sure what anybody will do or say anymore. And that includes me. The things I've accepted, gone along with, living here! They sometimes make me feel like a stranger to myself.

Oh, how I wish I was home sometimes! I read about the Movement (I love that name of it, by the way) and I want to grab Ursa-Bea and take the next plane headed north. So much is happening and I feel so out of it! I need to be marching or sitting-in or demonstrating somewhere. I should've been in Washington for the Big March. I should've been the one personally desegregating those rest rooms between Washington and Tennessee, as many times as you and I had to squat, Mama, behind some bush. And I should be in Alabama with Grady right now, right this minute working on the voter registration drive. And I know I sound like a broken record in every letter, but please tell him to be careful. And I wish the two of you wouldn't drive down home this summer. There're too many awful things happening down there for you to be alone in a car on those roads. Take the train or fly down this time. I'd feel easier in my mind if you did. Or take the bus. After all, you can sit up front all the way now!

Just think, homefolks, no more back of the bus, no more bushes, no more you can't eat or sleep here even if you do have the money. All of that finally at an end. I can't get over it. Black folks—no more Negroes or "cullud"—finally moving, a-movin', the Movement, I love it! I'm going to send Ursa-Bea to take my place at the barricades as soon as she's old enough. Nobody here knows it, but I've already got her in training. And I've also decided that she's to go to Weaver High when the time comes, like her mother and uncle before her. Especially now that it's more integrated. Primus is going to want to send her to some fancy prep school we can't afford, but I'm going to hold out for Weaver High so she can learn how to walk the walk and talk the talk. To get her ready for the barricades. As you saw in the picture of her I sent you last year she's already got her Afro.

As for your daughter, she'll stay put on the little atoll and continue to do what she can here. That's not to say I don't also feel like walking away sometimes, just like Primus. But I've really come to see things here and in the States in pretty much the same light. There's the same work to be done. I drive past Armory Hill, the big slum we have here, and I could be driving through all the Harlems in the States. And just as we're finally a-moverin' up there, *the Movement!* I keep telling myself that maybe, just maybe, we'll start a-moverin' down here and won't run and hide the next time the navy shows up on our doorstep. I know, Daddy, I can hear you know: the woman's an eternal optimist. And so I am. So I am.

Love,
Estelle

12

She sat with her breath sucked deep into the wells at the base of her throat and her collarbones standing out like the wings of a crossbow.

She had just announced that she had changed her mind and would not be going after all to the reception being given tonight by the Planning and Development Board.

(Early evening. It was an early evening long years after Primus Mackenzie had agreed to serve on the board.)

He appeared not to have heard what she said. His back to her, he was standing at the other end of their bedroom in the house on Garrison Row, slowly emptying his pockets onto a tall chest of drawers in front of him. He was almost finished. His wallet already lay on top of the chest, along with his keys and the two handkerchiefs he always carried.

"Did you hear me, Primus? I said I'm not going to the P and D's little affair this evening for the visiting firemen. I've decided to sit this one out. I'm going to the cropover fete in Morlands instead," she said, her voice raised slightly to reach him across the long, narrow room. "Ursa-Bea's been home almost two months and she hasn't been up to the to the country yet, so we're going to cropover. I just sent her before you came in to put gas in the car and to have it checked over. And she's picking up one of her cousins—probably Jocelyn—to go with us. We'll be leaving as soon as she's back. And Celestine's going too."

Still taking his time, he undid his cuff links, took off his watch, and placed them along with his tie clip into a beautifully carved accessory tray in front of him. A gift from her, done in mahogany from the slopes of Bush Mountain. After years of what she called "the three Ps"—pleading, prodding and pressuring—she and her allies on the Arts Council had finally gotten the other members to agree to an annual exhibit and sale of handicrafts from Morlands and the other country districts. She had bought the tray for him at the first exhibit seven years ago. The exhibit, as well as support for a drama group she helped to establish in town and a children's art program, were accomplishments she could point to for her years on the council.

At present, she and her friends were applying the three Ps to get the council to underwrite a touring theater for the countryside.

"This has been the third reception in as many months. Do you realize that?" She again waited. Then: "The P and D Board must spend nearly half the national budget wining and dining visiting firemen. And I have to ask myself if it's paying off. With all the money spent entertaining them and the really big money spent building a new main road, new airport, big new industrial park and what all to entice them, I still don't see that many of them rushing in to do business here, not even the small fish, which are the only kind we seem to attract. And the few who do come, try to make as big a killing as fast as they can and move on somewhere else. It's been more years of this than I care to think of. So I'm skipping tonight. In fact, Primus, I think I'm skipping all the nights from now on. I can't take it anymore. I've had it with the P and D Board and their give-away parties. And I've more than had it with the firemen."

Another long wait, and silence over at the dresser. Then, with the wells at her throat deepening as she drew in more air than she could possibly use, Estelle said, "Besides, if you must take someone, there's always Number Two wife. I'm sure she'd be glad to step out on the town with you this evening, since from what I understand she never goes anywhere."

"How can she stay cooped up in that place all the time?" she had asked Roy some years ago. "Working day in and day out like that? Never seeing anyone but the help and a parade of old retired white people. Does she ever go anywhere except into town to shop? Does she have a friend, a Roy-friend she can talk to? I find myself feeling almost sorry for her. It's true, Roy. I don't understand it, but that's about all I feel when I happen to think of that woman. . . ."

"I knew you'd come around to seeing her in a kinder light," Roy had said.

"Yes, why not surprise Miss Forde," she said, "and ask her to go with you to the little 'do' tonight and to all the other P and D 'do's' from now on? The firemen won't know the difference. And the natives have long since known the truth."

He had removed his jacket, tie and shirt by now and tossed them on a chair for Celestine or the maid to attend to later. The rest of his clothes slowly followed. It wasn't until he had stripped to his shorts and had taken a clean set of underwear from a drawer of the chest that he turned to her. Turned and stood with the late afternoon light in the room striking his impassive face and neutral gaze and ripening the dark plums stored under his skin. The flesh at his middle had thickened in recent years and was beginning to slip wearily over the waistband of his shorts.

"Look," he said, "I had to spend the entire morning showing these people from the States around, the firemen or whatever you want to call them. I couldn't even go to court. You know that. You had to put off the cases for me. And then this afternoon there was a meeting of the House. The whole afternoon spent listening to those jackasses bray. And now I've got to turn around and go to this reception. In other words, I haven't had a chance to just sit and blow for the day. So I'm not able for any dramatics this evening, Estelle. I'm asking you to take off those slacks you've got on, put on a dress, and come with me to this thing. They're expecting both of us."

"And I said I'm not going. Not tonight or any other night. I've had it with the board's brand of planning and development." She was thinking of the new section of the main road they had recently built to bypass Armory Hill. To spare the firemen and the tourists the sight of that eyesore. It had cost hundreds of thousands of dollars to cut through the far side of the hill. She sat firm.

He turned and disappeared into the bathroom nearby, leaving her sitting there in the slacks and the scoop-neck cotton blouse she had donned for the trip up-country. The cardigan she would put on once they reached the mountains lay across her lap. On her feet were the flat-heeled shoes she wore when driving. She was planning on letting Ursa drive as far as Marigot, and then she would take the wheel for the steep climb up Bush Mountain and on over to the town of Morlands farther north.

Ursa-Bea. The four years living with the homefolks and going to Weaver High had done their job. She had learned how to walk the walk and talk the talk well enough to get by. With relief and secret satisfaction Estelle had watched it happening more and more each time she came home. A new edge and quickness to her walk and gestures. A way of looking at and listening to you, as if to say, I'm listening to more than just the words. A subtle, necessary wariness. *"Damn!"* she would forget herself and say, and Estelle heard Hartford's North End. And she heard Grady as well. He said it that way. Grady . . . She would never forget her father's stricken voice on the phone telling her about the beating that would leave Grady partially crippled. *Tête chargé,*

Celestine would have said. She had been *tête chargé*, in a state; and although it was years now, she hadn't gotten over it. She still woke up occasionally to find Primus holding her, rocking her because she had been crying over Grady in her sleep. She had flown up to the States the same day the call came and the following day had gone with her parents to Alabama, where they had stayed until he could leave the hospital. Grady would try comforting them by joking that he now had a genuine hoodlum's walk, with the slight drag and dip to his step. Yes, it was good that Ursa-Bea had been around him during the four years at Weaver High, where Grady himself taught. He was living proof of what it had been like on the front line . . . And Ursa-Bea did well her first year of college. Has already, she told her, made a good friend. She's getting there, Estelle thought. Almost ready for the barricades or whatever . . .

The sweater on her lap, her breathing tight as a bowstring, she sat listening to the water in the shower. Years ago, she had complained about there being only one bathroom in the huge house, and he had had this one installed in their bedroom. And there was the large echo chamber of a room itself. She heard at least three other couples keeping them company when they made love, she once told him. Repeating them word for word. Echoing their cries, their moans, their laughter and sighs./"Estelle!" he had pretended to be shocked./"I mean it. This barn turns us into an orgy. We need to do something about it."/So that he had gone along with her converting the room into a small apartment. A sitting area with a rattan sofa and chairs, occasional tables and lamps took up one half of the space. The other half was filled with the expensive suite of bedroom furniture he had ordered from Conlin and Finch as soon as they bought the house. The white elephant, as she still called it. The sitting area also held a large television, one of the first on the island, as well as a console stereo and bookcases. In a window equidistant between the two sections sat a mammoth air-conditioner he had had shipped down from the States.

Anything so that she couldn't accuse him of not providing for her adequately. Anything that might dissuade her from driving out to the airport in the middle of the night again.

"I agree with you about the dramatics," she said the moment he came out of the bathroom wearing the change of underwear. "I'm not up to them either. That's another reason why I've decided to stay away from the P and D receptions from now on. I'm tired of putting on my same old act for the firemen each time. You know the one. My touch-of-home-away-from-home act. That's why you and the others on the board are always so eager for me to come to these little affairs. If I can make your guests feel more at home, then maybe, just maybe, they might be more disposed to investing some of their greenbacks. Even when the other wives aren't invited, Estelle is always asked along to do her little number."

"What the hell are you talking about?" Asked in an unperturbed voice. He began dressing.

Come to think of it, she went on, her voice carrying across the room on the hum of the air-conditioner, she was always being put on display. It had started the first day she stepped off the plane. Before she could get her bearings she had found herself up on a platform being shown off as the wife the PM "went and find in America." A honeymoon spent being hauled around from one meeting to another at all hours of the night. Always being made to stand up beside him like some door prize he had won on his Carnegie tour . . .

"You loved it, Estelle." Said quietly, his back to her again. "You couldn't wait to come up and say a few words."

Not only loved it! I used to feel we could move Gran' Morne just the two of us!

"Don't be so sure about how much I loved it!"

And it wasn't only the meetings. He had insisted on dragging her to every funeral, wedding, christening, prize day and house raising to make sure he didn't miss out on a vote. To every fete and dance, where to show how democratic he was he would hand her over to anybody who came asking for a dance. Having to dance with any old rumhead. The man who had been three sheets to the wind at the victory celebration that time in Pointe Baptiste had rolled his stomach like a nest of snakes against her, had breathed a distillery in her face, and she hadn't been able to haul off and slap him because he had voted NPP. That's the way it had been for years until he realized he didn't have to bother campaigning anymore because people in Morlands were going to vote for him no matter what. She had gotten a rest then. Until along came the P and D Board and she found herself being trotted out again.

"Do you know who I feel like at these receptions and do's for the firemen? Do you?" As she stood up abruptly, the sweater on her lap fell to the floor. "Like the tattooed lady at the circus, that's who. I've got the stars and stripes tattooed on me from head to toe. And there's this barker with a bullhorn calling for every Shriner and fireman in town to come have a look. Step right up, gentlemen, an honest-to-God piece of Americana, never mind she's not quite the right color beneath all the red, white and blue. Well, the tattooed lady is taking the evening off. She's going up to cropover where she won't have to be 'on.' No show tonight, or any other night for that matter."

"We'll go up to cropover tomorrow, Estelle." His voice patient, low-pitched, reasonable. His back still turned to her and the distance of the room between them. He was putting on his belt, completely dressed now except for his tie and the jacket to the suit he had changed into. And he was half-smiling, thinking perhaps: a tattooed lady at the circus. Only Estelle could think up something like that.

"We'll go to this thing tonight, Stel, leave early, get a good night's sleep, and drive up to Morlands the first thing tomorrow."

"I'm driving up today. The minute Ursa-Bea gets back here with the car we're leaving."

"We'll all go up tomorrow."

"The main fete's tonight, you know that. Everything'll be over by tomorrow."

"There'll still be enough going on. We'll go then."

"No, we won't. Something else having to do with the P and

D Board will come up. The board and all the VIP visitors keep you so busy you don't even have time for cropover in your own district anymore. So I'll go. One of us at least should be there. Especially this year, when the crops were nothing to speak of because there was so little rain. People need something to cheer them up. A man from Wellington stopped by the office today to tell me he scarcely made anything this season. He's so fed up he's decided to move to town and would like you to help him find a job. He's the third one this week to come in with the same story. You weren't there to hear them, of course. The P and D Board again. Personally, I think you should just come out and tell people in Morlands the truth: that you don't have time for the district anymore. Nor the interest. Just come straight out and tell them. That way they wouldn't expect to see you until a few days before an election . . ."

He finally turned to face her, and for a time stood looking across at her in that characteristic pose of his: as if calmly and confidently waiting for someone to appear and attend to the situation for him. Just take care of it for him. Someone who would draw those collarbones back under the buff-yellow skin and fill in the awesome wells at her throat, who would erase from her eyes the disillusionment he saw there that was only a fraction of his own. Someone finally, his guiding guardian spirit, his *chi* who would provide him with the words powerful enough, persuasive enough to get her to take off the damn slacks, put on a dress—that silvery gray one with the draped top that he liked— and come with him tonight.

He waited as if fully expecting the deliverer to appear.

Until: "I wonder, Estelle, if you've ever thought about how someone like myself—a so-called representative of the people— feels having to go up to a place like Morlands all the time with my two arms long down and my hands empty?" That voice of his that gave no more weight to one word than to another, that had the ability to make everything around him come to a halt whenever he paused and to wait patiently until he resumed speaking again. It happened at every meeting when there was an election.

Estelle heard it and wanted to clap her hands over her ears. Don't listen to that voice of his!

"Have you ever thought of that?"

"Of course I have!" She quickly bent and snatched the sweater up from the floor. Don't look at him either!

"Well, if you have, you don't seem to understand what it's like. You've lived with me all this time, slept next to me in this bed every night, yet you don't have a clue as to how someone like myself feels. A small boy walking along the road in Morlands with half the seat of his pants missing and his backside bare to the world probably understands better than you. He knows it's no joke for me to be running up there all the time when there's so little I can do for them. What I go through each time. It's been eight years now that I've been trying to get the electrification done. You know that. Eight long years, and only last month did they get as far as Government Lands with the lines. It might take another eight years for them to reach Morlands. The main town in the district still without a streetlamp! The small boy and everybody else up there sees how my hands are tied. And they know, even if you don't, that it's gotten worse since the damn people in the rest of the country took fright and let the DNP steal the election that time. As they've done every time since then by crying communist and threatening to call in the bloody ships again. They've found the winning formula for the cowards in this place. I'm not telling you anything you don't know."

And they understood—the small boy and the others—even if she didn't, that it made more sense for him to stay in town and try and talk to these people from Canada, the States or wherever in the hope that one of them, one day, might be willing to put a factory or plant up in Morlands. He wouldn't rest until he had at least seen to that. That's the only reason he had decided to serve on the board. Since it was to be independent of government, he thought he might be able to use it to get a little something

for Morlands. She knew that. They had discussed it any number
of times before he finally agreed. The board, the firemen was the
best he could do at the moment. Sometimes she acted like she
didn't understand the situation in these little poor-behind islands.

"Wha' the rass, Estelle, do you think that any of us, even the
hangmen in charge of the government, like having to run behind
these white people with our hand long out? Do you? . . ." His
voice rose. He stepped to the edge of the platform out at the
monument. His head came straining forward. She caught the
movement out of the corner of her averted gaze. The lasso of a
cane again! He had told her about it shortly after the night years
ago when they had been stranded on Bush Mountain. How that
mother whom he always spoke of with love, loyalty and dread
in his voice had reached out with the wrong end of the cane the
night before he was to leave for school in town, hooked him
with it around the neck, and, dragging him up to the counter as
if he was just another one of the little abandoned children who
worked in the shop, had laid down the law to him.

He had told her the story of the cane handle, and she hadn't
been able to rest until she convinced him to dismantle the shop
and turn it into his office up-country.

". . . And do you think I want to go to this thing tonight?"
He had crossed into the sitting area. "Not really. But these receptions are about talking business. As you know. And, yes, I
should be in Morlands saying a few words to try and cheer people
up. But I'm sure everybody there would want me to stay in town
and meet with these people from the States if they knew what I
have in mind . . ." He paused, drew closer to her. "I'm going to
talk to them about possibly starting a cannery in the district . . ."

"No, you won't! You'll talk about what they want to talk about.
Which, as usual, will be about what we're lacking. Infrastructure.
We never have enough infrastructure for them. How I hate that
word. I've seen it happen every time, and I've had it!"

She also thought about the sisal factory he had proposed at
the last P and D reception and of all the other plants, factories
and businesses he had sought to interest the firemen in over the

years, and she repeated, almost shouting, "I've had it, Primus! I'm not going anymore!"

". . . A cannery would be possible now that there's electricity as far as Government Lands." He continued as if she hadn't said a word. "It's criminal the amount of fruit that goes to waste when they don't sell fast enough or people can't get them to town. That's always been a problem up there. You know that, Estelle."

She saw them. She tried not to; she tried shutting her mind's eye, but she saw them: the spoiled, spotted mangoes, papayas and oranges; the once green soursops like brown deflated footballs, the pineapples and melons gone soft, and all the other carrion fruit lying where they had been thrown under the stalls in the large market shed at Morlands or along the small roadside markets. Sometimes piles of them as high as the pyramids they had once been a part of, which the hawkers lovingly erected each morning and maintained throughout the day.

She saw the rotting piles, the gaunt dogs who wouldn't even go near them, the clouds of flies; she thought of the lost money, the tin-ning roof that would not be repaired again this year, the school fees that could not be paid, and she slowly sat back down.

"And I'm thinking of something big. A cannery that would be able to switch from mangoes to guavas to hearts of palm or whatever according to the season. A plant that would run the year round. And right there on Government Lands, with the people who work in it living there also in the housing scheme we've talked about for years. An entire town built around a single big plant, like the kind of thing I saw in the States. I'm going to put the idea to these people tonight and see what they have to say. That's why I need you to come with me, Estelle." He was close enough now so that she caught, very faintly, a hint of the cologne he had dabbed under his arms. Guerlain Homme. She had given it to him as a Christmas present last year. And there was the stronger musk of his urgency. She kept her face turned aside. "Not to parade you around like a door prize or something in a circus—you can talk such damn nonsense when you're vexed—but to help me convince these people that something like the cannery could work. You know how to talk to them better than I do. You understand—since you're from the same place as them—what they're really saying behind the words. You know how their minds work. I need you to look at them, Stel, and tell me if you think they're genuinely interested or they're just talking. Drinking up the free whiskey and just talking. So put on a dress and come. Let's not have a big noise this evening. We'll go up to cropover tomorrow."

13

The plastics manufacturer from Wilkes-Barre, a slight, boyish-looking man in a tropical-weave suit and the beginnings of a reddish sunburn, had come hurrying over as soon as she fled the group that had been discussing the cannery; and in an effort to control the angry trembling in her limbs, she was trying to focus on what he was saying. The unions again. He had taken up where he had left off the last time he had caught up with her at the reception and was complaining about the high cost of doing business in the States because of the unions. He made shower curtain sets, tablecloths and covers for small home appliances. All of them plastic. He was hoping to add dustcovers for business machines and computers to his product line, but the unions were a problem. Estelle had made the mistake earlier in the evening of asking him about his company, and a steady litany of complaints had followed.

"Now you speak the kind of English I don't have any trouble understanding," he said, relieved, when they met, and ever since then he had claimed her ear whenever he got the chance.

They stood now, just the two of them, alone for the moment amid the sixty or so guests in the Windsor Room of the Triunion Royal Palm Hotel. Directly above their heads hung a huge globular chandelier—one of many in the ornate, high-ceilinged room. Over at the entrance, two caryatidlike statues on either side of the door held aloft giant candlebra that added to the glitter of the chandeliers, the opulence of the marble floor, the crown molding and the bas-relief columns around the walls. The Triunion Royal Palm. It was the oldest hotel on the island, built in the grand manner to accommodate royal visitors. Princess Margaret had stayed there when she came down for the independence celebrations over a decade ago. She had in fact opened the independence ball by dancing with the premier in the Windsor Room, which was where the P and D Board always held its receptions.

". . . They're enough to make you want to pack up your business and move it out of the country altogether," the man from Wilkes-Barre was saying.

Half listening, trembling, seething, Estelle kept her eye on the group she had just abandoned. He was still there; Primus Mackenzie—she couldn't believe it—was still there, his shoulders in the dark business suit he had on angled in such a way they partially blocked out the sight of her, his gaze carefully avoiding the spot, some ten feet way, to which she had fled. How could he continue to stand there? To be still talking and laughing with them? She had turned on her heel and left them flat, telling herself, No, Estelle, don't do it, don't even think of doing it, and the same voice saying, Yes, go ahead, do it! and he'll leave the crazy wife he went and find in America home from now on. Both voices raging in her, she had walked away, refusing to say so much as "If you'll excuse me . . ."

He should have done the same. Just turned his back on the six of them there helping themselves to the free whiskey and rum, and walked away. Instead, there he was, chatting, laughing with the very one among them who had dismissed out of hand his idea of the cannery. A sporting goods manufacturer from Chicago. A large, balding man whose face took its expression from either his wide, hail-fellow-well-met smile or his eyes, which were the color of the steel gray frames of his glasses. He was the spokesman for the entire delegation.

"Sounds like you're from our part of the world," he had said with the smile when they were introduced at the beginning of the evening, his hand engulfing hers.

The smile gone, he was the same man who no more than ten minutes ago wouldn't even let Primus finish telling him about the cannery.

No, he had said, cutting him off almost as soon as he began. No, he had repeated, the metal gray eyes taking over the expression on his face and the tone of his voice. What they needed to do first and foremost was to improve their port. Before thinking of a cannery or anything else, they first had to do something about their port. They couldn't expect to interest anyone in setting up any kind of sizeable industry in a place that lacked decent port facilities. It would pay them to put out the money and build themselves a deep-water harbor. He didn't know who had advised them to erect an industrial park before they had their shipping organized. That was putting the cart before the horse. A first-rate port. First-rate roads throughout the island if they were talking about having factories in the countryside. A telephone system that worked. It had taken him over an hour that afternoon to put through a call to Chicago. And they didn't have nearly enough hotels. Tourism. Now that's what they should really be pushing. And in a big way. It was a natural for the place. And it would provide them with the capital to do whatever else they wanted. They needed to get rid of a fancy relic like this place and bring in the chains. The Hiltons and Sheratons that were going up on the other islands. They were behind in this. But first, a decent port. Along with some healthy concessions on custom duties, taxes and the like. And everything nice and stable politically, no coups or government takeovers—his smile breaking, he had wagged a playful finger at them. Once all that was in place, and they could also offer the addicts like himself two or three first-rate golf courses—the smile taking over his face completely—they'd have more people than they could shake a stick at rushing in to build a cannery or anything else they had in mind.

"Well, here's one of your industries that's doing all right right now, as far as I'm concerned." This from the owner of a furniture company in Grand Rapids. He was holding up his glass. "I couldn't drink the rum in that last place we visited, but the stuff you make here tastes almost as good as old J&B."

Primus Mackenzie had laughed along with them. Not only laughed, but as the man who had spoken held out his glass he had touched it with his own; and trembling, enraged, Estelle had made her escape while they were all laughing and clinking glasses, saying, No, don't do it, don't even think of it, and in the same voice: Yes, go ahead, do it! and he'll leave the crazy—

Suddenly interrupting the plastics manufacturer and his talk of unions, she asked him if he had ever played "Statues" as a child.

"Do you remember the game?" Her voice loud enough to carry across to where he stood with his gaze averted and his shoulders trying to block her out. "Someone in the group would spin you around and the minute they let go, you were supposed to freeze into something—a chair, an animal, a bird, anything, or into someone famous, Hitler goose-stepping with his arm stuck in the air, maybe, and the other kids would have to guess who or what you were. You had to hold the pose without moving a muscle until somebody guessed right, and then you'd spin that person around. Do you remember the game?"

Before the puzzled man could answer, she began to turn in a slow spin, taking care not to spill the drink in her hand—her third rum and soda for the night. She did one complete turn, and when she came to a halt, facing him again, she already had the hand that held her drink, her right hand, raised straight up above her head, and her left arm was already bent at the elbow, and she was holding her evening bag as if it were a tablet.

She stood as if turned to stone. Even when the man from Wilkes-Barre, laughing uneasily and looking all the more boyish in his bewilderment, guessed who she was, she continued with the pose, standing rigid in the silvery gray dress with the draped top she had been asked to wear, the rum in her raised glass glowing amber in the light of the chandelier high overhead, and the last breath she had taken before becoming inanimate sucked into the hollows at her throat.

She was stone that couldn't see, couldn't hear, couldn't feel. So that she didn't, couldn't, see the growing stupefaction on the man's face or hear him asking anxiously if she was all right. Nor could her eyes follow his as they wheeled in alarm toward the group ten feet away, where *he* was still talking and laughing with the man in the steel-framed glasses and the others. The look on the boyish, sunburned face soon spread to the faces over there, and then slowly, in an ever widening circle, to every face in the room. Although Estelle couldn't see this. Nor did she hear when the conversations that had been going on slowly faltered and died, with the last shreds of laughter dying also, as everyone there, all sixty or more guests, also decided to play the game, all of them turning into statues of themselves: visiting firemen, hangmen who ran the government and the various ministries, the great people—them! from Garrison Row and Raleigh Hill, the moguls who owned Conlin and Finch and managed the banks and businesses in town, and the few wives like herself who were present. Even the waiters with the trays of drinks and canapés had joined in the game. Aghast black faces above their starched white jackets.

Everyone playing "Statues."

Minutes that lasted longer than all the years the Triunion Royal Palm had been there.

A hand on her raised arm finally, slowly forcing it down; and then just as slowly prying the glass of rum and soda from her stone grip. The drink disappeared and the hand returned to take her lightly by the elbow, a familiar touch except for the tremor she could detect now that the game was over and she could see, feel and hear again. And his head had come straining out of the socket of his neck. She didn't have to look to know that. Then, as if nothing out of the ordinary had happened and they were simply leaving the reception early as he had promised—"We'll leave early, Stel, get a good night's sleep, and drive up to Morlands first thing in the morning," said in the bedroom less than two hours ago—he was steering her across the Windsor Room in that unhurried way of his, over the marble floor and around the groups in their path; while those they passed, the firemen, hangmen, moguls and the rest who had joined the game, continued to wait for someone to come along and guess who they were so they could breathe and become animate again.

The silence in the room, the stillness followed them past the larger-than-life female figures holding aloft the candlebra at the door, and out into the lobby. The same lobby where no one his color had been allowed to enter either as a guest or a visitor when he was a boy, Primus Mackenzie had once told her. The Triunion Royal Palm. Princess Margaret and her entire entourage had stayed there.

From the lobby with its cool marble, columns and lights, the hand at her elbow led her into the heat and darkness outside and down the flight of wide steps to the driveway.

Ordinarily, she would have waited at the foot of the steps while he went to get the car. Tonight, as soon as they reached the bottom step she slipped her arm from his light hold and, without waiting, without looking back, started up the driveway alone, walking swiftly between the row of royal palms that gave the hotel its name. In the darkness their towering heads had merged with the moonless sky.

She had looked up at him after they made love on Bush Mountain that night long ago, and for a moment his head had appeared to be

*grazing the black dome of the sky and the white of his eyes had been
at the center of the starfield.*

If you think you're going to make me feel I wasted my life
. . . The words already forming in her head.

At the end of the driveway she turned left, in the direction of
Garrison Row, and kept on walking, staying close to the high
stone wall with shards of glass cemented along the top that separated the hotel grounds from the road. The hotel was in the
Raleigh Hill section of town, where the old Georgian and Victorian great houses all stood behind similar high, glass-topped
walls. The houses were already shuttered and dark, the road
deserted, the only light the nebula that came from the Royal
Palm. There was no sidewalk, only a narrow, grassy shoulder, so
that she had to step lightly to prevent the high heels she had on
from sinking into the soft places and slowing her progress.

It wasn't long before she heard the Buick, its motor sounding
as if it was idling as he took his time coming up the driveway.
Still acting as if nothing had happened. Just as he would act
tomorrow when he took his seat in the House. He would walk
into the chamber at his characteristic pace, she knew, take his
seat as if the election years ago hadn't been stolen from him and
the NPP, and he was, and had been since then, the legitimate
head of government. And no one there, not even the prime
minister, would dare say a word to his face about tonight.

(Later, he was even to bring the talk that raged behind his
back to a halt. To salvage her reputation and his own, he hinted
that the man from Wilkes-Barre was to blame. "The fella said
something or the other to her about black people in the States
demanding too much, and had her all upset. And you know
Estelle . . . Some these people don't know how to talk to you,
y'know. It's that racialism they still have up there.")

The high beams on the Buick flooded the road with light and
quickly singled her out as he made the turn at the end of the
driveway. The headlights were like two huge spots trained on
her on a dark empty stage. She kept on walking, making sure

not to bring her weight down fully on her heels. Almost tiptoe-ing. The car slowly followed until she reached the end of the hotel grounds and turned onto the sloping road that was called Raleigh Hill. Then the lights moved past her, dropping her back into darkness again, and he was pulling up just a yard or two ahead of her, bringing the Buick so close to the shoulder of the road that the door on the passenger side almost struck the wall of the house she was passing when he leaned over and swung it open.

The door blocked her path and she stopped.

"Get in the car, Estelle."

He spoke after a long wait, and the tremor she had felt in the hand on her elbow was in the choked voice from the driver's seat.

She ignored it, just as she was ignoring the opened door and the waiting seat. If he didn't move the car she was prepared to spend the night in the one spot. Her heels were already anchored in the ground. *I will not be moved./Just like a tree planted by the waters* . . . She would be like the tree in the old spiritual.

If you think you're going to make me feel . . .

By the time he finally slammed out of the car and came charging around to where she stood, Estelle had resumed the game of "Statues." Not a muscle moving. Her breath stored again in the deep wells at her throat. Her collarbones like a crossbow. And her eyes a pair of empty holes the sculptor had gouged out of the pale yellow stone and then flooded with tears. This time she was playing what looked to be a coachman, her arms bent at her sides and her clenched fists, which were turned upward, holding a pair of invisible reins.

The sight of the fists and the gouged and flooded eyes brought him up short.

That night driving down from the meeting in the foothills of Gran' Morne, he had reached over, taken one small, clenched fist in his hand and raised it to his lips. One of the fists she was using to keep the country boy in the donkey cart to the straight and narrow. And after kissing it, he had held onto it, had refused to let it go, so that he had been forced to drive the rest of the way with only one hand. "Merci, oui," he had said.

Long long years ago.

"If you think you're going to make me feel I wasted my life by coming to live with you in this place and putting up with you and your demons and contradictions and the Do-Nothings and the P and D Board and that cow of a woman over at Mile Trees all these years, you've got another think coming!"

Shouted into his face and into the night for all of Fort Lord Nelson to hear. Her voice spiraling high just seconds before he took and flung her toward the front seat of the car. On her way down her head struck the edge of the door frame. A glancing blow that would scarcely leave a sore spot tomorrow. Nevertheless, for an instant, she saw an entire galaxy of stars.

———

'Foreday morning and the familiar dove-gray light in the bedroom.

There were any number of things she could have said or done as she felt his hand on her stomach. A whole arsenal of no's she could have called upon. The simplest one would have been to ignore the hand, to hold herself like one of those cooling boards black folks down home used to lay out the dead on long ago, until the hand went away. Or she could have suggested in the mock-friendly, solicitous voice she reserved for this particular no that maybe he ought take himself and his honorable member over to Mile Trees, they were sure to find relief over there, and the hand would be quickly withdrawn. Sometimes she treated it like an old banana peel someone had thrown from a tenement window as she was passing by and it had landed on her, squeamishly picking up the hand by the least bit of skin and dropping it back on his side of the bed . . .

This morning she could have simply sent him back to the other half of the room where he had spent the night. She had gone to bed and left him slumped over on the rattan sofa, holding his head in such a way that his hands covered both his eyes and ears. Still hiding from the sight of her head striking the door frame. Still trying to block out the sound. "Stel!" he had cried and, lunging forward, had caught her before she fell completely. Had caught and held her, cradling her head against his shoulder, rubbing the place she had struck, his tear-filled voice begging forgiveness while she pounded him with the fists that had held the reins straight, cursed him and cried.

He had held her until they were both calm enough for him to drive home.

It would have been easy enough to send him back to the sofa. Instead, for whatever reason, she not only permitted him to stay but allowed the hand to remain where it was. Nor did she object when it began to gently knead the slight pouch of flesh across her stomach that had been there ever since she had had Ursa-Bea, the puffiness that refused to go away even when she scarcely ate for weeks at a time in protest over something or another. When she was naked or in a bathing suit she looked as if she had actually had all the children it would have taken to fill the hundred and one bedrooms.

She felt him struggling to ready himself—the hardness no longer came as easily anymore—and she turned to him. She closed her mind to the sight of him talking and laughing with the man who had dismissed the cannery without even hearing him out, closed it to the thought of him with the legion of firemen over the years, and turning to him in the bed she brought her face up to his face, her mouth to his mouth and her hands down to help him.

Later, when he told her that he loved her, she said almost impatiently, "I know, I know."

BOOK III

Polestar

1

Today, for the first time in months, Ursa is carrying her briefcase and she's wearing one of the three or four suits she kept from her NCRC days. This one's a lightweight navy blue wool gabardine with a loose-fitting, boxy jacket, the standard cut of all her clothes, deliberately chosen to disguise the evidence of Estelle's genes: this body, that looks as if it's still waiting to develop some hips, a definite waistline and breasts larger than the nubs she's had since age eleven.

To the suit she's added a silk ivory-colored blouse with a cowl collar, a pair of navy-blue-and-white spectator pumps with heels to give her a little height, and earrings. Celestine's braid flawlessly circles her head. Her watch, which she hasn't even bothered putting on lately, is back on her wrist, along with a filigreed bracelet in gold that matches the earrings. Both presents from the PM when she got the job at NCRC. ("The National Consumer Research Corporation. One of the Fortune 500, bo. She's second only to one of the big directors there," he used to boast to friends. Pleased. Proud. Her life set to his agenda.) And there's her Ghurka shoulder bag, numbered, embossed and registered. A present to herself when she turned thirty. She had splurged, spent the three hundred dollars and bought it. Had even had it gift wrapped . . . You're looking good, girl, she tells herself. Even Viney would approve of the way she looks today. No ratty-looking cape! And as she climbs out of the subway at Ninety-sixth Street and Central Park West, on her way to Lowell's with the good news, she has practically finished composing the letter that will grant her a reprieve, that will get her out of the promise she made two years ago.

Been holding off writing you, it'll say, because I didn't know for sure whether I'd be able to come down/say home/whether I'd be able to come home for the elections next month. I've been waiting around for some definite word on the follow-up study in Midland City I wrote you about back in February, the one I said I really wanted to do. It's been nearly four months without either a clear yes or no from the people at the foundation who have the final say. I had just about given up on its ever coming through when finally, only today, good news! They're going ahead with it after all. And guess who they called right away? The Mackenzies' girlchild. I've just come from a long meeting with the project director. And this time I'm to be one of the key people on the team./He'll like that./They liked the work I did on the first study four years ago, so I'm being asked to help with planning and coordinating the research for this one. I'll also be setting up the first phase of the fieldwork and conducting the initial interviews. I can't wait to find out what's happened there over the four years and to see the people I got to know then, especially my friend, Mae Ryland. She's the mover-and-shaker I used to write you about all the time. If I know her, she's probably running Midland City more so than the mayor. The other good news is that this is to be the first in a series of studies to be done there over a period of years, and I'm to be part of those also. There's even talk of a book about our findings, a kind of before-and-after study of political change in a small, mainly black city, and I would be involved in writing that too. I'm still pinching myself. At long last the kind of long-range, in-depth research project I've always dreamed of doing./Don't forget to mention the money./And you'll be pleased to know that I'm being paid well this time, not the pittance I had to accept on the first study because I had just started free-lancing. So I'm a respectable work-ing woman again. The only snag is that I have to start work almost immediately, which means I won't be able to get away for a while. I couldn't possibly ask for time off just as the study's getting started. In other words, Mr. Mackenzie, sir, you're going to have to get yourself reelected without my help this time, as difficult as that'll be./Good. The joke will help./I know you're going to be annoyed that I won't be there, but I'm sure you'd agree that business comes first and this is where I should be. TCB, as we say here, taking care of business . . ./What else? Talk about the resort./By the way, what's the latest on the resort scheme? How close is it to being built? Where's it to be? How much are you putting in it? . . .

Now to get all that down on paper and mail it off. A sudden flutter kick around her heart at the thought of his face as he reads it. She might not hear from him for months, as happened when she left NCRC. Standing on the southwest corner of Ninety-sixth Street and Central Park West, waiting for the light to change so that she can cross over and walk on the side bordering the park, Ursa feels the familiar disturbance in her chest, near to her heart. Quickly she stifles it. Oh, no you don't, not today! Noth-ing's going to spoil today!

The light changes, she crosses over and leisurely heads north along the cobblestoned walk found on this side of the street. Large, beautifully laid hexagonal stones that are like a honeycomb spread beneath her feet. And they're the same dark gray as the stone wall that runs the length of the park from Fifty-ninth Street up to its end.

Had it been an ordinary day she would have stayed on the train to the next stop, which would have put her only three short blocks away from Lowell's apartment building at 106th Street. But there's nothing ordinary about today. The job came through, and with better terms than she had expected. A copy of the contract she just signed is in her briefcase, along with her notes from the long meeting this afternoon. The letter that will save her from another end-of-the-campaign speech has been written, signed, sealed and already delivered in her head. And since it's Friday, the last Friday in the month, there's the bimonthly dinner to look forward to. It'll be a celebration. A fete. She's going to see that it is, no matter what mood the dinner partner is in!

By way of celebrating she'll insist that they eat *comidas cubanas* at Victor's on Columbus Avenue tonight. Fried plantain. Lots of fried plantain—her favorite since she was small. "*Mal élève! You gon burn off your mouth, oui!*" *Celestine would make as if to slap her hand as it edged toward the slices of plantain just out of the hot skillet. One moment she would threaten her and the next turn around and treat her to one of the golden slices after cooling it off. Blowing on it with thick pursed lips until it was cool enough for her to eat.* And I'll have an avocado salad. Then, as the entree, either *bacalao* in an onion and tomato sauce or king mackerel *écrevisse*. Mmh—some good eatin'! And rice naturally, with red or black beans. Everything smelling and tasting as if it's just come out of the kitchen at Morlands. And a split of Brilliante all to herself. Mr. Carruthers never touches it. Too sweet. And afterward, after the leisurely walk back up Columbus Avenue, a little whoopee.

No high-powered romance anymore, just a little something. This desert out here.

And the celebration will continue over in Brooklyn tomorrow. As soon as the meeting this afternoon was over, she called Viney with the news. "What'd I tell you? I knew it was going to come through. All that worrying for nothing." Viney always has to take credit for everything, always has to be right. Part of her has remained the RA in charge of the freshman dorm. "I'm going to fix a special dinner for you tomorrow. And we just have to have a little Moët," she said over the phone.

Bless her.

And there's the weather today, which is no ordinary thing either! All this spring green! Ursa stops to gawk like a tourist up at the trees, those lining the curb and the ones crowded just behind the stone wall of the park. The two sets of trees have mingled their branches to form a tunnel high above her head. And the tunnel holds a kind of silence in spite of the noisy traffic along Central Park West and the banshee roar of the subway that rises every so often from the grating set into the cobblestoned sidewalk. Over the past couple of weeks the trees have quietly turned green. The kind of green you never see in Triunion where every day of the year is summer. A mild tentative green that looks as if it hasn't made up its mind yet whether to stay. The blur of new leaves, the grass nudging its way up inside the park where, Ursa sees, a pair of lovers have already spread their blanket on the ground—Erzulie protect them! Don't they know this is the dangerous end of the park even during the day? The muggers, the rapists, the flashers and the bicycle thieves . . . —all this delicate, hesitant green could disappear overnight, it seems. She could wake up tomorrow to find bleak, dun-gray February again.

Last Saturday she saw her first flower of the season in Viney's backyard. A small crocus over near a part of the back fence that was closest to the swings and sliding pond and other play equipment. It appeared to be trying to hide itself by the fence, and with good reason. Robeson turned nine that week, and Viney threw the usual party for him on Saturday. (She went over to help.) His friends from school, from the neighborhood, from the cultural center he went to on weekends were all there—including, of course, Dee Dee from down the block. Black, white, Latina, Asian—a mini-U.N.—tearing around the yard in some free-for-all game.

Seeing the crocus and the horde of sneakered feet, Ursa went

Paule Marshall

over to the fence and announced, her hands cupped to her mouth like a bullhorn: "Anyone who so much as puts a foot near this crocus can forget about having any pizza or ice cream and cake later on."

They all steered clear of it.

She didn't realize it, but that lone flower last Saturday was a sign that this week would bring good news. Why do I always fail to pick up on the signs?

And I can't believe this sky! Stopping again to gaze upward, her head all the way back. Take away the traffic, the subway, the phalanx of apartment buildings across the street, and she could be standing gazing up at the sky above the beach at Government Lands. It's that clear and rich a blue today. A warm but rough wind that belongs more to May than to April has taken a broom to the usual fallout from the incinerators and cars and to the petrochemical drift from Jersey across the river, and has turned the sky over the city a Caribbean blue. Almost seven o'clock— she checks her watch—and there's still this much blue in the sky! This much daylight! The sun refusing to go down.

Spring. The old exhausted, maligned and cruel bawd of a city, which is as much home by now as anywhere else, has also like herself been granted a reprieve.

Hooray! Estelle might send her another *Hooray!* telegram when she reads the letter, as she did when she walked out on NCRC. To show that she approved and was pleased. Just the one-word message, *Hooray*, on the telegram, and signed *Love, Estelle*. Ursa hopes she'll send one this time too. She's never really been able to figure out that mother of hers, someone who set her asail in a rowboat before she could even manage the oars. Had simply pointed the bow in the direction of the North Star and said either sink or swim or learn how to row! Just go on up there! Always rushing her. Nor does she understand why Estelle has stayed on through all the shit the PM's laid on her. Why don't you leave him? Why didn't you years ago when you found out about Miss Forde? Instead of all the dramatics—driving me out to the airport in the middle of the night when I was only three scaring me half

254

to death and playing "Statues" at the reception that time and the hunger strikes and all the rest—why didn't you, why don't you just leave him? Nobody stays and takes shit anymore. That's passé. And why, goddammit, did you have to make me like you, so that I can't say *later* for Mr. Carruthers—never mind there're one or two things I still like about him. Just bless him and release him and split! And try and find myself a real oasis. There've got to be a few out here. Why do you still have me hanging in there with him? What's the point? Is there any use? . . . She sometimes finds herself shouting all this and worse at Estelle when she encounters her around a corner of her mind. "I've just never known how to take her, Viney," she's confessed more than once to her sister/friend. "I'm still trying to figure out Estelle. Don't get me wrong. I love her. I'd do anything for her and she knows that, but she's a puzzle. I needed to know her before the PM and Triunion and the keep-miss and everything else got to her. I wish I had known the PM in his 'before' days too . . . Anyway, that's another one of the things that's keeping me away from that place."

Doesn't she ever miss spring, Ursa wonders. She goes and sits on one of the benches that line the stone wall, places her briefcase beside her, crosses her legs and ignores the dirt, the splintered glass of wine bottles and the foul windblown scraps of newspapers underfoot—they don't bother cleaning the streets this far uptown. She keeps her eye on the green canopy overhead. Doesn't Estelle ever miss this new soft green? She doubts it. Estelle hardly ever mentions the States or anything to do with the States in the postscripts she writes to the PM's letters. And she never visits here anymore. Not since the accident. Ursa thinks back to the death of her grandparents—the fatal car accident that had killed both Booker and Bea Harrison. It had happened only months after she had graduated from college. Estelle had stopped coming to the States after that. She had flown up for the funeral; had gone through it looking as if she had also died and it was only her drawn and speechless ghost seated in the church between herself and the PM, her ghost out at the cemetery and at the wake afterward. A ghost that refused to be comforted. She and the PM returned to Triunion a few days later and she hasn't been back since. Over twelve years and she won't come near the place. Yet she's always made clear that this is where she wants her daughter to be. Estelle. A puzzle. She can only love her and hope to understand her someday.

At 106th Street Ursa again waits at the corner for the light to change. Lowell's building is directly opposite. Fifteen stories of elaborate masonry and large casement windows, and with an awning to the curb and a doorman at the entrance. It's the last of the old well-kept apartment buildings to be found this far north. Just four short blocks away the park ends and Manhattan turns into Dresden. She calls it Dresden. Whenever she looks north from Lowell's windows she recalls an exhibit of World War II photographs she had seen at the main library on Forty-second Street when she first moved to the city. There had been one photograph especially, taken of Dresden just after the war. Whenever she looks uptown from Lowell's twelfth floor she sees the same bombed-out, burned-out ruin as in the photograph. Someone sent in the B-17s. Had carpet-bombed it back to the Stone Age. "Nigger, I didn't leave my daddy's good house to come and live in no Harlem!" And the nigger, as if speaking to a hard truth others refused to see, would say that maybe there was no escaping Harlem, not even for the white folks, which would infuriate her all the more. So that one day, without even leaving a note on the kitchen table, his wife had helped herself to the best of the wedding gifts and moved back to Philly.

"Hi, Carlos. It'll soon be time for you to turn into my uncle again."

Ursa stops to chat briefly with Carlos as he holds the door open for her. Gray-haired, portly Carlos who plans to return to the Dominican Republic when he retires. He knows what she means and laughs. "It's getting there, all right." During the hot summer months Carlos leaves off his doorman's cap and exchanges the jacket of his uniform for a white Guayabera shirt. She's told him about her uncle Roy and his Spanish Bay shirts, how he wears them even to Government House . . . She had taken Viney to meet him that last visit home and he had shown them his garden—his stately cannas and the rare pagoda flowers he has cultivated for years—and afterward, on his deep, cool veranda, he had gotten them both more than a little sweet, more than a little salt on the rum punches he personally concocted.

She misses him. Misses them all suddenly—the PM, Estelle, Celestine, even Astral Forde. Misses the stone faces of Congo Jane and Will Cudjoe and the other two out at the monument. Longs suddenly for the little miserable two-by-four island she's been hiding from with tears in her eyes—as the old people in Morlands say—for the past four years.

As the longing floods her, she almost wishes for a moment that the study hadn't come through just yet.

2

"What happened?"

Ursa takes one look at the keloid of a frown swollen to twice its usual size and before moving away from the door of the apartment that Lowell Carruthers has just closed behind her or setting down her briefcase, she asks what happened.

"The bastard made his move."

"Davison?"

"Who else?"

"What'd he do this time? It's too soon for another one of his seizures."

"What he said he was going to when he held that meeting behind my back last month. Went and put someone in my unit who's to be second in charge, someone he's setting up to take over."

"Oh, no."

All right, Ursa, keep calm, she tells herself. Go and sit down first of all. Calmly walk past this man and across the foyer, step around the dog over there . . . /After sniffing indifferently at the hem of her skirt when she first entered, Mitchell has gone to lie down in the archway between the foyer and the living room. The archway is his sentry post. He spends the day there, poised to hurl his seventy pounds of packed muscles and bone at the door the moment he hears an unfamiliar footstep./ . . . Step around him and go sit down. Don't even stop to put down your bag or the briefcase, just go and sit and no matter what, try and hold onto the brightness you came in here with.

She does just that: calmly turns away from Lowell Carruthers, crosses the foyer, sidesteps Mitchell and the fixed snarl of his pit-bull mug, and goes and sits in the living room. A living room that always gives her the uneasy feeling that she's trespassing in a display room of furniture in a department store. Everything's that neat, that arranged, that organized. The sofa in soft Brazilian leather, the matching armchairs, the end tables and floorlamps all carefully positioned on the beautifully patterned area rug Mitchell has been trained never to go near. The entire living room, in fact, is off-limits to him. Not a book or record album leans out of place in the huge wall system that rises from the floor to the ceiling between the windows that overlook the city. Not a speck of New York's gritty fallout is ever to be seen on the dustcover to the stereo, on the glass-topped coffee table, the windowsills or anywhere else. The thoughtfully hung prints and few abstract originals are never so much as a fraction awry. But then, startling you, one of the prints rises above the neatness and the cordoned-off, unlived-in look of a display room to dominate the walls and the entire living room. It's a Romare Bearden collage of a mother, a midnight-black mother with a domed forehead similar to her own, reading to a child by the light of a kerosene lamp like the kind still used in Morlands.

Ursa always sits facing the collage. It serves to remind her— because she's always forgetting—that this too is Lowell. Just as is the framed photograph of his three nephews on an end table, his sister's children with whom he has spent nearly every other weekend since their father was killed in Vietnam. A devotion she resents at times, although it remains one of the things about him she still likes.

Lowell comes and sits quietly on the sofa opposite her chair, which faces the collage. His shapely hands, his long-limbed body that he keeps fit by working out at the Y, and his altogether ordinary, unremarkable black face that is the same deep-toned reddish brown as the leather of the sofa. And his receding hairline. He brings them all and places them across the coffee table from her. She sees that he hasn't changed out of the clothes he wore to work—the dark suit, the white shirt, the power tie—something he normally does as soon as he comes in. Glancing over at the liquor cabinet that is part of the wall system, she finds the drop lid closed. Too upset to fix himself a drink even. Or to ease himself with a little of the Mexican weed he keeps there in the handicraft box from Triunion she gave him. And no old Motown sounds from his high school days are on the turntable. Sometimes, after a particularly bad Davison day, he'll put on Marvin first thing when he comes in ("What's Going On?"), then some early Stevie Wonder or the Supremes. The same albums they used to play occasionally after making love back in the time of the free zone.

Oh, Lowell, why don't you quit that miserable job. You've let it run you into the ground. You've let it ruin everything.

"So he finally made good on one of his threats," she says. "Somehow I never believed he would. I thought the one last month had blown over like all his other little brainstorms. In fact, the last time I asked you, you said he hadn't brought it up again."

"He hadn't. I thought he had forgotten about it too and I'd

have at least three or four months of peace before he came up with something else to bug me with. But I guess he finally got tired of crying wolf all the time. Anyway, as of Monday the compensation unit will have a new assistant manager. I was told about it for the first time this afternoon."

"But how could he do something like that? Hire somebody without consulting you?" She is almost shouting and has to quickly remind herself: Stay calm, listen to him, he needs you to listen to him; say, do what you can to help, love him again if you can, but don't let this do in your good news.

"I asked him the same question."

"What'd he say?"

"He lied." Lowell's voice is curiously flat and distant, as are his eyes. "He said that when we discussed it last month, after the meeting I missed—we never discussed anything and I didn't miss any meeting, I was deliberately excluded—he assumed that I understood he would go ahead and find somebody on his own. So not a word all these weeks. Not even one of his famous memos. Just an announcement this afternoon. He called me into his office all smiles to tell me. The three of us are to sit down on Monday to work out just what my new assistant manager will be doing."

She can only shake her head in disbelief. "Who is it? Who'd he hire?"

"He didn't. He decided that instead of bringing in anyone new he'd move up somebody, which is what he intended doing all along."

"Who?"

"Who do you think? Someone from his little cabal, that's who. Some Ivy League type he brought in a couple of years ago to work with him coordinating operations. Nobody in the division can say what the cat actually does, although he's always all over the place. What we do know is that he's Davison's chief flunky and spy. And I know—as does everyone around there—that the cat knows absolutely nothing about what goes on in my unit. He's had no training, no experience in handling the kinds of cases we get."

"Didn't you point that out to the fool?"

"I must have talked till my black face turned blue. A waste of breath. He's made up his mind. And there's nobody to even appeal to. Because the bastard's already gotten the people upstairs to approve the move. The deal's gone down, in other words, and I'm to be saddled with some lackey who as far as my unit is concerned doesn't know his ass from a hole in the ground . . ."

How, she wonders as he falls silent, how can it still be so bright outside and yet seem so dim, so shadowy all of a sudden in the room? There's enough blue left in the evening sky that if she was to go over to the window with a book she would have no trouble making out the words. Yet it's suddenly dusk, almost night inside the living room. She can barely make out his face across the coffee table. Not that it matters. The frown's still there, she knows, looking like an old wound that's still compulsively piling on scar tissue, still trying to heal itself. And the bays at his temples that have left the tuft of hair she calls Triunion at the front of his head have deepened since the last time she saw him, two weeks ago. At least that's the way it looked to her when he opened the door to the apartment just now and she saw disaster writ large on his face.

And this flat, indifferent voice of his! This monotone! A Lowell incapable of his usual nonstop railing. He can't even manage the furious stage whisper she's used to hearing across the table in a restaurant when there's a Davison crisis. None of that this time. Only this emptied-out, detached voice and distant gaze.

She would have preferred one of the old harangues.

More shadows. She can no longer make out the mother reading to the child in the print on the wall behind him. And Mitchell over in archway has all but vanished. There's only the sound of the steady low-level growl that is part of his breathing.

"Why don't you quit that job, Lowell? Just tell that man and Halcon Electronics Inc. to take their little kiss-muh-ass job and do what they know with it."

She's surprised at how easy it is to say this out loud again. She repeats it to herself nearly every time she sees him, but it's been three years since she's actually said the words aloud. The last time being right in this room. They made a pact that evening. He had been going on again about her leaving NCRC when she finally blew up and told him she didn't want to hear it anymore. He was to keep his criticism to himself and to stay out of her business. Seizing on this, he in turn forbade her to tell him what he should and shouldn't do concerning the job. He was also tired of her advice. "I don't want to hear it anymore either. Just stay off my case, goddammit, and let me work things out . . . !" Both of them shouting.

Their voices drove Mitchell out of the archway and down the hallway that leads to the rest of the apartment. He always retreats when there's a quarrel.

"All right!" she cried. "From tonight on, not another word out of me on the subject. I kiss my right hand to God!" And in true Triunion fashion she kissed both sides of her right hand and raised it to heaven.

Her raised hand sealed the pact.

She suddenly breaks it now and surprises herself at how easy it is to do. "Just quit, Lowell. Enough is enough. There's no way you can go on working there after what that man's done. And the brass who went along with him are just as bad. All of them need to be told to take their job and shove it. I wouldn't even give them so much as a day's notice. Just leave and let the entire compensation unit collapse under the flunky."

"Just leave, right, and give the bastard the satisfaction of knowing he finally ran me out."

"I wouldn't care about that. Let him celebrate. That's not important. It's about being able to work someplace where every day isn't a pitched battle with some fool. So I'd let him have his job. You want it that badly? Okay, you got it, I'd tell him. And you won't have any trouble finding something else. Halcon isn't the only company with an employee relations division. And every office isn't a battlefield. Nor is everybody out there a Davison . . ."

Stop, she tells herself, you've said enough. But she can't stop;

it's been held in too long. "Or you could do what you've wanted to for years: set up your own recruiting outfit like the guy in Chicago you used to talk about. You could go back home and do that. I'm sure you won't have any trouble getting a start-up grant, so you wouldn't have to use all your own money. And you'd make a go of it what with your experience, and as organized as you are. I know you would . . ."

For long minutes there's only the sound of the belligerent breathing from the archway. Twelve floors below, a battalion of fire trucks roars past. Headed for Dresden. The darkness that fell prematurely in the room is rapidly spreading over the sky outside the windows, draining away the last of the blue. Dusk both inside and outside now. Silence and dusk, until there's a sudden movement across the way; a long, scarcely visible arm reaches out, and a lamp at one end of the sofa comes on.

The swollen knot between his eyebrows. The eye of a hurricane. Her little trash house of twigs and dried mud clinging to the side of some mountain in Morlands is about to be swept to the four winds.

"And if I don't make a go of it, if I lose my fucking shirt, I can always go home and take over running Daddy's hotel, right?" Said quietly, in the reined-in voice he reserves for public places. "I've always got that to fall back on."

"Okay, forget I said anything."

"No, I'm afraid I can't forget, because we had an agreement, remember? Something about keeping our two cents worth of advice to ourselves. And you've just broken it. Which means I can also go ahead and say what's on my mind. And I'm saying that if my little project doesn't work out and I lose every penny I've got, I won't have to worry because I can always go into the hotel business. I've always got that to fall back on, right?"

"Your sarcasm notwithstanding, I still say you should quit and do what you really want to. It'll be taking a chance, and that can be scary, but you should do it anyway . . ." Fear. She knows all about it. She wasn't able to get up from her desk chair that last day at NCRC. Had to wheel herself in the chair over to the

typewriter to do the letter, afraid, terrified that if she stood up
her legs would give way permanently under her. Her fear then
as palpable as his now. She can feel and smell it across the glass-
topped table.

"You need to go on out there and try, Lowell."

"You're really back to telling me what to do, eh? All right, I'll
just go on speaking my mind too. And I've got a whole lot on
it. Been had for the longest time." The same deadly conversational
tone. "First off, since you're being so free with your advice again
seems to me you should treat the gentleman I just mentioned to
some of it. I'm talking about the gentleman with the hotel. Looks
like he could do with some too. Why not write and say look
here, Papa-daddy, you've been in that government job too long,
it's about time you gave up your seat and let somebody else try
to do something for your poor constituents. 'Cause *you's* tired,
Papa-daddy. You need to throw in the towel, resign, retire, quit.
Now that's some advice that's really needed, if you ask me. You'd
be doing Papa-daddy a big favor."

"What is this? How did the PM get into this?"

"How? Simple enough. I just thought that since you've started
counseling folks again that you might also want to include him.
Tell the truth, I'm surprised you haven't offered him your services
before, seeing how important he is to you. First comes him, then
the little island in the sun."

"What're you talking about? What're you getting at?" Puzzled,
Ursa feels herself peering across at him as if the lamp hasn't been
turned on and she's having trouble making him out in the darkness. "I haven't been near that place in four years."

"You don't have to go near it. Your head's there. You think
I don't know that? Oh, sure, your body's around. Habeas corpus.
We have the body, but that place and De Lawd—especially De
Lawd—have your head. He alone comes in for at least ninety-
five percent of your thoughts."

"Wha' the rass are you getting at?" She's on her feet. Bewildered,
wary. "Why are you bringing up the PM? This isn't about him.
We were discussing—"

"Everything's about him!" He too lunges up, the storm that has been sitting waiting between his eyebrows erupting. Over in the archway Mitchell also leaps to his feet with a confused bark and quickly disappears down the hallway.

"Everything's about him! I've changed the subject, haven't you noticed? We're talking now about De Lawd, and I'm saying that not only does he come in for the lion's share of your thoughts but that everything you do, everything you've ever done, is about him in one way or another . . ."

Her quitting her job, for a starter. It wasn't only that the cigarette and whiskey surveys had gotten to her. She was also trying to stand up to De Lawd. To stop always doing what pleased him. She'd never admit it, but that was behind it. The same with her going back to school again. What does she need with another master's? De Lawd. It's not only about a paper she never got to write because of some racist professor, it's about Papa-daddy as well. Another degree to make up to him for having left the job. To get back in his good graces again . . .

"What're you talking about? Where're you getting all this nonsense from?" Please. You're not telling me anything I don't know.

". . . And why haven't you been down to Sun Island in all this time?" he cried, the runaway voice fully in gear now. "What's the reason behind your staying away so long from that place? I've got a theory. Him again. Something happened the last time you were there, I bet, to open your eyes to De Lawd. It must have finally dawned on you that there's probably no real difference anymore between his so-called opposition party and the ratpack in charge. I suspect the truth came and stared you in the face that last trip, and you've been hiding from it ever since . . ."

"Fool! Idiot! I don't have to listen to this nonsense!"

And all the running down there she used to do before. Every time he looked, she was taking off for *the* island. Even when they first started going together. Making it clear that there wasn't anybody all that important up here to hang around for. There were times when he thought she might not come back. That she'd just decide to stay and not even bother telling anyone, except, of course, her alter ego in Brooklyn. And who was she running down there so often to see? Him again. De Lawd had only to crook a finger and she went running. He was the only one who really mattered to her. Even if there was something halfway positive about someone else, she wouldn't be able to see it. She didn't want, she didn't need, she couldn't see, she wasn't really interested in anybody else . . ."

"I don't want to hear it!"

". . . Maybe if I was more like De Lawd I would have had a chance . . ."

"I'm not going to listen to any more of this garbage!" Well, then, don't! Pick up the damn briefcase and leave! You never took the strap to your bag off your shoulder, so you don't have that to bother with. It's just a matter of bending down and picking up your briefcase from the floor. It's right there next to your foot. Pick it up, walk, don't run—don't give him the satisfaction of seeing you run—across this room, through the foyer and out the door. And leave the fool raving to himself.

For some reason she can't get her body to bend.

". . . Then there're all the goddamn letters!" The whirlwind voice hasn't once paused. Nearly every time he sees her it's "I just heard from the PM again," and he's subjected to yet another report on the great man's doings. Every time he turns around, another letter. She must have a mountain of them by now, because he knows she never throws not a one of them out. "In fact I wouldn't be surprised if you don't sleep with the latest ones under your pillow . . ."

Pick up the briefcase!

". . . You probably do. Maybe that's why I'm not allowed near the place. It's not that it's too small and messy, but that you don't want me to see all the letters tied in a pink ribbon up under your pillow . . ."

Idiot! If you must know, I keep them in the headboard, in their own private compartment!

". . . Never once been near the place, can you believe it. I've yet to put a foot in the door . . ." Suddenly, his anger is greater than ever. And more physically threatening. He seems about to reach across the low table and seize her by the throat. "Don't know what it looks like. Never been invited over for a meal. Never spent the night there. Don't know what your bed is like. I think about that. How's that supposed to make me feel? What's it saying to me? Hey, I don't mind seeing you every once in a while, but you really don't matter anymore. That's what it reads like to me. You control everything, where we fuck—because that's all it is now—where we sleep, you pay for you when we go out . . ."

" 'How're you going to pay the goddamn bills?' You said it, not me!"

". . . all because I once asked how you were going to support yourself free-lancing. Always pulling out your wallet before I can even get to mine. *Ms.* Independent. Except, of course, when it comes to De Lawd. He has only to whistle and you do a Mitchell. You're like that place you're from, you know that. Sun Island and all the places like it you're always criticizing. Independent in name only. Still taking orders from Big Daddy England, America or whoever. Still got that mind-set. Would be scared shitless to stand on their own if they could. That's you all over—"

"Idiot! Imbecile! Fool! Shut up! Are you any better? Shut the rass up!"

Suddenly, as if obeying her, his voice does drop and his eye, Lowell Carruther's eye, seems to turn slowly on himself. "Okay," he says after a long, troubled pause. "Okay. I have some of that too. I admit it. I'm too cautious. Not the type to jump out there and try something on my own unless I'm a hundred percent certain that it'll work. And that's a handicap. It really holds me back. I need to get some help with that . . . Then, things have gotten so bad for us, the mean streets have gotten so much meaner, I have to wonder if it's not too late for my little project to make a difference. I worry about that a lot. And that holds me back all the more . . .

"But your case is just as bad, if not worse, baby!" The hurricane force of his voice again. "You need to come out from under certain people. Quit letting them run your life by remote control. You need to say Stop! in the name of love. You need to . . ."

The storm rages on for the rest of the night, all during the following day and for another night again. That's the way it will seem to Ursa in the weeks to come. Worse, even when her paralysis finally lifts and she's able to bend over and pick up the briefcase and to walk without hurrying, without bolting, across the living room and out into the foyer, it feels to her as if she hasn't really moved. Somehow, she's still standing there helpless under the tidal wave of his voice.

Halfway across the foyer she suddenly stops, turns and takes a detour down the hallway that leads to the bathroom at the other end. On her way there and back she passes the shadowy lump that is the frightened dog. His low-level growl. His labored breathing. He's lying outside the door to the bedroom midway along the hall, his other sentry post whenever she sleeps over.

The hurricane continues in full force inside the living room.

And again, when she's back in the foyer on her way toward the door, with her toothbrush and shower cap and the sheer, lacy scrap of a thing she puts on when they're being kinky stuffed into the briefcase, there's still the odd feeling that she hasn't moved an inch from in front of the coffee table.

There's an explosion behind her as she reaches the door. Everything inside the living room—furniture, books, records, paintings, the collage of the midnight-black mother and child—has suddenly picked itself up and is hurtling out into the foyer, it sounds like. A hand grabs for her shoulder, her arm; she dodges and it encounters only the strap of the Ghurka shoulder bag; that's all his hand can find and he grabs that, holds onto that, while she tries pulling it away. There're his enraged cries, his curses, his panicked voice: "No, you don't! You don't just walk out of here like this . . . If you do, if you do . . . I'm warning you, Ursa . . . !" And the two of them tugging furiously at the bag as if it's a spoil they both came across while looting a store during a riot uptown. Until, finally, Ursa finds herself thrown completely off balance for a second. She sees the bruising hardwood floor come rushing up at her for a second as Lowell Carruthers abruptly lets go of the strap to the bag and the next moment, almost in tears, snatches open the door. "Get the fuck out!"

And strangely enough, even as he slams the door behind her and she heads toward the elevator, taking her time, still refusing to hurry although he can't see her; even as she reaches the elevator and rings for it, waits for it, and then takes it down the twelve stories when it comes, she's still standing, it seems to her, in the middle of the living room, listening against her will to the idiot's every word.

Downstairs, crossing the lobby, she struggles to arrange her face for Carlos at the door.

Outside, all of the azure is long gone from the day.

3

Never even got to mention that the study came through after all. Or to show, as proof, her copy of the contract in her briefcase. Never got to say she'd been spared, reprieved, and wouldn't have to be going anywhere but over to Jersey come the end of May. The bastard didn't even notice the way she was dressed or the briefcase in her hand! Did she usually turn up to go to dinner wearing a business suit and carrying a briefcase unless she was working? Shouldn't he have at least noticed that, no matter how upset he was? Her good news swallowed up by a frown the size of a fist as soon as she stepped in the goddamn door. Never mind, Ursa, never mind. It doesn't matter anymore. That was it. Fini. Your toothbrush and stuff out of his bathroom! What should have happened years ago finally happened. Stasis. Viney had been right that time. A relationship like a bad case of constipation. Going nowhere. Good riddance.

Ursa checks her speed, eases up on the gas and reminds herself that it's time to be on the lookout for the Midland City exit. It should be coming up in another mile or two. If she misses it, she'll find herself headed toward Paterson, the next exit on the turnpike.

She maneuvers the small Dodge Omni she's rented through the late-morning traffic over into the right lane on the highway.

Somehow, though, she'd always thought it would have happened in public, with what he had been waiting for years to say, all that venom, coming at her in a stage whisper across some restaurant table. Or even on the walk back up Columbus Avenue afterward, with her finally heeding Viney's voice in her ear and abruptly heading off in the opposite direction, leaving him haranguing the air. She'd be gone! Gone for good! Somehow she hadn't expected the showdown to come at his place, in that living room that looks like a display room of furniture on Macy's eighth floor. With her unable to bend down and pick up her briefcase! Standing rooted to the spot taking in every lunatic word! Acting as if she actually wanted to hear the nonsense, the garbage, the shit! What had come over her?

Worse, she still feels at times, although two weeks have passed, that she hasn't really left that room. She's still there on her side of the coffee table listening to him raving.

That'll pass. That too shall pass. Forget it. Just try to put all of it out of your mind, Ursa. You tried to be helpful and got a kick in the teeth for your trouble. The man took all his misery out on you. It happens. So forget it. What's important is that you're working again. You'll pay this courtesy call on His Honor today, try to set up one or two initial interviews with key people like Mae Ryland, and the work will have started. It's Monday morning and you're working again. And you mailed off the letter early last week: . . . *Will miss being there, but I'm afraid it's business first right now. I know you'll understand* . . . That's done. And you're looking good again. The old NCRC suits have more than held up. In fact, the hemline is back in style. Your briefcase is next to you on the seat, along with your birthday bag . . . Then on top of everything, there he was trying to tear apart the three-hundred-dollar Ghurka bag! Wouldn't let go of it! It's a wonder the fool didn't break off the strap! Forget it, Ursa. Put that man and his insanity out of your mind. Stasis. You should have walked long ago.

She has paid the toll and moved into the exit lane, and as she approaches the turnoff to the ramp and has to gear down, her left foot comes off the floor, her right hand drops, both of them groping, searching for a second, until she remembers: the Avis near her on Broadway had only automatics when she went there this morning. She misses the clutch and the gear stick. It feels good, though, to be driving again, instead of being at the mercy of the subway or some reckless, bad-tempered New York taxi driver.

The ramp takes her in a sweeping arc down into the southeast corner of Midland City, and into the same disheartening scene that greeted her every time she came over during the first study four years ago. It's exactly as she remembers it from then, the same no-man's-land of abandoned factories and warehouses and defunct railroad lines; the weed-choked vacant lots that have become garbage dumps and junkyards piled high with the ca-davers of cars waiting to be compacted and recycled. Crumbling buildings and decay everywhere. And hardly a soul in sight. Hardly a truck or a car besides hers to be seen. A ghost town. And to think this had once been the industrial heart and muscle of Midland City!

If she was to turn right and drive over the old buried freight lines, she would soon come to the first little tar-paper shotgun houses that mark the eastern boundary of the sprawling South Ward. Or simply the Ward, as everyone calls it. "All of Midland City is the Ward, if you ask me. 'Specially since the folks with the money done move to the suburbs. Oh, they come back every day to make some more money. Downtown is crawling with them from nine to five. But that's it. They won't let night catch them nowheres round here. Ain't nobody left then in Midland City but us Ward chickens."

Mae Ryland not mincing her words. She was their chief informant on the earlier study, as well as her personal guide, mentor, adviser, teacher, taskmaster and friend. Mae Ryland. It'll be good to see her again. And she knows where to find her. There's no need to even telephone. Mae's always in the same place.

The street she is on, Allen Street, which branches off from the foot of the ramp, leads into the business district a few miles away. There's almost no traffic at this end of Allen or for as far ahead as she can see, so that it's not long before she's within sight of downtown Midland City. The skyline is a mix of the old graystone office buildings left over from the time when the factories to the southeast were booming, and the newer rectangular towers of glass that was the only building being done when she was here before. Part of the revitalization of downtown. Mae Ryland used to speak her mind about that too. Ursa spies a number of giant cranes against the sky to the north of Allen Street. More of the towers going up.

The main post office appears on her right as she reaches the heart of downtown. The Municipal Court is a few blocks ahead on her left, past the Midland City Bank and Trust Company and the two largest department stores in the city. The streets here are filled with people and cars. Then, just beyond the court building and set back from the street by a cobblestoned circular driveway, stands City Hall, a five-story neo-Gothic affair of elaborate stonework, turrets, vaulted windows and gloom. It could pass for a cathedral or a castle. It always reminds Ursa of the battlemented, ivy-covered buildings on the Mt. H. campus.

Leaving her car in the visitors parking lot adjacent to the driveway, she climbs the wide, steep flight of steps leading to the great doors at the entrance.

". . . Useta be the only black face you ever saw in there was the janitor's. That's the way it was when I first came to Midland City, and still is just about. But we finally got ourselves somebody who's gonna do somethin' about that, who's gonna change up, shake up the complexion of the color guard down there, starting from the top down. There's gonna be a lot more black, beige and brown to be seen up in all white that's been there since forever, a lot more of us having a say in what goes on in this city from now on. But there's only one way we can do that. Only one way to guarantee that'll happen. I don't have to tell you what that is, but I'm gonna anyway. Each and every one of you in this room tonight's gonna have to get up off your rusty-dusty—yes, that's right, I'm speaking plain, you know me—and get on down to the polls come November eleventh. You know I'm gonna be there. Soon's they open the door my foot'll be in it. And who's gonna be there with me? Who else can I count on? Who'm I talking about besides Mae Ryland? Talking about me too, you say? Well, lemme hear it! Lemme hear it!" And the cry would go up from the packed auditorium, hall, community center, church or wherever, "Talking about me! Talking about me!" Mae Ryland priming the crowd, warming it up, getting it ready for Sandy Lawson, who would then take over with the smile that had the slight gap to it, a hand raised in the V sign and that stride, that glide, that walk of his that had nothing to do with anything as ordinary as walking.

She's early for her appointment, and while wandering through the cavernous halls of the building, killing time, Ursa thinks back to the phenomenon that was Sandy Lawson moving from one point in space to another. The way he negotiated the distance between his seat and the lectern once Mae Ryland introduced him. Or worked a crowd shaking hands. The way he entered a room. The light fantastic he did coming down a flight of stairs, his body angled back slightly like Viney's when she puts that hand on her hip. Sandy Lawson used to make Ursa think of old Sidney Poitier movies on television. Poitier's long legs would carry him across the screen with such speed, deftness and grace she used to imagine that the elements in the room or whatever the setting weren't even aware of his moving through them. His was a lean, mean, racehorse swiftness; there was both a tension and a flow to his body that said to the air, light and dust particles around him, Now you see me, now you don't; I done been here and gone.

Sometimes she used to watch his old movies just to see him walk the walk.

The stride that brings Sandy Lawson around his desk as his secretary ushers her into his office twenty minutes later has lost none of its speed, fluidity and grace. He reaches her in seconds across the large room, is shaking her hand, clasping it between both of his; is leaning his tall, compact frame down from its rarefied height to buss her lightly on the cheek, is smiling with the little irresistible gap there to the front of his mouth, is exclaiming, his voice enveloping hers, "Ursa Mackenzie, where you been hiding? what you been up to? thought you'd forgotten about us folks over here, come on in, come on in, we only got a few minutes but come and sit and let's talk. We got us a whole lot to talk about . . ." In the same breath he's telling her that she hasn't changed: "Still your fine, petite self . . ."/"Neither have you."/"Are you kidding? This is only a shadow of the Sandy you once knew. You looking at an old man, Ursa. This job's turned me into an old man. Got gray all in my hair since the last time you saw me. That's what mayoring does to you . . ." And all the while he's moving her, guiding her, a hand at her elbow, making her part of his swift yet unhurried ballet back across the room, and all without disturbing a single molecule of air or displacing a mote of dust.

Sandy Lawson.

She finds herself in a tufted wingbacked leather chair facing him across a massive desk. His suddenly familiar long-jawed face, his wide, sloping nose and the eyes with their quicksilver energy. His Honor, wearing a brown pin-striped suit and a tie that matches his ginger-colored skin and hair. The blue and yellow state flag hangs on its stand a few feet to his right, against the wall behind him. The Stars and Stripes topped by a bronze eagle is to his left. The two flags framing him. The great seal of the city, showing a blindfolded Justice holding her scepter and scale, is on the same wall directly above his head.

"*. . . Useta be the only black face you ever saw in there was the janitor's . . .*"

Mae Ryland's voice in her ear once again.

"What d'you know. Ursa Mackenzie." For a long moment Sandy Lawson sits quietly taking her in with the smile that reveals the inviting space between his front teeth. As if the phenomenon of his walk isn't enough, there's also that slight space, that gap. He was thirty-eight at the time of the campaign; that gap, though, with its tiny teardrop of flesh in the middle, made him look ten years younger each time he smiled. Mae Ryland worried about that, Ursa remembers.

"You're not going to believe this," he says, "but I called your name it couldn't have been more than two weeks ago. I had no idea I'd be seeing you, but your name just came to me. It had to be around the same time you were writing me about the new study. We must have a little mental telepathy going for us."

"Could be," she laughs. She is sitting all the way forward in the high-cushioned chair to make certain that her feet are resting squarely on the floor. You can't expect to be taken seriously if your feet are dangling just short of the floor. She learned that long ago. "What was the occasion?"

"I was down in your part of the world for a few days. You couldn't call it a vacation. This job doesn't come with vacation time, I've discovered. I was just snatching a little much-needed R and R. One thing I've learned since taking over down here is that everybody in Midland City has a problem and they believe only one person can solve it and that person happens to sit in this chair. I haven't had a day off since the swearing-in. And that includes Sundays. Somebody should've pulled my coat about what I was getting into. Anyway, I just had to get out from under for a few days. So I called in my mother to look after the kids, put everything here on hold, and Dot and I took off for the islands."

"Where'd you go?"

"Someplace called St. Martin. You ever been there?"

"No, but I know of it."

"Nice little place, although we didn't really get to see it. It's half French and half Dutch, and no bigger than a minute. It makes even Midland City look big. We stayed on the French side at one of these places that has everything right on the premises. You don't have to step out the gate the whole time you're there. Everything you could possibly want right there. It was just the kind of place I was looking for, because I didn't want to go anywhere, talk to anyone except Dot, read a newspaper, or hear the monster ring. Nothing. I just wanted to laze on the beach and turn the world off. Which is exactly what I did. And one day I'm stretched out with my piña colada when your name suddenly pops in my head. I remembered that you were from one of the islands. Your father's even in the government, I remember you telling me once. Is he still in?"

"Oh, yes, and ever shall be." Mailed the letter. That's done. Reprieved.

"Still going strong, eh? Maybe I need to talk to him. He might be able to give me some pointers on how to hold up under the pressure. Anyway, I couldn't think of the name of the place you were from."

She tells him.

"That's it, Triunion. Couldn't think of it at the time. And I turned to Dot and said Ursa Mackenzie, she's from down this way. I wonder what she's up to. Called your name and then as soon as I'm back in the office I find your letter on my desk.

"So . . ." He leans back behind the huge desk, spreads his hands. "So you folks are planning on running another study on us. I guess to see what's happened to Midland City since Miz Lawson's boy, Sandy, took over."

"Something like that. With your approval, hopefully."

"No problem. You've got it. I haven't forgotten how helpful you people were during the campaign. Besides, the study can't help but show how we're trying to turn this city around. So go right ahead. I'm all for it. You've got carte blanche to talk to anybody here in City Hall or any other city agency. I've got nothing to hide. Naturally, I don't have to tell you that you're going to run into all shades of opinion as to how I'm doing. There're some who'll rate me pretty high. Those're the folks who understand I've only really just come on the job and I'm not some kind of miracle worker. They're willing to be a little patient to see how I do. Thank God for them. Then there're the ones who've already decided that Sandy Lawson is the worst thing that ever happened to Midland City. And all of them don't happen to be white either. In fact, most of those giving me a hard time right now are Folks. So you're gonna hear a whole lot of bad-mouthing, especially over in the Ward. Some over there who were a hundred percent behind me, who were like family to me, don't even speak to me anymore . . ." His gaze shifts slightly. "Our friend Mae Ryland, for one."

"What?"

"I know," he says, his high energy, his almost exhausting enthusiasm suddenly collapsing. "I didn't think it could ever happen either."

". . . They don't know what to make of it downtown 'cause it's no big-money, fat-cat, party-run campaign. It's no slick, high-tech TV and radio campaign. It's strictly The People—with a capital T and capital P—of the South Ward's campaign. An I'm-tired-of-being-stepped-on, pushed-around-and-ignored campaign. An I'm-a-part-of–Midland City–too campaign. It's a door-to-door, let's-get-out-every-last-vote campaign. It's an I-want-to-see-more-than-just-the-janitor-looking-like-me-down-at–City Hall, as Mae Ryland says, campaign. It's a coalition-of-every-organization-in-the-Ward—thanks again to Mae Ryland—campaign and a coming-together-of-Black-Folks—with a capital B and F—from-all-over–Midland City campaign. So tell me, how is anybody gonna stop us? Ain' no way!"

"He's doing good," Mae Ryland leaned over to whisper to her. Instead of remaining on stage as she usually did after priming the crowd, she had come down to sit beside Ursa in the front row of the Elks hall, where the meeting was being held. "He's got a nice beat going. Got the preacher in him warmed up. And he's giving off enough electricity to light up between here and Paterson. He's doing all right."

"And don't forgot the smile," she whispered back. (One night at a long strategy meeting in Mae Ryland's storefront on Howard Street in the Ward, which had been their campaign headquarters, a tired Sandy Lawson had stood up, stretched his six-foot-plus frame, yawned, and smiled, and for a moment, looking up at him, Ursa had wondered what it would be like to fit just the tip of her tongue into the gap between those teeth to the front and to tease, play with, the tiny stalactite of flesh there. Had he read her thought? Caught a whiff of her lust? She could have sworn she saw his smile widen. Too bad, she had thought, that there was Dorothy Lawson to consider. And Lowell Carruthers.)

"Yeah, he got that smile working for him too. Onliest thing, he needs to be talking more about the issues, and I just wisht he looked a little older."

And she thought yes, the PM would probably consider Sandy Lawson "a small boy," someone who would be no cause for worry if he was running against him in Morlands.

Mae Ryland whispered back and forth to her in their seats up front; then as Sandy Lawson ended his speech and, amid the applause, held out a hand in her direction, calling for the Coalition Lady to join him, she had taken a few brisk Congo Jane steps over to the stage and climbed the stairs there to stand beside him—a chunky, solidly built woman of about sixty, with surprisingly small hands and feet, and wearing harlequin-framed glasses, support hose and her trademark: a blouse with a lace-trimmed ruffled jabot under the matronly suit she had on. Standing there a little winded from her swift walk, her hand joined and raised with Sandy Lawson's, and her glasses filled with every face in the hall. The applause had become deafening the moment she stood up, and someone who had been waiting for her to return to the stage started in with a tambourine. The joined hands held high, the voice of the crowd raised even higher, and the tambourine racing./Mother Ryland, the old people at the senior citizen center called her. Old enough, most of them, to be her mother or father, they nonetheless called her Mother. "Oh, oh, here come Mother Ryland. I wonder what she got for us poor old folks to do today?" She had come with more boxes of envelopes for them to stuff. "Put away the bingo for a while— you don't have no place to go to spend all that money you winning nohow—and come help me with these envelopes."/ "Where Miz Ryland at?" He came up to the door of the community center where Ursa, along with another member of the study team, stood waiting for Mae Ryland to arrive; a bean-pole he was, with the bill of his cap twisted around to one side of his head and wearing what looked like a pair of weighted space shoes with the lacings untied. He was one of Mae Ryland's grands. ("The Lord didn't see fit to give me no babies of my own but I got me more grands and great-grands than I can count. And they your grands too—" pointing with a small forefinger, the nail painted pink, at the audience she was warming up for Sandy Lawson one night. "Never mind what mess they might be into or how much stuff they on or how much you'd like to disown them sometime, they still all of us grands. Who else we got? So I'm looking for you to be down to the polls come November eleventh, cause it's ain't just Sandy you gon be voting for but all these grands out here look like they trying to do away with theirself and us too. Think about it." The finger reaching out to each and every forehead to press home the thought.) "Where Miz Ryland at?" He peered past Ursa down to the front of the community center where Sandy Lawson and his wife, Dorothy, stood amid a small crowd of early arrivals. Everyone waiting for Mae. When she told him that Mae Ryland had gone to bring over a group from the east end of the Ward, he had turned away. "I be back." Trudging back up the street in the sneakers that made him appear to be fighting weightlessness on the rock fields of the moon. Mae Ry-land was the only one who could get those like him to attend a meeting occasionally or to come in and operate the copier and other machines the Meade Rogers Foundation had purchased for the campaign headquarters. She had them handing out leaflets, serving as couriers, and driving the older people to meetings in the VW van that the foundation had also bought./Miz Ryland. Mother Ryland. The Coalition Lady. At the end of every meeting and rally she came and stood next to Sandy Lawson, and they held each other's hand high.

"You didn't know, did you, that I had her down here with me for a while." Sandy Lawson speaking in the suddenly subdued voice. There's both sadness and defensiveness in his face and voice.

"No, I hadn't heard." Shock and disbelief are still in her own voice, she knows, and probably all over her face as well. Be neutral, she reminds herself. You're supposed to be neutral and objective. Keep your feelings to yourself.

"Yes, she was down here for well over a year as liaison person for the Ward. Had her own office, secretary, a city car whenever she wanted it, an expense account, you name it. She was all set. It was one of the things I had decided to do as far back as the campaign."

"What happened?"

"That expressway behind you."

Because of the way he swept her across the office when she came in, she failed to notice the back wall. She quickly took in the rest of the room—the tall stately windows with their drapes, the polished brass chandeliers and the paneled walls to the side hung with any number of plaques, citations and photographs of Sandy Lawson shaking an array of hands, nearly all of them white. Everything seen at a rush as she was being escorted across the floor. But she missed the back wall and an artist's rendering of a six-lane expressway that confronts her now as she looks around the wing of her chair.

The drawing, complete with speeding cars, a landscaped median and a sky with a few peaceful clouds, takes up most of the wall.

"She was against it from the get-go," Sandy Lawson says. "There was no need for it, according to her. Although people can hardly get downtown to work because every road is practically gridlocked, she didn't see the need for it. It was being built for the white folks out in the suburbs. Well, let's face it, those folks just happen to be our biggest tax base right now. And without some taxes coming in we can't hope to do anything for anybody. Besides, with the expressway we'll stand a better chance of attracting more business. I'm about getting this city moving again, putting us on the map. I'm tired of people saying when you mention Midland City, Oh, you mean that *town* not far from Paterson. She refused to see the logic of that. She didn't want to hear about priorities. I should put the expressway on hold. There were more important things to be done. Giving orders. You know how Mae loves to give orders. Then when she found out we were going to have to route it through part of the Ward, that really did it. It's a wonder you didn't hear the fireworks all the way over in New York."

"When did all this happen?" Her voice is as it should be: neutral, objective, calm.

"Early last year. The day the council voted for it was the day she left." Sandy Lawson spreads his hands resignedly. "The problem with Mae when she was down here was that she only thought about the Ward, everything was still the Ward, and everybody was to think that way too. She couldn't understand that you're dealing with an entire city when you're sitting behind this desk, and that sometimes you have to—"

The phone rings with the muted sound of a cricket chirping. Sandy Lawson picks it up, listens, utters a terse "Okay, thanks," and before he puts it down he has already recovered much of his characteristic enthusiasm. He smiles apologetically across at her. "The folks I'm having lunch with are on their way over." He's on his feet. For a second or two he stands motionless between the flags and under the great seal; then in single fluid movement he is around his desk and taking her elbow as she also rises. There's a reprise of the walk that's more than just walking back over to the door. The leave-taking comes in a rush on the way there. "I haven't said my last word on Mae and that expressway. We need to have a much longer session so I can really explain my position on it. And once that's out of the way I'm taking you to lunch"—the smile again, with the gap and its tiny teardrop —"a lunch just to eat. No heavy talk. I don't know the last time I've done that. One thing I've learned about white folks since taking this job is that they don't eat. Not the ones I have to deal with anyway. They never sit down just to grease and make a little small talk. They always got some agenda to go with the meal. Now that you'll be around again, we have to get together every so often for a lunch that's strictly about food and chitchat. That's if you don't turn ag'in' me too after Mae Ryland and the folks in the Ward get through bad-mouthing me."

The smile becoming shadowed once more as he ushers her out.

Back in the car Ursa sits with one hand on the key, which she has managed to put in the ignition. Her other hand is on the steering wheel, her foot is poised above the gas pedal, but she's unable to complete the motions needed to start the engine. Her gaze is on one of the new rectangular towers north of Allen Street, a building completely sheathed in mirror glass. The midday sky is reflected there in flawless detail.

It has rained off and on for the past two days—April showers in mid-May—and although this morning saw the end of the rain, the sky hasn't cleared completely. There's a thin, pale cloud cover like a drop scrim on a stage, and behind it the sun is a washed-out yellow disk, its light a diffused glare. The glass walls of the building are a diorama of the overcast sky. That sky has trailed her all the way from West 101st Street this morning, trying to forewarn her. Why does she always fail to notice the signs?

As she sits there immobilized—paralyzed for the second time

in two weeks!—Sandy Lawson's car with his official seal on the fenders back and front pulls up in the driveway. Minutes later, he appears at the top of the high, wide steps fronting City Hall. He's accompanied, she sees, by two men whose white faces and dark suits look almost interchangeable from where she sits in the parking lot.

They move in close formation down the steps, the two men —one on either side of Sandy Lawson—crowded in on him, almost shouldering him between them. And both of them are talking to him at once. His head is turning from one to the other, back and forth repeatedly like someone at a tennis match. There's his smile. And then all three of them are laughing.

They keep to the same formation as they enter the limousine. The man who was on his right on the steps enters first, Sandy Lawson follows, and the other man climbs in behind him. The chauffeur closes the door, and the three disappear behind the car's dark-tinted windows.

Only after the car itself disappears in the noon traffic is Ursa finally able to turn the key in the ignition and put her foot on the gas.

4

Sent For You Yesterday, Here You Come Today reads the familiar sign on the door of the storefront at 3790 Howard Street, the South Ward. Closed. But Will Be Back Soon is on the reverse side of the sign, Ursa knows. On the plate glass window to the right of the door can be seen the faded remains of a painted-on barbershop pole. That's also familiar. Mae Ryland's husband had cut hair for over thirty years behind that window. After his death, when the store became the headquarters for just about every grass-roots organization in the Ward, his widow had left the striped pole on the window with Jack Ryland's name and the words "owner and proprietor" printed under it. She had also kept his red-leather-and-chrome barber's chair jacked all the way up over by the window, so that everyone passing could see it sitting there like a throne.

And there *she* is—Miz Ryland, Mother Ryland, the Coalition Lady. Peering through the glass panel of the door, Ursa finds her where she had expected her to be, in her old swivel chair, behind her gnawed-looking, overflowing desk in the middle of the room. Two girls are seated beside the desk, one of them holding a baby, and Mae Ryland, her head bent, is busy filling in a long official form. There she sits, intact, wearing a white blouse with a lace-trimmed ruffled jabot unfurled like a pair of butterfly wings down the front. The same small neat hands, pink-tipped. The dark face with the high cheekbones and wide nose looking not a day older than it did two, three centuries ago or will look the next time it manifests itself. The chunky body not having gained or lost a pound since the last time Ursa saw her. And there's the familiar chain on her glasses—like the pull chain on a lamp—to keep them around her neck when she takes them off. The only thing different are the glasses themselves. She's exchanged her old harlequins for a pair with frames that are attached to the bottom of the lens, so that the glasses look as if they're being worn upside down.

Mae Ryland. She looks up as the door opens, peers forward, frowns and becomes very still; then: "Wait a minute . . ." Taking off the upside-down glasses. "Wait a minute . . ." Putting down the pen in her hand. "Is that who I think it is? That can't be who I think it is standing in my door . . ."/"Yes, it is."/"Ursa Mackenzie?"/"In the flesh."/Another instant of disbelief before Mae Ryland is on her feet, around the desk, and hurrying toward her, exclaiming, already fussing with her, "Sent for you yesterday and here you come today. Late! Our folks just *will* be late! Come on in here!"

The arms gather her into the ruffled folds of the blouse and into the faint, suddenly familiar smell of talcum powder and the Dixie Peach she uses on her hair. Mae Ryland wants to know how she's been, what she's been up to, and how come she's back in Midland City. She's scolding her for being out of touch for so long. She's telling her like Sandy Lawson that she hasn't changed and then in the next breath declaring that she has. "Looks to me like you growed some. And I see you still got your braid." Embracing her again. Exclaiming over her again.

The greeting goes on for some time, before Mae Ryland finally leads her over to the desk. There, she introduces her to the two girls. One of them, wearing a maternity top and drinking a soda through a straw stuck in a quart container, says "Hi" without removing the straw from her mouth. The other, the smaller, darker and younger-looking of the two—perhaps fourteen to the larger girl's sixteen—is holding the baby. Mae Ryland even introduces the baby, who is fussing. Its small testy cry was the first sound Ursa heard as she opened the door. "And this little fella doing all the complaining is Mr. Michael Lamar Wilson."

Bustling about, Mae Ryland opens a metal folding chair, places it across from her desk, settles Ursa in it, then excuses herself: "Be with you soon's I finish helping Miss Wilson fill out this here paper."

Seated back at her desk she takes up her pen again.

The office, the old campaign headquarters, the former barbershop looks larger than Ursa remembers it. Perhaps because it's empty; nothing's there aside from the barber's chair over by the window, Mae's cluttered desk, a few folding chairs and rusted file cabinets, and an office-size refrigerator at the back of the store. Where's all the equipment from the campaign—the typewriters and mimeograph machine, the Addressograph, and the computer and copier that the foundation supplied? She glances up at the transom above the door, which held the old air-conditioner that leaked on you as you entered. Even that's gone. A square of warped plywood covers the hole. Lord, they must have ripped off Mae! Gone too are the blowups of Sandy Lawson that had covered the walls and filled the window. His smile. That irresistible cleft to the front . . .

If possible, she would take back the momentary lust she felt that night when he had stood up—right in this very room—and stretched, yawned, and smiled.

The sound of the fretting baby.

Dee Dee, she thinks. The girl holding it doesn't look that much older than little Dee Dee. She even has her hair done up in beads like Dee Dee's. And the baby, bundled in a sweater set and a not-too-clean receiving blanket, couldn't be more than a month old.

Filling out the form is going slowly, mainly because of the girl. Every time Mae Ryland turns to her with a question—"They want to know where you lived at before you moved over to Vanderbilt Street?"—the girl seems to have to rouse herself and travel a great distance before she answers, before she's even able to hear what's being asked of her. With each question there's the same long journey. And each time Mae Ryland takes down her glasses and patiently waits for her to arrive.

The baby's colicky little cry fills the room, along with the sound of the other girl sucking on the straw she never removes from her mouth. Super Big Gulp is printed on the oversize container she has propped on her high stomach. Soursop juice, it looks like through the clear plastic straw. Whatever the girl's drinking—Seven-Up or Mountain Dew—looks just like the almost colorless soursop juice she used to love when she was small . . . Or like what had looked to be frozen grapefruit juice in the two vials Viney had shown her in the refrigerator freezer that time. "The closest you can get to an immaculate conception," she had said . . . At her checkup down on West Fifty-eighth Street last month, they told her everything was fine. There was no need for her to come back. Why, then, does she find herself still wondering whether they actually did anything? Why does she continue to feel at times that whatever it is, is still there? . . . As a parting shot she should have told him about the trip downtown back in March, and let him really have a seizure. Ursa, forget him. Past history. Lowell Carruthers is past history.

The fussing continues until finally Mae Ryland puts down her

pen, pushes back from her desk, and, reaching over, gently takes
the baby from the girl and places it on her lap. With fingers made
for picking the tiniest bit of lint off a wool skirt or dress, she
unwraps the blanket, unbuttons the sweater, unties and slips off
the little cap. Talking to him as she does: "Mama, you should
have said when she was dressing you to bring you over here, I
don't need all these clothes. It's almost summer out here and
here you got me all hot and mis'rable in all these clothes . . ."
Cupping the small head in her equally small hand, she dabs the
perspiration from his face with a tissue from a box on her desk.
The face has yet to turn as dark as the rim of his ears or the
cuticles of his tiny nails. With a fresh tissue she wipes the hair
that has not yet turned nappy.

"Now that should end all this fussing."

But it doesn't, and as the fretful cry persists, Mae Ryland
suddenly bends closer to the small skewered face, as though
alerted to something she missed before. She's listening intently
now and watching the twitching, the little Saint Vitus' dance the
limbs can be seen performing now that the blanket is off. A
stillness comes over her, a stillness so wide it seems to reach out
and silence everything for miles around, except the loud intermittent sucking on the straw. Then, loosely wrapping the blanket
around the baby again, covering up the dancing limbs, she hands
him back to the girl.

She scarcely seems aware that he has been placed in her arms
again.

*The woman on King William Street had lifted the cloth from over
the sickly baby only long enough for them to glimpse the sores covering
its face, and then had held out her hand.*

The scene four years ago superimposed suddenly on Mae Ryland's office, the baby and the girl. She's seeing double again.
It's always happening to her.

When the form is completed and the two girls and the baby
leave, Mae Ryland doesn't turn to her for some time. She's forgotten she's there, it seems. Still holding the pen, Mae sits with

her gaze on the door, looking at it through the top of her bifocals. She asked them when they were leaving to turn around the sign and to release the catch on the slam lock. And for a long time she sits gazing across at the locked door.

There's the wide wide silence again.

Until finally she takes off the upside-down glasses—just lets them fall on their chain down to the ruffles and lace covering her chest—and she slowly turns to Ursa. Her altered face. All her sixty-odd years, as well as the years of her several other lifetimes, are suddenly visible on her face.

"Tell me somethin' good."

Ursa spreads her hands. All she can offer is the emptiness of her short hands with their stubby fingers.

"You over here fixin' to do another study, I bet."

She nods, and for a moment wants to take herself, her little Ghurka bag, briefcase and NCRC suit out of there.

It's Mae Ryland's turn to spread her hands. Hers in comparison are almost dainty, the nails done in a shade of pink you'd expect to find next to skin that is all peaches-and-cream. They offer Ursa the sight of the stripped room, herself behind the cluttered, dog-eared desk, and the two empty chairs the girls have vacated.

"Well, here we are, all o' us, right where you left us. And in my case right *back* where you left me. 'Cause if you had come year before last this time you wouldna found me here. I was over on Allen Street, I'll have you know, in that building look like a church—you know the one—hanging out with all the big shots there."

"I heard," Ursa says. "I just came from over there and Sandy told me."

"Oh, you shoulda seen me!" Mae Ryland exclaims, a mocking brightness taking over her voice. "Had me this office with a rug on the floor, pretty pictures on the walls and my name and title on the door: Mrs. Mae Ryland, Liaison—whatever that means—Officer, Community Relations, the South Ward. Had me a brand-new desk and one of them phones with all kinds of buttons and holds and flashing lights on it, and a ring sound just like a cricket. Had this nice little white girl at my beck and call. My secretary. Even had a city car I could use whenever I wanted. Oh, I was somethin'! All I can say is I'm sorry you didn't get to see me in all my glory."

"I am too," she says. "You should still be there, Mae."

"Well, I'm sure Hizzoner told you why I'm not. The little disagreement we had. Tell me, does he still have up that picture in his office? The one that takes up damn near a whole wall?"

"Yes, it's still there."

"It's a pretty road, ain't it? When it's done, certain folks'll be able to zip in and out of downtown without having to so much as glance at the rest of Midland City. And you saw where he's running part of it, didn't you? I know you had to, being as you had to cross DeSalles and Marion—or where they used to be—to get here."

"Yes, I saw it."

On her way over to Howard Street, she suddenly found herself on an overpass that hadn't been there four years ago, and when she pulled over and got out of the car to look over the guardrail, there was this trench, this long, wide, deep trench where DeSalles, Marion and the streets on either side of them had once been. Below she saw an array of heavy earth-moving equipment and men in hard hats at work. Only one or two black faces among them. This section of the expressway was still just a raw gash in the earth. It had yet to become the picture on the wall.

Triunion! Triunion all over again! While she was still in high school, the P and D Board had completely rebuilt the road between the airport and town, turning it into a highway for the benefit of the tourists and the would-be money people, with a section that bypassed Armory Hill altogether, and that had cost a fortune. Where am I? Which place? What country? Is there no escaping that island? . . . She stood for the longest time on the overpass above what had once been DeSalles and Marion streets, putting the questions to herself.

"The day they voted for that road was the day I relocated back to 3790 Howard Street, the South Ward," Mae Ryland is saying.

Then abruptly she's on her feet. "Before I get started on Sandy Lawson and his road I'm gonna feed us," she says. "I know you need a little nourishment after what you been through this morning, and I always got enough for company. Besides, my hypo is telling me it's time to eat again."

Ursa suddenly remembers: Mae Ryland's hypoglycemia, and the small frequent meals she eats to combat the weakness and fatigue that will overtake her should her blood sugar drop. "People would pass by the store and see me stretched out like I was dead in that barber's chair," she once told her. "Just too tired to even move. Or I'd be sleep. I really knew somethin' was wrong then, 'cause I'm not somebody to be taking no nap during the day. And then I'd get the blues so bad. And I'm not someone to be down all the time. Didn't know what was wrong till I went to this doctor told me to cut out pork, sugar and fried everything and to eat mainly rabbit food. Which is exactly what I did, hard as it was. I still can't lose no weight even with the rabbit food, but I feels so much better."

She goes to the small refrigerator in back and in a few minutes a meal and two paper plates appear in a hastily cleared space on the desk. There's an already prepared salad in a saran-wrapped bowl, thin slices of turkey breast, dark sprouted bread and a bottled dressing that reads No Oil on the label. And there's tea—dandelion tea/How could I have forgotten the dandelion tea?/—being brewed in a hotpot on the desk.

Dessert will be a large Winesap apple that sits waiting on a paper towel. A knife to cut it in two lies next to it.

"Now, if you had come year before last I coulda treated you to lunch in one of them fancy restaurants downtown, 'cause I also had me an expense account. You'd have eaten in style. Now you have to settle for hypo food."

"It's a feast," Ursa says, and getting up she goes over and embraces Mae Ryland again.

* * *

"Useta be I couldn't swallow my food if I happened to think of that road while I was eatin'. Nothing would go down. But I'm getting better. I can talk about it now and still eat."

The hands made for picking off near invisible bits of lint, for undoing impossible knots in a thread, fashion an open-faced sandwich with a slice of tomato, turkey and a slice of the dark bread. A large paper napkin tucked into the neck of the blouse protects the fall of lace-trimmed ruffles.

"To think that the onliest thing Sandy Lawson has done so far for the South Ward—the place that put him where he is— is to run a road through us like we ain't even here. Oh, that thing hurts me. 'It's a question of priorities.' Just listen at him! After folks that never went near a poll in their lives was running to vote for him—'Going to vote for Sandy'; 'Miz Ryland say vote for Sandy'—he turns around and sends in the bulldozers on us. And when we got out there to try and stop them they started dragging us off to jail right and left. It was the sixties all over again."

"But why didn't they put it on the other side of Allen where the new office buildings are going up? That would seem the logical place for it."

"To me too. That's if they needed it in the first place. But no. They went and brought in some big-time consultants and according to them it would cost the city less to run it through part of the Ward. So before we knew it they was throwing peoples out of their houses and DeSalles and Marion and those other streets was gone.

"I don't know," Mae Ryland says and pauses. She slowly chews on a piece of cucumber from the small salad she's served herself. "Seems like the minute he took his hand off that Bible at the swearing-in, Sandy Lawson got to thinking different. Or maybe that's the way he thought all along but knew better than to come out with it before. Or maybe he right away started letting the white folks downtown do his thinking for him. I don't know.

That city manager they got down there—what you need a city manager for if you got a mayor?—and the folks run the banks and the chamber of commerce 'n' such. The ones always going out to lunch with him. In no time he got to acting like some simpleminded woman a man can sweet-talk into throwing open her legs before she knows what's she getting into. Just started letting those folks mess with his mind . . ."

Plainsclothesmen! Ursa suddenly thinks. The two men crowding Sandy Lawson as he came down the steps and talking all up in his face, who had then seated themselves on either side of him in the limousine, had looked like plainsclothesmen. It suddenly comes to her that that's what they were like.

". . . They've got him down there thinking he can turn little Midland City into Paterson or New York. And the collar-and-tie black folks don't want nothing to do with us in the Ward are also tight with him. Never gave a dime to his campaign but they're all around him now. They was pushing for that road as much as the white folks 'cause they out there in the suburbs too."

She puts down her cup of dandelion tea and her hands open out again. "So that's how it went down. After all the time and hard work peoples over here put in—I wasn't the onliest one—and after all the help you all at that foundation gave us, that's how it went down. The folks been running Midland City since forever still running it and they got Sandy Lawson going along with their program, listening to them with his head going every which-a-whar. You remember my which-a-whar story?"/"I remember."/"The one about the colored station conductor?/ "Yes."/"Poor fella was too old to be still calling the trains. Well, one day so many trains was coming in and out of the station, just flying in and out, he couldn't keep up with 'em. His old gray head was turning every direction at once. 'Traaains going east, traaains going west, traaains going south, train train traaains going *ever' which-a-whar*!' You remember that one, don'tcha?" She didn't hear Ursa before.

"I remember," she repeats. Mae Ryland used to tell it about the black candidate handpicked by downtown to run against

Sandy Lawson. It was one of the stories she would use to warm up the crowd before he came on.

"Well, they got Sandy like that old station conductor, head going ever' which-a-whar, thinking he's the one building that road and the one gonna be putting up this big convention center that's next on the agenda. A picture of that'll be going up in his office soon, taking up another wall. And how much you wanna bet they'll be tearing down some more of the Ward to build it."

"He didn't tell me about that."

"Course he didn't. Too 'shame of hisself. And they got rid of the troublemaker. She's back on Howard Street and good riddance. That city manager and those other white folks on the council couldn't stand the sight of me down there. But they don't know who they playing with. I'm like the Vietcong back in the war. Remember how they useta do? No, you was too young."

"No, I wasn't. I remember."

"Well, then, you know how they wouldn't come out and fight fair and square. They'd just lay up in the jungle hiding till they saw their chance and then *whoomp*! Oh, that used to get to the generals. They talked about those Vietcong somethin' terrible. Called them cowards. Said they wouldn't stand and fight like men. Called them sneaky. Called them gooks. Well, I'm a gook. Just laying low over here in the jungle for a while. Trying to get my strength back after the hurtin' Sandy Lawson and his friends downtown put on me. I be back, though. Don't have no choice. 'Cause things in the Ward are worse than ever. I don't know if you could see it driving over here, but it's a fact."

"I saw it."

Dresden, she said to herself and then immediately changed it to Beirut. On her way to rent the car this morning she passed a newsstand on Broadway and saw a picture on the front of the *Times* of a bombed-out section in Beirut. So that when she entered the South Ward she found herself thinking "Beirut." Beirut as she drove past the run-down or burned-out frame and shingle houses and the walk-ups leaning and sinking in on themselves, past the boarded-up stores and the idle men holding up the sagging walls. And more men waiting on certain corners; and boys in space sneakers, their caps turned to the back or side of their heads, waiting also. The women and girls waiting. *". . . Anything you head desire, darlin' . . ." Whispers from the sagaboys in their dark shades limning out on King William Street, in front of Conlin and Finch and the banks.* There seemed to be more decayed and gutted houses and stores this time, more waiting men and boys, women and girls, more broken glass and debris, garbage and stray dogs everywhere, and more children playing amid it all under the glare-filled sky that trailed her from New York trying to warn her. Beirut. And Armory Hill along the old abandoned section of the main road. Driving over to Howard Street an hour ago, there was no separating the landscapes that filled her mind.

"But I be back," Mae Ryland is repeating. " 'Cause it ain't about Sandy Lawson got his head all turned around. It ain't even about Mae Ryland, 'cause she's about ready to join the bingo game over to the senior center. I don't have to tell you who it's about."

"No."

"You see the grand just left outta here? The one with the baby? Well, she's the third one been in here this week with some form to fill out so's she can get her a little somethin' and can't make head or tail of it. And the other grand pulling on that straw'll be back here shortly for me to do the same for her . . ." A pause; her gaze travels back to the door. "Some of 'em come in here you can't hardly tell which one's the mother, which one the baby. Or which one's more strung out than the other . . . They shouldna never let her take that baby out the hospital so soon."

A longer pause this time during which her gaze leaves the door to slowly pan the room. "Then there's the ones that broke in here one night and cleaned me out."

"I was going to ask you what happened."

"The grands," she says simply. "They took everything but what little you see here. Woulda even taken that barber chair if it hadn't been bolted down. I never had that to happen before. I useta could go out and leave the door unlocked. Just turn around the sign and not bother locking up, 'cause the word was you's not to steal from Miz Ryland. You's not to touch nothing belonging to her. That's finished now. These little great-grands coming along don't care who or what you are when they need money for the stuff. Will stomp and rob their own mother look like. Don't care nothing about their ownself, don't care nothing about you."

"The woods are on fire." Viney's voice comes to her.

"Where you get that old down-home saying?" Mae Ryland asks, surprised.

"A sister/friend of mine," she says. "Her grandfather in Virginia used to say it all the time."

"Well, never was a truer word. Fire. It's raging out here."

Mae Ryland falls silent, and for a time sits staring down into her cup as if reading the tea leaves. She has finished the sandwich and the small salad. Silent, until her head slowly comes up. "I take back what I said just now about Sandy Lawson," she says quietly. "It's about him too. 'Cause he was once one of my grands. I was to his graduation there at Rutgers. Saw him get that law degree and cried I was so proud. Was to his wedding when he married Dot. And was there when both their babies was baptized. And not to say I'm taking the credit, but I'm the one helped him build up his practice. When folks would come in here with a problem needed a lawyer, I'd send 'em to Sandy. So I just can't dump him like that. I don't even know as I'm all that angry with him. I'm disappointed in him. I'm disgusted with him. I'm ashamed of him. I could take that Lady Justice seal in his office and go upside his head with it. But I don't know as I'm ready to give up on him yet. Sometimes you have to try and work with what's there. Try to see what's good in the person and work with that. 'Try to find a little good in everybody even if it takes a spyglass to make it out,' Jack Ryland used to say. 'And if you can't find nothing even with the spyglass just make up somethin' good about 'em.'

"So I keep telling folks here in the Ward, keep telling myself, maybe we ought not to give up on Sandy Lawson just yet, even with the hurtin' thing of that road. Maybe we need to let him run with it awhile till he sees for himself what those folks downtown are up to. He's young. Maybe he can learn . . . But if we find he can't learn and keeps on doing like he's doing"—her tone has suddenly changed; her face has tightened—"if we see he just ain't no *use* no kinda way, we'll vote his little gap-toothed self outta there the same way we voted him in, and find us another grand. And if that one don't do right neither, we'll vote his butt out too, and just keep on till we find us the right one. The right one's got to be out there somewheres . . ."

"Tell me somethin' good . . ." This time with a smile. They have shared the apple by now and have talked about the study. Mae Ryland, her mood brightening, has teased her, saying she would cooperate only if certain conditions were met. Teasing but also being serious. "That foundation you work for will have to fix up this office, first thing. Get me some typewriters, desks 'n' such in here again, and a nice computer and copier like before, and a security gate front and back to keep out the great-grands. And I need me a air-conditioner right away—and one that don't pee on you as you walk in the door."

Ursa laughed. "No problem, Mae. They'll do it. We'll have even more funds to work with this time."

"Oh, yeah!" Mae Ryland's eyes narrowed. Then, with an edge of bitterness: "Tell the truth, what these foundations 'n' such need to do is give me the money they be spending on all these studies. That's right. Just hand over the millions to Mae Ryland. I'd show 'em what to do with them. First thing, I'd throw up a real heavy security gate, like you see on the liquor stores, around the whole of the South Ward. Not a dealer would be able to get near the place. Then I'd get to work inside. More detox, more rehab, more outreach and job training than you could shake a stick at. More housing, clinics, schools, factories, day care . . . You name it. I'd have me a regular Marshall Plan going on in here, like this country had for Germany and them other places in Europe to build them up after World War Two. And I'd bring in Ursa Mackenzie to work with me. That's right." A solemn nod in her direction. "It'd be a better job than what she's got now. Oh, I don't mean no offense, baby," she added quickly. "I know you out here trying to do a little somethin' that's about somethin' till we can get to the real work. And that's what I mean to do: give you some *real* work! Yeah, these foundations oughta get some sense in their heads and hand over the big bucks to Mae Ryland. Let somebody who knows what needs doing TCB."

That said, she has then turned to Ursa with a sudden smile: "Tell me somethin' good. You married yet?"

Caught off guard, Ursa laughs nervously. She hears her little nervous laugh. "No. I haven't gotten around to that yet. If ever."

"You ain't shacking up with anybody, is you?"

"Mae! It's not called that anymore."

"Do tell! I still calls it that. Is you?"

"No, I haven't gotten around to that either."

"I ask 'cause that's all you hear about nowadays. Just 'cause the white folks are doing it we got to run behind them and do it too. Useta be only our folks—the ones couldn't do no better—lived common-law. Now it's the style. It's got so you can't tell who's following who anymore, whether it's the white folks running behind us in everything or we running behind them."

Then, in her abrupt way: "What about that fella you was going with when you was over here before?"

That's finished and done with and good riddance is what she should say. That's what's on the tip of her tongue to say, yet she hesitates, can't manage it.

"Don't want to talk about him, eh? All right. I only asked," Mae Ryland says, " 'cause I wouldn't like to think that any of these mens out here was messing over you. After all, you's one of my grands too."

* * *

"I see you still got your little accent," she says. "You slips into it every once in a while." They're on their way across the room. They've set a tentative date for the next meeting, and Mae Ryland is seeing her to the door.

"How's your family in the islands doing?"

She hesitates again, thinking of the letter that should have arrived by now. Oh, God! He might not write for months! Then: "Fine. I haven't heard from them for a while, but I'm sure they're fine."

Saying this as Mae Ryland turns around the Sent For You Yesterday sign and unlocks the door.

5

. . . The elections, the elections, *oui*! that's all the talk these days, never mind everybody knows it's gon be the same old *histoire* all over again—Celestine going on to herself as usual. Every time you turn on the radio, that's all you hearing. That's all you seeing on the television when the news comes on. And all of them— they could be DNP, NPP or Independent—they all promising you the sun, moon and stars. *Seigneur!* How they can lie so? Is a wonder You don't strike down every last one of them, save the PM. Is only the PM that talks straight to the people. He's doing his best, he tells them. He's still trying after all these years to improve conditions in the district. And he's gon keep on trying, but they know what he's up against with the thieves and Do-Nothings that's been in charge all this time. He stands out at the monument and talks to them straight. And the people know he's speaking the truth. They trust him. He's Mis-Mack's boychild, after all, born right there in Morlands, near where the old market used to be. But the rest of them? *Mes amis!* They're just putting on a big show to get your vote.

And the one putting on the biggest show of all is this Mr. Justin Beaufils who calls himself running in Morlands. You don' know how he could feel himself so powerful as to put his name up against the PM's. Some little schoolteacher fella, his father came from up Gran' Morne as a boy. But every time you look he's holding a meeting or printing up a paper criticizing the PM and giving it out all over the district. And he has the brass face, *oui*, to send a copy of the papers all the way to town, right here to the house to make sure the PM sees them. One came last month asking when's the last time you saw the Honorable Member of the House for Morlands? When's the last time he set foot in the North District? No respect! And another one came this month calling for a debate. He wanted the PM to come and debate with him up at the monument. He even had it print up big in the newspaper for everybody all over the island to see. Is the first time we ever hear about a debate in Triunion. "The schoolteacher fella must think he's running for the White House, Celestine. He's been watching too much television from the States." That's what he said when he read the paper, and he take and throw it to one side. He don't have the foolish boy and his papers to study. But not so with the *blanche neg'*. Ever since this Mr. Justin declared himself, she's made it her business to find out everything about him. What I don't know to tell her she gets from people in the district when they come to town and stop by the office. You have to ask why she's concerning herself with him, some little ringtail boy who don't have no better sense than to run for the PM seat. "Since you're so interested I'm going to arrange for you to meet the gentleman." He was right to tell her! "Oh, good, because I just might vote for him if I like what he has to say. That way the poor man can at least say he got one vote." She talks to him any way she feels to . . . Wants to know the boy's life history now! Why, you have to ask. One thing I know about him: he was one in the gang of little fowl-yard children she used to let come in the yard to play with 'ti-Ursa when she was small. That's who he is. She don't remember his face, but I do. And if my memory serves me right he's the one that pelt the rockstone at the gate that time when the PM came home and found them all over the place and ran them out. When I told her that she laughed and said no, that this Mr. Justin is one of my *'ti-garçons* from years back, but I don' want to claim him now 'cause he's running against the PM. Teasing me, *oui*, always teasing me. "You need to laugh more, Celestine. You're too solemn." That's all I hear from her . . . But I believe he's the same wicked little boy that pelt the stone that time. Who would think he would've amounted to anything, an upstart who don' know his place. But his father worked day and night at the sugar mill in Morlands to send him to school in town and he get to be a schoolteacher and then the government sent him to teach in Spanish Bay. He was down there teaching for a good few years before he decide to move back to Morlands. He and the wife. Some woman he went and find in Spanish Bay. She's in everything with him, I hear. She was to some big school in Cuba, they say, and feels herself to be as powerful as him. Is the two of them standing up to speak at a meeting, *oui*, and she has as much to say as him. Is the two of them writing all these papers against the PM and printing them up on some machine they got from America. I wonder how they would run the machine if the PM hadn't kept after the Do-Nothings for years to put in current up there. *Les ingrats!* And is the two of them driving all over the district in a piece-a old car giving out the papers. They's in everything together, this Mr. Justin and the wife he went and find in Spanish Bay. And they got a few hotheads that believe as they do backing them up. Not only in Morlands but in some the other districts too. All of them calling themself Independents and wanting to change up everything one time. *Mes amis!* They gon have the *Woody Wilson* pulling in here again ready to rain fire on us, like what almost happened years back. And this time it would be worse, 'cause they've changed up the guns on it. The *blanche neg'* told me it now has some missile somethin' on it that's a hundred times worse than the guns. *O ciel eternel*, it could be finish with Triunion!

"What to do with the schoolteacher fella, Celestine?" He was laughing. This time a letter had come to the house. This Mr. Justin wrote to tell the PM he should come and join in with him. Give up his seat in the House, leave the P and D Board and join in with him. *The brass face!* "You say I had to run him from the yard when he was small, Celestine? Well, it looks like I'm going to have to do the same thing again." The PM's not taking him on, *oui*, 'cause he knows people in Morlands have better sense than to listen to some hothead. I hear that scarcely anybody comes to the meetings he holds, and they say that as soon as he gives somebody one of his papers criticizing the PM, they take and tear it up right to his face! Serve him right! The PM just throws his to one side for the *blanche neg'* to read and goes on about his business. He has more important things on his mind than some small boy who all of a sudden feels himself so powerful. There's the government big resort scheme. Every day he's down to the P and D Board helping out with that. That thing don't give him a moment's rest. On top of that he has to be in the House and in court back and forth. And there's Mile Trees to see to. Not a moment's rest. And he has his child on his mind. *Tête chargé*, *oui*, 'cause she sent a letter here the other week saying she won't be coming down for the elections as she promised. She just start a big job and she can't leave just now. He was glad to hear about the job, but he's upset all the same that she won't be here. Four years, *oui*, and she hasn't set foot near Triunion. You don' know what's keeping her away. As regular as she used to come before. Now, it's like she don't want nothing to do with the place. Oh, that thing hurts her father. All he writes to her, she won't come. It must be some man that has her so she can't leave him not even to come and see her own father. I know the PM wun like to hear that. Or maybe it's the States. If you ask me, that's what it is. Living up there all these years has changed her, *oui*! Has turned her from us. Is true! I saw it happening from when she was in high school and would come home for her long holidays. I could see all the way back then she was changing. It's the *blanche neg*'s fault! She sent the child to live up there when she was too young. She's to blame! She was always in a hurry to send her away. *Seigneur!* Is a wonder You don't strike her down too! And now hear her! When the letter came from 'ti-Ursa, the PM said he was gon write and tell her to come down if only for the weekend of the election itself, but the *blanche neg*' told him no, not to write, not to call. I heard her with my own ears. "Just let the woman be, Primus. Let her live her life. She'll come when she's good and ready. There must be something she's trying to work out in her mind about us or this place or whatever. Who knows? She'll come when that's done. I know her. Besides, it doesn't make any sense to spend all that money for her to come just for a weekend . . ." *Mes amis!* The woman acts like she don't care whether or not she sees her own child! And the only one she ever brought into this world! An unnatural mother, *oui*! What else can you call her?

All these years, all these years, and there's still no understanding the *blanche neg*'.

6

"... The resort scheme! The government's big kiss-muh-ass resort scheme! That's the only thing he talks about these days. He
don't have Mile Trees to study anymore. He could lose the place
tomorrow and he wouldn't care. You hear what I'm saying, Malvern? He could lose Mile Trees tomorrow-self! and it wouldn't
matter to him. All because of the friggin' resort scheme!"

The angry flush beneath the cream-colored skin, and her outrage, resentment and fear. Since her last visit to Armory Hill
three months ago Astral Forde has tried holding them in. She
has sought to relieve their pressure on her spirit by heaping abuse
on the heads of the maids, the cook, the yardboys. She has gone
to sleep each night with them stampeding through her dreams
like the two horses he used to whisper about in bed years ago

—the trampling, the screams of the young mare, the blood in the yard of the house at Morlands—and she has awakened to them each morning. The outrage, resentment and fear. Until finally this evening, unable to keep them penned up any longer, she stripped off the neat skirt and blouse she wears as manager, threw on one of the nice-nice dresses from Conlin and Finch she seldom has occasion to wear, telephoned for a taxi and when it came and deposited her at the foot of Armory Hill she climbed past the fowl yard and hellhole at the bottom of the hill that has gotten more dangerous over the years—more gun, more knife, more bare murder; more ganja and worse. Triunion coming like Jamaica these days. And the disgrace known as Armory Hill has grown larger, the scab of scrap houses and shacks having spread in recent years to within sight of Fort Lord Nelson.

She climbed in the nice pair of shoes up the rutted path to Malvern's house, her flashlight in hand, the stampeding in her head and her back turned to the darkened vista behind her: Cannon Beach in the near distance, where she went walking out with the footballer she'd met at the dance that time, only to have the brute tear the nice new dress half off her. Long years ago; she seldom thinks of it anymore. And to the right of the beach, past the old fortifications, she could have seen, had she looked, the lights of the deepwater harbor the P and D Board got the government to build. And out in the harbor were the even brighter lights of a cruise ship, two or three freighters and the refurbished *Woody Wilson* with its Tomahawk cruise missiles in place of the old 16-inch guns.

The *Woody Wilson* will remain in port until the elections are over.

Seething, Astral Forde didn't so much as glance over her shoulder on the climb up. Her eye remained on the lookout for Malvern's small house on the upper ridge. It is one of the few houses on Armory Hill that has current. And the moment the door opened to her knock and she stepped inside, it was as if a corral gate had burst open.

"... Every word out his mouth is the resort scheme! That

comes before everything nowadays. I tell you, if I had the will of the banks and the big people from Canada and America who're partners in this thing I'd have them decide not to bother with it and take their money and leave. The whole thing cancel and I'd never have to hear another word about it again in this life!"

She sits back in her chair. Fleshy thighs and hips crowding the seat under her. A congested face framed by the wealth of Spanish Bay hair.

"They had it on the television the other day." Malvern. "They was stopping people in town and asking them what they think about the resort scheme. Some was for it, but a good few they asked was against it, saying there's too many hotels in the place as it is, and what we need with anything that's gon be almost the size of Fort Lord Nelson."

Malvern's voice is barely audible, and it takes her a long, painful time to utter the words. And she herself is barely recognizable. Malvern who used to be all restless energy, who would be on her feet doing a carnival jump-up and keening *voilà* at a choice piece of news, is nothing more now than a near skeleton with dull, lifeless eyes and ashen skin, a body bag of bones covered in a cotton shift and laid out on a Barcalounger that is reclined as far back as it will go.

She's been sick for well over a year.

"In and out of the hospital all the time. They cutting and cutting, they giving me different treatments and all kinda medicines and I'm still ailing. And all the medicines do is make me sleep. They like they don't know what it is wrong with me or they not saying," she had said in disgust to Astral Forde the last time the latter came to visit. "But I've made up my mind about one thing: I'm not letting them put the knife to me again."

"I'm tired of the government horse-pital," she complained to her husband during her last stay there, and the bus driver fella, who had been a dispatcher for some years now, signed her out, brought her home and put their youngest child, a girl of twelve named Grace, to look after her. To give her the bedpan and the pills and to bathe what is left of her.

(Tonight, as soon as Astral Forde entered the house, Malvern sent Grace out of the sitting room, out of the big people talk.)

"The same with the bed," Malvern also complained. "I'm tired of it morning, noon and night." And her husband wrote to the older children, nearly all of whom had emigrated to the States, and they sent down the Barcalounger. Just as over the years they had sent the color television Malvern keeps at the foot of the recliner, the stereo console nearby and money for a suite of up-holstered living-room furniture to replace the cushionless sofa and chairs. Everything crammed into the small sitting room. The wedding picture with the round-faced groom has been moved to the top of the stereo. The wax anthuriums in their vase are gone.

"One man they asked was against it 'cause he said is the gov-ernment gon lose out and not the banks or the people from Away if the resort scheme don't work. They had it right on the television—"

"It's not only the government gon lose out!" Astral Forde cries before Malvern finishes bringing out the last slow word. "It's all those *in* government that're putting money in the thing that're going to lose out too. And Primus Mackenzie is one of them. Instead of him adding on to Mile Trees like I been begging him to do for years, he's planning to put money in something that don't even exist. That's the thing that has me so vex."

"Is true." The slurred, feeble voice from the recliner. The sunken eyes. "He should've add on to Mile Trees long ago and made it into something big."

"The P and D Board is to blame!" An even angrier outburst. "That and the bogus election years back. He was all set to do it when they stole the election and he was so down his mind turned from everything. And then when he joined the P and D Board and they started building new airport, new highway, new deep-water harbor, one big thing after another, all that was more important to him than Mile Trees. That's the way it's been for years. And now with the blasted resort, it's worse yet. He don't care nothing at all about Mile Trees anymore. He wants to be up with the white people in this big multimillion-dollar thing. To hear him, you'd think he's in charge of everything concerning it. The thing has put out his head. And he's running about now trying to borrow money for his share in it. Running. All the time running. Killing himself. You should see him, Malvern. The resort scheme has heaped years on his head. The worries have tired him out, licked him down. He needs to go away someplace and rest. If the so-called wife cared anything about him she'd see to it he had a rest. I know if he was somebody belonging to me that's what I'd do. But what she care so long as he keeps her in the swell house on Garrison Row . . . Running. He stops by Mile Trees and he's rushing off again in no time. And as for having anything to do with me? Don't ask. I couldn't tell you the last time." Angry hurt like cream that has clotted and turned sour beneath the near white skin. "And even when he does come holding onto me he's no use anymore. The worries. And he's not lingering. His clothes are back on as soon as he's done, and he's on his way home to the little dough-off wife. Like he can't wait nowadays to get home to her."

Malvern can barely lift her hand in a philosophical wave. "That's the way it is. When they start to give out they run looking for the wife again. They make the best of husbands then."

"And what about the beautiful-ugly daughter? What you hear concerning her?" A flicker of the old hunger for news stirs in her drugged gaze. "Is a good few years she hasn't been down on a visit. I can't remember the last time you telling me she was here."

"How you could forget that?" Astral Forde looks at her in disbelief. Actually looks at and sees Malvern. Because from the time she entered the house, already raging as she stepped in the door, she has been blind to everything except her own sense of injury, her own outrage. Now, though, for a moment, her eyes clear long enough for her to actually see her friend: *Oh, God, Malvern's looking bad, in truth. She's gone down down to nothing.* Then, because the thought that follows is too frightening, the thought of no Malvern, her gaze quickly becomes blind and self-absorbed again.

"Four years," she says. "It'll be four years this August since she was here last. That's the time she came with this friend of hers I told you about, the one like a long drink of water, and the friend's little boy, a force-ripe little man who had to have his say in everything. It was the first time she ever brought anybody with her on a visit. Don't you remember me telling you that the three of them came over to Mile Trees and how she and the friend was strolling about the place and lying out on the beach laughing and talking. No man. I has yet to see her bring a man down here."

"True? I wonder why? You would think she woulda married long before this. Some rich fella up in the States or the father would've found some big shot for her here."

"But what's wrong with you?" the old impatience with Malvern flaring up. "Don't you know that the man ain't born yet that's good enough for the great Mistress Ursa! If you ask me, he wouldn't care if she never marries. All the same, it's funny: I has yet to see her with a man-friend. She only came down that last time with this woman, this tall something in a pair of sunglasses that took up half her face. For all you know, they might be two good wickers you see them there. The wick of the lamp might be all they care about. The only thing to satisfy them. They might not have any uses for a man."

Malvern manages another philosophical wave with her bony hand. "What to do? Is the modern times. Everybody doing as they feel to and saying to hell with whoever don't like it. And who's to say, maybe those women God made so have the right idea. At least they don't wake up one morning and find themself saddled with a head of children draining every ounce of their strength and their life gone. That's one thing you can say for them."

Astral Forde shrugs. "Bare bare wickers, the two of them, if you ask me. And if you had seen how friendly they was being with me that day. Kept trying to get me in a conversation and to come and have a drink with them, never mind Mistress Ursa will think nothing of putting me out in the road the day she decides to leave America and come back to take over Mile Trees . . ." It's an old obsession, an old dread. "And she's another worry on him. He don't say nothing, he keeps her name to himself as always, but I know it grieves him that she don't seem to want to come near the place anymore."

"Is only natural that it would grieve him," Malvern says. "After all, it's his only child. All these years and you still don't seem to understand that."

"The government resort scheme and the great Mistress Ursa!" Her eyes are completely engulfed. "Those are the only two things on his mind. And it's like the resort scheme means more to him right now than her even. Take yesterday. He stopped by all excited to tell me they gon be printing up some prospectus something that will tell all about it. They're to decide in the next day or two where they're gon build Mr. Resort, and as soon as they know that they'll print up this prospectus. And the minute it's ready he's gon bring me a copy to read. Who the rass tell him I want to read about that thing! Who, I ask you! The minute he leaves, I'm gon chuck it in the trash. I tell you, if I had the will of the banks and the big people from Canada and America . . ."

After a time the sedated Malvern dozes off, although her eyes remain partly open. Two thin, dull-yellow crescent moons beneath her lowered lids.

Meanwhile, the voice beside her stampedes on.

7

Hélas, hélas, hélas! She wouldn't even open it! The PM came and set it down next to her plate before he sat to the table, and she wouldn't so much as open it. Wouldn't touch it, *oui!* this book that tells all about the resort scheme. Wouldn't even look at it. You would think the PM had come and put some nastiness a dog had left in the road down in front of her. And after all the trouble he had getting the thing for her, 'cause the public is not to know about it until after the elections next week. The P and D Board are gon keep it secret till then because of the bad-minded people that are against it. But he managed to get a copy for her to read. And I know she sat there at the table refusing to look at it. "Don't worry, I'm going to read it, and from cover to cover, but right now I want you to tell me where they've decided to build it." That's the only thing she wanted to know. He must tell her that first off. And when he said for her to look in the book, that it was there—you could see he didn't want to tell her himself—she refused. He even gave her the page number where it was. "No, I'm not looking in the damn thing. I want you to tell me." The woman talks to him any way she feels to. "Where, Primus? Just tell me where they're putting it?" Well, she kept on persecuting him till he had to tell her. And then *mes amis*! it was like the *Woody Wilson* had fired one the missiles it's got now into the dining room. She was in a high high state! *Tête chargé.* The news came as a shock to me too, but she was like somebody out of their head. All the PM tried to explain that he wasn't the one behind it and it was the others who had decided, and that maybe, who knows, it might even be a good thing for Morlands—all he's saying she's not listening. She's calling him and the P and D Board and the government and the white people that encouraging them in this thing all kinda names. Oh, she performed! 'Buse-ing everybody right and left. I never heard so many bad words in my life. You have to ask what fowl yard in America she came out of. And the PM's not doing or saying anything to stop her. I don't understand it, *oui*! He lets her say whatever she pleases about his affairs. Is almost like he wants to hear her *bêtise.* Then all of a sudden she stopped and just sat there staring off. Staring far far off like she did that time when she took the man's child and his car and drove to the airport in the middle of the night, and when we got there she was parked near the runway —*Seigneur!*—and staring far far off. She had the same look for the longest time yesterday. Till she finally came to herself. "Celestine!" Calling me. I must come and take away her plate. She hadn't touched the food on it, but I must take it away. Starting up that again. You don't know how long it'll be now before she eats more than a mouthful of food for the day. The well of her neck will be deep enough to hold water. Her arms will get like two yellow sticks. *Toujours une histoire!* Always upsetting herself. The woman could be happy if she would just leave off the man's affairs. But no, she has to have her say about everything concerning him. And it's not that she doesn't have her own affairs. She's high high now on the Arts Council. Yet she has to be in his business too. Always getting on like she's a Congo Jane marching next to him with a cutlass and gun. The *blanche neg*! A cross, *oui*. She's been nothing but a cross from the day she set foot in Triunion.

8

After nearly a hundred city blocks—at least five miles—the man is still muttering foully at her in his language. He's sending the taxi hurtling down the last stretch of Canal Street toward the bridge, and still cursing her under his breath.

Go ahead, bitch all you like, speed all you like, Ursa exhorts him, clinging to the strap by the backseat window, her eyes closed. Make like you're at the Indy 500. That's exactly what I want you to do. Because I know you're not about to kill yourself too. You can't be that stupid. So go ahead. See if you can't go even faster. Put wings on this thing if you can. I'll get there all the sooner.

"Oh, God, Viney," she had said over the phone. "I'll be right over! I'll get a cab and be right there!"

"Not going Brooklyn." A heavy Eastern European accent and an unpronounceable name on the lighted ID card on the dashboard. And the look the man had given her as he turned and saw her face through the Plexiglas screen. That's what had greeted her twenty minutes ago when she climbed into his cab at the corner of 101st Street and Broadway and announced her destination. "Not going Brooklyn." He had refused to budge from the corner.

They're scarcely off the goddamn plane from Transylvania or wherever before they know who they're going to let ride in their cab and where they will and won't go. "Look," she had said, "you are required by law to drive me anywhere in this city I want to go once I'm in your vehicle, and that includes all of the five boroughs. So you can either take me to the address I've given you or we can go to the nearest police station and have it out there. Either one, but I'm not getting out of this cab."

Who was it the actor Godfrey Cambridge the one who dropped dead on the set in Hollywood a while back heart attack the papers said who used to try running them down when they refused to stop for him? Would throw his black self up on the hood if they happened to stop for a light and try clawing his way through the windshield. Playing tackle with New York's yellow cabs. That's enough to give anybody a heart attack sooner or later . . .

She thinks of Godfrey Cambridge whenever she has a run-in with some taxi driver.

"I don't know what your immigration status is, but if you break the laws in this country you'll find yourself deported in no time. I've already taken down your name and ID number to give to the authorities, so that if you don't want to find yourself on a plane back to darkest Europe you better drive me to where I want to go." Trying to make her voice sound like a gun she had pressed up against the back of his head.

Something ugly in his language had come back at her through the speak holes in the Plexiglas. Then the man was slamming his foot on the gas, the cab was bounding forward, and she grabbed for the strap and closed her eyes.

And she has kept them closed all during the breakneck ride down through the city. The chaos of the careening taxi joined to Viney's distraught voice in her ear.

Oh, God!

They've reached the bridge, she can tell. There's the high metallic hum of the tires on the steel roadway and the echo of the giant cables reverberating overhead. There's the dark plangent voice of the river below.

For less than a minute she hears the sounds above the turmoil in her head; then they're gone, and the taxi is roaring through the streets of downtown Brooklyn. The muttering up front continues unabated. A dime. That's all you'll be getting, buddy. After paying her fare, she always leaves a tip of one thin dime in the slot when they've been particularly nasty. A dime, or better yet ten pennies if she has them. Viney worries that someday one of them is going to jump out his cab and attack her. Once, another Slavic type had shouted nigger bitch after her. She had had to laugh: the man could hardly pronounce either word. Yet another had hurled the dime at her retreating back. This City. Fun City. The Big Rotten Apple. Home.

Oh, Viney!—the greater part of her mind remains on the stricken voice on the phone telling her about Robeson. Robeson! How could something like this have happened to Robeson?

———

They hold each other for a long time in the entryway under the high stoop, where the sign on the wall reads V. Daniels and Son. Unable to speak, they simply hold each other, their silence part of the silent stone out of which the house is built and the night silence beyond the basement gate that Viney has just closed and locked behind her. Standing there with their arms around each other until Viney steps back, reveals her tear-swollen face, her stricken eyes, says, "He's upstairs. He finally dropped off to sleep a little while ago. I had to give him a sleeping pill."

They enter the basement hallway and in silence start the climb up to the bedrooms on the third floor. Viney, wearing the long denim skirt that is part of her at-home outfit, climbs slowly, her tall frame slanted forward. She looks almost bent over with age. Another thirty, even forty years might have been added to her thirty-seven since Ursa last saw her.

"Dee Dee's with him," the bent figure says as they reach the parlor floor. "He asked if she could come and spend the night."

Robeson's room is the first one off the landing on the third floor, right next to the bathroom and at the back of the house. His door is partly open. On it hangs the copy of an old theater poster showing his namesake as a scowling Emperor Jones. Like Napoleon, the actor has one hand thrust inside the tunic of his uniform and his lower lip is curled all the way down, just like Robeson's when he can't have his way.

Inside the room Dee Dee is awake in the slide-out half of Robeson's trundle bed. As they enter she turns from the television. She's watching a ball game being played out on the West Coast, where it's still daylight. Those eyes of hers that appear to be on twenty-four-hour guard duty beneath her beaded hair. Red and green beads against the black twigs of hair. She orders them to be quiet with a finger to her lips. She herself has turned off the sound on the TV and is silently calling the plays on her own.

A few feet away Robeson sleeps curled up on the main section of the bed. He is lying more on his stomach than on his side, and he has burrowed his face deep into the pillow. Ursa can make out only a small portion of it as she goes and leans over him and places her hand lightly on his head. A nostril, a closed eyelid, one corner of his mouth and a cheek the color of the coffee from up Gran' Morne are all that's visible in the light from the TV screen. And these look surprisingly untouched. She had somehow expected to find bruises, welts, a wound that might perhaps never heal; or at least the skin at his wrists scraped away by the handcuffs, exposing the raw flesh. Some outward and visible sign of his ordeal that would have sent her rushing out into the streets to commit mayhem. Instead, he appears unscathed; simply asleep in his bed, in his department store, which is what she calls his room. She likes to tease him that she knows where to come to do her shopping. Everything in his room is a floor model of what's in stock down in the cellar, she tells him—his desk, books and the set of Junior Encyclopedia, his Apple PC and printer, his home science lab, his math games, erector sets and the model spacecraft he and Viney assembled together; his large aquarium of tropical fish, which is still lighted up, and next to it the collection of shells he brought back from the beach at Government Lands, mounted in a glass display case; his baseball gloves and bat, tennis racket and his lacrosse stick from the junior team he's on at school; there's the complete set of Corgi cars and the Lionel trains that were his passion for a time, the shelf of dog-eared stuffed animals—Pluto, Pooh-Bear, Babar and the others—that used to trail around with him when he was small; another shelf of dolls, chocolate-colored boy and girl dolls Viney had encouraged him to play with, along with the dollhouse she gave him as a Christmas present when he was three, which was large enough for him to crawl into back then. A room like a department store.

He sleeps surrounded by it all, his face burrowed in the pillow.

Ursa remains with her hand resting lightly on him for some time.

"He hasn't slept like that, curled up and on his stomach like that, since he was a baby," Viney says on their way back downstairs.

He was arrested that afternoon on his way home from day camp. School for him had ended the first week in May and until it was time for the sleep-away computer camp, Viney had put him in day camp, the one at his school. And on his way to take the bus home that afternoon, he was seen attempting to break into a number of cars parked along Hicks Street in Brooklyn Heights, according to the arresting officer; and when questioned he was uncooperative, full of back talk, insolent. Moreover, he refused to be searched and became so belligerent—again, according to the officer—that he had to be forcibly restrained and taken to headquarters.

". . . Threw him into the patrol car, Ursa! Took him in hand-cuffs to the police station! And had him there for over an hour before they even let him call me! Just kept him sitting there in handcuffs like some hardened criminal!"

They are on the sofa in the second floor living room, and Viney is struggling to be more coherent than she was earlier on the phone. Hers was the only voice on the machine when Ursa came in. She had gone to dinner with the members of the research team for the Midland City study, and when she got home around ten o'clock there was Viney's distraught, scarcely coherent voice on the tape saying "Ursa, Ursa, where are you? Why aren't you ever there when I need you? Call me, please call me. It's about Robeson. They arrested Robeson!"

The flutter kick jarring her heart, she dialed Brooklyn and stood listening to Viney telling her some impossible tale about Robeson caught trying to steal, Robeson in handcuffs, Robeson at the police station . . . and minutes later she went rushing over to Broadway in search of a cab.

"This cop swore he saw him trying the doors on all the cars along the block to see if any of them were open. And that he had what looked like a knife he was using to jimmy the locks . . ."

"What! What knife? That's a lie! Didn't Robeson tell him he was just playing a game?"

He calls it his odometer game. Viney calls it dawdling. On his way from school or when she sends him to the store, he some-times plays his odometer game. He'll see a car parked at the curb and will try to guess how many miles it has on it from the condition it's in, and how old or recent a model it is. Then to see how close he's come to being right, he'll look inside at the odometer. If he's way off and there're far more miles than he had judged, he'll make up the difference by imagining all the places the car's traveled to on vacation: Disneyland, the Grand Canyon, Marine World in Florida, the Kennedy Space Center. He sometimes plays the game with all the cars on a block.

"Of course he told him. But do you think that cop believed him? All he saw was some black kid looking in a row of cars when there was nobody much around, and right away he thought, 'Got him! Got me one! Little nigger trying to steal somebody's tape deck to buy drugs.' Robeson said he was yelling at him before he even got out of the patrol car. Jumping all over him before he could say a word. He tried telling him he wasn't doing anything, that he was on his way from day camp at his school, told him which school, and that he was just playing a game. Even tried explaining the game to him, but he said the fool was so busy yelling and calling him a thief he didn't hear."

"Oh, God, and if I know Robeson, he started yelling too."

"He had a right to!" Viney cries. Her voice quickly drops, though. "Naturally, that only made the so-and-so all the more angry. Some smart-alecky black kid up in his face telling him it's a free country and there's no law against looking inside a car, that he has his constitutional rights—which is what Robeson said he told him. Some little minority in sixty-dollar sneakers and a twenty-dollar Izod sports shirt who says he goes to the Belfield School and who looks and sounds like he just might, standing there giving him word for word. Sassing some flatfoot who's probably up to his eyeballs in mortgage payments and bills out in Queens and can only afford to send his kids to Catholic school, if that. Can you imagine what was going through that man's mind, Ursa? *Do you realize what could have happened?*

"Ursa, I'm talking to you!"

"Don't say it." She wants to run from the look on Viney's face and from the scene inside her own mind: Robeson, that lower lip curled all the way down, his shoulders slanted back like his mother's when she puts that hand on her hip, and his voice raised to an angry white man with a gun. *Oh, God.*

"Don't say it."

But Viney does: "He could have killed him, Ursa. That cracker could have blown my child away. He could've sworn he saw him reaching for this knife he was supposed to be using to jimmy the locks or that he had started to run, resisting arrest, or he had tried grabbing his gun when he went to search him—anything —and blown him away!

"It happens, Ursa!" Screaming it at her as if she doesn't know. "You read about it, you see it on the news. It still happens in this city, in this country. Are you listening to me? It could have happened!"

Once again, there are no words. All Ursa can do is to move close to her on the sofa and to hold her as she did that night in the pool at the Parkview years ago, when she saw the river on Viney's face and felt her hurt and despair over Willis Jenkins like weights on her ankles, threatening to pull them both under. All she can do is to hold as much of her as she can with her abbreviated arms. And to sway with her. Because after a while, without being conscious of it, Viney begins the slight swaying that overtakes her whenever she's upset, that transforms her into an elderly Mother of the Church moanin' low in her pew up front.

It's a long time before she speaks again.

"I couldn't tell you how I got from work over to that police station. I must have taken a taxi, but I could just as well have run all the way from Manhattan my heart was pounding so when I got there. I can't tell you the state I was in. And by the time I arrived they had changed their story from the one Robeson had told me on the phone. The precinct captain realized he had trouble on his hands, so they were saying then that Officer Pirelli—that's the animal's name; you should have seen him, some Neanderthal type—hadn't really arrested him . . ."

"You put handcuffs on a nine-year-old, you throw him in a patrol car, you haul him off to the police station, and it's not an arrest. Wha' the rass do you call it?"

"That's what I wanted to know. But no, all of a sudden it hadn't been anything that serious. The only reason Officer Pirelli had brought him in was to give him a little scare so that *if* he had been up to something he wouldn't try it again. That's all it had been. Not really an arrest. No harm meant. No harm done. Just giving him a little scare.

"And oh, God, did they ever succeed! If you had only seen Robeson when I got to the station." The stricken, choked-off voice again. "He was terrified. I've never seen such terror in his eyes. And he'd been crying so hard before I got there the tears had left long white streaks down his face. And he couldn't stop shaking. Even when I got him home and he had calmed down some, he'd all of a sudden start shaking again. And the fear wouldn't leave his eyes. Even when Dee Dee came over and they were watching the game together, there it was again—the fear. And it's still there, Ursa. If you had raised his eyelid when we were upstairs just now you would have seen it for yourself. . . ."

"It'll go away, Viney. He'll get over it."

"You think so?" Said wistfully; then she's shaking her head. "Me, I'm not so sure. Something like this could mark him for life. I'm sure of one thing, though"—and the mouth that calls to mind the curled striated petal of a hibiscus suddenly tightens; a drawstring running through Viney's full lips might've been pulled tight, gathering them into a set, grim line—"Pirelli is out of a job. If it's the last thing I do I'm going to see to that. I'm not settling for him to be demoted or disciplined or transferred to Central Harlem as punishment. Or for him to undergo sensitivity training on how to deal with black folks. He's to go to court, stand trial and lose his job. He's to join our folks down at the unemployment insurance office and see what that feels like."

"Have you spoken to Harold?"

(Harold, her lawyer and a former boyfriend in the years before Willis Jenkins.)

"You know I did. I called him from the station, and I talked with him again when we got home. He says it's a clear case of unlawful arrest and the abuse and intimidation of a minor. Robe-

son and I are going to see him in the morning. And I also called
Sharon. She was out of town at a conference, but I spoke with
Margaret, who's going to have her call me as soon as she's back."

(Sharon, a friend of theirs from college who's a child psy-
chologist. And Margaret, who has been Sharon's lover ever since
their junior year. The two were regulars at the soul table in the
dining hall.)

"You have to go with us to see Harold tomorrow, Ursa. I
know you're working again, but you have to go with us."

"You know I will."

"He says that one of his partners is close to the police commissioner, so he's going to bring him in on the case. Pirelli doesn't
know what he's in for. I'm going to pull every string, use every
contact, spend every penny I've got to see to it that that animal
never wears a policeman's uniform in this city again!"

Viney jumps up, and for the rest of their time in the living
room she alternates between pacing the floor and sitting next to
Ursa on the sofa. She'll sit talking for a while, and then as if an
invisible hand suddenly yanks her to her feet she's up and pacing
again, the Swedish clogs she wears at home keeping time on the
parquet floor to her voice. Sometimes it's the voice on the answering machine—high-pitched, distraught, almost incoherent.
Then it'll drop and sound close to normal. There're even periods
when it's silenced; when Viney just comes and sits and says
nothing. Simply sits, swaying lightly, gazing off. Then, abruptly,
she's up again, back and forth across the room, raging: ". . . Does
that humanoid know how hard I'm trying with this child? What
it takes for me to keep this show on the road for his sake!? The
mess I have to put up with at Metropolitan, a company that
wouldn't even sell insurance to black folks years ago. We couldn't
even buy a little fifty-cents-a-week policy. And some of those
white coworkers of mine still can't stand the fact that I'm a vice
president. Does he know how often I want to pull your
number"—she comes to an abrupt halt for a moment, turns and
faces Ursa—"and just walk, *resigning as of this moment*, but know
that I can't . . ."

* * *

". . . I should've kept him riding the school bus and this wouldn't have happened." She is sitting down this time and her voice is calmer. "I shouldn't have listened to him last year when he said he was old enough to take the city bus. I should've gone on paying the money and had him picked up at the door and brought back to the door each day."

"Stop blaming yourself, Viney."

She doesn't hear her.

Nor does she hear her minutes later when she asks, "Did Robeson say if anybody saw what happened? You're going to have to have a witness."

She has to repeat the question. Finally a nod. "We might have one. He said a woman came out of her house when he was being thrown into the patrol car and asked what was going on. She must have seen everything from her window. We'll have to find her. But she was the only one who bothered. He said the other people who passed by didn't so much as say a word. They didn't even stop. Can you believe that?" Her voice rising again.

It's Ursa's turn to nod.

"They see some hulk yelling at a kid, roughing him up, putting him in handcuffs, and they don't stop to ask what's up? They just assumed like Pirelli that he was out to steal something. Those people could have seen Robeson blown away, Ursa, and not said or done a thing! When I think of that—"

Viney's abruptly on her feet again and across the floor. She comes to a halt at the back of the room, and for a time, after she turns around, she just stands there watching those people today pass by with wild, angry eyes. In front of her stretches the entire living room, a long stately room with a pair of tall narrow windows at the front, crown molding around the high ceiling and the ceiling itself covered with a bas-relief design of garlanded flowers and fruit. To make the room appear less formal, Viney has decorated it in warm tones of sand and terra-cotta. The large sectional sofa, covered in off-white Haitian cotton, serves as the centerpiece. And there's the evidence of her hard work in the paneling and woodwork and the two sets of double doors in the room, all of which she single-handedly restored to the original oak.

Behind her, through one set of doors, lies a smaller, more casual room that contains her books, a desk for the work she brings home from Metropolitan Life in the evenings and the piano she bought when Robeson started taking lessons three years ago.

"You were right that time. I should never have moved over here. I should've taken the money I made on the apartment and gotten out of this city altogether. Bought a house in Teaneck or on Long Island—Hempstead or someplace like that . . ."

"It could have happened there as well, Viney. You know that."

"Where're you supposed to go, then? The moon? Go live on some other planet?" Shouting at her across the thirty or so feet separating them.

"I'm going to be all right." Said quietly by way of an apology ten minutes later when she comes and sits back down. "The worst didn't happen. Robeson's asleep upstairs and you say maybe he'll get over it. I'm going to take him to see Sharon anyway. You're here. I talked to my mother earlier. Naturally, Jewell Daniels wanted me to pack up and come home for good. As if Petersburg is any better. And I've spoken with Harold. And you're going with us to see him tomorrow. So I'm going to be all right."

"Of course you're going to be all right."

Then: "Oh, Ursa, you think of all our folks out here who don't have a Harold to call!"

"I've been sitting here thinking the same thing."

Later, in the same reflective tone, Viney says, "You know, I see the way some of the black mothers in the walk-ups on the block, where Dee Dee lives, treat their kids in public, yelling at them over the slightest thing, threatening them with a whipping, going upside their head—just so quick with that hand. And it always makes me so angry. I want to go over and slap them. And so ashamed, especially if there're white folks around. To have them see us treating our kids that way. You've seen it."

Ursa nods, puzzled. "It makes me angry too, but what made that come to mind?"

"Well, I'm thinking that maybe they're not just being too strict or taking out their frustrations on the kids," Viney says. "Maybe it's their way of teaching them how to behave around the Pirellis out here. That might be part of it. So they'll know better than to go up in some white cop's face talking about their constitutional rights and running the risk of being blown away. Maybe I haven't been teaching Robeson what he really needs to know. I've let him think the world is like this house and this block and the Belfield School where all the little white kids and the teachers think he's so great. Perhaps I'm not such a good mother after all."

"Don't do this to yourself, Viney."

"Lemme say it! I need to say it! I'm not like you. I can't disappear down some manhole when something happens and not say a word to a soul. I can't keep things bottled up inside the way you do. I've got to get them out, if not I'll go crazy!"

Leaping up again. Up and down the floor again, from the tall windows overlooking the front yard to the double doors at the back of the room. The long skirt flaring at each agitated step. The clogs a loud metronome on the parquet. Until she comes to a halt at the doors, which are open, and stands looking inside the adjoining room, her gaze on the piano, a small baby grand with its graceful lid propped open and Robeson's lesson book on the stand above the keyboard.

"I should never have given him that hard-luck name. Look at what they did to the real Robeson. Took away the man's passport. Wouldn't let him sing. He couldn't even make a living finally. I should've named him after someone else."

"You know you don't mean that, Viney. Come on and sit down."

" 'Is it Mrs. or *Ms.* Daniels?' " Viney says.

She hasn't moved from the doorway, although she has turned to face the living room and Ursa over on the sofa.

"That's the first thing the precinct captain wanted to know. 'Is it Mrs. or *Ms.* Daniels?' And every time he called my name he made a point of stressing the Ms. I could hear it. He was trying to smooth things over, hoping I wouldn't make trouble for him, yet he couldn't resist getting in his little dig. *Ms.* Daniels, just to let me know that, yes, I might be a hotshot VP at Metropolitan, I might make twice his salary, but I was still in his book just another welfare mother standing there with her little ADC child and no father in sight.

"And do you know something? . . ."

"Please come and sit down, Viney."

This time she obeys her, slowly crossing the room, the hem of the skirt scarcely moving, slowly sinking down onto the sofa, slowly turning to face her. The Chickahominy nose that belongs on Mount Rushmore. The face the color of caramel candy.

"And do you know something," she repeats. "I would've given anything to have had a Mr. Somebody standing beside Robeson and me in that police station this afternoon. I felt this awful space, Ursa, this hole the size of me next to me, could even feel the wind pouring through it . . . I remember my mother used to buy me these paper-doll books when I was small. I used to love them. All the dolls were white, naturally, but it never occurred to me, or to her either, I guess, that it should be otherwise. There were usually two dolls on the first page, sometimes a boy doll along with the girl, and then pages and pages of pretty clothes to dress them in. When I'd cut out one doll there'd be this empty outline left next to the one I hadn't gotten to yet. That's what that hole next to me today felt like, the outline, the space where some decent, halfway-together black man should have been. Okay, someone with a few problems—who doesn't have a few?—but with enough there for you to work with. Someone useful. And it's not that I can't manage on my own. Hey, I'm doing it every day! It's about dealing with what's still out there—that Neanderthal who could've blown my child away and that precinct captain with his *Ms.* Daniels. Someone next to me to deal with that! Instead"—her voice curves downward—"there was only this blank space, this hole next to me and Robeson.

"And he felt it too, because we weren't in the house five minutes before he didn't ask *the* question."

"Oh, Viney!"

Viney nods. The river that had turned into a hard, clear finish over her eyes that night in the pool has turned back to a river again.

"What do you think he's like, Aunt Ursa?" Robeson even subjects her to the question at times. And her answer is always the same as his mother's; simply, that whoever he is, he just *has* to be like the man he was named for. A very special and gifted black man.

" 'Is it Mrs. or *Ms.*?' " The rage in Viney's spent voice.

She sits, gazing through the river at her handiwork, the beautifully restored paneling that reaches to a height of about four feet along the walls, the woodwork around the windows, the baseboards that run the length of the floor, and the pair of tall, arched double doors like the doors to a sacristy, one at the back of the room and the other in the middle, directly opposite the sofa and opening onto the hall.

The doors alone took her almost four months to strip and refinish.

She gazes at the one across from the sofa for a long, long time.

"They can just take all your little shit and turn it to shit."

Viney who seldom if ever curses.

———

"I'm sorry," she says. "All this time and I haven't even asked you if you want anything. A drink or something to eat?"

They have left the living room and are standing in the large parlor-floor hall, which looks more like a second living room than just a mere hall. A floor-to-ceiling gilt-framed mirror is to the right of the front door, which is paneled with beveled glass; while a elaborately carved built-in bench is to the left. The light fixture is a converted gasolier, and the huge newel post at the foot of the stairs leading up to the third floor repeats the design of garlanded flowers and fruit on the living-room ceiling.

"I've got all this food left over from dinner because neither Robeson nor I could really eat."

Ursa shakes her head. "I'm not hungry. I had a late dinner with the group who'll be working on the first phase of the study."

"How's that going?"

"We're only just discussing how to go about things. We won't really get down to work until after Memorial Day. I plan to take the people I was with tonight over to meet Mae Ryland then. She's going to be a big help as usual. God, it was good seeing her! In fact, she was the only positive thing about that first visit. As you know . . ."

On her way back from Midland City after her first trip there the week before, she had driven straight over to Brooklyn, had let herself in the house with her key, and had sat waiting in the kitchen. When Robeson came home from day camp she listened to his account of the basketball game he had just played and then to him upstairs practicing for his piano lesson. Then, when Viney got in from work, she told her about that first day on the job. Went on and on about the day. How she'd been overwhelmed —being back in Midland City again—by a sense of her life being a series of double exposures. Everything—elections, roads, the

South Ward, Armory Hill, the PM, the Do-Nothings, Sandy Lawson, the white people–them! still running things in both places—everything superimposed on everything else. Inseparable. Inescapable. The same things repeated everywhere she turned. ". . . It's like I keep running, Viney, but I can't hide . . ."

"Which one of us can?" Viney said gently. Then: "Stay over. You can take back the car tomorrow morning, but stay over tonight."

"Any word from home yet?" she asks now.

"Not yet. I might be in for the silent treatment again. I was hoping I'd at least hear from Estelle. But not a word from her either. I don't know what's going on. I'll wait until after the elections this weekend and try and get through to them on the phone."

"How I wish the three of us—you, me, Robeson—could take a plane out of here this minute and go camp out on your beach. . . ." Said wistfully. "Just tell the world go hang for a few days and camp out on Ursa's beach. And we'd take Dee Dee along this time."

"Have you heard from Lowell?"

They're upstairs now, in the much narrower hall outside the bedrooms, with Robeson's half-opened door at the head of the landing. Inside his room the television is off, as is the light in the fish tank, and Dee Dee is asleep on the slide-out bed. Her face, which is turned to the door, is dimly visible in the light from the hall. Asleep with her eyes still keeping vigil behind her closed lids.

Robeson is burrowed even deeper in his pillow.

Viney asks about Lowell, and for the first time that Ursa can remember she does so without her usual Lowell tone and her lip curled down.

"No, I haven't heard. Nor do I expect to."

"All right. I just thought I'd ask."

* * *

In the restaurant tonight she put him at a table not far from where she sat with the group from the foundation, and she had him complaining about the usual to the empty chair where she would have been. Until the waiter appeared with the main course. He ceased his angry stage whisper then. Hands clasped, head bowed as if saying grace, he inspected the food the way he would a still life in a museum. A long, loving appraisal. And when he finally looked up, there it was: the smile, the silent word *perfect*, and his forefinger and thumb joined in the sign of wholeness and unity . . . She saw him so clearly that for a moment, distracting her from the conversation at her table, she felt it: the hollowness. It comes and goes. Some days it shrinks to almost nothing, and feeling nothing she says to herself, Free at last. Why did it take me so long? Why did I think it would be so hard? Other days the hollowness is the size of the canyon in Robeson's odometer game.

"Do you need something to help you sleep?" Viney asks. "I'm going to have to take a couple of pills."

She says no.

"I'm going to have it together again by tomorrow, Ursa."

"Don't I know it!" she says and holds her for a long minute.

Before turning on the light in the hallway bedroom to the front of the house where she sleeps whenever she stays over, Ursa goes and stands at the one window in the room. Her gaze falls on the gas lamp burning in the yard below. The lamp was added as a final touch when the renovations were done. A buoy. She's always thought of it as a buoy marking the channel that led to the harbor of Viney's house. After the long subway ride, she'd see the lamp up ahead as she turned the corner onto the block, and minutes later there would be Robeson shouting "Aunt Ursa!" as he unlocked the basement gate. Welcoming her with the latest dance craze and those unmarred eyes of his.

"Mes amis! *A big girl like you in a flood of tears! And over what? What do you? Who trouble you? Not a soul* oui, *and you's in a flood of tears.*"

And Estelle, that strangest of mothers, would sometimes say, "Let her cry, Celestine. Let her get it out of her, whatever it is."

9

It's late afternoon, almost five o'clock, by the time Ursa finally reaches 101st Street the following day. And as she stops to collect her mail in the vestibule of her building, she finds a yellow "attempt to deliver" notice amid the bills and letters in her box. There's a check mark next to the word "package" on the slip and a long, multidigit claim number. A package is being held for her at the post office on 104th Street near Broadway.

Coffee, she thinks, quickly calculating the time since the last supply arrived. No letter, but at least he's decided to send the coffee, so he can't be all that annoyed. He has it specially shipped through a friend of his at the Coffee Exporters Board in town. A three- or four-pound package of the choicest beans from the foothills of the old graybeard mountain. Enough for both her and Viney and sent faithfully every three months.

"You need to say Stop! in the name of love." The lunatic's voice in her ear for a second and then it's drowned in the relief she feels at the yellow slip in her hand. Relief, love and a tinge of annoyance. The odd mix the PM never fails to arouse in her. What does a Lowell Carruthers know or understand? It's more complicated than you can understand, fool! she should have told him.

She checks her watch, quickly stuffs everything but the notice back into the mailbox, and is out of the vestibule. The front door slams behind her and she's hurrying, almost running up the steep incline of the street toward Broadway and the post office, the river at her back.

The sky over the river and the city has cleared up again. It's been a day divided between sun and clouds. Bright summer sunshine reigning for a time, only to be overtaken by a mass of rain clouds moving in from Jersey, being driven by a warm May wind. She looked up once to find thunderheads like the kind seen in Triunion during the rainy season rolling in over the city. Yet there's been little or no rain for the day. The thunderheads roll in, the May wind keeps them moving out over the Atlantic, and the sun reappears almost before they're gone. It's been like this since morning, a day that has kept shifting between sunlight and clouds.

Most of the morning was spent in Harold's office in Lower Manhattan, not far from the State Supreme Court Building on Centre Street. She and Viney with Robeson seated between them facing Harold across his desk. Dark-skinned, preppy-looking Harold Newsom with his trim mustache, flared Benin nose, and a manner that took charge. He had been one of the Beautiful People at the bar for the BPs close to Viney's old apartment. Married, though. "He might not leave her, Viney." Ursa had tried warning her. But Viney had believed otherwise and had let herself in for a whole lot of grief. Surprisingly, though, she and

Harold became close friends after the breakup. He's one of Robeson's "uncles." And once in a great while, when the celibacy gets to be too much, Viney gives him a call.

She sat in his office this morning looking as if the day before hadn't happened. The impeccable going-to-meet-the-Met clothes, the sleek flyaway hair, and the polyurethane finish in place once again over her eyes. Only a trace of the puffiness from last night was still visible on her face. Viney intact, yet old Mother Daniels was doing her little nervous sway inside. Ursa felt it across Robeson seated between them.

"You're to tell your uncle Harold everything that happened, Robeson," Viney instructed him.

As always, Robeson took his cue from his mother, so that aside from the change to be seen in his eyes, there was no other visible sign of what he had been through. Viney had made him put on shoes instead of his sneakers, a pair of dress pants, a tie and his school jacket with the Belfield crest on the breast pocket. The same way he would dress for every court appearance later on. He sat there this morning, his back held straight, recounting his ordeal in his best Belfield School voice and manner. Viney's boychild. Except that occasionally there would be a catch in his voice, a sudden sharp intake of breath he couldn't control. His body undergoing a brief but powerful shock every so often. Dee Dee or one of his other friends might have sneaked up behind him and cried "Boo!" startling him and causing him to recoil.

Later, when they returned to Brooklyn, they treated him to lunch at Junior's, his favorite restaurant downtown. He liked their cheesecake with the cherry topping. He hardly ate his sandwich, but asked if he could have dessert anyway. When the slice of cheesecake arrived, he actually smiled and did a little jig in his seat. He ate less than half of it, though. Then said he wanted to go home. They were due to return to Harold's office at two o'clock to meet with his partner who knew the police commissioner and then to go in search of the woman who had witnessed the arrest. He would do both, he said, but that wasn't until later.

They had over an hour before they were to leave for Manhattan again, and he wanted to go home until then.

They did as he asked.

———

At the post office Ursa is handed a package wrapped in brown paper. This can't be coffee. The package is the wrong shape and size. She stands weighing it in her hands, puzzled. From the look of it, it could be the telephone directory for a place with the population of Staten Island or Midland City. But it's certainly not coffee. A letter is scotch-taped to the outside. It's the familiar blue envelope, yes, but without the government seal. And the handwriting—a large hurried scrawl—is the one she's used to seeing only in the postscripts to the PM's letters.

Estelle.

BOOK IV

Tin Cans and Graveyard Bones

1

" '*Ti-garçon!*"

As if conjured up on the spot, the boy instantly appears at the back door of the office in Morlands, which Celestine still thinks of—and still privately calls—the shop, Mis-Mack's shop.

"The place needs airing out, *oui*."

She gives the terse order, and with the same swiftness that brought him to the door the boy moves across the room and promptly sets about opening the three tall double doors to the front that face onto the square.

He's a long-limbed, broad-shouldered, muscular sixteen-year-old wearing a pair of cutoff jeans and a faded T-shirt from the last election, five years ago. Vote the PM! The PM *Toujours*! can still be faintly seen on the front. The shirt has to be a hand-me-down, since it would have been sizes too big for him back then.

With his build, height and age, he's a far cry from the *'ti-garçons*, or small boys, who usually serve as Celestine's helpers. That army of six- to nine-year-olds with ashy stick-figure legs, potbellies and bung navels she has hired over the years to fetch and carry for her. They often arrived on the job with patches of ringworm on their heads, their backsides bared to the world in a pair of ragged shorts and their hair rust red from a lack of protein, as hers had once been. *" 'Ti-garçon, vini m'pale ou!"* she would call, and whoever happened to be her little helper of the moment would come running to do her bidding.

This boy today might have been all of the *'ti-garçons* and small boys from over the years who had finally managed to put flesh and muscles on their bones and grow up.

Having speedily opened one door, the boy starts on the second, first removing the long iron bar that secures the door from the inside, then swinging open the two halves and latching them to the wall on either side. Celestine watches. The doors to the shop haven't been opened, she knows, since the last time she was up-country, a good six months and more. The caretaker, who was one of the doormouth children from long ago and this boy's grandfather, knows better than to disturb the place when she's not there.

Before calling the boy she stood reverently in the dim, sealed-up room breathing in the smells only she can detect. All the smells from the old shop are still there as far as she's concerned: the saltfish, kerosene oil and penny bread smells ingrained in the walls and floorboards and in the old scarred wooden counter that was the only thing the *blanche neg'* spared when she turned the place into an office years ago. Always interfering! Celestine stood for a long time breathing it all in, her feet planted on the floor, her hair that has gone from red to black to gray over her lifetime braided around her head—a single braid like a wreath. And she's wearing one of her black-and-white print dresses in which the black predominates. In mourning still for Mis-Mack.

And there, seated in her high chair behind the counter at the cash drawer had been Mis-Mack, Mis-Mack clear as life, with the cane she used as a hook-stick lying near to hand . . . Out of all the little children who were abandoned from time to time outside the shop, she, Celestine Marie-Claire Bellegarde, was the only one who had never tasted the cane handle around her neck. The only one, *oui*! Mis-Mack had always treated her special. Right from the beginning she had put her above the other doormouth children, even above the maids she had working in the house. When anything important needed doing she always called on her. "Celestine!" She would hear her name before Mis-Mack even finished calling it, and go running. Mis-Mack had trusted her, had depended on her, had *chosen* her. Look how she put her in charge of all three children. Had ignored the grown maids about the place, *oui*, and as soon as she borned each of the babies, she had handed them over for her to care, never mind she was only eight when the PM was born. It was like Mis-Mack had been waiting all along for her to come. Special. She had always been special.

"Don't you ever want to take a day off, Celestine? Please take a day off."/"Take today off, for God's sake, Celestine. Go to town, window-shop, buy yourself something pretty at Conlin and Finch. Or just sit and do nothing for the day."/"I'm taking Ursa-Bea to the movies this afternoon, Celestine. Come and go with us. Please. Wouldn't you like to go to the movies if only once, just to see what it's like? . . ."

Always after me to do this or do that like she feels I missed out on something in this life. What does the woman know!

The third and final door stands open, and without having to be told the boy has started sweeping out the room. Outside, empty and almost treeless under the early morning sun, lies the square where the open-air market used to be held long years ago. Celestine goes to stand in the center doorway, remembering. Hawkers from all over Morlands and from all up Gran' Morne gathered in the dust and broiling sun. Even back then you could count the few trees on the fingers of one hand. All day out under the sun until finally the market shed was built and the PM named it after Mis-Mack. The *blanche neg'* kept after him to keep after the Do-Nothings till it was built . . . She has a good heart. That's one thing you must say for her. And with everybody. I was to sit, *oui*, and learn to read along with 'ti-Ursa. And I was to have a proper bed and my own furnitures bought from Conlin and Finch in my room. A good heart. But there's no understanding those American ways she's got!

Shading her eyes, Celestine gazes across the square at the old parish church where the PM received his pet name. Its discolored limestone walls stand pockmarked and weary, its carved weather-beaten doors are out of alignment. It had gone from being Catholic to Anglican and back again over twenty times. Had changed hands over twenty times in two centuries during the long-ago wars.

"When you finish sweeping you's to start measuring out the rice."

"Yes, Miss Celestine. I already cut the paper to suit."

A bush broom of palm leaves in his hands, the boy is sending the dust flying out the three doorways where it turns into gold mica in the sun.

Celestine likes this '*ti-garçon*. You don't have to tell him every little thing. He's like she was at his age. Special.

The hundred-pound bags of rice that will be parceled out at the final meeting this Sunday arrived from town in the same van she traveled in yesterday. The boy's task will be to measure out the rice in two-cup portions and afterward wrap the portions in the squares of brown paper he has already cut and put aside. Then, come Sunday, the packets of rice will be handed out to the women before the meeting out at the Monument of Heroes begins. Rice for the women, two or three shot glasses of white rum for the men, bought from the distillery in Morlands, and a Bic pen for everybody for as long as the supply lasts. A box of the pens also came up on the van yesterday. No longer are the rice and rum enough, not even in Morlands. Last election it had been the T-shirts. This time the Bic pens. Even those that can't even mark X for their name gon be grabbing for one to clip on their clothes where everybody can see it. *Mes amis*, good money gone! But what must the PM do? He knows he must come with an extra little freeness these days, never mind everybody's gon give him their vote.

Leaving the boy to his tasks, Celestine steps out the back door of the shop into the courtyard the size of a parade ground that is the hub of the old house. The yard holds the kitchen, a small stone house unto itself./"No more cooking with charcoal! It keeps the kitchen too hot and sooty. And it's destroying all the trees." And I know she made the PM put in a gas stove. Always interfering!/And the horse stalls from long ago are still in the yard, standing empty except for the jeep that remains up-country. For the bad roads the PM is still after government to fix. *Hélas!*

She climbs the stairs to the living quarters on the second floor. There're the bedrooms to be seen to—the floors scrubbed with white lime and sand, the mosquito netting taken down from their hoops and given a good shaking to remove the dust and any dead insects caught in the mesh, and the mattresses put out to air. The glass jalousies the PM had had to expense himself putting in at all the windows to please the *blanche neg'* are to be washed. The house made ready.

For a long time Celestine stands in the doorway of what had once been the nursery and is now Ursa's room. One of the maids has already taken out the mattress and the mosquito netting. The floor has been scrubbed down and the windows washed. The work done. It's the room where for years she slept on a pallet next to the crib, which had held first the PM and then his two sisters, and where she would have slept with 'ti-Ursa had not for the mother. She wasn't to sleep in the same room with her. "She's to sleep by herself, Celestine. You can be next door but not in the same room." What kind of mother would do a thing like that? Put a child to sleep by itself from the day it's born? *Mes amis!* That must be the way they do things in America. Mis-Mack now was different. She had her to sleep right next to all three till they were of an age to have their own room. And even then they hadn't wanted to leave her. The PM had cried long tears, and every chance he got would find himself right back there. The door would open a crack, a blade of light would reach across to her pallet on the floor, and a familiar foot would briefly appear in the light before the door closed again.

"Where it 'tis you going with your mannish self?"

Whispering it—she always whispered it—so as not to wake his sisters.

Years later, she had only to touch herself and there he would be again. Right there with her. And not as some little seven- and eight-years-old boy, but the PM grown and a man . . .

"Oh, come on, Celestine, there must have been someone. Some beau when you were sweet sixteen."

Always teasing her, *oui*. Always thinking she had missed out on something. What did the *blanche neg'* know?

———

"Celestine, my love, guess who's changed her mind and will be coming down after all to see me chase Mr. Justin from the yard again?" Smiling, *oui!* It's been a long time since he's smiled like that. And he was waving the telegram like it was a flag.

Merci en pil, Seigneur! Her prayers had been answered.

The telegram arrived yesterday morning, and in the afternoon she set out for Morlands to get the house ready, traveling in the same van that was bringing up the rice and the Bic pens.

2

Nothing's changed.

As always, he had alerted his friends among the airport officials of her arrival, so that as she stepped off the plane, one of them —the short, gray-haired director of customs who had known her since she went off to high school—was standing waiting on the tarmac to take care of the formalities for her. After they greeted each other, with the man playfully scolding her for having stayed away so long, he escorted her past the long lines in immigration and saw to it that her passport and landing papers were stamped before anyone else's. Her carry-on bag, which was the only piece of luggage she had brought—since she'd be here less than a week—passed through customs without being opened.

She had begged him not to do it when she was in college. "I really don't mind standing in line with everyone else."

"But why, when there's no need?" He had been genuinely puzzled. "What's the point of my being in this so-called government if I can't get a little VIP treatment for my child at the airport? That's about all that seat I occupy is good for. In fact, I'm thinking of having a steel band greet you the next time you come down. And a red carpet spread from here to yonder." Said with the smile there was no resisting. And which, in the shadows behind it, betrayed how much the little influence he wielded at the airport meant to him.

She didn't bother to openly object after that.

And her picture has been taken. Standing waiting with him and Estelle as she came through the arrivals gate was a photographer from the *Triunion Daily*. Her picture taken as soon as the embraces were over. He had arranged for that also. Her face will appear in the Visitors to the Island column on the front page of tomorrow's paper. "Miss Ursa Mackenzie, daughter of the Honorable Member from Morlands and Mrs. Mackenzie, in the island for the elections" will read the caption, and the accompanying article will also, as always, list her degrees—her little B.A. and master's—and make mention of her present job. And if she knows him, he will have inflated her position on the Midland City study. That man.

Nothing's changed. Not even the car. There, sitting waiting for them as they left the terminal, was the black Buick sedan from four years ago, the latest in the line of oversize gas guzzlers from Detroit he has insisted on driving against all logic all these years.

It was parked in the area reserved for official cars.

Estelle insisted that she sit up front. "Your father needs you next to him so that he can reach over and pinch you every once in a while to make sure you're real. He still doesn't believe that you're actually here."

"True!" he exclaimed. "You don't know it, my lady, but you came to within an inch of being kidnapped. That's right. I was all ready to fly up to New York and kidnap or shanghai you, one, if you hadn't formed yourself back here."

The playful smile, his arms around her again in another massive hug, and then he was holding the door on the passenger side open for her.

To reach the house on Garrison Row they had to take one of the lesser roads instead of the highway between the airport and town. And no sooner were they under way than the all-too-familiar scene began to unfold. There they were: row after row after row of little pitched-roofed houses of sunbleached pine-board or unpainted concrete blocks, with bare front yards and rusted tin-ning roofs, all of them crowded together under the bright blue perfect roof of the sky and a sun that is the color of a ripe mango. Faces in every shade of black streaming past, black in all its *terribleness*, as they used to say when she was in college, during the last days of the Movement, meaning in all its variety and beauty. Our folks come in every shade but green, her grand-father used to say. Meaning, also, in all its angers and pain. They flood past—men, women, children. The little ragtag boys hail the Buick, which Ursa knows looks like a stretch limousine to them. A city vendor with a basket of yams on her head quickly takes to the ditch along the road as she sees it approach. The smaller English and Japanese cars scramble out of its path. Only the buses and vans just down from the country with their ov-erload of people and freight refuse to give way. And the donkey carts. After all the years and any number of P and D projects, the donkey cart is still to be seen, even in town, and it's not about to move out of the way for anything, not even a big motorcar from the States.

Unchanged. Everything unchanged except that there is more of the same. The overcrowding is worse than ever. They're run-ning out of room on Triunion.

Ursa closes her eyes for a moment. The South Ward. The double exposure beginning again. Ke'ram. Ke'ram. She asks for strength to see her through the next five days.

"I should warn you right off, Ursa-Bea, you won't be hearing much out of your father today," Estelle is saying.

"How come?" She sits around in her bucket seat to better see the face thrust between hers and the PM's. The moment they left the airport, Estelle had sat all the way forward on the backseat so that her face is lodged between theirs.

"Because I've made him take a vow of silence on certain subjects."

"Not just a vow. Your mother's put a muzzle on me, Ursa. You can't see it, but I've got a muzzle on." Winking over at her as he steers the car with effortless, unerring grace and authority.

She used to love watching him drive when she was small. Once, when Estelle took the wheel on the long drive up to Morlands, she had cried, "*No!* You're not to drive. Only the PM. Let the PM!" He had laughed and quickly pinned her to him as she tried pulling Estelle's hands from the wheel—and then laughed some more, pleased.

What did I know, Viney?

"And I took the same vow," Estelle says. "We both agreed not to spoil your first day back by immediately burdening you with all that's going on in this place. So not a word for the time being about the election. You'll hear enough about that when we go up to Morlands tomorrow. We also agreed to call a moratorium on all talk about the resort scheme. Your father can't wait to show you the prospectus that's just been issued, but I've made him promise to also hold off on that till tomorrow. Besides, if you were to see that thing right away, you might just turn around and take the next plane out of here."

A laugh from the driver's seat. His head comes edging forward, though, and there's a sudden strain in his voice. "As you can tell, your mother doesn't approve. In fact, she hasn't had a kind word to say about this particular project from the beginning. And for some reason she feels I'm the one behind every decision that's been made about it. She won't believe there're some things I don't go along with either. Take the business of the—"

"You're breaking our agreement."

"True. I beg for an excuse, madam." He turns briefly to the face next to his, genuinely contrite. "It won't happen again. But come tomorrow I'm going to have my say. My daughter and I are going to sit down—just the two of us—and have an ol' talk."

"Fine. Just so long as it's not today. No mention of the unmentionables for the next twenty-four hours. Today's to be strictly fun and welcome home. Your uncle Roy, Ursa-Bea, has invited us over for drinks around five, and we're having dinner at your favorite cousin's."/"How is Jocelyn?"/"Fine. She's pregnant again, and she and her husband have just bought a new house. The woman's a veritable baby-making machine. Thank God, my daughter didn't choose that as her life's work. The entire clan will be there tonight, so you'll get to see everybody one time. But right now we want to hear about you, only about you. You're the only subject that's permitted for the day. I can't tell you how happy we were when that telegram came yesterday. It's the first time in months I've seen your father smile."

"From ear to ear." He grins at her across the face separating them.

"And as soon as Celestine heard, she took off for the country to get everything ready for her 'ti-Ursa."

"I told her to have plenty of fried plantains and soursop juice on hand."

"He did," Estelle says. "It's going to be quite a homecoming. But as I said, right now we want to hear about you. How's the study going? We were so relieved to hear that it came through. Have you seen your friend over there yet—the woman you used to write us about all the time before? And how's Viney and Mr. Precocious? And when's the last time you visited your uncle and cousins in Hartford? . . ."/She's going to ask about Lowell. Please don't let her ask about Lowell Carruthers./"And how's your love life?"/"Estelle!" A rebuke from the driver's seat./"Your father doesn't want to hear about it, doesn't want to know that you even have one, but I do. You hardly ever mention that beau of yours in your letters. And what's going on in the dear old U.S. of A. these days? I don't read the papers anymore. I decided to write off the eighties the day Bonzo's friend was sworn in. And to think I used to love those Grade B movies he played in! I just drew a line through the entire decade . . ."

Her mother's voice in her ear, and her face—the buff yellow of a file folder—only inches from her own. She sees the lines and shadows there: faint half-moon shadows she doesn't remember ever seeing before under the eyes, and the two lines that shape Estelle's wide, upstaging smile have dug in around her mouth, to become age lines. Close up, her skin looks as if a very fine hairnet her exact same color has been drawn tightly over it. The subtle webbing and creasing already under way. She won't be one of those black women who never shows her age. Not enough melanin . . .

When she was small she used to divide the people who mattered most to her according to the two sides of her hands. There were those of the plum dark back of her hands: the PM, Celestine, her favorite cousin Jocelyn; and those of her pale, pinkish palms: Estelle, Astral Forde, her uncle Roy and the little colored-white girls at St. Gwinevere's Girls School in town. Her classmates. And for the longest time she had longed to be numbered among those of her palms and had been secretly angry at Estelle for not having made her the same yellow as herself . . . What did I know, Viney? What did I understand back then? All that shit! I know, you say cut it loose, just cut it all loose. That's easier said than done, sister/friend.

. . . and Estelle's gotten thinner. When they embraced just now inside the terminal, her bones felt as light and hollow as a bird's and smaller than her own even. And the wells at her throat are deeper. Every tendon and cord there showing . . . She's at it again: piling her plate with food at each meal, but eating only a mouthful or two before calling for Celestine to take the plate away. It could go on for weeks.

Oh, Estelle, why won't you just leave?

She knows better than to seek the answer in the face next to hers. Perhaps his, the PM's, will offer a clue. Something other than the charm that has seduced them all over the years. Her gaze shifts to the other side of the car. All she sees, though, is the same aging. There's more gray to his hair than she remembers from her last visit. More slack, tired flesh around his middle under the shirt-jac suit he has on. Back at the arrivals gate, when he held her and kept on holding her, there had been so much exhausted flesh enveloping her she hadn't been able to see anyone else, including Estelle waiting her turn to greet her . . . Long ago, she used to look up from the pool at Mile Trees and not be able to see the trees or even a patch of sky. His body would be in the way, his head blocking out the sun. The annoyance she used to feel! She would have done anything some days to make him move, to get out of her way. She felt a tinge of the old annoyance just now in the terminal as he kept on holding her. As well as anger. The angry question she's been assailing him with ever since the prospectus arrived had flared up. How could you have agreed to it? Government Lands! Don't hold me. I don't want you to hold me. Both annoyance and anger there for a moment and then gone, swept away by the sheer pleasure of seeing him. And by the perspiration on his face. Perspiring, she knew, not only from the heat inside the crowded terminal but from worrying while he stood there waiting that she might have changed her mind again and would not be on the flight.

She wanted to take a Kleenex from her bag and, before even turning to embrace Estelle, wipe the perspiration from his face.

What did a Lowell Carruthers know or understand?

"And how's the work on the degree going? Have you started writing the thesis yet? You never mention that in your letters either . . ."

"One at a time, Estelle! You're not giving her a chance to answer question one, never mind two. I haven't heard my child's voice yet."

He complains but is smiling; he approves of this exaggerated welcome.

These two. Nothing's changed.

Estelle is leaning so far forward by now she's practically sitting up front with them. Her profile is superimposed on the PM's,

Ursa notes, the side view of her face and head taking up more than three quarters of his. Their two profiles like bas-relief heads on a medallion or a specially minted commemorative coin. And their heads are in turn superimposed on the parade outside the Buick—on the dark, fleeting faces, the woebegone little houses, the cars, buses and donkey carts, and on the trees Estelle is always trying to save.

The struck coin of those two heads . . . *Why won't you just leave?* Ursa becomes very still inside. She's as close as she'll ever come to an answer, she senses, watching them, the one head framing the other. Estelle's not going anyplace. She'll never leave. And another hard truth: What she has tried for years to understand about these two is perhaps none of her business.

"Everything," Estelle is saying. "You're to tell us everything. And you can start with whatever you like. We're both starved for news of Ursa-Bea."

"True!" he cries and reaching over pinches her lightly on the arm. A love pinch to make sure she's real.

3

"... No experimental farm, Ursa-Bea. No agricultural station. No small farmer's cooperative such as your father and I talked about for years. No model village, housing scheme or hospital. No cannery or sisal plant or any other kind of factory or plant. Instead, Government Lands is to be a playground for the Fortune 500 and friends."

Ursa's old bedroom in the house on Garrison Row. It's a smaller version of the huge echo chamber of a room down the hall—the master bedroom—that Estelle had converted into an apartment. She's seated in an old-fashioned morris chair a few feet from Ursa's bed, the same chair, in fact, she used to curl up in to read the nightly bedtime story years ago.

It's past midnight. Ursa in her gown and robe had been sitting on the edge of the bed, the light in the room on, unable to even think of sleep when Estelle tapped on the door.

That was a half hour ago.

"I saw light under your door and thought I'd come visit awhile. Your father's fast asleep." Standing like a wraith in the doorway in a filmy blue dressing gown and a pair of satin mules in blue also, and with a fuzzy pom-pom on the vamp and Louis XIV heels. She hasn't changed her style slipper over the years. Without her makeup her face looked more creased than in the car earlier and the shadows under her eyes more pronounced. "And I'm breaking my vow of silence on certain subjects," she said, entering the room and closing the door behind her.

She brought along her copy of the prospectus. She hasn't stopped inveighing against it since she came in. ". . . The filet mignon flown in fresh every day from Miami. And Dom Pérignon served as a matter of course at the built-in bar in the swimming pool. Daddy Warbucks will be able to swim over and sip a glass of the bubbly between laps. And not one but two huge pools, I'll have you know, Ursa-Bea, one saltwater, one fresh, never mind the place will be on a beach that has the best swimming in the world.

"And after the gentleman has his swim? What then? Why, there'll be the eighteen-hole golf course—two of them also—the tennis courts, the health club, the stables, the marina with his yacht waiting, and on and on. And let's not forget the conference center where Mr. Warbucks can mix a little business with his pleasure if he likes. It's to be the largest of any resort in the islands. It says so right in this thing." She snatches up the prospectus from her lap, shakes it by the spine so that the pages flutter and snap like bedsheets in a wind.

"And did you read, Ursa-Bea"—she lets the prospectus fall to her lap again—"that the place is to have its own airfield. They're going to fly the moguls straight up from the airport so they won't be subjected to that miserable road we'll be taking tomorrow or to the sight of some little boy missing the seat of his pants. Their own private plane service! You must have seen that . . ."

"Yes, I saw it." She had read and reread her Xeroxed copy of the prospectus that came in the mail on Tuesday, two days ago. There was a bookmark in the page that discussed the building site, and she had read that page first, as soon as she came in from the post office and opened the package. And afterward she sat for a long, long time, unable to read any farther. The last of the daylight faded outside, the streetlamps on 101st Street came on, and still she couldn't go on to read more.

How could you? The anger that slowly engulfed her as she sat there!

"And did you also see where there's to be a casino? Some huge Monte Carlo–type casino. Strictly high-class gambling. We've never allowed anything like that here before!" Every cord in Estelle's neck is visible.

"How could he have gone along with it? That's what I don't understand." Don't hold me! I don't want you to hold me! she had almost shouted at him at the airport, even as she was flooded with pleasure at seeing him again.

"Ask him! When the two of you have your talk, ask him! See what he says. He's only going to repeat what he keeps telling me: that having it in Morlands might just benefit the district. How, I'd like to know, in what way, when all the help—maids, waiters, maintenance, security guards, everybody—are to come from the hotel training school in town? Did you read that, Ursa-Bea?"/She can only nod./"People in Morlands won't stand a chance at a job cleaning the toilets even—"

Then abruptly: "I wonder what Mr. Beaufils would have to say about it?"

"Mr. Beaufils?"

"Your father's opponent," Estelle says. "He's the young teacher who's running as an Independent in Morlands this time."

"Oh, yes, the PM mentioned him in a letter, but he didn't give his name."

"I'm not surprised. He doesn't think much of Mr. Beaufils. I'd love to know, though, what that young man would have to say about this prospectus. I'm sure if he saw it he'd call for a referendum so people in Morlands could decide whether they want some big resort that won't benefit them in their backyard. Government Lands is, after all, public land, meaning belonging to the people. Something the P and D Board doesn't seem to understand . . . Yes, if you ask me, Mr. Beaufils needs to see this thing—" Then abruptly again: "You used to play with him when you were small."

"I did? What's his first name?"

"Justin. You probably don't remember him, but he was one of the children I used to invite in to play with you when we were up-country. I don't remember him, but Celestine does. She even swears he once threw a rock at the gate when your father came home one day and chased them all out. I remember the incident—I was furious with your father—but I couldn't say who actually threw the rock. If she's right and it was him, he's remained true to form, because he's still throwing rocks in a manner of speaking. He keeps bombarding the district with flyers criticizing everything: your father, the government, the P and D Board, the U.S. Navy coming to supervise the elections each time, the big estate owners, the moguls in town, and the great people–them! He actually talks about class and color in this place! Something nobody's ever dared to do openly before. Mr. Beaufils is something else. A bold one. He even put an ad in the paper challenging your father to a debate."

"What! What did the PM do?"

"Ignored him. Said he must think he's running for the White House. A bold one, though," Estelle repeats. "And his wife is also something else, from what I hear. She's from Spanish Bay, an agronomist who went to Cuba to study. The two of them are all over the district giving out their flyers, holding meetings. They're quite a team, I understand. And they have a solid plat-form, Ursa-Bea. I like what they have to say . . ." A pause, a lifting of the shadows around her eyes, a wistfulness in her voice: "Your father and I were like that. I've told you how we spent our honeymoon campaigning. And to show you what little prog-ress has been made, we were calling for much the same things then as they are now. The need for a change from the ground up and for people in Gran' Morne and Spanish Bay and the rest of the island to come together, really come together. It was four months on the go morning, noon and night. I wouldn't have exchanged it for anything in the world."

A thin, fleeting smile and the shadows descend again.

Their profiles in the car earlier. Like two heads on a commemorative coin. She'll never leave him or this place . . . "Does he have any supporters? This Mr. Beaufils."

"Not really. Only a few young people like himself. Hotheads, as they're called. He must know he doesn't stand a chance, but he's giving it his all anyway. I like that," Estelle says. And Ursa suddenly remembers the man on hot, crowded King William Street four years ago, who had drawn her away from Viney and Robeson. A man her age with missing teeth and wearing a rag of a Hawaiian shirt that exposed his bony chest. Did she remember him? "I was one the little children your mother uses to let come and play with you in the yard when you all came to spend time in the district." She did not remember him. Then: "Things hard in the Fort, Miss Ursa. I have a mind to move back up to the country . . ." She had given him money for bus fare out to a stone quarry where he said they might be hiring and to buy himself something to eat.

Nothing's changed.

"Mr. Beaufils has even written to your father, you know," Estelle is saying. "He sent a letter last month telling him he should resign his seat in the House, quit the P and D Board, and join what's left of the NPP with him and the Independents. I told you he was a bold one. Your father could be the honorary head of the party and their principal adviser. They feel he still has a lot to offer the country. He's just never had a chance because of the stranglehold the DNP thugs have had on us all these years. It was a very respectful letter, Ursa-Bea. Well, I needn't tell you what your father did with it."

"I can well imagine. Although, to tell the truth, what they're proposing might not be a bad idea . . ." She's thinking of the slack, overweight body that had enveloped her at the airport. Its exhaustion. An exhaustion of more than just the flesh. "It's something he should at least think about."

"I told him the same thing," Estelle says. "Because Mr. Beaufils is right. Your father's not through yet, although he seems to feel that he is and that this resort is his last chance to be part of something big. There's enough of the old PM there. I wouldn't still be with him if I didn't believe that. But right now he can't hear, see, think, feel or even dream about anything except the P and D's latest, quote, development scheme. I bet he's in there right now dreaming about the damn thing.

"And you know of course he's planning on putting money in it."

Ursa sighs. "Yes. That was in his last letter. Where's he going to find it?"

Estelle spreads her hands—small, veined, tan-yellow on both sides. "Nowhere that I can think of. This white elephant is mortgaged to the hilt. Mile Trees also. So he can't borrow a cent more on them. And the house in Morlands belongs to your aunts as well, so he can't sell that. Where's the money to come from? I don't know, but he keeps running from one bank to the next and meeting with some financial adviser he's putting his faith in."

"Oh, you've got that breed down here too now?"

"I'm afraid so. In fact, he has to see this adviser tomorrow first thing, so he won't even be going up to the country with us in the morning. He's running so much I doubt the two of you will have a chance to talk. The ol' talk he promised you. Besides, I'm sure he's not all that eager for you to get him alone. He knows he's going to be in for it about Government Lands and that beach you love so much. Anyway, we'll see what time he turns up in Morlands tomorrow.

"Always somebody to see about money!" Her outburst is loud enough to carry to the master bedroom down the hall. If awake, Primus Mackenzie would have heard her. "And the frightening thing, Ursa-Bea, is that he's beginning to sound like he'll do anything to get it. Money to sink into something that might turn out to be a bust. He might lose every penny. He—"

Estelle stops herself, and after a long moment, when she's somewhat calmer, she slowly rises. She stands there, a short distance from the bed, looking ghostlike in the filmy dressing gown and holding the prospectus like a book of bedtime stories in the crook of one thin, anorexic arm. "And to think I was the one who said we weren't to burden you with our troubles your first day back. How's that for keeping my word?"

"It's all right, Estelle."

"It's just that this Government Lands thing has really hit me hard. This is the worst to have happened since the elections were stolen that time. It's gotten so I'm afraid of my own thoughts when it comes to the P and D Board and your father. I feel positively murderous some days. That's why I wrote you. I needed you here. I knew you weren't ready to come back to this place yet for whatever reasons, but I decided to write anyway . . ."

"I'm glad you did. It's time I came back."

". . . Because something has to be done to stop those people on the board and to bring your father to his senses. I don't know what, exactly. Worse, I'm not sure I could do it, even if I did know."

Estelle said as much in her letter. ". . . I don't think I can manage this one on my own. You have to come down here, Ursa-Bea. Maybe you can think of something. And you have to come right away!" That sentence had been underlined twice. Ursa had read and reread the brief letter any number of times, along with the page in the prospectus that had the bookmark, and while seated in her darkened apartment on Tuesday she silently offered herself for whatever would be required of her.

She voices that offer now, thinking of that twice-underlined sentence. "I'm here," she says and turns her hands palm up and holds them out slightly as if waiting to receive her orders in a sealed envelope.

Estelle quickly crosses over to her, ready, it seems, to slip the envelope from between her breasts. Instead, she reaches out her free hand and Ursa feels it lightly touching the braid that circles her head. The tips of Estelle's fingers trace and retrace the thick plait that starts at her forehead and trails down behind her ears to the nape of her neck where the two halves are joined.

"I like it," Estelle says, repeatedly touching it. "I meant to tell you earlier how good it looks on you. Your father was a little taken aback, I could tell, but I like it. How I wish I had your nice thick hair! And wait till Celestine sees it. She'll be pleased no end."

Then: "Well, I guess I should let you get some sleep." Reluctantly Estelle withdraws her hand; reluctantly she starts toward the door across the room.

"You asked me about my love life in the car this afternoon . . ."

Estelle immediately comes to a halt, turns, and quickly retracing her steps comes and sits down beside her on the bed.

4

Taking her time, the sullen-faced nurse slowly pulls the bed curtains closed, sealing off Malvern's bed from the thirty or so others in the overcrowded ward. An agitated Astral Forde waits for the woman to be done, 'buse-ing her for her slowness under her breath: "One step today and the next tomorrow. You could be dead and buried waiting for her to bring you a glass of water or a bedpan." Then, as the last curtain is drawn into place, shutting out the rest of the ward, and the nurse disappears, Astral Forde almost hurls the upper half of her body across the bed and grasps Malvern's bony arm, actually touching her friend for the first time ever. "Oh, God, Malvern, listen, nuh!" Her voice a desperate whisper. "Can you hear me? Listen to what I'm telling you! The man is thinking of selling Mile Trees! You hear what I'm saying?

He's thinking of selling the place. Some person he has advising him said he'll have to sell it to find the money for the resort scheme. And he's thinking of doing it, just selling the whole place. Can you hear me? Malvern! Listen to what I'm telling you! I might find myself out in the road!"

Not a sound from the motionless figure on the bed. Not the flicker of a closed eyelid or the least twitch of a muscle to indicate the distraught voice is even being dimly heard. What is left of Malvern is as inanimate as the pallet mattress under her and the peeling iron bedstead at her head and feet.

"That's the news he came with this evening. There I was getting the bills and receipts ready to send to the accountant when he stop by to tell me this thing. And all in a rush. And his eyes not meeting yours. He wouldn't even stay to hear what I had to say about it. He didn't even ask. Just announced it so and gone. Rushing up to Morlands. The great Mistress Ursa finally decided to come home—they had her picture big in the paper this morning—and all of them will be up there until after the elections are over. And as soon as they're over he's gon make up his mind about Mile Trees. That's the piece of news the man came and dropped on me this evening. How he could think of doing such a thing, Malvern? Tell me! The one business that's made him a little money over the years. And what will he have to leave when he dies? What's his own child gon have? The man's not even thinking of providing for his own child! You must know he's out of his head not to be concerned about her. It's the resort scheme. That thing has put him clean out of his head. Somebody needs to take drastic measures with that man. You hear what I'm saying, Malvern?" Shaking the stick-figure arm. "Drastic measures!"

Again no sound or movement. The only faint signs of life are an occasional shallow breath that barely disturbs the sheet covering Malvern, and the slow, slow drip from the catheter trailing down into the bedpan on the floor near Astral Forde's foot. Urine the color and consistency of molasses.

"Thinking of selling Mile Trees! That's what the madman

stopped by to tell me no more than a half hour ago. I could find myself out in the road. The job I had all these years gone and I'm out in the road. Malvern, say something, nuh . . ." The panicked voice, the congested face the color of cream that has clotted and gone sour.

Malvern maintains her neutral silence. But from all over the ward, where it is already bedtime, the other patients speak for her. The groans and outcries of those asleep, the unanswered calls for the nurse from those awake drift in over the curtains that are as patched and dingy as the sheet covering Malvern. The sounds come, along with the smells of unemptied bedpans, unwashed bodies and floors, and the sight of the flaking water-stained ceiling around the dangling light bulb that has been left on over Malvern's bed.

The government horse-pital, as it's called. You's guaranteed not to leave there alive. So goes the saying.

"Instead of him building up the place into something worthwhile, he's thinking of selling it to put the money in something that's only a lot of big plans in a book. There's not a stone or a brick with the word resort on it anyplace. The blasted thing don't exist. You understand what I'm saying, Malvern? Instead of him looking to what he has . . ."

The old complaint. It becomes part of the furious outpouring she's helpless to stop. "Mile Trees gone! I'll find myself out in the road! Listen, nuh, to what I'm telling you . . . !" Over and over again in Malvern's already sealed ear.

"The doctors are saying she won't last the night."

The gray-haired, sorrowing man in a dispatcher's blue uniform has slipped up behind her chair. He stands, his head bowed and his official cap in hand, gazing past Astral Forde's large body flung on the bed to his wife's motionless form. With him is the youngest child, the daughter they call Grace; and next to her, wearing a bus driver's khaki uniform, stands the son Malvern insisted on naming *The* Woody Wilson. He's a slightly built man in his mid-thirties with his father's mild, dark, moon-shaped face and Malvern's spare limbs. He and his sister are the only two of the children left in Triunion.

Husband and children had quickly relinquished their place beside the bed and gone to sit in the hall when Astral Forde, the crazed look on her face, came rushing in, led by the nurse who then closed the bed curtains.

The three have quietly slipped back now to gather behind her chair.

"Whatever this thing is, it has eat her down to nothing," the man says.

For a dazed moment, as the already grieving voice sounds behind her, Astral Forde looks at Malvern as if she's the one who has spoken. Her friend has finally heard her and spoken, until her overturned mind registers who it is: the beautiful-ugly bus driver husband with the face like a cow stepped in it his picture sitting up big in the middle of the little two-by-four house on Armory Hill all these years. She could count on the fingers of one hand the number of times she overstayed her visits and he came in from work and found her there.

Astral Forde pulls back from over the bed. Sits up straight in her chair.

"The doctors are saying she won't last the night. That's why they're letting in anybody that wants to see her."

The voice like a church bell already tolling, so that in one of those rare moments of clarity, when her mind briefly shifts from Mile Trees and her own preoccupations and fears and she can actually see past the all-absorbing universe of herself, Astral Forde actually *sees* Malvern for the first time since she burst into the ward—her still, wasted form under the dingy sheet, her shuttered eyes and the face that has already assumed that look of absolute indifference and repose.

For a single clear moment she sees her friend, and then she is leaping up, almost knocking over the bedpan, and trying to tell the dispatcher whose mourning is already under way that he must send one of the children to tell her when Malvern, when Malvern . . .

She can't bring herself to say the word.

———

"*Wha' the rass*! Is this what Mr. Mackenzie is paying you good money for? Tell me! I would like to know. Is this why he's giving you a salary every fortnight, for you to come and stand at his gate and sleep? . . ." She had caught the night watchman at it again as the taxi bringing her from the hospital pulled up. ". . . Nearly every night the same friggin' thing. I come out here making my rounds and find you taking your night rest. And I has never seen anybody who could sleep so good standing up. A thief could come and walk away with the place, could murder every last one of the guests in their beds, and you'd never know. I tell you, I have a mind to give you whatever money's due you and run you from the place tonight-self. Just give you your money and let you g'long home so you can sleep proper in your bed. 'Cause you's no use. No use atall. You's too old for the job!" she cries. The man quickly leans away from the onslaught of her voice in his face. He's a thin, scarecrow figure of a man, wearing a threadbare jacket and a hat against the night dew and carrying a truncheon in his hand. He looks to be in his late fifties, not that much older than herself. "But just you wait"—Astral Forde brings her congested face even closer to his; her voice drops to a furious half-whisper—"just wait till he sells the place and you find yourself out in the road with the rest of us. I'll see then where you gon find a watchman job that'll pay you to come and spend the night sleeping!"

———

Out in the road!

Her distraught steps take her through the grove of mile trees that separates the guest cottages from the manager's house. The old-style bayhouse and bungalow she has loved ever since she laid eyes on it some thirty-odd years ago. Its thick stone walls built to withstand a hurricane. Its double set of wooden shutters at each window. And, at each entrance, an extra pair of doors made of metal and studded with rivets. At night, when all the shutters and doors are closed, bolted and latched, the place sealed up, not even God himself could find a way in. *Out in the road!* It could all be taken from her. The house sold along with everything else.

Inside, she charges from room to room, closing up for the night. In her rush to get to the hospital, she had stopped only long enough to lock the inside shutters at the windows and the inner doors. But now, beginning at the front of the house, she attacks the tall metal outer doors, first unhooking them from the wall, then slamming them into place with the force and clang of an iron door in a dungeon. Some prisoner has been condemned for eternity. Afterward, still raging—*Out in the road!*—she throws the heavy crossbars that secure the doors into their housing, and once again closes and latches the inner doors.

She does the same at the back of the house. There're six doors in all.

Next, turning to the windows, she takes down the long poles that keep the night shutters, which are made of solid wood, open during the day. And instead of easing them down as she usually does, she lets each of them fall of its own weight, setting off a series of thunderclaps that add to the clanging of the doors that is still reverberating through the house.

(Years ago he offered to install glass jalousies at all the windows and in the slatted panels on the inner doors, to let more light and air in during the day and, he said, to modernize the place. He was also thinking of putting an air-conditioner in the bedroom for her. She stood for some time pretending to be considering his offer. "I don't know," she said finally in that seemingly don'-care voice of hers. "If it was a house belonging to me I don't think I'd bother putting in glass everywhere, 'cause the first hurricane to come along is only going to send all of it flying. Good money gone. As for these air-conditioners, all they do is use up a lot of current and keep you with a cold all the time. I don't have no uses for them. No, I'd leave the place just as it is." Loving the metal, the wood and the thick stone.)

With all the windows and doors in place, the house battened down, Astral Forde comes to a halt in her bedroom, and for some time stands looking wildly around her, as though searching for something else to slam shut, to bolt down, and latch furiously into place.

The bedroom is the only room she actually ever uses. The desk where she keeps the accounts is here, as well as the large console television the PM presented her with years ago, but which she seldom ever turns on. Presents large and small over the years: the silver vanity set on its tray on the dresser, the digital clock-radio beside her bed and the five-piece Mediterranean-style bedroom suite itself; the heart-shaped boxes and tins of candies and chocolates that still arrive regularly from Conlin and Finch and the nice-nice jewelry box for her earrings and gold bangles, presents also. The offer of the air-conditioner, the offer of a car as well, which she had also refused. He then arranged for a taxi service in town to send a car for her whenever she wanted to go out. Gift offerings to delight, to honor, to appease . . . One half of a huge old-fashioned armoire holds the white shirtwaist blouses and schoolteacher skirts she has always worn as manager. The other half is filled with the nice dresses she would put on when going to visit Malvern. The rest of the space in the room is taken up by the suite of bedroom furniture with its queen-size bed.

Not far from the bed stands the valet.

It's the third one she's bought for him over the years. In addition to the usual features, this one also comes equipped with a pantspresser. A panel on one side of the valet opens to reveal a built-in ironing board. The pants are inserted, the panel closed, the automatic timer set, and all wrinkles are removed, the crease made razor sharp, and the pants emerge looking as if they've just come from the dry cleaners. She had come across the model in a magazine from the States that one of the elderly guests had left behind and had sent for it. When it arrived she unveiled it for him and then stood watching while he repeatedly opened and closed the panel and toyed with the dial on the timer. There was no hint of a smile, no sign that he was pleased. *One thing, I know he don't have nothing like it in the house on Garrison Row.*

"America," he said finally.

"How you know so good?" She laughed uneasily; he must not like it.

"Something like it could only come from there," he said. "Not only that, I bet the fella who thought to add on this ironing board is a millionaire today . . ." Then, finally looking at her and smiling, a little self-deprecating smile: "And Astral Forde is going to see to it that I at least look like one. *Merci, oui.*"

If I had the will of him! She can almost feel the handle of the ax in her hands and hear the valet splintering into a thousand pieces . . .

She flees the bedroom.

Out in the road! Taking up the litany again as she goes and sits in the unused living room, amid the most recent set of furniture. The matching sofa and chairs, the floor lamps and tables look as if they've only just arrived from Conlin and Finch, although they were presented to her several years ago. They have yet to be properly arranged around the room.

Out in the road! Thinking of that deaf ear just now at the hospital and the look of total indifference on the face. Malvern gone far far off! Oh, God!

Out in the road! Her eye falls on her copy of the prospectus lying on a console table across from the armchair where she will spend most of tonight. "I'm going to get a copy for you," he had said. "You're to read it and let me know what you think. You're the one with a head for business." And he had kept his word. Only last week, he stopped by all smiles to give her the friggin' thing, and when he left she read it up to the page that mentioned Government Lands. She read that page twice to make sure she was seeing right; then with a loud suck-teeth had flung the thing aside and forgotten about it.

Now, though, she sits gazing long and hard across at it. *If I had the will of him!* Her head filled with the sound of wood being splintered beneath the hurricane roar of her thoughts.

5

Ursa parks the jeep on the Government Lands side of the road, and in what will be her first stop for the day she starts across to the monument that lies on the opposite side of the old north/south colonial highway that runs from Morlands to Spanish Bay at the other end of the island. She has to skirt a large pothole filled with water, water the same grayish brown as the broken surface of the road and of the dust that will start to fly as soon as the sun, which has been up for less than an hour, reaches its full strength and quickly dries everything.

It rained off and on during the night, a series of noisy thunderstorms that added to her sleeplessness. As she lay listening to each downpour or waiting for the next to begin, it didn't seem that the thunder and lightning and the bursts of torrential rain were coming from the sky but from the heights of Gran' Morne a few miles to the north of the house, the hoary old mountain taking her to task for having stayed away so long. Chastising her, even as it welcomed her back with the lightning flashes like a fireworks display in her honor.

Another rain-filled pothole the size of a small crater and she's on the other side of the road. Her short legs somehow manage to make the leap over the flooded drain alongside the shoulder, and then she's walking across the stony pasture that lies between the road and the steps leading up to the monument about fifty yards away. The Monument of Heroes. The only worthwhile thing the DNP has done in all the years it's been in office, the PM used to say, Ursa remembers. And not only him but others as well. And look, people would say, how the scamps went about it: how they put Congo Jane and the others all the way in the country, behind God's back, where scarcely anybody can get to see them, so as not to offend the white people in town. And they still wasn't satisfied. They then went and put Jane and the others far far back from the road, so that not even the few people passing by can see them. The scamps! The vagabonds! The Do-Nothings! They's a cross we have to bear.

Nonetheless, there it stands, the monument, hewed out of the pitted volcanic rock from the old mountain that overlooks the entire North District. Tomorrow night, Sunday, nearly all of Morlands will be gathered at its base for the final meeting of the campaign. People like peas, like coffee beans in a sack, crowded together on the dark pasture and spilling over onto Government Lands across the road. The entire district come to see and hear the member from Morlands and to let him know by their applause and shouts of "hear-hear!" and the drumroll of their bare feet on the ground that they can't help but love him. Mis-Mack's boy-child. He's still trying his best for us, never mind what this Mr. Justin and the wife he went and find in Spanish Bay and the other hotheads like them running about the place giving out these papers against him are saying. And he's still the PM up this way, bo. The one and only PM as far as the North District is concerned, never mind who those DNP thieves that keep on stealing the elections each time put in his place.

Black faces indistinguishable from the night. Ursa knows she won't be able to make out a single face tomorrow night. The fireflies will be more visible than the citizens of Morlands. Thinking of this, she climbs the steps to the platform where she, Estelle and Celestine will sit over to one side, just out of reach of the one spotlight on the PM. It's unlikely that any other members of the family will come up from town.

And there *they* are, looming above her on their base at the rear of the platform as she reaches the top step, the four who will also be part of his cheering section tomorrow night. The old man, Pere Bossou, to the left of the statue, will blow his conch shell for Morlands's favorite son; on the far right Alejandro, the boy-soldier from Spanish Bay, will hail him with his conquistador's sword; and in between those two, ready to do battle for him with cutlass and gun—cutlass in one hand, stolen musket in the other, both of them similarly armed—will be Congo Jane and Will Cudjoe, coleaders, coconspirators, consorts, lovers, friends: Jane, a Congo woman who loved the look and feel of pretty things, wearing the shawl of Alençon lace she had taken as the spoils of war and as compensation in part for the nub of a breast that had been left in shreds; and Will Cudjoe with a bandage made from the shawl binding up the gunshot wound on his forehead.

The four heads graze the early morning sky.

"See if you can touch her toes, Ursa-Bea! Reach up and try and touch her toes!" And perched on Estelle's narrow shoulders she had strained all the way up until she could just reach the tip of the stone foot thrust out from the edge of the base. Warmed by the sun, Congo Jane's toes had felt as alive as her own. She must have been no more than three at the time. One of her earliest memories.

She gazes up at the stone face as black and wide-nosed as her own. And at the eyes that appear to be one dark, far-seeing, all-seeing pupil. The wings of the shawl crisscross Jane's chest like bandoliers, hiding her loss . . . Estelle had waited until almost time for her to go away to high school before telling her about the whipping and what it had done. Up till then, that part of the story had always been omitted.

The morning after the full story she woke up to find she had slept with her arms folded tightly over her chest.

Jane. Jane *and* Will Cudjoe, she quickly adds, reminding herself of the old saying about those two: You can't call her name or his without calling or at least thinking of the other, they were so close.

"I like that," Lowell Carruthers had declared back in the days of the free zone. "We need to get back to thinking like that, being like that again if we're ever going to make it."

It was unacceptable, the man had said, handing the proposal back to her the moment she stepped in his office. The thought of a paper on Congo Jane and Will Cudjoe and the others like them had turned him against her. Professor Crowder who had always been so friendly . . . Bastard! Twelve years and it still rankles. And now that she can finally write the paper, she hasn't as yet put down the first word. Reams of notes all over the apartment and not even the introduction written. That part of her life still on hold for some reason. The Janes and Will Cudjoes still waiting on her to tell about them . . .

Ursa sees the bird droppings like chalk tears on the faces that look to be just inches from the sky, and she can no longer meet their eyes.

Back in the jeep she puts it in reverse and backs up until she reaches the turnoff to Government Lands and the beach at its other end. The road that will take her there is little more than a dirt track that last night's rain has turned into a bog. She has to use all the skill she can muster with the steering wheel and gears to prevent the jeep from going into a slide and crashing head-on into a tree. Each time it strikes one of the deep ruts that litter the track, the muddy water flies up like a geyser. She has to roll up the window next to her to keep from being spattered. Puddles as large as lakes and patches of soggy ground that suck at the wheels like quicksand. The jeep pitches and rolls like a ship in distress. An abomination, this road. All the P and D projects and this road is still as it was before she was born. It will soon, though, be a wide, well-paved, tree-lined driveway for the Fortune 500 and friends. *How could you be party to it? . . . Don't hold me!*

The swill continues for close to two miles before the road peters out at the solid wall of trees that borders the beach at Government Lands. Coco palms, sea grape and almond trees. Ursa parks at their edge and, taking the keys to the jeep and her beach bag, heads toward the sound of the surf and the salt drift that have taken over the air.

And there it all is as she emerges from the trees: the wide white-sand beach that follows unerringly the curve of the bay, the overarching sky that is absolutely clear except for a ridge of clouds, left over from the rain, that can be seen hovering along the horizon; and there's the wide, wide sea spread before her. It still contains traces of the night so that it's a deeper, richer blue than the sky. The scales of morning sunlight on its surface are like a fleet of paper boats a child might have fashioned from the pages of a notebook and set adrift.

Not a soul in sight. The beach empty from one great wing of the bay to the other. She's too late for the fishermen who left at dawn and too early for the women who will come later in the morning to help with the catch when the first boats return around noon. Tomorrow, Sunday, will be another matter. Sunday is sea-bath day at Government Lands beach. People like peas on the beach from the time God's sun rises. All those who don't spend the day in church coming to have a sea-bath. The children running and flinging themselves half naked into the surf, and the grown-ups—the small farmers, the cane cutters on the big estates, the coffee growers from up Gran' Morne, the men and women who work the rice fields in the wide valley below Bush Mountain—all of them performing a careful ritual before actually going for a swim. They will stand waist-deep in the breaking waves, scoop up water in their cupped hands and splash it over their arms and shoulders and chests, and in great handfuls over their heads, while keeping their faces turned to the horizon and beyond. Only after thoroughly splashing themselves will they then go for a swim. Some never even bother. They simply remain in the surf anointing themselves with seawater until they decide to come out.

Ursa sits—cool, slightly damp sand under her and between her toes as she takes off her sandals. She's wearing a loose-fitting cotton jumpsuit that is almost the same shade of blue as the sky. Behind her, just above the tree line, hangs a temperate seven o'clock sun. About ten feet below her the waves are quietly exploding with the sound of Ke'ram. They heave themselves onto the shore, there's the soft muffled explosion, the foam spreads like the lace of Jane's shawl, and the wave recedes. Ke'ram. They're breaking and receding with the sound of Ke'ram, saying it for her. She sits listening for a long time, her mind gathering the calm she will need today and her gaze on the low ridge last night's rain clouds have formed on the horizon. It's like the landfall of an island that came into existence during her absence.

"You sit on this beach and feel like the world's been created no more than ten minutes ago. Everything and everybody's brand-new," Estelle had said. She might have been sitting on this very spot when she made her pronouncement. She was wearing, Ursa remembers, a black two-piece bathing suit, the waistband cutting into the puffiness across her stomach, and she had on a straw hat with a brim so wide it shaded both their faces whenever Estelle bent over her.

"How old are you, Ursa-Bea?" Bending down to where she sat on the sand beside her, and bringing the cool shadow of the wide-brimmed hat over her face.

"Four." And to prove to Estelle that she knew exactly how many that was, she had held up the appropriate number of fingers.

"No, you're not. You're not even a day old yet. You only just got here ten minutes ago. You're brand-new. How old are you, Jocelyn?"

Paule Marshall

Jocelyn, her roly-poly cousin, was spending time with them in Morlands.

"Five and a half," Jocelyn had said.

"Nope. I'm afraid not. You're also only ten minutes old. But you're not to feel bad, either of you, because it's the same with me. As old as I look to you, I'm brand-new too. So are all the trees behind us and the sky, the sand crabs, the sun and every grain of sand as far as you can see. And don't forget this wave just coming in. Everything's just been created."

And there was Viney. Their last day on the beach she had suddenly stood up, taken off her designer sunglasses, spread her arms in the batwing-sleeved caftan she had on and had tried to embrace it all. Saying after a long, reverent silence, "We should have headed straight here the minute we got off the plane . . . and not budged for the entire two weeks."

Viney. She, Robeson and Dee Dee are in Petersburg by now, spending the Memorial Day weekend at her mother's. Viney had come to see her after she called to tell her about the prospectus and the letter from Estelle. Upon hearing that she had changed her mind and would be going down for the elections after all, Viney had also decided to go home for the long weekend, and to take Dee Dee. That had been on Wednesday, three days ago. Viney had taken the afternoon off from work and come up to 101st Street.

"Both Robeson and I could use a few days away from these mean streets, too, now that I think of it," she said. "And it'll help having Dee Dee along. Besides, I need to go sit in my old church and ask for strength to deal with Pirelli and the New York City police department." Saying this with the evidence of Monday's ordeal faintly visible behind her carefully made up face and with the windy hole next to her, the outline where some halfway-together, useful somebody should have been.

Viney's down home, in the house that sits directly across the road from a Civil War battlefield. A few doors down from the house is the church where she was baptized, the Triumphant Baptist Church, which faces the same battleground.

380

("Home sweet home," Estelle said on the way from the airport when Ursa told her about Robeson's being arrested. Her face disappeared from between theirs in the front of the car, and she sat drawn up into a corner of the backseat, saying nothing more, but thinking, Ursa knew, of her brother—her uncle Grady—whose hip had been broken in an Alabama jail back in the sixties, and of her mother and father—her grandparents—dead on the road to Tennessee when Booker Harrison suffered a massive stroke at the wheel. He had refused to take the train or bus down to Tennessee each summer even after they were integrated. "Home sweet home," said again from the backseat, the voice bitter, despairing. "How does that saying go? The more things change the more they remain the same?"/"Estelle," the PM called gently to her over his shoulder. "Don't upset yourself. You know what those people up there give. Besides, Ursa says the little boy's all right. Come and sit up close again. We miss your company.")

"And what about Lowell? Don't you think you should let him know what's come up?" Viney had suddenly asked as they were saying goodbye Wednesday evening.

"Why do you keep asking for him? No, I'm not telling him anything! I haven't even thought of that man." Which was true. She hadn't been conscious of Lowell Carruthers crossing her mind since the prospectus arrived.

"All right, there's no need to get annoyed, but you could at least phone him before you leave. I'm sure he'd want to know about what's happened down there."

"Are you kidding? The only thing he would want to hear about Triunion is that it had sunk to the bottom of the sea taking the PM with it. I told you the ugly things he had to say."

"He was upset over the job, Ursa, you know that. He probably didn't mean half the things he said. I think you should at least call him before you go. Just a call. That won't take anything from you. You know he's sitting in that apartment of his waiting, hoping that you'll call."

Viney speaking of Lowell in this strange new way, without

her customary disdain and the lip. She had stood over by the door, her attaché case at her side, dressed in the killer clothes she wore to work—another Congo Jane who loved pretty things—had stood there pleading Lowell's cause.

"I mean you don't just up and walk away from somebody you've been going with for over six years because of a quarrel, I don't care what was said. Who knows, it might even have been a good thing. The two of you might be able to really talk to each other now. That's what happens sometimes. People blow up, say things that've been festering for years, and afterward they find they can be straight with each other. No more playing games and hiding behind egos. Sometimes the whole relationship takes a turn for the better. It happens. It can happen if there's enough there to work with . . . Was it just a quarrel—and maybe one that was even a good thing—or am I really through? You need to ask yourself that, Ursa . . ."

(Estelle said as much two nights ago in the house on Garrison Row. "Are you sure you're finished, Ursa-Bea, or was it one of those quarrels that just seems like the end because you're still so angry? There's a difference between the two." Then, suddenly turning on herself: "I shouldn't have insisted that you come! Here you've got your own troubles and I practically ordered you down here to pile more on you."/And shaking her head, Ursa repeated what she had said minutes before. "No, it was time I came down.")

"Call the man! Just pick up the phone and call him!" Viney had finally lost patience on Wednesday and reverted to her old RA, den mother ways.

"I can't, Viney. I can't deal with Lowell Carruthers right now. I'm not even sure I want to ever. Certainly not while he's still on that job. He'd have to make a move first. He knows that. Or who knows, maybe it's really over. He said what he had to say and what I needed to hear, I guess, from someone other than myself, and maybe that was it. He served his purpose, and it's done. I don't know.

"Sister/friend," she quickly added, and to escape the frightened look on Viney's face, quickly embraced her. "I really can't deal with it now. We'll talk when I get back. Maybe by then I'll have things straight in my mind."

A perturbed Viney left, and she began packing, barring Lowell Carruthers from her thoughts, but feeling the hollowness again. And that night she dreamed that they were walking along Columbus Avenue, with him going on as usual—the Davison jones on him—when he suddenly stopped and groped for her arm. His hand on her arm, holding it against his side and refusing to let go of it even though she began angrily pulling it away. But he held on as though her arm, which was scarcely half the length of his, was a stick being held out to someone drowning. The tug-of-war over her arm soon turned into an all-out brawl. A stadium-size crowd quickly gathered, all the YRUMS—the Young and the Restless Upwardly Mobiles—of the Upper West Side stood in a circle around them, with Professor Crowder in their midst, jubilantly waving the rejected proposal, and all of them egging the two of them on, throwing pennies at their feet and taking bets as to which of them will go down first. Go to it! Go to it! A battle royal. A nigger show. Until Pirelli pulled up in his squad car and led both of them away in handcuffs. A Pirelli who was the surly taxi driver from Monday night dressed in a policeman's uniform . . .

To shake the thought of the dream and the hollowness that had caused it, Ursa abruptly gets up and starts walking along the beach in the direction of Gran' Morne to the north. With the help of the ground mist, the mountain has begun its morning's levitation, along with everything else. Trees, houses, rocks—all slowly taking to the air.

She's left behind her sandals and the beach bag well out of reach of the surf. All the bag contains is her copy of the prospectus and the jeep's ignition key. No bathing suit, no towel, not even a pair of sunglasses. She got up at dawn, put the prospectus in the bag first thing, quickly showered and dressed, and with the flutter kick around her heart—where it will remain all day—she left the house before even Celestine was up. An early morning swim, they'll think, when they wake and find her gone. When she used to come down faithfully three or four times a year, she was known to take off for Government Lands beach at 'foreday morning sometimes. She and the fishermen the only ones out in the cool, dove gray dawn.

Walking, trying to rid herself of the dream, she comes to a pile of rocks set back near the line of trees. 'Ti–Gran' Morne. Everyone calls the rockpile, which slopes up to form a miniature hill about twelve feet high, Little Gran' Morne. It's been there for as long as she can remember. Later in the morning, the women who come to help with the catch will wait for the boats there, seated on the patches of sedge that grow amid the rocks nearest the ground and shaded by a large almond tree, part of whose trunk lies embedded in the pile.

And tomorrow, Sunday, sea-bath day at the beach, Little Gran' Morne will be alive, she knows, with any number of boys and one or two tomboy girls scaling its heights in the game they call Monument. It's been so since she herself was a girl. Skin glistening from the sea, they'll clamber up the jumble of rocks, and once they reach the top they'll play Monument, slashing away at an invisible foe with Alejandro's sword and the cutlasses belonging to Jane and Will Cudjoe, and strafing the air with musket fire. Standing on a large flat rock near the summit, they'll turn their cupped hands into conch shells and become old Pere Bossou rallying slaves into soldiers.

Slowly Ursa climbs the 'ti-mountain and sits on the same flat rock near the top. She breathes deep the salt breath of the sea. Takes in the flawless curve of the bay below her. And slowly puts aside Lowell Carruthers as the canyon inside her begins to shrink. Up here the sky seems closer, bluer. Ke'ram. And the sunlight appears to be refracted through the puffed-out throat of a lizard. True, they used to make her skin crawl, yet she had loved a lizard's throat. They would come to rest on a sunny patch of ground or a wall or rock, close their bulbous eyes, raise their squashed green heads, and as if by magic their throats would swell till they became a thin, sheer, translucent fan, and the sunlight passing through it would be transformed. Ke'ram. Thinking: just as the children playing Monument tomorrow will be transformed, becoming even the old man with a conch shell for a bugle. I'll come back to see them in the morning. Thinking too: there won't be many Sundays left for them. The uniformed security guards patrolling the beach will be enough to discourage the rock climbers and everyone else from coming near the place. In short order, Government Lands beach will be the exclusive property of the NCRC types flown in on the private planes. *How could you? . . . And about to put your money in it too! Selling Mile Trees! . . .* She finally gives way to the thought, no longer able to stave it off. *Selling Mile Trees!*

He arrived in Morlands late last night to announce that this was what he intended doing. Then, in the next breath, before either she or Estelle could utter a word, he turned from them and was calling for Celestine to bring his supper. They would discuss it in the morning, he said, but he was too tired, too blasted tired, to talk about it tonight. What time in the morning, Estelle wanted to know, "when your lieutenants will be here at the crack of dawn and the last-minute two-day campaign will be in high gear. What time, I'd like to know!" He ignored her anger, her sarcasm and turned to Ursa: and the two of them would also have their ol' talk in the morning if he got the chance. Don't think he had forgotten. He and this daughter of his—this busy American Ms. who doesn't have time for her own father anymore, won't even come to see the poor fella—are going to take some time for themselves tomorrow. He'd love for them to go and sit in the sea with two or three mangoes and have their talk there. Did she remember when they used to do that?/She remembered. The mangoes would be sweeter after he dipped them in the surf. Nectar. And when they were done eating he used to scoop up the water like the bathers on Sunday and wash around her mouth./"Just sit in the sea with my child and dip mangoes and ol' talk . . ." Talking faster last night than they had ever heard him, his voice hoarse from exhaustion, his face haggard. But right then, right then he needed to eat and to look to his bed.

"Celestine!"

She appeared before he finished calling her name, and after eating he went immediately to bed.

He slept, and she and Estelle sat on the veranda overlooking the parade-ground yard, a lighted mosquito coil on the floor between their chairs, the smoke twisting straight up in the windless night. Silent. Both of them feeling too hopeless to even try to speak. Down in the yard a bulb had been left on over the door to the one bathroom in the house, to light the way there. The small stone house of a kitchen over near the stairs stood dark and shuttered, the tank of propane gas for the stove gleaming white against the wall outside. Several yards away the ancient stalls held the Buick, the jeep and the Nissan Estelle now drove—the PM's latest gift—and at the back of the huge yard the two-story-high wooden gate that turned the house into a stockade had been secured by an iron crossbar.

The old house sealed for the night and silent. And the night silent except for the steady din of crickets and tree frogs, cicadas and the wildly zooming hardback beetles—sounds that went unnoticed, that were simply the pulse of the darkness, the silence.

Both she and Estelle remained part of the silence for the longest time until Estelle surprised her by quietly saying, "That poor woman. What's going to happen to her, Ursa-Bea? That's what I'm sitting here thinking about." Estelle turned to her. In the faint light reaching them from below, her face appeared to be lit by a candle whose glow was so feeble it did nothing but create dark holes where her features should have been. "Oh, I'm sure she's saved enough over the years to live on. I'm not talking about that. I mean Mile Trees. The job. She's been married to that place for so long. That's the way I think of her, you know—when I think of her at all—as being married to those dozen little cottages. I suspect they've been more important to her than your father even. That's the way I see it. Maybe I've *had* to see it that way in order to have gone along with our quote arrangement all this time.

Who knows?" This with an almost indifferent shrug. Estelle talking to her about Astral Forde for the first time ever.

She was again grateful for the letter ordering her home.

"One thing I do know," Estelle said. "Ursa-Beatrice doesn't approve—and has never approved—of my having gone along with the arrangement. You've never said anything but I know. I even worry that that's the reason—or one of the reasons— you've taken to staying away from the place. Just fed up with your mother . . ."

"It's that I didn't understand why you put up with it."

A rueful laugh. "You're not the only one! I'm not sure I do. And yet I can't tell you the last time I've felt the least twinge of jealousy or whatever toward that woman. Or anger anymore with your father over it. How is that? Now, that I don't understand!" she cried, angry with herself suddenly. The thin thread of smoke from the mosquito coil quickly shifted out of her way. "What happened to my ego, my pride? Why is it that all I've felt for Miss Forde for years now is sympathy and a little curiosity? What's the woman like? How could she put up with someone who's never taken her anywhere, never spent a night with her? I doubt if your father's ever sat down and had a meal with her. How could she take that?" Estelle answers herself. "She had Mile Trees. That made up for everything. But what'll she have now that he's thinking of selling it? She won't find another job that easily at her age. And why am I sitting here worrying about her instead of myself? That I don't understand either." Then: "You're to go by and see her before you leave, Ursa-Bea."

"I will," she promised, "although I won't get two words out of her as usual."

"Go anyway," Estelle said.

By now the sun has cleared the top of the almond tree that is part of the small mountain of rocks, and Ursa's seat at the summit has become unbearably hard. Getting up, she slowly picks her way down 'Ti–Gran' Morne, thinking of Astral Forde. Astral

Forde forced to stand beside him at the pool each Sunday holding the towel and the glass of soursop juice on a tray. A maid's work. The manager turned maid on Sundays. And because of that the look directed at her in the pool that had said, If looks could kill, bo, you'd be dead.

And yet, sometimes, there had been the hint of another feeling behind that look. One that used to puzzle her even more when she was small. That other look, that other feeling would be there one instant and gone the next, so fleeting she was sure Astral Forde wasn't even aware of it . . .

And then, late yesterday morning when they arrived in Morlands, there was the same look, the same feeling in Celestine's eyes, only completely undisguised. By the time the stockade gate was opened and she and Estelle drove into the yard, Celestine was already out of the house and waiting over by the stalls. There she stood in the familiar dress of mourning, her gatepost legs rooted to the ground, and the sunlight striking the face—black, smooth, high-boned—that would never age. Everything about her unchanged, except for the braid like a heraldic wreath around her head. It had turned completely gray over the four years.

After they embraced, Celestine stepped back to inspect her version of the braid. She gazed at it in silence for a long time, reached out and touched it the way Estelle had done the night before, turned her around to see how well she had joined the two plaits at the back. Then: *"Mes amis!"* Uttered with her face lifted in praise-giving to the sky. Flesh of her flesh might have returned to stand before her. *"Mes amis!"* Celestine embraced her again, ignoring Estelle nearby.

But Estelle refused to be ignored and, placing her arms around them both, said, "I've always believed in sharing the wealth."

She has prepared his morning cup of coffee by now. Coffee that is half milk and with a layer of coarse brown sugar like a bed of sand at the bottom, which he will stir himself, as he liked to do when he was a boy, Celestine once told her. This morning before the cook was up, she had unlocked the kitchen, ground the coffee beans in the hand mill, scalded the milk, and prepared it. Whether in Morlands or in the house on Garrison Row she always has the coffee brewed and waiting for him the moment he awakes . . . Last night she had appeared with the food before he even finished calling her name . . . "Please come go with us to the movies, Celestine." Or: "Come go shopping with us, please," she used to plead along with Estelle. All to no avail.

Ursa, if you think about Celestine's life you'll never come near this place again! Suddenly, instead of slowly picking her way down the rockpile, she lets her legs take off under her and she's rushing downward in a headlong plunge she can't control—that she doesn't want to control—down the last six or seven jagged feet to the bottom. For seconds at a time she's almost airborne; she's like the children on Sundays whose feet barely touch anything solid as they come flying down from their minimountain. Gone! 'Ti–Gran' Morne will soon be gone. Along with the almond tree wedded to it. The bulldozer will make quick work of them both. Gone also the women who wait here each morning and the fishermen who set out each dawn. Their smelly boats will be the first to go! The management of the resort scheme will see to that. She charges toward a large patch of sedge she sees between two rocks near the ground. But instead of serving as a footing, the grass made slick by the rain last night simply slides out from under her. It's there one moment—damp and rough under her bare feet—and then gone the next. Her arms fly out. In her panic she tries grabbing hold of the air, the morning light, the sky, a lone plover flying overhead, only to come crashing down, with her hands splayed open, on the grassy patch. Her right hip strikes the edge of a rock, pain knifes through her, and then she is free-falling the last foot or two to the ground.

"Shit!"

She lies sprawled on the sand, cursing and clutching the struck hip. And then rubbing it. "Rub it, Ursa-Bea!" Estelle would say whenever she fell and banged an elbow or a knee. "Don't cry. Just rub it and it'll stop hurting." And it nearly always did. Estelle getting her ready, from the day she was born practically, for the lone voyage in the rowboat.

It takes a long time, even with the rubbing, for the pain to subside enough for her to move. When it finally eases after nearly a half hour, Ursa slowly picks herself up, brushes the sand off her clothes, her arms, her hair, and holding her side starts back to where she left her sandals and the beach bag. Inside the bag, the prospectus she plans to drop off. No matter how much she's hurting, there's still the main task of the day to be done. She limps forward on the injured hip.

———

By late that night the soreness and stiffness have set in, and the pain returns full force. She's about to take off her robe and climb into bed when it hits her again. And for a long time all she can do is sit doubled over on the edge of the bed, holding herself and rocking. A version of Viney's moanin'-low sway, only her movement is back and forth, not sideways. And the pain isn't just in her right hip, as it was earlier on the beach. It starts there. She feels the edge of the rock cutting into the same place again. But in a matter of seconds the pain leaves there and begins moving slowly across the well of her stomach to her other hip. Sweeping across at intervals, in wave after wave, and lancing her as if somebody has taken a knife to her. Sometimes no sooner than one wave reaches her left side, another begins on her right. It's what her grandmother used to call a traveling pain. "Got this traveling pain across my back, don't know what it is," Bea Harrison would say and take a hot bath with Epsom salts.

She should do the same, she tells herself, bent over and rocking on the bed. A long soak in a tub with some salts. Then remembers that there's only a shower in the one cavernous bathroom down in the yard. She'd have to wake Celestine, whose room is next to hers, and ask her to put one of the galvanized tubs used for washing clothes into the shower for her; it's the way she used to be given a bath when she was small, seated in a washtub in the shower stall. No, don't bother with the tub. Let Celestine sleep. Let her get her rest. There's the coffee to be made at the crack of dawn for the boychild none can resist. Rocking, still rocking, as the pain cuts across her again. I'll just get a couple of aspirins from Estelle. No, let her sleep too. She has scarcely seen Estelle all day. By the time she returned in the jeep, the task she had set for herself completed, Estelle had gone out. The stall that held the Nissan stood empty. The one for the Buick also. His right-hand men in the district arrived early in the morning and the all-out two-day campaign—as Estelle called it—has gone on all day. No ol' talk. She had been forewarned. When Estelle came in she complained of the heat and a headache and went to her room. And she has stayed there for the rest of the day. Let her sleep. There might be another bottle of aspirins in the bathroom or some kind of salve. Maybe even a heating pad.

Doubled over on the bed, Ursa watches herself walk out of the bedroom and along the veranda until she comes to the stairs leading down to the yard. She sees herself going down the worn, noisy stairs, guided from below by the light above the bathroom door. She feels her legs carrying her across the yard to the door and over the threshold into the damp stone bathroom, where she turns on the light inside and searches in the medicine cabinet for something that will get her through the night.

She thinks of doing all this, sees herself doing it, but does nothing. Instead, when the next wave of pain wells up and explodes across her belly, she just lets it take her, simply lets it take and fling her onto the bed the way a piece of coral caught in a heavy surf is flung onto a beach. And when the pain subsides she doesn't try to sit up again; she just lies there waiting for the next wave, drawn up in the robe she didn't even get to take off.

She had awakened that Saturday morning in late March to find she had slept in her coat.

Viney, do you think those idiots might've only half done the job, and whatever it is, is still there? . . . That crazy thought again. Two whole months have passed, and it still comes back from time to time to hag her spirit.

6

If only you had heard her, *oui*! "There's nothing more to be done, nothing more to be said, so all of you might as well go home. It's been a long, exhausting day—both today and yesterday—and we could all do with some sleep. You can stop by later in the week, if you like. We'll be here. We're going to stay right here in Morlands for a while getting some much-needed rest, so there'll be plenty of time for you to stop by and talk. And you're welcomed to take whatever's left in the van. The rum's gone, but there's some rice and a few of the pens left. Just help yourself on the way out." If only you had heard her! She told everybody that was sitting with him in Mis-Mack shop the same thing—Trevor Yearwood, Cyril Payne, Pierre Armand from up Gran' Morne and all the others, people that's been close to the PM all these years, helping him with the elections and looking after the district for him when he's in town. The *blanche neg'* just come right out and told every last one of them to go home, saying tomorrow it's back to work and she knows they need their rest. What's done is done. Come back later in the week. Putting people out the door! *Mes amis!* Talking to them nice and polite but putting them out all the same. And the PM's agreeing with her. Thanking them and saying they could as well go home 'cause sitting around is not gon change anything. He was gon study the returns one last time and then look to his bed too. "This is the kind of news you got to sleep on, bo. It takes a good night's rest to tackle this one." *Tête chargé, oui*, in a state, you can tell the man's in a state—he can't believe it, nobody can believe it —but he's still trying to make a little joke for them so they won't go away feeling so bad. That's the way he is. But not the *blanche neg'*. She ain't making joke one. As soon as six o'clock come and it turned dark everybody was to leave, and the minute the last person was out the shop she called for the *'ti-garçon* to come and lock the doors. And she was there helping him. If only you had seen her! The arms like two sticks from starving out herself, and she's trying to close those heavy doors. Then the boy was to go and close and lock the big gate to the yard. Nobody else is to set foot in the house tonight. Everybody gone and it's only her one in the shop with him now. And you can tell she's gon sit there till Thy Kingdom Come if need be. She's not gon budge from his side now that she's got her way . . . She even sent away the man's child! *Seigneur!* 'Ti-Ursa must leave too. She was there trying to comfort her father, but I know after a time the *blanche neg'* told her like she did the others: There's nothing more to be done, nothing more to be said, and she best get ready to go back to town. She was to take her car. *Mes amis!* Sending the child to drive her one all up Bush Mountain at this hour of the night! She has to get back to her work. The plane to New York is leaving first thing in the morning and she needed to go to town tonight and get a good night's sleep there. She needed her rest. If only you had heard her! Not that that ain't true. 'Ti-Ursa needs to rest. I don't think she closed her eyes all of last night. *Tête chargé* like everybody else over what happened yesterday. Then she get a fall on Saturday morning that kept her up all that night too. Fall and hurt her hip out at Government Lands beach. I was gon make a green-leaf plaster to draw the pain or boil some bush tea for her to drink, but she said no. She's refusing to take anything for it. Not so much as an aspirin. It'll go away, it'll go away, she's telling you, but you can see it's giving her trouble. She could scarce climb the steps to the monument last night. *Mes amis!* Everything happening one time! 'Ti-Ursa fall and near break her hip and the PM lose his seat. *The PM lose his seat!* You say it but you still can't believe it. What I has seen in Morlands these past two days! People wicked, *oui!* This Mr. Justin got his hands on the book that tells all about the resort scheme and he went and copy the page concerning Government Lands and give it out all over the district. How he got hold of it, who wicked person give it to him or send it to him, you don't know. The people in the shop tonight was saying it's one of the Do-Nothings on the P and D Board who's vex 'cause they're not putting the resort scheme in his district and he's the one sent it up to him on the bus must be Saturday. But if so, you have to ask yourself why he waited till then when this book-thing was ready over a week now. You just don't know, *oui*. Nobody knows. You don't even want to think who the person could be. *Seigneur!* In this life you have to run from your own thoughts sometime . . . The whelp took the page from the book, copy it just as it stands with the page number big on it, and gave it out all over the place. From early early yesterday they was all over the district handing it out, he and the wife he went and find in Spanish Bay and the pack that's joined in with them. All over, even down on Government Lands beach where people was having their sea-bath. Every last man, woman and child in Morlands was to have a copy of the thing. And they was telling those that can't read to find somebody who could, to read it for them. Running all over giving out this paper. They even had the brass face to bring one here to the house. When the *'ti-garçon* went to open the shop yesterday morning, there it was slide under the door, and he run with it to the PM who was having his coffee on the veranda. *O ciel éternel!* If you had seen the PM's face when he read that thing! Is a look I'll take with me to the grave. It gave him such a turn he couldn't do or say a thing for a time. Just sat there holding it in his hand and staring at it like he couldn't believe what he was seeing. *Tête chargé!* It was a long long time before he could come to himself. "Celestine!" Calling me. That's the first thing he did. The *blanche neg'* was sitting right there with him asking him what happen, over and over what happen, what the paper said, but he's not answering her, he's not even looking at her, just calling me. "Celestine, you see this? It looks like the school-teacher fella has pelt another rockstone at the house . . ." Trying to laugh, *oui*. "I'm gon have to talk muh talk tonight to explain this one, bo." But do you think those brutes out at the monument last night gave him a chance to speak? Not them! They wasn't satisfied to spread the papers all over the district and have people all upset over Government Lands, they had to come and mash up the meeting too. This Mr. Justin had his henchmen all through the crowd, and the minute the PM stepped forward to speak, one of them held up his paper. And then a next one held up his, and when you looked again, a next, and on and on. And as soon as the papers went up they started shouting all kind of questions at him. What about this paper? Tell us about what's on this paper—the resort scheme and where you and the P and D Board are putting it. They din want to hear any ol' talk about he's still trying his best for them or about the thieves and Do-Nothings in government that keep him from doing anything, they only want to hear about what's on the paper. Why was he hiding it from the people? He din have a right to do that. Hiding it because he knew people in Morlands would be against it. Tell us about this paper! And they heard his name and money are all up in it too. Tell us about that. *Mes amis!* One call out one thing and a next something else before the other one even finish. Shouting at him to explain himself and then not giving him a chance. The brutes din mean for him to speak! 'Cause they knew if he was to explain things in his way the people would go along with him. So they just kept it up till everybody there was so worked up they decide to join in with them and started holding up their paper too. All you could see was these sheets of white paper all over the place. You couldn't see not one face out there in the dark, only the papers. And they're shouting at him too. Saying they heard the resort scheme is not gon benefit them in any way and how he could go behind their back. Everything the henchmen saying they're repeating. After drinking up the rum and helping themself to the rice and the nice Bic pens the PM gave out before the meeting, they start 'buse-ing him right and left. *Les ingrats!* How your own can turn against you! And after mashing up the meeting, the henchmen then call for everybody to go with them to where this Mr. Justin was, to hear him speak. He and the wife was all the way down in Government Lands putting up a trash house. They say they gon live there till the P and D Board agrees to consult with the people in the district about the resort scheme. They're not budging till then. And anybody that want, can come and put up a trash house too. They're calling on everybody in Morlands to do like them. *Mes amis*, the resort scheme finish, *oui*, 'cause you know the white people are not gon put their money in anything where there's all this confusion. The meeting spoil, the resort scheme finish, and the PM left standing out at the monument with only a few old people that was gon vote for him no matter what still down in the pasture. *Seigneur!* Is a good thing Mis-Mack din live to see last night. She must be grieving over it, though, in her grave. The shame of it! It was enough to make the stone people up on the statue behind him shed tears. I don't think 'ti-Ursa raised her head the whole time we was there. She couldn't bear the sight of it. As for the *blanche neg'*, don't ask me how she stood, 'cause I never so much as let my eye catch hers. You have to run from your own thoughts some-time. Morlands people turning their backs and walking away from the PM to go and listen to some small boy schoolteacher fella that don't have no background! And then turning around again today and giving him their vote! Ungrateful whelps! And this Mr. Justin still ain't satisfied. He stole the vote, he took the PM's seat, and he's still persecuting him. As soon as the returns was in this evening he sent one of his henchmen over here with another letter asking the PM to join in with him. *The brass face!* Saying he's gon need his help. And you watch, if the *blanche neg'* has her way that's just what's gon happen. She's gon do and do till she has everything her way. Tonight was the start. Putting everybody out the door! Sending away people that's been with the man for years! Go home. There's nothing more to be said. And then putting her own child on that ol' road in the darkness. Kissed her and told her it's time to leave, what's done is done. *Mes amis!* an unnatural mother . . . As for me, I was to make coffee for the two of them and leave it on the stove along with some food—she'll start eating again, you watch—and g'long to my bed. Giving orders right and left. But I don't care what she says, I'm gon sit out here in the yard all night if I have to, 'cause the first thing he's gon want to know when he comes to himself is where's Celestine. *Celestine!* I'll hear him before he even opens his mouth good to call my name. What does the *blanche neg'* know? . . .

7

Ursa has to tap the car horn a third time before the night watch-man's head finally comes up with a jerk. She has pulled up no more than ten feet from the man, yet he hasn't heard her. Asleep on the job, his truncheon hanging by its strap from his wrist, almost touching the ground, and his arms hanging limp at his side. You better not let Miss Forde catch you, or it'll be "Come get your money and get from round the place"—thinking this as the man stumbles forward from the closed gate.

He's an old man, she sees, as he brings his sleepy face down to hers at the window of the Nissan. Or someone who's just old-looking before his time. She can't tell. She doesn't know him. There was another guard the last time she was down. She'd hate to think of the number Astral Forde has hired and fired since then.

She tells the man her name, and the sleep instantly vanishes from his face and from the pair of rheumy eyes under the hat he has on. He can't quite find his voice to say anything, but he brings the truncheon in his hand up to his hatbrim in a confused little salute, and then he is hastening back to open the gate. He gives another little salute as the car glides past him.

Ursa waves in return.

At the end of the driveway she parks in front of the open pavilion that connects the two rows of cottages that make up the Mile Trees Colony Hotel. Together the buildings form a U around the swimming pool the PM insisted on having. Went into debt for years to install it, although a perfectly good beach borders the place. The bathing here is almost as good as at Government Lands.

Why did he have to have the pool, which the guests hardly ever used? Why was certain "stuff" so important to him? It might have been one of the questions she would have put to him if they had gotten around to their ol' talk.

As she enters the pavilion she finds everything in darkness. Only ten o'clock, but the elderly guests are already bedded down. Not a single light to be seen in any of the cottages. There's the moon, though. A large, bright, three-quarter moon. It has accompanied her on the long drive down from Morlands, and it now sits high above the tall tropical pines that surround the hotel. She can hear the familiar tête-à-tête the mile trees keep up with one another day and night, whether there's a breeze or not. And there's the intermittent surge of the waves nearby.

She stands listening for a time, trying to rev up her nerve. Because Astral Forde over in the manager's house might well refuse to see her or to talk to her, might refuse to even open her door. All right. So be it. She'll wish Miss Forde well and head on over to Garrison Row and her bed. She'll at least be able to tell Estelle that she tried.

Moving a little stiffly because of her hip, which is still sore, she leaves the pavilion for the work area and outbuildings behind the cottages. Beyond these lies the manager's house off to itself behind a large grove of the mile trees. The work area is also in darkness, except for the kitchen, she discovers. There's light on in the kitchen—which is a separate building, like the one at Morlands—and the door is open. Someone in there at this hour? It can't be the cook. She and the rest of the help would have gone home long ago. It must be Astral Forde making her nightly rounds. She's in there counting every grain of rice to make sure not a single one has been stolen. Ursa! She chides herself for her uncharitableness, and then quickly steels herself as she approaches the lighted doorway. She might not even get the usual three or four grudging words out of the woman this time.

To her surprise, it's the cook whom she finds there. The cook along with one of the maids. She knows both women. They have worked at Mile Trees since before she went away to high school, the only two to have survived Astral Forde's tongue that many years. There's fervently religious, gray-haired Daphne, whose cooking the guests are always praising, and the maid, Alberta, a workhorse who never gives Astral Forde anything to criticize.

They're both seated in the kitchen as if holding a wake, silent, solemn-faced. Dressed in their street clothes, their hats on against the night dew, ready to go home, yet sitting there.

What's going on?

She steps in the door. For a moment the women are too startled to speak—she might have been an apparition of herself, a duppy, a *loup-garou*—and then their voices quickly converge on her, with both of them speaking at once: "Miss Ursa, is that you? Is that you in truth?"/"God bless my eyesight! Miss Ursa in the flesh!"/ "Why you stay away from Triunion so long?"/"We saw in the papers that you was back and was hoping you'd stop by."/"Is it true what we heard on the radio this evening, that your father lose his seat?"/"What a thing, eh! Who would believe such a thing could ever happen to Mr. Mackenzie?"/"And is trouble we have here too! Trouble all today."/"Is a good thing you're here."/

"Is God Himself send you!"—this from Miss Daphne, the cook, her eyes closed for a moment, her hand raised in witness to the fact. She's a devout member of the Brethren.

The trouble, Ursa learns, is that Astral Forde has refused to leave her house all day, and Mile Trees has been left to run itself. She appeared briefly in the morning. But even then, according to the cook, there were signs of trouble. "She start the morning with hard words. Nobody was doing anything right. I had on the little radio I keeps here in the kitchen—waiting for news about the elections—and she come and turn it all the way down. She din want to hear nothing about the so-and-so elections. Then some young fella in a bus driver uniform came to see her and after he left she was even worse. Just 'buse-ing everybody without any cause . . ."

"More fowl-yard words than we ever heard before . . . ," the maid, Alberta, adds./"I had to stop up my ears," the other woman interrupts her briefly./". . . And saying we was gon find ourself out in the road. The place was gon sell any day now and we would all be out in the road. On and on about that till she all of a sudden dropped what she doing and went and shut herself in the house."

"She hasn't even come back to lock up the place, the kitchen and so," Daphne says. "And we don't have the keys."

"And we know better than to go near that house to ask her for them. And we can't go home and leave the place open so, 'cause the night watchman we have this time is no use. The others left, but the two of us that's worked here so long can't do that. We must sit and wait till she decide to come out."

"And not a meal for the day!" Daphne, the cook, exclaims. "Food cooked and left for her and she won't come and eat. Since morning it's been nothing but trouble here."

It's then that Ursa tells her to prepare a tray and for the two of them to go on home once that's done. She will get the keys and lock up. Sounding like Estelle. She knows she sounds like Estelle just hours ago. "There's nothing more to be done, nothing more to be said, so all of you might as well go home."

A relieved Daphne quickly rises to prepare the tray.

Fifteen minutes later, holding the tray as if she's Astral Forde beside the pool years ago, Ursa slowly makes her way through the grove of pines, her path lighted by the not-quite-full moon. When she reaches the end of the path, the moonlight also presents her with the completely shuttered darkened bayhouse.

The woman might slam the door in my face . . .

Astral Forde more than fills the narrow space of the one door she finally opens.

Ursa had to knock several times and call out her name before she finally heard the inside door being unlatched, and then the dungeon sound as one half of the metal double door to the outside came open and Astral Forde appeared. Her angry, aging, grief-stricken face. Her eyes that darted a look at both her and the tray and now refuses to look at either of them. Her Spanish Bay hair—a dyed black in the light from inside the house. And her fleshy cream-colored body filling the doorway, barring all entry.

Ursa thought she would have found her in a nightgown and robe. Instead, Astral Forde has on her manager's outfit—the neat white shirtwaist blouse and black skirt from Conlin and Finch, with a lacy handkerchief that might have come from part of Congo Jane's shawl tucked in at the waistband, next to the key ring that holds the keys to the principal doors at Mile Trees.

What to say? I should have thought of what to say on the drive down! "Hello, Astral, how are you?" she says. "Forgive me for barging in on you so late, but I wanted to say hello. I'm going back to the States in the morning and I didn't want to leave without at least stopping by . . . It's been a long time. How've you been?" Then, saying it Triunion style and with the proper accent: "How you been keeping?"

"Fair for the time being."

The familiar don'-care, expressionless voice. The grief and anger in her face is nowhere evident in that voice. The flat gaze remains off in the distance.

Ursa holds out the tray with the food, which the cook has covered not only with a *couvre-plat* but with a clean dish towel as well, for extra protection against the hordes of insects.

"Daphne thought you might like something to eat, but she didn't know whether to bring it over. So I volunteered. I found her and Alberta waiting up for you in the kitchen. They were afraid to go home and leave the place open, so I said I'd come get the keys and lock up . . . If that's all right with you."

Astral Forde makes no move to take the tray or to give her the keys or to step back out of the doorway. So that for a moment Ursa has to fight the impulse to give up and walk away. To just turn, the tray in her hands, and walk. For an instant she could curse Estelle for insisting that she come. And then it passes. Both feelings quickly pass. Because what had she expected? Astral Forde is just being herself.

"I don't know if you've heard the news," she says.

"What news?" The grudging voice again.

"About the PM losing his seat."

Before Astral Forde can control them, her indifferent eyes come wheeling around. Confronting hers aghast. Her mouth opens, but it takes a long time before she can actually speak, her disbelief and shock are so great. "How you mean he lose his seat?" It's a choked, incredulous whisper. "How that could happen? You standing there telling me your father lose his seat!" Ursa nods, and a stricken Astral Forde staggers back out of the doorway, permitting her to enter.

Inside the front room of the house Ursa takes a seat, places the tray on her lap, and for the next half hour and more recounts for Astral Forde the events of the past two days in Morlands. Everything that happened there from the time the flyers appeared early yesterday morning—Sunday—to the final vote count this evening. She leaves out her part in it. Talking while discreetly inspecting her surroundings. This house that she's never been in before, but used to wonder about. The PM's other home. She takes in the thick stone walls—bare, not a picture on them; the battened-down windows, the plastic-covered furniture that looks brand-new. There's the same unlived-in feeling to the place as Lowell Carruthers's living room . . .

"Your father . . . ? How he stands . . . ?" The choked whisper again when she's done. Astral Forde, across from her in an armchair, has sat listening with her face bent and a hand covering her eyes. "How this thing leave him?"

"He can't believe it, but you know the PM, he'll recover."

She had sat with her arm around him in the shop, saying what she could to comfort him, promising to come down more regularly from now on—and loving him as much and in the same way perhaps as this woman, until Estelle sent her away, along with everyone else.

There's a sudden violent movement in the air; everything in the stone room might have suddenly exploded, as Astral Forde brings her head up. "The resort scheme! The P and D Board and their kiss-muh-ass resort scheme! That's what caused him to lose the seat!"

She's herself again: Astral Forde of the fowl-yard tongue. She used to sneak behind her and listen, Ursa remembers, and take in every word.

"He was all ready to sell Mile Trees to put money in the friggin' thing!"

"Well, that's out now that he's no longer in the House. He won't be selling anything," Ursa assures her. She sees the lingering doubt, though, in the congested face, and the lingering fear.

"Instead of him doing what he should have years ago—fixing up the place, adding onto it!"

"It'll happen. He'll be free now to put his mind to that and other things."

"You would think he would want to leave something big for you to take over and run . . ." Said with a certain slyness—the eyes averted again—and with even greater fear.

Ursa smells the fear like a musk off the woman's body, and

she says with a laugh that she hopes will reassure her. "Me! I'm not one for the hotel business. It's not my cup of tea. I'd never come back here to run this place. My life is in the States, for better or for worse. Besides, I've always thought of Mile Trees as belonging to you . . ." She stops and waits until Astral Forde turns her astonished eyes her way. "That's right. Oh, I knew of course that the PM owned it and all, but somehow I always thought of it as really belonging to you."

Then, quietly, her head bowed, her eyes on the dish towel covering the tray: "I used to hate that you had to stand there on a Sunday holding that towel and tray. Even before I was old enough to understand, I didn't feel it was right . . ."

"Always getting on like he thought you was some child I had for him!"

Who said that? Astral Forde looks wildly around her as though the outburst had come from someone other than herself. Some Judas with both longing and rage in his voice had spoken, betraying feelings she kept secret even from herself.

"He didn't mean to insult you, Astral. You know that. What he would have liked, I guess, was for all of us to be together in one happy compound. He was born on the wrong continent"— she can't even smile at her own wit. And then she adds in the formal way it's put in Triunion: "I beg for an excuse for him."

Silence. Astral Forde, her wild gaze turned aside, has retreated into her customary silence once again. And there's a sense of her fiercely holding onto the silence, afraid perhaps that if she doesn't she'll find herself betrayed a second time.

All right. It's all right, Ursa. Let it be. Don't push her. She's said far more than just three or four words this time. Besides, you wouldn't want her to behave completely out of character.

Getting up, she places the tray on an end table next to her chair. Before leaving she tells Astral Forde she'll see her the next time she comes down on a visit—probably at Christmas—and like a loving daughter she urges her to eat.

8

Midnight. Alone in her bedroom in the house on Garrison Row, Ursa takes her sore and exhausted body and gingerly lowers it to a sitting position on the edge of the bed. She then bends over and lifts one leg, literally takes the leg in both her hands, raises it until it's parallel to the floor, and, shifting the rest of her around slightly, she stretches the leg out on the bed. She's now partly facing the footboard in the darkness. The room is in darkness. She does the same with the other leg: bends over, lifts it, places it next to its mate. Treating the abbreviated legs she used to angrily blame on Estelle's genes as if they're no longer connected to the motor center of her brain and thus have to be moved manually.

Next comes the trunk of her body, that short, shapeless block from her neck to below her navel that looks as if it's still waiting for the laws of puberty to catch up with it. No waistline or hips to speak of; not a trace of the high, rounded ass that should have been her birthright; and two nubs for breasts. A body like a study in underdevelopment . . . Never mind, Ursa. Just lay it to rest. Slowly she eases the block down on the bed, only to feel a sharp twinge in that right hip the moment she's completely supine. There's still an occasional twinge. I don't understand this pain! The worst of it had all but disappeared by yesterday morning. Then, last night, just as she was climbing the steps of the monument with Estelle and Celestine, the final meeting about to begin, it flared up again. She was to welcome it, though, as the evening unfolded. The waves of pain cutting across the well of her stomach not only drowned out the catcalls and accusations from the crowd, they also blinded her to the sea of flyers being held up in the darkness and to the sight of the PM alone at the front of the platform, under the rigged spotlight. His Gethsemane as he stood there unable to get in a word.

". . . Tell us about what's on this paper! We want to hear about how you're letting them give away Government Lands! . . ."

Even those who couldn't help but love him started shouting.

The pain returned last night to blind and deafen her to all that, and then vanished again this evening when the final count came in from the polls.

Now there's only an occasional twinge and the soreness.

She places one pint-size arm alongside the naked torso she's just deposited on the bed. Her clothes are in a pile on the floor. Tired—she was too tired after undressing to even walk over to the closet to hang them up. Too tired to bother putting on her nightgown or to turn on the light.

In the darkness she arranges the other arm on her other side.

With her arms, legs and torso in place, there's only her head, with its version of the PM's forehead, to be settled on the pillow. With him that high domed forehead was seen as a sign that he had been born to occupy some equally high office. "He's the PM, bo, the one and only PM as far as the North District is concern. He was from a boy and will always be!" Said at every victory celebration she had ever attended. In her case, it just made her look slightly hydrocephalic—so she thought—and worse, it overshadowed those parts of her face that took after no one but herself. That were simply Ursa. She'd catch her reflection in a mirror and all she would see for that first moment was his forehead, sitting like the dome of the Sistine Chapel on top of her face.

Turning over, Ursa burrows it deep in the pillow, closes her eyes, and places her mind and thoughts on the road out to the airport tomorrow morning. She'll leave Estelle's car at the house, call for a taxi or for one of her cousins to drive her, and head out to the airport at dawn's early light. To take the plane nonstop back to the City. And upon reaching the City after the three-hour flight, she'll have the cab bringing her from Kennedy stop off at the natural-foods store not far from her on Broadway. There she'll buy a large packet of herbal mineral salts. Which herbs? She'll decide when she gets there. And the first thing she'll do when she reaches the apartment is to fill the bathtub with water as hot as she can stand it and take a long, delicious soak in chamomile, rosemary or comfrey scented salts. To get rid of the last of the soreness. That before anything else. Ke'ram.

Paule Marshall was born and raised in Brooklyn, New York. After graduating (Cum Laude, Phi Beta Kappa) from Brooklyn College in 1953, she worked as a magazine writer and researcher and eventually began work on her first novel, *Brown Girl, Brownstones*. Since the publication of that famous book, she has published two more highly acclaimed novels, *The Chosen Place, the Timeless People* and *Praisesong for the Widow*, as well as a book of novellas, *Soul Clap Hands and Sing*, and *Reena and Other Stories*, a collection of early writing. Paule Marshall has taught at several universities, and is now Professor of English at Virginia Commonwealth University in Richmond, Virginia. She divides her time between Richmond and New York City.